WHO'S STILL AFRAID?

MARIA LEWIS

Copyright © 2020 by Maria Lewis

All rights reserved.

No part of this book may be reproduced in any form or by any electronic or mechanical means, including information storage and retrieval systems, without written permission from the author, except for the use of brief quotations in a book review.

ALSO BY MARIA LEWIS

Who's Afraid?

Who's Afraid Too?

It Came From The Deep

The Witch Who Courted Death

The Wailing Woman

The Rose Daughter

For Quentin Kenihan, who thought everyone had a story that mattered.

1

A trickle of icy rain ran down my back and I shivered involuntarily. It was the first of many raindrops as the light pitter-patter picked up to a full-on downpour. Ignoring the increasing amount of water now saturating my person, I focused on the view in front of me. What had once been a prestigious boarding school was now a crumbling building on the outskirts of Galway. Vines crept up the side of the five-storey brick structure as the earth attempted to reclaim it. A lone sheep bleated as it limped by the entrance. I was crouched in a heavy thicket and waiting for a sign from Jakea, who was positioned on the opposite side of the building. A slight movement behind an old garden shed alerted me to Lorcan's movements. He was ready.

My hair was pulled back in four tight braids and I wished I hadn't turned down the beanie Clay had offered as a cold wind rustled the bush I was hiding in. The time was upon us. I wiped a stream of water from my eyes as I tightened my grip on the machete resting at my side and squinted through the storm, ready for action. The single squawk of a bird was all it took for me to launch from my crouched position and sprint for the black, open space where there had once been a doorway. Mud sloshed up my tights as I darted across the ground and into the interior of the building.

It was considerably darker inside than it was outside – despite the Irish weather being gloomy as all heck these past few days. My irises contorted as werewolf vision did the adjusting for me and the shadowy layout became illuminated. Taking the first left, I pounded up a stone spiral staircase that would lead me to the top floor. There was a heavy-looking wooden door at the final landing. I didn't hesitate for a second as I kicked it from its hinges. It flew forward with force and knocked one very surprised – and now unconscious – werewolf from his previous position near the entrance.

Three Laignach Faelad were sitting in the centre of the room around an altar that I could only assume was used in worship of the God Crom Cruach. Red wax spilled down three tiers of creepy, evil craftwork with various feathers and objects dangling from it. The centrepiece was a small, human skull that sat atop the pillar much the same way an angel would sit on a Christmas tree. Oil was spilling from a metal container and running down the bone grooves. I should have been disturbed by this – deeply horrified, even – but this was the fourth and final Laignach Faelad camp we had stormed in the past three months and I was prepared. The baby-killers in training, however, were not.

They leapt from their positions on the floor into defensive postures and snarled at me. Two could play at that game. I snarled back and caught a glimmer of surprise cross their features before I launched into the fray. Sprinting towards the one closest, I switched directions at the last minute and caught the brunette by surprise as I wedged a blade into his trachea. He gargled for a few awful moments before I was able to yank the machete free and complete the execution. My dummy target tossed himself at my waist, pulling me down to the ground in an attempt to disarm me. It worked, but in the process I was able to wedge my foot underneath and kick him backwards as we fell. Landing on the ground solo, I rolled out of the way just as the third man tried to bring the altar crashing down on my head. Pouncing up in a squat, I kicked the vat of oil in his direction as it descended. He screamed as the searing liquid burned his flesh, leaping backwards and clawing at his face in agony. I carpe diem-ed the moment and came up behind him quickly, shifting my hands into their werewolf claws and grabbing either side of his head. With one swift twist I broke his neck. Dead. As his body dropped, I rested a foot on his shoulder and twisted again, decapitating him completely.

Wiping the blood spray from my face with my elbow, I looked up to find myself in a now-empty room. The third comrade had fled, which was honestly the only sensible thing to do. The unconscious werewolf lay near the doorway and I swiftly brought my blade down on his neck. Cleaning the machete on the leg of my tights, I turned and headed for the stairwell, taking the steps two at a time as I passed the fourth and third floors. I could hear the fleeing man tearing through an entrance on the second floor: now my destination. He must have heard the ruckus from the others downstairs and assumed he wouldn't make it through the front door. Given the twins were on ground duty, that was an accurate assessment.

The second floor appeared empty. Only a long hallway stretched before me, with dozens of doors peeling off it. I could barely hear him. The soft dripping as rain leaked into the building and splashed on to the floor was cloaking the frantic puffs of the Laignach Faelad as he hid somewhere on that level. I made my way towards the first two doorways, which were both open and facing each other. Pressing my back against the wall, I took a calming breath before dashing into the first room and across to the other side of the space where I could protect my rear. He wasn't in there. Instead I was looking at an abandoned classroom with a dozen or so desks in various states of disrepair tipped over on their sides. I scanned the space and – satisfied he wasn't hiding anywhere – made for the exit.

I was nearly at the doorway when a figure appeared, right out of thin air. Jerking back in shock, I raised my weapon as a reflex but quickly realised it was useless. Floating a metre or so off the ground was the image of a young boy, I guessed about ten or eleven years old. A ghost. I had never seen one before, yet there was no mistaking what it was. He was almost entirely see-through, with the room behind him visible through his frame. His body was an unnatural combination of whites and blues. Even the garden shears that were protruding from his stomach and the blood that decorated the wound was a dark navy colour. He said nothing at first, just floated there, slowly shifting from side to side. He didn't look sad exactly, more like he was bored and keen for this drama to unfold so he could go back to haunting the old school. My weapon was still raised and I lowered it, even taking a step closer to examine the ghost.

'He's in the third room on the left,' he said, in a soft voice.

'Er, thanks . . .?'

'Seamus. My name is Seamus. And yours is Tommi. I heard one of the men downstairs say it.'

'Are you a, uh, friendly ghost?'

He smiled, slowly. 'To you.'

I shrugged. 'Good enough. Third room on the left you say?'

'Yes, and he has an axe. He's waiting on the inside of the door.'

'The fuck? When did he have time to get an axe?' Sighing, I slipped the machete into a sheath at my calf and grabbed two drop point knives instead. This was going to be a close combat situation.

'Righto.'

'I shall be interested to see how this goes,' said Seamus floating out of the room after me as I made my way down the hall.

'Aye, you and me both, dead kid,' I whispered, crouching as I neared the entrance.

Diving into the room, I forward rolled once, twice, until I was on the opposite side of the doorway. The werewolf hadn't expected me to come in so low to the ground and had foolishly swung the axe forward at the unexpected movement. It had gone right through the ghost as he followed into the space.

'Hey!' I shouted, realising too late that it wouldn't actually hurt the haunter. I rolled my eyes at myself and tossed the first throwing knife from a crouched position. It wedged just above the Laignach Faelad's elbow – not my best shot – and I offloaded the second quickly, which landed in a much better position between his neck and shoulder muscles. The blades were what Clay called 'Texas toothpicks' and they ended in a narrow point that sank comfortably into the flesh. The werewolf shouted and sprinted in my direction, clutching blindly at the knives sticking out of his skin. I jumped out of the way but wasn't quick enough to avoid a glancing blow to the jaw as he thrashed wildly. Ducking swiftly, and annoyed that I'd copped a hit, I used an old desk to launch myself from and utilised the momentum to elbow him in the back of the head. His skull made a sickening sound and he stumbled forward, leaning over his knees. I landed on my feet, unsheathed my machete, and inched towards him. He spun around suddenly and hurled both of the knives that had been previously embedded in him. Pivoting to the side, I narrowly avoided the first by blocking it with the machete; the second sliced along my collarbone but didn't stick. He had nothing left and lurched towards me like a drunk rugby player. His hand hadn't managed to transform, but his nails had elongated into werewolf claws. I sprinted in his direction, then leapt in the air at the last minute and flipped over him, ignoring the sting of his claws as they grazed my shoulder. I landed squarely on his back, the werewolf crashing under my weight as I drove the machete through the rear of his neck. We landed with a hearty thump, and years of classroom dust shook free. I coughed as a cloud descended over me.

'Blergh,' I wheezed, finishing off the Laignach Faelad. A weird smacking sound came from behind me and I turned to see Seamus attempting to clap.

'You are very good,' he said. 'You're one of them, aren't you? A member of the Praetorian Guard?'

'Nope, I'm a wolf-for-hire type.'

'A werewolf . . . what pack are you affiliated with? One of the Highland packs?'

'I am Scottish but no, I'm not with any pack. I'm rogue.' The confused expression on his face made me continue. 'A lone wolf.'

'Oh,' he said, nodding.

I tilted my head, taking in his old school uniform, which

clearly dated back to the Victorian era. 'You sure know a lot for a wee solo ghost boy. Are you here by yourself?'

He nodded. 'Yes, I have been since the day I died.'

'You're a lone wolf too, then.'

He looked delighted at that.

'Who shanked you?'

'My teacher, Mrs Humphrey. She always said I asked too many questions.'

'That nasty wench! How did she get away with something like that?'

'Oh, she didn't,' he said quietly, smiling.

A shiver ran down my spine that had nothing to do with the cold. 'So, Seamus the friendly ghost helper, is there anyone else on this floor that I should be killing or are we good?'

He darted out of my field of vision for a moment, disappearing beneath the floorboards. I shrieked, not expecting the ghost to act so ... well ... darn ghostly.

'Tommi?!' Sanjay's voice sounded out before his fast steps brought him around the corner. He took in the scene as if it was exactly what he expected, then looked at me, confused. 'What happened?'

'There was a ghost,' I said, gesturing wildly. 'He just went *whoooosh* through the floor.'

Sanjay nodded solemnly. 'Yeah, they do that.'

'Of this, I'm now aware. How'd things go with you?'

'Good. Heath and I wiped out the third and fourth floor. The twins cleaned up the ground and Clay and Lorcan are still on perimeter, but no one escaped. You?'

'Four on the fifth, took out three and chased a straggler here.' I nudged the corpse with my foot. 'Seamus said this floor is clean.'

'Seamus?'

'The ghost boy.'

'Interesting. I've never actually seen a gho— ARGH!'

Sanjay screamed as Seamus appeared through the wall next to him. I jumped, but counted my lack of yelp as a small success. The ghost appeared unfazed by our reactions and merely gave the additional werewolf a passing glance.

'Everyone in your party is unharmed,' he said. 'Excluding the loud man who appears to have broken his wrist.'

'Clay? How did he get hurt?' I asked, assuming the identity of the 'loud man'.

'One of *them* had hidden on the ground floor and waited until it was calm to try and flee. He took your friend by surprise and knocked him over.'

Sanjay and I shared a look, before making for the stairwell. 'If one of them escaped—' he started.

'He did not,' interrupted Seamus, who was floating happily along behind us.

As we jumped off the final step and walked out through the open doorway, I saw what he meant. The rain had eased and I scanned the faces of my friends until I caught sight of a body laying spread-eagle on the grass. A large spear was protruding from his back, pinning him to the ground. He was still wriggling slightly, snarling and swearing as Jaira approached him with a short sword. He barely gargled a word at her before she silenced him permanently, her twin Jakea watching at her side. I turned back to the group gathered: Lorcan, Sanjay, Heath, and Clay nursing a wrist that was slowly turning purple.

'Who just turned him into a rotisserie chicken?' Sanjay murmured.

Heath looked particularly pleased with himself as he raised his hand. 'That would be me.'

I had been around plenty of weapons in my time and was proficient in dozens, but I had never seen a proper spear before – let alone someone who could use it.

'I— I just . . . Cannot. Even,' I spluttered.

'Javelin-throwing was one of the four exercises all Pictish boys had to master in their training. It's so rare one has the opportunity to use it these days.'

My mouth was hanging open and I shook my head at the huge, immortal warrior. I turned to check on Clay.

'*Hijo de puta,*' he cursed through gritted teeth as I softly prodded his wrist, which was sitting at a right angle. 'He shouldn't have caught me unaware like that.'

'It's okay. I got nicked too,' I said, gesturing to the blood that was streaking down my chest and the golf ball forming on my jaw.

'Eh, that makes me feel slightly better.'

'I'm gonna set it before your super spiffy werewolf bones start healing wrong. Be brave?' I asked, positioning my hands into the right spots.

'Please, I was born bra— *LA MADRE QUE TE PARIÓ!*'

I smiled at him, rubbing his shoulder as he attempted to murder me with his eyes.

'Get it in a brace,' Lorcan said from behind us. 'It will help the healing.'

'How are you, Lo?' I asked, looking around.

Lorcan was staring out over a muddy paddock in the distance. He didn't have a cut on him. 'Fine.'

His answer was abrupt and I tried to ignore the pang I felt in my chest when his eyes met mine. He hadn't wanted to come on this expedition; he had made that very clear from the moment we left Treize HQ in Romania. Yet he'd done it anyway and I felt like a large part of that was because of me. Things had been tense between us since this mission started, but I had hoped once we took out this last pocket of survivors he'd be happy. Instead . . . he just looked *over it*. I sighed and glanced back at the rundown school. Seamus was floating patiently at the entrance, watching us as a small smile played on his lips.

'And what are you so happy about?' I said, starting towards him.

'They are defeated. You have killed them all and they will no longer plague this place.'

'You have an impeccable vocabulary for a kid.'

'Thank you.'

'And have they been plaguing "this place" for a while?'

'Yes. They are evil. I might not be a natural thing, but I saw what they did. I know what they intended to do. I'm glad they are vanquished.'

'Talkative little bugger, isn't he?' said Heath.

'He helped me scout out the second floor.'

'He spooked the final one out of hiding,' added Lorcan, joining the three of us as we stood before the ghost boy. I was the werewolf meat in an immortal sandwich and that wasn't even the weirdest part of the day.

'What's the deal, Seamus? You're the first ghost I've met – are they all as nice as you?'

He looked down at his feet at that comment and if he could have, I'm sure he would have blushed. 'That's very kind of you to say.'

'Ghosts are often trapped within the confines of a site,' Lorcan said, nodding at the garden shears jutting out of the boy's gut. 'Especially if it's the site where they were murdered.'

'Only a medium can move them on,' added Heath. 'Or a specific completion.'

'How did you make that sound dirty?' I muttered, crinkling my nose. 'What kind of completion, like, unfinished business?'

Heath chuckled. 'You've seen too many horror movies, pet. This isn't *The Sixth Sense*.'

'I know that,' I snapped, before glancing at the creepy house. 'It seemed much more like *The Others*, anyway.'

'There is something you could help me with,' Seamus interjected with a smile, which was a disturbing sight given his several missing and broken teeth. 'The day before, I lost my ball when we were playing cricket. I was looking for it in the garden at dusk when Mrs Humphrey followed me out. I never found it.'

'That's your unfinished business?' huffed Clay.

I shot him a look that silenced any further comments. 'A general direction?' I asked. 'We owe you for helping us.'

Seamus raised a ghostly arm and pointed to the left of the shed. I nodded, making my way over towards it. Lorcan kept pace with me, whispering as we walked.

'The odds of us finding his ball—'

'I know, I know. At least let me look, okay? Who knows how long Casper here has been haunting around waiting for someone to just *try* and search for it.'

I met Lorcan's stare and saw that he disagreed with me. 'I understand that you want to try and help, but I think this is futile.'

'The *real* Casper might be better suited for something like this,' added Clay, as he searched the brush with one arm. He was referring to the German woman I'd met while working at his supernatural bar, Phases. She was a powerful medium and one of the last of her kind. She was also one of the few friends I'd made since relocating to Berlin.

'Unless you have her stashed away in the van, three werewolves and four immortal warriors is all we've got.' I looked over my shoulder to see Heath chatting with the ghost, which worried me. 'Great, now Heath is probably going to try and recruit him to the PG.'

An hour later our quest was looking pretty fruitless. Resting my hands on my hips, I sighed and kicked the dirt with my foot. Seamus was still floating in the same spot.

'We need to call it,' said Jakea, who had been taking care of body disposal.

I agreed, and made my way over to the poltergeist of the former schoolboy. 'I'm sorry, we looked really hard and can't find anything.'

He didn't look disappointed, rather, deeply saddened. 'That's all right. It was kind of you to look.'

'I'm sorry,' I said again, feeling extremely useless. 'I'll come back, I'll find a way to . . . We know a woman, a medium, she might be able to—'

'Thank you, it is fine. I appreciate your effort. You killed the monsters and that's the most important thing.'

I returned his smile feebly. Lorcan's hand on my shoulder was a subtle reminder that we needed to go. 'Thanks again, Seamus.'

'You're most welcome, Tommi . . . ?'

'Grayson. My name is Tommi Grayson.'

'Best of luck to you.'

We made our way to our hired van: all of us wet and dirty and bloody in equal measure. Once we were loaded into the back of the vehicle, Heath sped down the uneven country road and we bounced around in the seats. I caught one final glimpse of the school before we turned the corner and the eerie, blue figure that was barely visible in one of its windows.

2

—————

'SHOTS! We're doing shots!' shouted Heath, banging on the bar with his fist. 'Line 'em up, blue eyes.'

The bartender – a shapely girl in her thirties with sparkling blue eyes – beamed as she poured our drinks. I was sitting on a bar stool and watching the twins with amusement. Jakea and Jaira didn't like being surrounded by large amounts of people, let alone in a rowdy Irish pub on a Thursday night. They were standing so close together their shoulders touched. Heath had insisted everyone meet downstairs at the hotel we were staying at to celebrate the completion of our mission for the Treize, the bosses of the supernatural world.

They were the ones who had hired us to track down the Laignach Faelad, the last members of a creepy-ass were-wolf cult who had wreaked havoc in Berlin, although 'hire' really only applied to Clay, Sanjay and myself. We were rogue wolves, not part of their organisation in the same way Heath, Jakea and Jaira were members of the Praetorian Guard – the immortal soldiers of the outfit. Lorcan had been once too, but gave up his title under rather contentious circumstances to join the Custodians, those who focused on peace and guardianship of other supernaturals. He didn't want to fight after centuries of doing just that and his presence in this hunting party felt like a weight on me. If I hadn't agreed to come on this trip, neither would he, yet as my Custodian he was essentially forced to.

An excited yell in Spanish distracted me from my grim thoughts and I smiled as I watched my friend. Clay – despite his injury – was in a good mood and on the prowl for someone to share it with. He was wearing a deep-green turtleneck and making eyes at a pretty guy across the bar who had been subtly returning his interest with measured glances. By contrast, Sanjay seemed ready for bed without any amorous interludes.

'Right,' said Heath, sliding our shots of tequila along the bench and passing out the lemon slices and salt shakers. 'Two shots each. Down them and shut up. Whether this was duty or a temporary assignment for you, together we've achieved something important. It was hard, dirty work but someone had to do it. *We* did it splendidly and the world is better for it.'

'*Arriba, abajo, adentro!*' shouted Clay.

With that, we clinked glasses, licked the salt on our hands, and downed the shots, complete with obligatory grimaces and grunts. I shook my head as the liquor ran down my throat, savouring the lemon and the burn in equal measure. Lorcan didn't touch his follow-up shot, so I knocked it back. Clay barely blinked as he finished his, slamming the salt-shaker down on the bench with emphasis.

'If you'll excuse me,' he started. 'It has been lovely spending these past few months with you all, but there's an

Idris Elba doppelgänger who needs my immediate attention. Good night and good luck.'

'Wait,' said Heath. 'Irish handcuffs.'

He loaded each of Clay's free hands with a Guinness and patted him on the backside.

'You tease.' Clay grinned dangerously before weaving through the crowd.

'I'm out too,' said Sanjay. 'But to an empty bed.'

I was unsurprised to find the twins had already vanished. I felt Lorcan shift behind me as he prepared to head upstairs.

Before he could open his mouth to say anything, I pre-empted him.

'Oh, come on, you can't be calling it quits? We've been in hit-squad lockdown the entire time we've been here, this is the moment to let our hair down. Get a lil' blootered. Become wise beyond our beers.'

Lorcan looked like he'd rather shave his hair off than let it down. He peered at me and I could sense an argument forming. Just as suddenly as it rose, his chest deflated and he gave me an unusual look.

'You stay up. I need to talk to Sanjay about some arrangements.'

'Fine,' I replied, frowning as he disappeared into the crowd. Considering he had been so hesitant to go on this kill quest, now that it was over I'd thought he'd want to celebrate. Maybe a part of me thought he'd want to celebrate with *me*. I kept thinking it was too much, the two of us being so close but so far away from each other. We'd kept our clothes on, kept things strictly professional and stayed true to our decision to end it – whatever *it* had been. There had been a lot to keep our minds busy, thank fuck, yet that didn't mean I hadn't caught him giving me significant, lingering looks. They garnered little more than frustration from me these days as the tension was exhausting and I felt like I was constantly walking on eggshells around him. Working with your secret ex wasn't supposed to be easy. Thankfully I had a physical outlet.

Our first Laignach Faelad targets had been in Berlin, where we had tidied up the last two remaining members of the pack there who had been in hiding. Then, with Clay and Sanjay having to take a break from running Phases – the Berlin nightclub they owned with the rest of the Rogues werewolf pack – Yu, Dolly and Gus had stepped up into full leadership mode. The rest of us hit Ireland with the first stop on the list, Cork, before we slowly worked our way up to Northern Ireland, investigating possible outposts in Derry, Clonmacnoise and Sligo. The mastermind of it all, Kirk Rennex, hadn't been lying when he said he had a small army ready to go. There were some twenty-five Laignach Faelad in various stages of preparation that had been spread out across the country. Luckily, they had all lost contact with their leader – and each other – so they'd had no idea we were coming. From the stakeouts and early mornings to vicious fights and long nights, it was a relief to be finally done with the evil pricks.

Sighing, I turned back to the bar to find Heath smooth-talking the waitress. I figured the weeks upon weeks of trying to keep a single-minded focus had taken a toll on all of us. Flagging the other bartender, I ordered a rum and coke. It was only a few seconds before I felt the presence of someone at my side, and I didn't have to glance at the newcomer to know it wasn't one of my friends. The man smelled of cigarettes and garlic. I ignored him as he leaned closer. The second my drink was placed in front of me, the words 'Can I get that for you, love?' spilled out of his mouth.

'Thanks, but I'm good,' I replied, sliding a note into the bartender's hand and smiling politely at my unwelcome guest. Of course, he hadn't come alone. Two of his equally leery mates were at his shoulder and eagerly watching his display of manhood.

'Ah, a Scottish lass. How is it across the sea?'

'I wouldn't know,' I said, sipping my drink.

'I love Scottish women. So fiery.'

I noticed Lorcan had returned to the bar with his coat on, obviously en route to somewhere. His attention had naturally been drawn to my interaction with the three men. Ignoring the 'fiery' comment, I muttered: 'Mmm-hmm.'

'How about you? Are you a fiery Scottish lass? Are we gonna find out?'

He nudged me with his elbow, causing me to spill a few drops of my drink. Swivelling on the stool, I slowly spun to face him. He was grinning stupidly, pleased to have finally got a response. Lorcan was inching closer to the scene and I felt Heath's eyes on my back.

'Do you know what I did to the last man who tried to make a sexual advance towards me without my consent?' I asked, keeping my voice neutral.

The bar idiot raised an eyebrow at me suggestively.

'I ripped his head off.'

The men stopped giggling abruptly, unsure about how to proceed after my comment was delivered deadpan. I wasn't joking. I grinned at him: a big, toothy grin. I made sure to shift my teeth ever so slightly so they elongated into delicate fangs. He dropped his glass with shock, stumbling backwards as it shattered at his feet.

'Tommi,' came Lorcan's warning tone.

I couldn't help but chuckle as the man grabbed his buddies by their sleeves and made for the door as quickly as he could, casting a terrified glance back at me over his shoulder. My body rumbled as I broke out in laughter, shaking as my teeth slid back into place and my face formed a genuine smile. Heath's laughter joined my own.

'Aw, come on, Lorcan, lighten up,' Heath said, through breaths.

Lorcan didn't reply, shifting his gaze to me instead. 'I'm going out.'

I was still giggling as I returned to my drink and found a second one sitting there.

'You deserve it,' said Heath. 'For that display alone.'

'Cheers,' I replied, watching as he settled next to me on the stool. 'What is this I'm about to drink? And where did "blue eyes" go?'

'Alchemist whiskey, 3Souls. And her shift finished. We're meeting up later.'

He smirked as he waved a napkin with her number on it.

'Is that a love heart around her digits?'

'What's wrong with that?'

'Nothing, it's very . . . cute. I'm sure you two will be perfect together.'

He laughed into his glass of whiskey. 'So, Tommi, how have you found your first time in Ireland?'

'Très conventional and touristy, really,' I answered, sarcastically. 'I've enjoyed the vacation.'

'We've got two days before we fly back to Berlin, you can take polaroids then. Lorcan can show you his old haunts.'

'He already did that, back in Cork.'

'He did, did he?'

'"*We lived near here, I fought near there*",' that kind of thing.'

'I'm sure that was satisfactory for your insatiable curiosity.'

I cast a glance at Heath, who seemed like he was about to burst out laughing at any moment. 'You're funny.'

'Looking?'

'Obviously, but no. You're *funny*. I just . . . I never would have imagined that a Pict could have a sense of humour.'

'Aye. Well. You haven't met many Picts.'

I snorted. 'Excluding yourself and I dare say a few members of the Treize and PG, who has, Heath?'

'Everyone goes with the stereotype. 'Picts! Warriors! Blue tattoos!' There was so much more to the culture.'

'Like?'

'*Like* wit and intelligence and a sharpness of the mind. They were just as valued as the arts of war.'

'Really?'

'Yes, we were raised that way. All noble sons were fostered by other families and began their physical training around nine or ten. You learnt the four exercises of weapons: archery, sword, sword-and-buckler, and javelin-throwing.'

'You demonstrated that one.'

'There were six feats of activity: hurling weights, running, swimming, leaping, wrestling and riding. You didn't get to move on until you mastered each one. There were three rural games and seven domestic games, but cleverness of words and sarcasm were expected of a warrior.'

'Huh. And what about this overwhelming sense of confidence and swagger that you have? I suppose that all stems from your formative years as part of a pagan warrior tribe living in the Highlands?'

'No, that stems from centuries of kicking ass and taking names.'

'Ugh, come on,' I groaned, slapping my hand down on the bar. Heath's reply was dead serious, but I did see the hint of a smirk as he took a sip of his beverage. 'You were *so* close to being slightly less of a wanker.'

He grinned outright as he ordered two more drinks for each of us. 'Maybe I like being a wanker.'

'Aye, maybe. Listen, what's going to happen to Seamus?'

'The ghost boy? There's not much that can happen. He's some one hundred and seven years old and his life force is tied to that ball, which was the centre of his last physical and mental activity on this plain.'

'You got all that from just chatting to him?'

'I've dealt with *a lot* of ghosts. They can be malicious little cunts if they want to be or, like your friend, helpful.'

'I just feel so sad knowing that this kid – who was on the receiving end of a fucked-up situation – is stuck like that indefinitely because his essence or whatever is glued to a ball like wet grass on the bottom of your shoe. Who even knows where it is?'

'The ball is there, which is why he remains. If you move the ball, you move him. He's strong enough to not be confined to the property.'

'It could just be buried deep, right? Or covered in undergrowth?'

'Sure. It's only a matter of finding it and returning it to him. If you kept the ball you could have a murderous ghost pet.'

'Murderous?'

'He killed that teacher, the one that got him.'

'I don't – wait, what? Did you flat-out ask him? You were speaking to him for, like, two seconds?'

Heath shrugged. 'Ghosts have a very clear sense of justice. They're vengeful buggers and not ashamed to admit what they've done.'

I leaned back on my stool, considering the information.

'You know . . . I can't say I'm sorry for her. She got what she deserved.'

Heath clinked my glass with his own. 'Atta girl, embrace the justice boner.'

His approval made me feel uneasy. 'I'm not saying killing is the answer.'

'The longer you're a part of this world, Tommi Grayson, the sooner you'll realise that it has to be. You can't work through the emotional issues of a ghoul. You can't rehabilitate baby-eating werewolves. You can't peacefully negotiate your way through a corrupt system. You start trying to counsel Bigfoot and people are likely to end up dead. More often than not, running someone through with a sharp implement is the only solution.'

In a lot of ways – most ways – he was right. Yet his words had me thinking about some good I might be capable of doing instead of continuing my role of executioner (no matter how desperately that role was needed). I sculled the rest of the unusual whiskey he seemed to favour and got to my feet, only a touch woozy from the alcohol.

'Uh-uh. No. I can see some of sort of righteous resolution in your eyes and that never leads to anything good,' said Heath, watching me carefully. 'Not for *your* family, anyway.'

'As of six hours ago you are no longer the boss, Mr Darkiro. If you'll excuse me, I have a ball to find, while you have a sweet, blue-eyed waitress to seduce.'

I didn't even bother grabbing my coat, figuring that I could do with the ten-kilometre jog to the school.

'You're going to look for a ball in the rain? Plastered?!' Heath called out after me.

'YUP!'

I heard him mutter the words 'completely radge' before I stepped out of the pub and into the night.

~

'THIS – WAS – A – FUCKING – STOOPID – IDEA!' I shouted into the darkness at no one in particular, but feeling all the better for it. Collapsing on all fours in the mud – and it was thick mud now – Heath's 'radge' comment was sounding reasonable. I sighed, arguing with my drunken self.

'No, come on, you ran all the way out here and have been digging through the dirt like a wild dog for a reason, Tommi. It's here, just find it.'

Hauling my ass up, I raised my face to the sky and savoured the sensation of the rain washing away the dirt. I hummed a Hilary Duff song, which seemed appropriate for the moment but was also a clear indicator that I'd lost it.

'*Let the rain fall down . . .*' I trailed off.

Sealing my lips, I looked down at the pile of brown and black mud that seemed to be taunting me. Seamus' glowing spirit form was visible as he hovered at one of the windows, probably wondering what the heck this werewolf was doing back in his garden in the middle of the night. No, he knew what I was doing. He was probably curious as to why I was doing it now.

Right. I dived back in, almost literally, as I shifted my werewolf claws and began ripping up the earth. I dug deep, throwing up all sorts of roots and discarded material in an effort to find the ball. Thankfully the rain softened the ground, making it easy to move large amounts of soil. Unthankfully it also turned everything into liquid, making it hard to grip any passing objects. I had mistaken rocks for a ball that many times I was about to discard the latest one when I noticed its unusual texture. I took pause, fingering some of the mud on its surface so I could see exactly what it was.

'If this is another fossilised cow turd . . .'

It was. Supremely shitty, I hurled it into the night with an angry scream. It was then that I sensed a presence behind me, my body stiffening before I recognised the unique blend of scents: tobacco, faint vetiver, and something zesty like bergamot. I spun around and it was testament to how drunk I was that I hadn't noticed Heath leaning against the exterior of the building earlier. He too was drenched and I tried to ignore how his wet clothes clung to that impossibly large frame, telling myself it was just the beer googles. Any warm feelings were immediately replaced with rage as I caught sight of what was in his hands, casually being tossed up and down in the air. It was a cricket ball, a faded red kid's toy, buried for over a century.

'Looking for this?' Heath asked, the amusement practically dripping from every syllable.

'How long have you been standing there?' I growled. 'You dick!'

I stormed towards him, hand extended for the ball before he raised it above his head and clicked his tongue.

'Uh-uh, not so fast.'

'Seriously? You might be six-foot-six, but that's not out of reach to me. You wanna test how high werewolves can leap, Heath?'

'You wanna test how hard Picts can fight, Tommi?'

His eyes glittered with the threat, as if he actually *wanted* me to agree to a showdown. I was vicious and, heck, had the added assist of werewolf superpowers. But Heath was a massive, ancient warrior with thousands of years of experience. I'm not sure what the over under on a match between the two of us would be, but I wasn't dumb enough to think I could take him . . . at least not under these sloppy conditions. He must have seen the doubt in my expression, a smile creeping on to his face as the seconds ticked by. I wanted to scratch it off.

'You're smarter than they give you credit for, you know?'

'Who's "they"?' I snapped, offended.

'Argh, brush it off, blue. It's a good thing: you want them to underestimate you, think you're nothing but a mindless soldier.'

'Stop with the riddles, you twat! Give me the ball.'

'*This* ball?' he chimed, holding it out for me to inspect, daring me to snatch it from his clutches.

'Well, I don't mean the two pebbles between your legs now, do I?' I replied, crossing my arms.

His laughter broke through the night like a boom of thunder, his chest rising and falling as he cackled at my barb.

'Aye, that was good,' he puffed. 'I needed that. And *you* need this ball to liberate The Flying Irishman.'

I looked over his shoulder at the silhouette of the crumbling structure. Seamus' figure was glowing in the window and I realised with a jolt that I'd never actually thought I'd find the ball. I'd figured if I tried really hard I would earn some sense of resolution before enlisting the superior skills of Corvossier von Klitzing, aka Casper.

'So, let me make you a deal,' Heath continued. 'I'll give you the ball, you liberate the ghost, and owe me a favour in return.'

'You're manipulating my moral compass.'

'Totally. Do you know how rare it is to find a supernatural with one these days? Took me a minute to remember how to exploit it.'

He had me. Worst of all, he *knew* he had me.

'Fine,' I sighed. 'Ya minger.'

Holding out his free hand, we shook without another word. Our grip was damp from the rain, but I noted his hands were mud-free. He passed over the ball and I took it, weighing the spherical object in my fingers.

'You've had this since we raided the place, haven't you?'

I looked up at his face, which was frozen in his usual mask of smugness, but otherwise gave nothing away.

'Ugh,' I groaned, stomping away from him and through the mud. 'Seamus? Oh *Seeeeamus!*'

I saw the kid disappear from his point at the window only to reappear at the main entrance instantly. As I neared closer to the door, his ghostly form became less transparent. The whites and blues solidified, turning into real colours. The dark, navy blood was now a rich red. His formerly white cheeks were now a soft pink, growing brighter with every step I took closer to him. His mouth popped into a small 'O' shape as he caught a glimpse of the object I held in my hands.

'You found it,' he whispered, evidently unaware that he was no longer floating. His body had slowly descended to the ground where he now took careful, uneasy steps. I didn't hesitate as I held out the ball to him. It rolled slightly in my palm before he snatched it up. Perhaps he was afraid that I would keep him, like some perverted genie master. I squinted as his figure glowed a little bit brighter. He was enraptured with the object, cradling it in his hands like a newborn chick. Just as he had become more real physically, he faded as quickly. I was rooted to the spot watching with morbid fascination as the ghost boy disappeared. Seconds before he vanished completely, he raised his head to look at me.

'Thank you. Thank you so much. We'll keep an eye on you, Tommi Grayson.'

'We?'

My question fell on dead ears, ironically, as Seamus evaporated entirely and I was left at the abandoned school: wet, muddy, and still a touch tipsy. I began the walk down the gravelly road that led to the perimeter of the property, digesting everything that had just happened. Heath fell in step beside me as we started the long trek back to town.

'I don't suppose you followed me here in a car, per chance?'

Heath's look dashed my hopes. 'Bit noticeable, that.'

'You could have stalked behind me in second gear, lights on full beam as I jogged through the difficult terrain. The Paulie to my Rocky.'

'More like the Rocky to your Adonis, but sure.'

I let out a surprised giggle, unable to help myself as he matched my punning. Eventually our steps quickened as we picked up the pace, legs striding as we ran. My vision was heightened and perfectly functional in the dark, meaning this Scottish werewolf could comfortably sprint through the night without fear of stacking it. Heath's wasn't, but he was clearly able to manage as he kept pace and rarely stumbled. Part of me hoped he'd roll an ankle, the injury getting me out of whatever I was indebted to.

'This favour,' I started, the words coming out between pants. 'I'm gonna regret it, aren't I?'

'Actually, I think you'll enjoy it.'

'So why trick me?' I answered, annoyed as I cast him a sideways glance.

'Because it's so *easy*.' He grinned. 'The way you care for others is an advantage to your enemies.'

His statement hit me harder than I wanted to admit,

largely because it was true. When my half-brother Steven Ihi had set out to hurt me, he'd used my friends Mari and Kane to do it. They were both dead now. I was alive, but permanently changed from not just the grief of their loss but what I'd done following it, the path of destruction and bodies I'd left in my wake.

'What's the answer, then, be like you? Care about nothing and no one?'

'You think that's what I do?'

'That's what I've seen.'

'Maybe because that's what I *want* you to see.'

'Or maybe you're just another bro posturing to appear deeper than he actually is,' I puffed. 'That's why people start vaping, Heath.'

He laughed, the sound fading as we both lowered our heads and charged up a rise that seemed to go on forever. As we mounted the crest, the glimmer of lights from the outskirts of town became visible. We didn't speak for the rest of the journey thanks to a combination of fatigue, remaining alcohol, and a not-so-subtle increase in speed as I tried to creep ahead of him and Heath matched me. The petty back and forth went on for a few kilometres, until the point where we were both sprinting through the streets of Galway and dodging revellers in an attempt to make it back to the hotel first. It was a dead heat, which annoyed me even further as I leaned against an outdoor bench and tried to catch my breath.

'Tomorrow,' he panted, his visible exhaustion providing sweet satisfaction. 'Meet me in the car park at eight, sharp.'

'Ew, that's so early. You're not even gonna tell me what this favour is?'

'You're picking up an old friend.'

'Who? And why?'

'Firstly, you'll see. Secondly, because they like you better than me.'

'Like that's hard,' I snorted. 'How long have you been scheming this?'

He winked, straightening up as he pulled his wet, blond hair back into a bun at the top of his head. Spinning around, he strutted away from the hotel and I couldn't help but admire the view I just *knew* he was putting on for me.

'Where are you going?' I called. It was already well past 2 a.m and we'd both need as much sleep as we could get with that horrific start time. His response was little more than a whisper, with a normal person unable to hear it given the distance he'd put between us and the liveliness of punters beginning their journey home. But I was not a normal person and my werewolf hearing picked up the words perfectly.

'Blue eyes,' Heath said, before disappearing around the corner.

3

———————

It was Saint Patrick's Day, because *of course* it fucking was. The day I had to get up early and owe Heath some kind of shady favour just *had to be* Ireland's biggest national day to get sloppy. Even though I was grumpy about the start time, I was still waiting in the car park ten minutes earlier than I needed to be and trying to ignore the stench coming from an overflowing dumpster.

Stupid bloody werewolf senses.

I recalled the time before I knew what I was, before I had experienced my first transformation. I had gone through life unable to smell the plethora of scents the world seemed to be emitting at all times, let alone trace them back to their source. I hadn't been able to use my werewolf hearing, for example, to make sure everyone's breathing was deep and steady in sleep as I snuck out of the hotel that morning. I guessed that if I were somehow able to go back to regular humanity – reverse the lycanthropic clock – it would feel like I was navigating life underwater, my senses muted to *everything* that was out there.

It was one of those new senses that told me my ride was

coming, albeit not in the vehicle I expected. I could hear the gravelly engine from a few blocks away and I tracked the sound as it moved closer and eventually crawled into the car park. Heath was crouched behind the wheel of a vintage Volkswagen Beetle in a matte gold colour. His huge body was crammed into the driver's seat and looked downright comical from my vantage point. He leaned over, throwing open the passenger door for me as I crept forward.

'Like the ride?' He grinned.

'You're driving Ted Bundy's car, you know that, right?'

'Just get in, will ya?'

I did as he asked, noting that he had an Irish band – Fontaines D.C. – playing from the vehicle's sound system, which was the only modern addition to the vehicle. We were quiet for a moment as he manoeuvred the gearstick around his seemingly endless legs, the Beetle chugging its way through the outer streets of Galway. It was still approximately two hours before the first person in this city would be vomiting into a gutter, but those smart enough to be making money off the revelry were awake and setting up for twenty-four hours of non-stop-partying. Decorations had been visible since we arrived in town and I watched green streamers fluttering in the breeze, counting the number of cartoon leprechauns I saw displayed out the front of bars, businesses and homes as we passed. There wasn't a single cloud in the sky, with the dreary past few days having given way to what looked like idyllic weather.

'Anyone see you leave?' Heath asked.

'Nope.'

'Anyone hear you leave?'

'Nope.'

'Aye, good.'

I didn't add that Lorcan wasn't in the hotel. Often, I

found myself subconsciously listening for the rhythm of his breathing, noting whether he was awake or asleep. It comforted me, even if we weren't what we once were. That morning he hadn't been in his room. After seeing him leave the bar the previous night, I was bothered by the fact he hadn't returned. Yet I kept that information to myself. Lorcan had secrets *on top* of secrets and I had learned from experience that the harder I pressed him, the tighter he would lock down. I had to trust that whatever he was up to, he was safe. And he'd tell me when I needed to know. Maybe. Probably.

'You gonna dish on where we're going or nah?' I asked, wanting the conversation to take my mind off *him*. 'And what's with all the secrecy? You know I hate being treated like a mushroom.'

'Kept in the dark and fed shite?' he questioned.

'Aye.'

He chuckled. 'All right then, flower. We're going to Galway Airport.'

I frowned, immediately confused as I knew for a fact it was closed to commercial flights. Jakea had said as much when Clay complained about the length of a road trip from one kill site to another, whining that we should have just flown into Galway instead.

'Chartered flight,' Heath said, as if reading my mind. 'Should land about 8.45 a.m on the dot. As for the secrecy, you're assisting me with a young bird who needs help. The less people who know, the better.'

I snorted.

'What?' he asked, feigning shock.

'And you're just doing this out of the goodness of your heart? What's in it for you, Heath Darkiro? Did you get this young bird in trouble in the first place?'

'Aw, come on, a girl in peril? I thought this would be right up your bleeding-heart alley, Tommi Grayson.'

'Why trick me into doing this favour for you? You could have asked anyone.'

'Did you bring a weapon?'

I retrieved the Glock that was tucked into the waistband of my jeans and concealed by the vintage letterman jacket I was wearing, resting the gun on my thigh so he was able to see it clearly. He nodded and I put it back.

'That's why "you". This favour could have been picking apples from an organic orchard or some crap, but you came armed anyway. I needed someone who would be on their guard.'

'Are you expecting trouble?'

'Besides you, no. But that's usually when it shows up.'

'I have Hunga Mungas with me as well,' I said, patting the backpack at my feet and feeling the stiff outline of the African fighting tool.

Heath gave me an incredulous look.

'What? They're a lot easier to conceal than a machete!'

'You're right, even on Saint Paddy's people would have noticed if you were walking through the streets of Galway with a *freakin' machete*.'

I barked a laugh, unwinding the window and relishing the sensation of air whipping through my hair as we drove.

'Just . . . be on alert,' Heath continued. 'I'm not expecting an outright assault, but are there eyes on us? Is there anyone paying more attention than they should be? What can you hear, smell? *Anything* that doesn't feel right, isn't. Trust your instincts.'

'Usually I have to suppress them,' I mumbled, thinking of the countless times I'd been asked – even ordered – to reign in my natural compulsions.

'Fook that.'

The car slowed, Heath dropping down into second gear as we neared what looked like little more than a large shed in a paddock. It was gated and on the other side of a chain link fence was a small runaway. I understood now why Galway Airport was closed to commercial flights: it didn't look like there was the infrastructure to support them. There were about a dozen light aircraft positioned around the perimeter and I scanned the faces of the few people milling about.

'They a threat?' Heath asked. I knew he was testing me.

'The first rule of flight club is you don't talk about flight club,' I replied, noting the logo and words 'Galway Flight Club' on all their shirts, caps, and jackets. Out of the corner of my eye I saw him nod, satisfied. We came to a stop at what had once been a taxi rank. With no incoming passengers, there was little point for it now and it was empty as he turned the car's ignition off. The music continued to play as we sat there and I tried to ignore Heath's stare. Finally, I gave in and twisted in my seat to face him, arms crossed over my chest.

'That's quite an egg,' he said quietly. To my surprise, he reached out and gently ran his thumb over the swelling at my jaw where I had been popped by the Laignach Faelad. I froze, not able to muster a reaction in the close confines of the car. His forehead creased with a scowl and I couldn't tell whether it was anger or confusion. Suddenly, he pulled back and spared a glance in the rear-view mirror.

'There she is.'

'She?' I questioned, swivelling around and following his gaze. With a start, I realised I knew who *she* was. My feet pulled me out of the car and down the walkway before my mind had a chance to catch up, my body seemingly drawn to our visitor by instinct.

'Sue!' I exclaimed, shocked in every way that mattered as the Paranormal Practitioner strolled towards me, rolling a suitcase behind her.

'Doctor Sue Kikuchi at your service,' she said, straight-faced. 'It's good to see you, Tommi.'

'You too,' I murmured, unable to stop the lie as it left my lips. In truth, the two occasions when I'd had dealings with the doctor both just so happened to be after the worst events of my life. First, almost two years ago as I recovered from the mental and physical of trauma of learning that I was a descendant of the world's most powerful werewolf pack, the Ihi family. Second, when I woke up in a Dundee hospital following my final showdown with Steven Ihi and knowing that Mari and Kane were dead.

Please don't let that be an omen for today. Please.

As I lifted her luggage and an overnight bag into the boot of the Beetle, I noted that she wasn't surprised to see me. I was exactly who she had expected to collect her, which meant that whether the ghost of Seamus had appeared or not, Heath had been looking for an opportunity to have me indebted to him. I recalled what he'd said about Pictish culture over drinks the night before, how wit and intelligence were just as valued as physical strength. I was learning that the hard way. Dr Kikuchi shook her head when I offered her the front seat, taking the backseat instead as we all folded into the vehicle and took off towards our next destination.

'Nice touch with the car,' she said, the comment directed at Heath. 'And the girl.'

'I thought you'd appreciate a familiar face. And I know the only thing you like more than vintage Volkswagens and girls is basketball. But getting Steph Curry to pick you up was beyond even my capabilities.'

'I hate the Warriors anyway,' Dr Kikuchi mumbled.

'How's the Mrs? How's the practice?'

I was confused, naturally. Dr Kikuchi was a lot of things, but she wasn't young: with her silver-streaked hair I knew she couldn't be the 'girl' Heath had told me was in trouble.

'Fine and fine,' she replied, short. 'Did you locate what I need?'

'Of course. A state of the art, privately owned doctor's surgery that's closed on Saint Patrick's Day. The wailers are coming early afternoon, so that gives you enough time to tinker with whatever doctor things you tinker with and for Tommi to give the place a thorough sweep.'

I had been listening to every word, trying to put together as much as I could from their conversation. Watching Dr Kikuchi in the mirror, I noted how her shoulders seemed to slump ever so slightly as she relaxed.

"Long as we weren't followed and this whole thing remains off the radar,' she said.

'Not in the air, you know my pilot's good for it,' Heath answered. 'And on the ground . . .'

'We're alone,' I stated, sensing my cue. I had been monitoring surrounding traffic for a tail ever since we left the airport, searching for anything unusual.

'Good. We're twenty minutes out. When we arrive, the address is a short walk from the car. Tommi, I want you to assess the exterior and then the interior. If all is safe, you text me on this burner and I'll bring over the doc.'

He handed me an ancient Nokia so large it barely fit in my hand. When I'd got up this morning, there was a note under my door from Heath telling me not to bring my phone, so I hadn't. Examining this brick, I couldn't help but think mine would have at least been more reliable.

'Uh—'

'Don't be an umpchay, just use it,' Heath snapped, interrupting my objection. 'Can't be tracked and my number is the only one in there.'

He waved his own phone by way of explanation.

'*That* is not *this*. Look at your screen! You can make video calls.'

'You just need to send a text, not browse Tinder.'

'I feel so safe,' Dr Kikuchi muttered from the backseat. 'So secure with this top-notch team.'

'Hey, you had the choice of Atlanta bringing you over and you declined, so this is what you've got.'

'Being deep underwater is starting to look appealing.'

I got the address from Heath and practically leapt from the car before it had stopped moving down the narrow alley he had turned into. The two had descended into full bickering. Saying Dr Sue Kikuchi liked me better than him wasn't much of a compliment now that I thought about it. *So why is she here?* I asked myself. She was clearly risking something, as was Heath. What that 'thing' was . . . I didn't have all the pieces yet.

I took a left onto one of the busier streets and was unsurprised to find it filling up with tourists. There were some locals among the fray, but it was mainly travellers who'd come to Ireland specifically to get drunk on the 'funniest day of the year, brah!' as I heard one lad shout. I looked longingly at the massive pint of Guinness he'd just emerged with through a swinging pub door. I didn't even like Guinness under usual circumstances, but I was Scottish. We start drinking whiskey from the bottle at two. Lager straight from the mother's breast.

I ignored the thirsty itching in my throat; I had a job to do, after all. The entrance to the doctor's surgery was one street over and I took a wide loop. My bright hair would usually stand out in a crowd but in the Saint Patrick's Day rainbow of green, orange, white, glitter, you name it, I actually blended in . . . for once.

There was so much commotion, so much noise, I had to sort through everything to determine if there was a threat. I did another lap just to be safe, before ducking behind a convenience store and waiting several minutes to make sure I wasn't followed. My spidey sense was not tingling. Shifting my claws just enough, I launched up the side of a brick building, my boots digging into the grooves of the structure as I climbed quickly. I would have been a blur of movement to anyone watching, but no one was watching. It was a weird human trait: rarely did someone look above their natural eyeline. The higher I climbed, the further I was beyond that. I saw the window that I wanted, spreading my legs and using the strength of my thick thighs to hold my body in place at the window frame. It was locked, but not very well. I didn't even have to break the glass, just a swift tug and the mechanism was broken.

Climbing inside, I heard the rhythmic beep of the surgery's alarm going off and followed the sound. I hit the entry code Heath told me and spent another few minutes checking then double-checking every room, every cupboard, every bathroom, every office and even the manhole to make sure the premises was safe. It was. Safe and empty and boring. I sighed, frustrated with myself. Was I looking for action? After three months on the job, was I an adrenaline junkie now? No, I wasn't like the twins. I would never become one of those Praetorian Guard soldiers speeding from one fight to the next, chasing the next battle, the next high. I waited an additional twenty minutes to see if anything popped up, then deemed the place safe and texted Heath to bring the doc around.

They'd be coming through the front door and I jogged down the entrance staircase to meet them, pausing near the handle to listen for their approach. It wasn't hard to discern.

'No fucking way can you tell me Kevin Durant has a shot.'

'You already said you hate the Warriors, you're biased!'

'I'm also logical. A few good seasons does not a GOAT make.'

'Excuse me, Jordan back-to-back '96, '97—'

Rolling my eyes, I yanked open the door and interrupted the middle of Heath's spiel.

'*You're* into basketball?' I asked. 'You?'

'Of course! With my height and ability to shit-talk, you can understand why I'm naturally drawn to the sport.'

I was about to shake my head in disbelief, but then I digested what Heath was wearing. He had an Irish flag draped around his shoulders like a cape, with a pair of glittery green, heart-shaped sunglasses pushed back to keep the hair off his face.

'This . . . is a new look for you,' I managed to choke out, biting the inside of my cheek to prevent a stream of laughter escaping.

'I'm blending in as a bellend,' he said, with a wave of his hand. As if on cue, a guy sprinted down the street in a green G-string, fuzzy red wig and bare chest decorated with paint that was presumably supposed to resemble a four-leaf clover. He had two lit sparklers in each hand and was waving them above his head triumphantly as the crowd cheered him on his route. I met Heath's gaze, neither of us needing to acknowledge the incident.

'You need to step up your hair game, then,' I muttered, letting Dr Kikuchi past me and into the surgery and gesturing for Heath to bend down. I did what I could with the spare hair ties I had on my wrist. With his blond locks now split into two, even buns on each side of his head, I couldn't help but snigger as Heath examined my handiwork in the reflection of a window.

'What the hell is this supposed to be?' he huffed.

'Nek level man buns?' I offered. 'Scottish Spice was always my favourite.'

He flinched, but looked resigned to his fate. 'You head in and watch the doc, I'll stand guard out here until our party arrives. I'm the only one they know on sight and I'll be the only one they trust.'

'All right.'

'Once they're here, we swap. And you take my phone.'

'Why?'

'Because there's music on it and I've got headphones.'

'You . . . you don't want me to listen to whatever happens inside?'

'I know you won't be able to help yourself. My way gives you plausible deniability.'

'And it also cuts off one of my senses. I don't wanna be Jessica Biel in *Blade: Trinity*, Heath. That shit's dumb!'

'I don't understand what you just said, but I trust you enough to pick up any incoming danger without needing to hear it. You have the ability to scent, that keen eyesight, and instincts most Praetorian Guard soldiers would kill for. Rely on those. Now, shoo.'

He shut the door in my face and I huffed with annoyance.

Fine. I stomped back up the stairs and into the surgery. Dr Kikuchi had set herself up in one of the examination rooms and seemed busy doing whatever it was she needed to do, so I located the staff kitchen and made us both cups of coffee. I didn't know if she took sugar or not – I had four – so I brought the container with me just in case.

'Thanks,' she said, as I set the mug on the desk.

'I can't tell you it's good,' I replied, taking a sip from my own mug and wincing. 'But it *is* caffeine.'

As I settled into the patient's chair opposite her, there was an easy silence as we both drank our coffee and she went through a folder of notes in front of her. I knew better than to ask what she was looking at. Odds were I wouldn't understand it anyway, even though I was more well-versed in medical jargon than some due to my best friend Joss having an ongoing battle with cancer.

'Do you play chess?'

'Huh?'

Dr Kikuchi didn't look up from her paperwork as she repeated the question.

'Uh, no,' I replied, thinking back. 'Maybe a few times with my grandfather, but I was always more of a cards person. You know, any game where I could skin the opposition.'

'You're living a chess game right now. Heath mightn't want you to know that, but I don't think ignorance makes anyone safer. I've seen too many innocent people become collateral damage regardless.'

'Innocent is not a word I'd use to describe myself,' I murmured, thinking carefully about what she was saying. Dr Kikuchi looked up then, examining me with her sharp gaze.

'I feel sorry for you, Tommi. I felt sorry for you from the first moment I met you. You're Ihi blood, but also not. You're one of us, but also one of them. You were born in a state of in-between and eventually one side's pull is going to be greater than the other's.'

'I—'

My response was stunted, as everything she had just said was loaded with meaning that I couldn't possibly comprehend.

'Why are you telling me this?' I asked. 'You know I hate this riddle shite. If you have something to say, just spit it out.'

'Keep an open mind,' she responded. 'Not everything is as it appears. And even when you have all the pieces, that doesn't mean a choice is going to be any easier.'

'A choice between what?'

She opened her mouth to reply, but I held up my hand to stop her. I could hear voices outside, Heath greeting whoever our guests were.

'They're here,' I said, shrugging out of my jacket and tossing it in the reception area on my way out. Dr Kikuchi called after me.

'Think about what I said, Tommi.'

'Think about making sense,' I muttered. I paused, eavesdropping on the conversation as the visitors chided Heath's ensemble. With a smirk, I opened the door just as one of them was acknowledging his camouflage.

'Camouflage is a little hard when you're eighty-two fookin' feet tall,' I said, scanning their faces. 'I tried to talk him into a leprechaun outfit, but he said it was too conspicuous.'

'No bawbag of mine is squeezing into sequined hot pants, you're having a laugh.'

'Technically we'd *all* be having a laugh, but sure – hold out on us, Heath.'

These guests weren't exactly the company I was expecting.

Spending the past few months as part of this contract kill squad for the Treize had thrown me, I guess. I'd forgotten that not everyone in the supernatural community was a cold-blooded killer. There were just two women. The first lass had beautiful tattoos snaking down her arms, which almost made up for the excessive amount of fake tan she was slathered in. Her bleached blonde hair was styled in the kind of pixie cut everyone with my type of bone structure *wished* they could pull off (we couldn't). The second woman was wearing a loose, flowing floral dress and barely looked out of her teens with her chubby, baby-faced good looks. She wouldn't stop staring at me and it was her eyes that told the truth: this kid had seen some shit. *You and me both,* I thought, immediately sympathetic. Out of the two of them, there was no need to guess who the 'girl in peril' was.

'Go on in,' I said, addressing my comment to her. 'She's waiting for you upstairs. The surgery's closed today so it's just us.'

They duo filed inside, the young girl last, and I felt her sad gaze linger on me. My ears were straining to pick up every potential threat, every nearby risk, and I had to work to mask my surprise as I heard something unexpected.

'You put that flag round my shoulders and we're gonna have words,' I growled, my distraction giving Heath the opportunity he needed. He beamed, ignoring my threat and doing exactly what I'd asked him *not* to do. He added the sunnies for bonus effect.

'You couldn't even dye your hair green for the occasion? Now we have to cover it up.'

I pouted. 'The hair stays blue.'

'Yeah, all right. Remember what I said? Headphones in.'

'And Charly Bliss all the way up, bruv,' I answered, taking the phone from him and wedging the earphones into my ears. As he shut the door behind me, I switched my attention to the street where things were getting expectedly wild. So, I watched. And I waited. Then I waited some more. The sun had properly set by the time the door opened behind me, the pair emerging from the doctor's surgery with Heath in tow. The youngest among them had been crying and even though her eyes weren't puffy, I could smell the salt.

'We'll talk,' the blonde told Heath, surprising me with an Australian accent.

'Aye.' He nodded as the women stepped into the crowd of Saint Patrick's Day partiers. I tracked their movements through the packs of people, many of whom were singing incoherent versions of what I had to assume were Irish classics. From the stance of the blonde, it was clear she was the muscle. She put herself first, leading the way. She was protecting the younger girl whose ginger hair eventually disappeared out of view as they turned a corner. Dr Kikuchi joined us on the landing, our trio taking off in the opposite direction towards where Heath had parked the car. We took the doctor straight back to Galway Airport, where Heath's pilot was clearly still waiting for their sole customer. She wasn't an overly affectionate woman, so instead of a farewell hug, I helped offload her luggage and walked with her to the tarmac.

'One more stop,' Heath said, when I got back in the Beetle. 'Then we're done.'

'Did you knock her up?'

'Whoa, what?' He stalled the car as I barked my question at him.

'She looks like a schoolgirl, Heath! I know you're a scoundrel but Jesus fucking Christ.'

'How did you know she's pregnant? I trusted you to keep the earphones on!'

'I did! But I couldn't help what I heard when they got there. *And* when they left.'

He looked confused for a moment, glancing away from the lights of incoming traffic to gawk at me. Then understanding washed over his features, his mouth popping open with surprise.

'The heartbeat,' he sighed, as if annoyed at himself.

'Heartbeats,' I corrected. 'She's pregnant with triplets. What kind of Scottish super-sperm do you have, anyway? She's tiny, your giant babies are going to tear her apart! I thought you'd be smarter than this.'

Heath couldn't form a proper response, he was laughing *that* hard. Tears were spilling down his cheeks and it just made me angrier.

'This isn't funny!' I said, whacking his shoulder. 'I didn't think a "favour" would be an entire day spent helping sort out your love children!'

'Tommi,' he wheezed. 'I'm not the father.'

'Bullshit.'

'I'm not, I swear it on . . . on the finest single malt whiskey you can imagine.'

I was about to continue arguing with him, but I knew how sacred *good* whiskey was to Heath. Besides, it was hard to get a word in over his continued laughter.

'They're really not your babies?' I asked, straining to hear his heartbeat quicken and sniff out a lie.

It was steady.

'No, they're not my bairns. I lived through the Middle Ages, okay? That was *peak* syphilis era. I'm no glove, no love all the way.'

'Accidents happen and condoms aren't always effective.'

'Oh, God,' Heath chuckled, his chest rumbling. 'I haven't laughed like that in a century. I'm so glad I brought you.'

He pulled over, the Beetle bumping over uneven ground as we came to a stop in front of a river. It was quiet, the sounds of the city partying somewhat distant as lights from nearby homes reflected on the surface of the water.

'Wait here,' he told me. 'I'll only be a few minutes.'

'Yes, sir,' I said, sarcastically. I was getting sick of following orders.

'Impregnate Sadie Burke,' I heard him mutter to himself, his laughter starting up again as he walked towards the riverbank. He didn't slow down at all, his legs carrying him right into the water and then beyond as he dived under the surface. I sat up, shocked to attention. He didn't reappear for almost a minute. I knew, because I was counting the seconds in my head. I had just unbuckled my seat belt in order to dive in after him when he broke the surface. Gulping a breath of air, he turned around and spoke to a woman who surfaced behind him. As Heath walked out of the river, fully clothed and completely drenched, the mystery figure remained. She only revealed as far as the tops of her shoulders, which were bare and looked almost grey in the evening light. I thought seaweed was trailing behind her, but with a start I realised it was hair.

'I think that broad is naked,' I whispered to myself, watching in awe. She and Heath exchanged a few more words before he strolled from the river entirely, the conversation coming to an end as he jogged back to the car. Leaning into the boot, he pulled out two enormous beach towels and wrapped them around himself. Part of me – the part that hadn't been laid in three months – waited for him to take his shirt off, so I could finally get a proper glimpse at that body. He didn't and my eyes flicked back to the surface of the river as he squeezed back into the vehicle. I sat up, startled to see the woman had disappeared. My eyes scanned the surface of the lake but there was nothing. Only ripples.

'Bit nippy,' Heath said, starting the car.

'Um, am I in an Arthurian legend or was that not the Lady Of The Lake?'

He chuckled. 'Afraid not. That, young lassie, was a selkie.'

'A . . . selkie?'

'Mermaid by any other name. Although they don't really like that term and technically it's not acc—'

'*Heath. Did I just see my first mermaid?*'

He blinked at me, looking uncertain before he shrugged. 'Mazel tov?'

4

———

It wasn't super late by the time we made it back to the hotel, but I was exhausted. It was like all the exertion of the past three months had caught up with me, not to mention a day running around doing weird shit for weird people on very little sleep. It was testament to how tired I was that I skipped the bar altogether, mumbling a farewell to Heath in the car park and stumbling to my room. I wanted to be alone. I needed it. There was too much to process, too much to understand, just . . . too *much*. Heath had sworn me to secrecy and I agreed, but the events of that day had left me feeling sticky. It was like I had been running through a web of fairy floss, unable to dislodge the strands. Not that my usual life wasn't complicated, it was messy as fuck. Yet it felt like after nearly twenty-four months as part of this supernatural world, I was at least beginning to comprehend my place in it. Or so I'd thought.

I ditched my clothes at the door and spent longer than I should have in the shower. After wiggling into a pair of flannelette pants and a singlet, I collapsed on the bed, pulled my regular phone free of the charger, hit Joss' number and waited for him to answer. I needed my best friend. I needed to hear his voice, see his face, and be comforted by something familiar. The screen shifted as we were connected, his mug appearing on the screen and mine in a much smaller window in the corner. I looked like shit. Joss, more importantly, looked great.

'I was just talking about you!' He grinned, the interior of his hospital room back in Berlin coming into view as we FaceTimed.

'I know, that's why I called.'

'Really?'

'No, ya bampot,' I laughed. 'Werewolf hearing doesn't cross countries, fark.'

'I know, I know,' he said quickly, in attempt to cover the fact he really didn't know. It made me laugh longer, my stomach muscles burning with the movements. Calling Joss had definitely been the right move – I immediately felt better. My hand had been forced when it came to introducing him to the world of the supernatural, but now that he was aware of the basics I was finding myself exceedingly glad. He was fascinated by the whole thing and had proven himself useful when it came to the research so often required. That wasn't my strong point but Joss loved it. If it hadn't been for him, we would never have cracked the Laignach Faelad case and made the connection to Kirk Rennex, who was the puppet master of it all.

Joss' treatment for Hodgkin lymphoma was continuing at Mechtilde General and his results were getting better every day. He was looking better *every* day, as I could clearly see through the screen. The way things were tracking, it seemed as if he'd be able to spend one or two days a week outside of the hospital. His doctor thought his improvements had a lot to do with a positive attitude and his happier demeanour: things that were new for a with-cancer Joss. I had a sneaking suspicion the cause of his advances was having an unbelievably exciting distraction. He was diving headfirst into the supernatural world and interested in every aspect he could learn about. His life or death battle seemed less important to him now that he had made friends with the Rogues and, to my surprise, a few Berlin Askari. The Askari were the nerds, mostly mortals, and did the groundwork for the Praetorian Guard and Custodians – who in turn reported to the Treize. They kept tabs on all the supernaturals, liaised with them if need be, and reported to the relevant PG or Custodian officials. They also tended to get killed more frequently, given they were more adept at research than wielding weapons. They were usually the first point of call when it came to dealing with volatile beings, so it figured.

As a general rule, Askari tended to be stiffs. Yet if there's one thing Askari loved it was knowledge and Joss had so much enthusiasm when it came to learning from them, they couldn't help but like him. I'd been surprised to learn that, along with Officer Dick Creuzinger, some had even taken to visiting him in the oncology ward. It was a relief to me because he'd had a considerable lack of company since I'd been out on the Ireland mission. It was one of these Askari who popped into frame now, waving at me cheerfully. That answered my question about who he'd been discussing me with.

'Hi Tommi!'

'Oh, hey, how are you?' I asked, waving back. Her name was Tulc, I thought, or maybe Tulcie? I could never bloody remember, so I always dodged addressing her directly. She was often wearing overalls, so in my head I just called her 'dungarees'.

'I'm good! Joss is helping me with some research.'

I snorted. 'Of course. How very Joss.'

'Hey, I'm useful!' he protested, taking up the rest of the screen and blocking out Tulc/Tulcie/dungarees as he shoved his face closer.

'I knooooow, mate. Not disagreeing. Just, take the afternoon off or something? Watch some episodes of *The Good Wife*.'

'We finished that. We're on to *The Good Fight* now.'

'Season four!' the Askari chimed.

'I'm very happy for you both,' I smiled, completely sincere. It was good to see Joss happy, even if I wasn't there and his present company meant I couldn't dive into any deep subject matter.

'You look shite.'

'Joss!' I snapped, even though I thought exactly the same thing.

'What? You do! Friends don't lie.'

'They do if they want to stay friends.'

'I thought you'd all be finished by now. Haven't you had a chance to relax? You're such a hypocrite, telling me to take the afternoon off meanwhile you're looking like Werner Herzog in a wig.'

'The *rudeness* that comment had,' I whispered, not even slightly stung. 'The audacity.'

'Just sayin'.'

'Fine, I'm going to put some cucumber slices on my eyes or some crap. Sleep in.'

'Attagirl.' He beamed. 'You're back in a few days, yeah?'

'Aye, a few days.'

'See ya then.'

'See ya, wee friend.'

'Oh! And tell Lorcan I said hi!'

I opened my mouth to respond, but the call disconnected before I had a chance. Great, now my mind was whirring with *Lorcan* thoughts. I slowed my breathing and closed my eyes as I sorted through the various sounds of the hotel and searched for him among it. He was there and I exhaled, more relieved than I would like to admit. He was listening to Nina Simone and as she sung about the colour of her true love's hair, I couldn't help but be transported back to my old apartment in Dundee. It was night, Mari and Kane had been shagging in her bedroom, and Lorcan and I had been left in the kitchen, both of us pretending not to know what they were up to. He'd asked me to cut his hair, which had been down to his shoulders when I'd first met him. So I did. Goosebumps rose on my skin as I thought about touching him that night, running my fingers through his hair and sweeping away the loose strands from the base of his neck. I was so tightly wound, the memory was turning me on. I touched myself – despite all the other problems I had, at least there was something I could do about *this*.

By the time I woke, it was late afternoon and our last official day in Ireland. My tummy rumbled when I looked at the clock, as if it knew I had skipped multiple opportunities for food in my unconscious state. Kicking the covers free, I stumbled from the bed and stretched my body as I moved. We were all flying back to Berlin tomorrow and at the end of the room sat my half-packed suitcase. I stared at it blankly, thinking about how nice it was going to be not to have to live out of a bag for the first time in months.

I dressed in a daze, lacing up a pair of thigh-high black boots. My fingers were as preoccupied as my mind, thoughts whirring as I thought about Dr Kikuchi, Heath's secrets, the young woman pregnant with triplets, and the *freakin' mermaid* of it all. Among all of that was the ghost boy, Seamus, and the last thing he'd said to me:

'We'll keep an eye on you, Tommi Grayson.'

'We,' I muttered to no one, shaking my head slightly. *We.* I checked the date on my phone, unsurprised to see the full moon was fast approaching. I was filled with a restless energy that coursed through my veins and made me feel overwhelmingly anxious. Or maybe this had nothing to do with the impending full moon at all. Maybe my anxiety was being caused by the million and one things I had to be anxious about.

Instead of addressing those issues, I decided to eat.

I took to the Galway streets in search of food, marching by many hungover people and envying them slightly. The scent of a delicious curry coming from an Indian restaurant made my mouth water, but I ended up the only patron in a divey pizza joint instead. It was licensed and that was what was most important. Left with my thoughts, a bevvy, and an entire meat lovers', I mentally drifted back to Seamus and the rundown school. The ghost wasn't there anymore, but since this was my last day in the country, I decided there was something about the place that made me want to see it again. I paid up and left the restaurant, realising with a jolt that in the past few days I'd seen both my first ghost *and my* first selkie. *Joss is going to lose his shit when I tell him about Seamus,* I thought, not sure how much I was going to be able to say about the second.

I walked slowly through the surrounding streets, trying to come up with a way to get around the secrecy I'd promised Heath. It felt as if I was in a trance, barely aware of my surroundings as my body moved forward while my brain was somewhere else entirely. There was a light breeze that ruffled my hair around me and I came to a halt. At first, I wasn't sure what had stopped me, just instinct, but then my werewolf senses took over. I had picked up a scent, a familiar one: Lorcan. Frowning as I looked down a dank alley where the trail led, soon I was following it before I even questioned whether or not I should. He had been on my mind and in my head. I took a left turn here, swiftly dodged a feral street cat there, then two right turns before my ears twitched as I picked up the sound of his voice deep in conversation.

'A whole family of missing banshees is unusual, I'll give you that, but—'

'That's why I think you should come. No one else is better suited for this and others are dropping off the radar quicker than we can track, not just the girl and her sisters.'

'It's not what I imagined my next assignment would be,' he sighed.

'Why not? You were able to find Tommi and get her away from the Ihi pack when no one else could.'

'That was different.'

Now it was her turn to sigh. 'You want out of this? Away from fighters? Any Custodian would consider hunting down a teenage banshee a piece of cake compared to a blood-thirsty werewolf. A little boring, even.'

'Boring can be good.'

I stepped out from behind the wall I had my back pressed against and took in the scene. It was a full few seconds before they noticed my presence, with her arm resting on Lorcan's and the pair of them barely more than a few inches apart. Lorcan stiffened as if he sensed I was there before he physically saw me. Eventually his head snapped in my direction. I couldn't meet his eyes as my own continued to run over their physical postures. Jenica's head slowly turned towards the alley's entrance where I was standing out in the open, all sense of casual discovery gone.

'Tommi?' she said, surprise rich in her tone. I was surprised too. The last time I'd seen the Berlin-based Askari, she'd been cosying up to Lorcan at Phases. He'd told me their outward affection towards each other was part of a cover when we'd fought about it. It was the easiest way to misdirect anyone from realising that my Custodian was also my lover. As I looked between the two of them, I wasn't so sure that was just a cover anymore. Lorcan's mouth moved as if to say something, yet no words came out.

'Your next assignment?' I asked, ignoring her and addressing the question directly to the man I cared about.

'I haven't had a chance to talk to you yet—' he started, before I cut him off.

'Or at all, really,' I snapped. 'It's hard to say a lot in four-word sentences sprinkled out over the course of days.'

'Listen—'

'Are you here on official Askari business?' I asked Jenica, sharply. 'Work not pleasure?'

She blinked before replying. 'Yes, I was sent to see if Lorcan and the Custodians could help with an incident.'

'What kind of incident?'

'That's . . . that's not for me to say.'

My skin itched with anger and I felt heat rising in my blood. Lorcan's green eyes were penetrating right through my very person and I couldn't maintain his gaze. I was afraid the wolf would be looking back at him, rather than the woman. I spun on my heels and walked away from the pair of them as quickly as I could manage without running. He muttered something to her, I didn't establish what, before taking off after me.

'Tommi, wait, we need to talk,' he huffed, jogging alongside me as I refused to slow my pace.

'You don't talk to me, clearly. You talk to her, the diversionary tactic, remember?'

'She's not here for that, she's on assignment.'

'Aye, it *definitely* looks like that way,' I snorted.

'I haven't had a chance to explain this yet—'

'You want away from fighters?' I barked, coming to a sharp stop. 'What about me? You're my Custodian, I'm your ward!'

'I . . .'

Whatever he was about to say died on his lips as I stared at him, trying to decipher the repeated puzzle of his actions and the contradiction of his words. She had said 'you want out of this', but what did that really mean? This PG kill squad was a temporary thing, it had always had an expiry date. Deep down I knew – from the second the sentence hung in the air – that Jenica didn't mean our Laignach Faelad mission. She meant me. *He* meant me. I couldn't process that yet. So I did what I often did in difficult situations: I bailed.

'Where are you going?' Lorcan called as I left him where he stood.

'To get some space,' I shouted. 'From you.'

I DRAGGED myself back to the school, back to where Seamus had haunted for so long and back to where the last of the Laighnach Faelad had been slaughtered. It made sense once I was there, having walked the entire distance because I remained a fucking idiot. When I'd said I needed space, it wasn't a metaphor: I walked and walked and walked until I had plenty of it. The air was sharp on my nostrils as I breathed it in, the weather noticeably cooler than it had been on Saint Patrick's Day. It was a relief: I preferred the cold. I missed the Berlin weather, I missed Scotland, and as the green paddocks stretched out in front of me, it felt like I got a tiny taste of home. Walking through the ruins of the old structure, I ran my fingers over the claw marks down the walls from the earlier battle. There was a deep groove in the floor, and I knew that was from my machete where I had pivoted on the spot. There was even blood soaked into the rotting wood – though it looked like nothing more than discolouration as it dried a deep-brown. I could sniff out the truth, however.

Three months of this, I thought, as I sat on the ledge of a window frame on the third floor. Even if I hadn't enjoyed the labour, it would have been worth it. My involvement on this job meant my half-brother, Quaid Ihi, would officially have a chance at release from supernatural prison Vankila. He had been fourteen years old when they threw him in there because of me, and now he was sixteen or so it was my responsibility to try and get him out. Hunting down the Laignach Faelad gave me the bargaining power to do that and I'd watched those around me carefully when it came to negotiating with the Treize. I didn't have a lot of power as the secret love child of a werewolf leader they once feared, Jonah Ihi, but I did have some: it was all about leveraging that capital.

It must have been later than I thought, and as the light dimmed on the horizon I knew I should be making my way back. To the hotel. To Lorcan. Would he even be there when I returned, or would he be off on one of those mysterious sojourns I now suspected had *a lot* to do with Jenica? I sighed, knowing my frustration wasn't with her. She was no one, just another Askari in the way. It was Lorcan I was frustrated with. And myself.

With a lurch, I leaped from the third storey and flew towards the ground, completing a perfect superhero landing. It was a shame there was no one there to see it. I called Yu on my walk back, who despite not being a werewolf was as much a member of the Rogues as anyone. She put me on loudspeaker so I was able to chat to Dolly, her partner, at the same time. They'd already spoken to Clay so knew we were coming back soon, but it was nice to have some idle chatter about the supernatural community and all of the hot Phases gossip as I journeyed back. I didn't want to think anymore. They were low-key two of my favourite people to talk to, Yu being former Praetorian Guard herself and Dolly a werewolf. I was able to fill my mind with their voices rather than my own thoughts, which was exactly what I wanted.

I hung up once I got back to the hotel, thinking that I would get changed and then head immediately down to the bar. Distractions and booze: I could figure out the rest later. Yet as soon as I entered my room and saw Lorcan sitting on the edge of the bed, hands resting between his knees, my stomach clenched. Given the things I'd seen him do, the question of how he got in without a key seemed redundant. I glanced from his face to the packed duffel bag at his feet and back again. His usually emerald-green irises seemed duller somehow, and I didn't miss the tinge of red around the outside. He was upset.

'What's going on?' I started, skipping the pretence.

'Like I said, we need to talk,' he replied, sounding sombre.

'Don't,' I said, laughing at the most over-used relationship cliché in the history of over-used relationship clichés. I could hear the sound of my own voice and I knew it sounded bitter. 'Just be straight with me.'

A shiver of hurt crossed his features and before I could react, he was up off the bed and across the room. With him suddenly in front of me, the heat that flushed in my cheeks as he touched my face was a reminder that, of all the problems we had, physical attraction would never be one. My breath caught as his lips moved to mine in a kiss that barely touched and I couldn't help but kiss him back, fingers running along his jawline. It should be illegal for a man to have bone structure like that.

'I'm leaving,' he whispered, pulling back slowly.

I heard what he said but at the same time, I didn't hear it. Relief poured through me at his words and I frowned, recognising the sensation. This was not what I should be feeling. We had been living in this weird state of flux, knowing that we weren't 'ex' anything but at the same time grounded by our history, the battles, the sex, the complications. So much of 'us' was unresolved and I think part of me just expected it would always be that way.

'And when are you coming back?' I replied.

He paused, letting the silence hang between us. My frown deepened.

'You want out, away from *werewolves*,' I said, speaking Jenica's words back to him. 'I assumed that was a temporary thing.'

'It's not.'

I stared at him in disbelief, waiting for Lorcan to add something else. Anything else.

'Let me guess,' I snorted. 'It's not you, it's me?'

'No, because it's not me. It's you.'

'I – what?'

'I've tried, Tommi. I've taught you and I've supported

you but this . . . this life? What you're becoming? It's everything I vowed to leave behind.'

'Hold up, you didn't have to come on this trip. We had this discussion back in Berlin. I was more than happy to finish the job on my own. Sure, it's always better if you're around but no one asked you to come.'

He snickered. 'I was your Custodian, Tommi. I've been trying very hard to be just that and *only* that. I couldn't trust Heath and the others to look after you and maintain your training.'

'You don't have to trust them, you just have to trust me.' I saw a flash of something in his eyes then: a pang of truth, perhaps. 'You don't, do you? You don't trust me.'

'I don't trust what you're becoming,' he said quietly.

'And what's that?'

'A monster, Tommi.'

My own breath snapped back into my throat as his words hit me harder than a thousand roundhouse kicks to the tit. I tried to formulate a sentence as my mouth opened and closed, yet no words were forthcoming. I felt like I was going to vomit.

'Was,' I said, my mind pricking on the past tense. 'You are my Custodian, we've given up *everything* to keep that one element the same, so why are you using "was"? Things might have changed with us, but fundamentally nothing has changed with this.'

'You refuse to see it. You left Dundee because you thought you gave in to your wolf that night at the warehouse.'

'I left because there were too many ghosts for me there,' I rebutted.

'In Berlin you were supposed to learn how to survive from the Rogues,' he continued, ignoring me. 'All you did was learn how to be a better killer. Now the past three months have been spent as part of an assassination unit. You're shifting multiple parts of you every day, multiple times, and you don't even blink when you harness your inner wolf.'

'Things YOU taught me how to do!' I shouted, not caring how loud my voice got or how many other werewolf ears in this hotel heard me. 'You're the one who encouraged me to seek out the Rogues, you're the one who taught me how to reach my inner wolf and try to use it. And now you're throwing this back in my face? YOU are the one who taught me how to kill, Lo, now you're saying these skills have turned me into a monster? How could you even use that word when you know the kind of real monsters we've faced?'

'It's the only thing I thought would get through to you. That, and me leaving.'

Another jab, again of the non-physical kind. It hurt just as much.

'Are you leaving or breaking up with me?'

We weren't together, but there was no phrase that better encapsulated what he was doing. He was breaking up with me personally and professionally.

He paused for a long moment, before finally saying: 'Both.'

I took three steps back from him, my mind racing. 'To do what? Follow Jenica on whatever mission she has chased you here for?'

He refused to meet my eyes as he ran a hand through his hair. 'As of an hour ago I resigned from my duties as your personal Custodian. It's the only thing to do, Tommi. This life is turning you into all the things I swore to myself I wouldn't be anymore. After Amos died, I changed everything about who I was and who I had been for over four hundred years. I found hope and a life in helping others instead of cutting them down. I found that in you. Now I'm back at this place where I swore I'd never be again: a lackey for the whims of the Praetorian Guard. I can't do it. It's not who I want to be.'

'And where do I fit in?'

'You don't. It's becoming clearer and clearer to me that this is what you are, where you belong.'

'I thought I belonged with you,' I muttered. 'Romantic or otherwise, I thought I belonged with you by my side in any capacity. And now you're calling me a monster . . . how does it change like that? How do you disregard everything we've been through and just quit, just walk away? Was it all a lie?'

'No, it's—'

'If you say the word "complicated" I will scream.'

He said nothing instead. We stood there, the two of us, metres apart in the shitty hotel room. It could have been oceans apart for all it mattered. Every line he spoke pushed us further and further away from each other. He said more words, but they ceased to matter. By the time he was done it felt like we were on different continents.

'I'm flying back to Berlin tonight, then . . . on.'

'Where will you go?' I asked, my voice sounding foreign to me. 'Oh wait, I'm sure you can't tell me that.'

'You know I can't.'

'I know that if you really wanted to, you would.'

He picked up his duffel bag with a sigh.

'A banshee is missing,' he said. Upon seeing the look on my face, he added further detail. 'Banshees were banished to Australia many years ago. They can't leave the continent. One went missing years ago, now a second from the same family is gone, along with ... others. There have been unconfirmed sightings internationally and they need someone to look into it.'

Anyone could do that job, I thought to myself as I crossed my arms and leaned against the wall behind me. But he was choosing to do it. I watched Lorcan make his way to the door and I felt myself shake as I realised the moment that he was leaving was *this* moment. How could this be it? How could we have fought side-by-side and lived side-by-side and loved side-by-side and then *this?* Lorcan turned and looked at me with a pity that made me want to slap his face, no matter how beautiful it was. I saw a tear streak down his cheek and I hoped it burned like acid.

'For the record,' I said, keeping my voice neutral, 'if I'm a monster, then I'm the monster you made me.'

With that he was gone, the door closing softly behind him as I stood there in silence. Somehow we'd managed to have one of the most devastating conversations of my life with the lights off, only the glow of the setting sun casting the odd shadow here and there. I'm not sure how long I stood in that position, glaring at the door Lorcan had just walked through. Hours, I assumed, given how the racket from the heaving pub downstairs rose and fell as the patrons came and left. Eventually I began to move, packing the rest of the few possessions I had brought with me on this trip. Unable to stand the quiet much longer, I pushed my headphones into my ears and turned up DJ Khaled as loud as I could stand it. When I was done, I showered, changed clothes, and headed out of the hotel with my gear in one hand. There were still a few more hours before we had to be up and on our way to the private plane that would take us back to Germany. Yet I knew sleep was pointless. The only thing I could bring myself to do was plant my ass on the kerb next to my bag and watch the sun come up.

5

When a pair of long limbs stretched out on the concrete next to me, I didn't have to raise my head to know it was Heath.

I did, however, cast a cursory glance his way when he passed me an unopened bottle of Patrón . I arched a single eyebrow, and my expression was met with a devilish grin as a cigarette dangled between his lips.

'Irish breakfast?' he offered.

'Do you just add "Irish" in front of everything to make it a cute phrase?'

'That's not stopping you from opening the bottle.'

'Oh look, an Irish werewolf,' I said, gesturing to myself as I snatched the alcohol from him. 'Ah, this here is what we call an Irish doorway.'

As the booze hit the back of my throat, it acted as a physical slap to my senses.

'I don't suppose you've got any Irish salt and lemons to go with this?' I asked, taking another huge gulp.

'That would be an Irish no.'

'Where did you even buy Patrón at this time of the morning?'

He just smiled by way of response. I offered him a sip from the bottle and he handed me his cigarette in return. Looking at the burning embers and the paper curling away from its base, I did something I hadn't done in years.

'Fuck it.' I shrugged, taking a long drag.

'When was the last time you smoked?' he asked.

My mind stretched as I thought back. 'Maybe . . . a bit over two years ago? Three? When Joss was diagnosed the first time.'

We remained where we were in comfortable silence for a while, the sounds of the town slowly stirring around us. Heath was first to break the quiet.

'Do you want to know where he's going?'

'Not particularly,' I said. 'I think it's probably better if I don't.'

'Cold turkey, huh?'

I tried to muster a smile but the attempt made my face hurt. 'I guess I should be completely unsurprised by you knowing that he left.'

Heath shrugged, unapologetic.

'And that he resigned as my Custodian.'

Another shrug. 'If you're waiting for me to say "I told you so" then you're going to be here a while.'

'You kinda just did, actually.'

'I told you back in Berlin that Lorcan and I mightn't be friends anymore, but I would never get in the way of his happiness. He does a good enough job of that himself.'

'"You played yourself",' I quoted.

'What?'

'Never mind,' I said, shaking my head with the knowledge Heath would never get the reference. 'Do immortals use Facebook? Insta? Don't give me that look, it's a genuine question.'

'Not . . . recreationally. Why?'

'It's just gonna be really hard for me to be a bittersexual and creep on what he's up to if he doesn't have a digital footprint.'

'Why would you care? Man routinely lies and leaves.'

'And you tell nothing but the truth, the whole truth, so help you, God?'

'This isn't about me,' he said, holding his hands up in a truce gesture. 'But aye, I've never pretended to be the good guy.'

'Thank Christ for that,' I murmured, taking the opportunity to reach into the depths of his coat and retrieve the packet of cigarettes I could smell there.

'Sure, sure, help yourself. "Thanks for the Patrón, Heath, you're welcome, Tommi. I'm very good at anticipating people's needs."'

'Thanks for the Patrón, Heath.' I smiled, this time for real, as I pinched his lighter too. 'You're very good at anticipating people's needs.'

He leaned in to shelter the flickering flame as I lit my cigarette. 'You're welcome, Tommi. And this is the last thing I'll say: when people walk away from you, let them go. Your destiny is never tied to anyone who leaves you. Their part in your story is over.'

'There's no way you came up with that.'

''Course not. Some pastor, Tony McCollum.'

I let pastor Heath's words sink in for a moment and I'll admit, I felt foolish. More than anything, I felt resignation and my usual dose of anger simmering under the surface. Yet foolishness . . . it was there too. I thought about the men I had been with in the past, the ones who I had been able to endure for more than a one-night stand. My former flame Poc sprang to mind, still back home in Dundee and actually in a *real* relationship now with a chick who seemed pretty damn deserving of him. I knew this because we still spoke occasionally. We were friends. Before anything else, we had bonded over a mutual love and appreciation of art, music, movies – the usual pop culture identifiers. Those had been a bridge to mutual attraction and yeah, he was fit. The feelings I'd had for Poc never came close to what I felt for Lorcan, but Lorcan and I were never friends. We'd been thrown into a situation together that was extreme, and it brought out the extreme in us.

I loved Lorcan, I was fairly sure of it. I'd risked so much for him. Yet just because we were undeniably attracted to each other, did that mean we should be together? Were we actually good for each other? Were we good *together*? Did we bring out the best in ourselves? I couldn't say that was true. And in a world where I'd initially known nothing and no one, Lorcan had always held so much power over me. He had all the information and all the answers. I had always pushed him about the things he kept from me, but now I felt deeply foolish for never once having taken the time to stop and ask myself the questions I was asking now that he had left. I was hurting, and I knew these scars were different from the ones on the outside of my skin. That sense of abandonment wasn't going to slip away easily. Thankfully, I had alcohol and an abundance of distractions for that.

'Is it dangerous?' I asked Heath, noting the strange look a woman gave us as she hurried along on her way to work.

'Hmm?'

'This missing banshee. Banshees.'

'Not for him. It's gobshite in a teacup, honestly. They've enlisted Lorcan way too late in the game to pick up a trail.'

I cast Heath a sideways glance, analysing him through narrowed eyes. He knew Lorcan had planned on leaving, and he likely knew Jenica was in town. He also knew as part of his new assignment Lorcan was supposed to be tracking down one, potentially other, missing banshees. All I knew was that as a species they had been banished to Australia at some point. Well, I'd just met two mysterious women a few days ago, one who had an Aussie accent and another who didn't speak. I had been sworn to secrecy about the encounter, so Lo didn't know what I knew. But Heath did. He must have known I'd connect the dots, yet he was trusting me to stay quiet all the same. I opened my mouth to say as much, about to flat-out ask if he'd intentionally run such a masterful shell game.

'What?' he asked, watching me as keenly as I was watching him.

'Nothing,' I sighed, thinking better of it. I didn't want this added drama. Maybe there actually were some things I was better off not knowing.

'Attagirl,' Heath said, slapping me on the back so hard it startled me into a coughing fit that most definitely didn't have anything to do with the cigarettes. Probably. 'Now, shall we see where the others are so we can get out of this depressing town?'

An elderly man cast Heath a disgusted look and muttered something under his breath as he strolled past.

'Oh, what? Like this is Hawaii? Fooooken hell,' he called after the older gent.

I whacked him playfully on the arm as I got to my feet, stretching out my limbs, which were stiff and cold. It would be a full moon tonight and I knew my body was going to pay for it during the transformation. Clay and Sanjay rolled out of the hotel entrance. As in, literally rolled: both had matching suitcases on wheels that looked more like mini-refrigerators from the fifties than luggage. In fact, Clay had mocked Sanjay ruthlessly months ago when we first started this trip . . . until Sanjay had shown him all the lightweight storage functions and the portable phone charger hidden under one of the straps. Two days later they had identical luggage, with Clay unashamedly admitting, 'when you're wrong, you're wrong, chica'.

'You two are up early,' said Sanjay, 'I thought we'd beat you down here.'

'Is that . . . tequila? Are you drinking tequila for break-fast, Tommi?' Clay asked, nudging the now empty bottle with his toe.

'Technically we both had tequila for breakfast,' Heath replied.

'Tequila is my lady,' I sang by way of response, 'my laaaady.'

Clay bopped his head in time with my terrible attempt at rhythm while Sanjay looked around us.

'Now if only our transport was—'

His sentence was cut off by the screech of tyres as our hire van pulled up at the intersection, Jakea at the wheel and Jaira in the passenger's seat.

'Get in, losers,' I murmured, hauling my bag up and following the boys. 'We're going shopping.'

WITHIN TWO HOURS we were on our designated PG plane and flying back to Berlin. And I was hella jaked. Heath had come through with another bottle of booze – that Alchemist whiskey – and the two of us had taken a seat at the back of the plane to finish it off. The others were sitting up front playing an increasingly strained game of poker as Clay continued a reign of dominance. Why anyone dared go up against him, I had no idea. I considered myself a decent player, but even I wasn't that stupid. Sipping slowly from my glass, I pressed my forehead against the plane's window as I looked out at the mass of white and pink swirling clouds. When you looked at them long enough, you lost touch with the reality of what they were: they appeared almost solid at times, like huge scoops of mashed potato in the sky.

'You know what's funny?' I said, keeping my eyes locked on the endless expanse of clouds and atmosphere.

'What's that?' murmured Heath in response, not looking up from whatever he was reading on a tablet.

'No one has asked where Lorcan is.'

I could feel Heath's eyes on me as his silence confirmed what I suspected. They already knew. No one had asked where Lorcan was because they *already* knew. My mind was my worst enemy in that moment, as I imagined him working his way through the group over the past few days, maybe a week, telling them one by one what he was intending to do, telling them to keep it secret, keep it to themselves, so that the very last person to know he was leaving was me. There was something about that which hurt more than anything else that had unfolded in the past twenty four hours. Closing my eyes, I let the vibrations of the plane rock me to sleep as my body finally gave up on everything that had been keeping it awake.

WHEN I STIRRED, Heath was taking me into Phases in an approximation of a fireman's carry. Waking slowly, I raised my head to see Yu and Dolly trailing behind us with our bags. My first instinct was to scream and squirm and kick until Heath dropped me, but I could feel another instinct too: something deeper and more primal. My wolf was stirring and my body's time in human form was about to take a backseat. The knowledge of what was to come left me pre-exhausted and out of fight before I even had the energy to arc up.

'Evening, Sleeping Beauty,' said Dolly, meeting my eyes with a small smile.

'Dolly, I'd say it's nice to see you and I've missed your face, but you look way too amused with this situation for me to do that,' I huffed, my words coming out funny as I tried to arch my back off Heath's shoulders.

'You owe me five bucks,' Yu told her girlfriend. Dolly chuckled as she slipped a note into Yu's extended hand.

Confusion obviously evident on my face, I glanced from one to the other and back again.

'We had a bet,' Yu explained, 'on what kind of state you'd wake up in.'

'That's putting it lightly,' Heath chimed in. 'They were aiming to profit on my likely disfigurement.'

Dolly shrugged unapologetically. 'I thought if you woke up to him carrying you to the cells like that, less than half an hour before transformation, you'd kill him.'

'I wagered you'd be too hungover to give a fuck,' Yu countered.

'Fight or fatigue,' I groaned, flopping back down against the broad expanse of Heath's back and letting my arms dangle in front of my face. Smooth skin brushed against my own as Yu reached out a hand, briefly squeezing mine. There was something about the small gesture that made tears prick at the corner of my eyes, something I wasn't sure I was able to hide so well in my vulnerable physical state.

The movement descending the final staircase to the cells that would hold us for the next three nights jostled our hands apart. Heath didn't let me down until we were already inside one of the rooms, surprising me with his graceful movements as he slowly – and gently – lowered me to the ground. My legs were so shaky I was barely able to stand and I allowed myself to slide down the wall into a sitting position.

'How long have I got?' he asked.

I searched internally for the answer, almost visually able to see my wolf pacing back and forth with impatience.

'You know I can hold it back,' I answered. 'I've changed in front of you before.'

'Technically you were behind me and I was driving,' he said, referring to the time I'd had no choice but to shift into werewolf form in the back of a moving van. 'And there was a steel grate between us.'

'Which wouldn't have stopped me if I wanted through.'

'Which *definitely* wouldn't have stopped you if you wanted through. I've been around enough werewolves to know not to push my chances, even ones with as much control as you. So, I repeat: how long have I got?'

'Ten minutes,' I whispered. 'Maybe less.'

'Aye,' he answered, rummaging through a bag at his side. 'We got here a lot later in the day than I would have liked, but Yu was able to pick up some prime cuts.'

He held up a massive bag of red, bloody meat for me to see. I nodded by way of response, my mouth watering at the very thought of being able to tear into that soon.

'I wasn't sure if you had passed out or fallen asleep. Seemed best to let you rest as long as possible before the full moon.'

'Thank you.'

With a brisk nod, he headed for the door. He was about to shut it when he hesitated, looking back. He was a hulk of a man: tall and blond and wide. Blocking most of the doorway with his physique, he looked more like a linebacker than someone willing to gently carry me inside so I could stay unconscious for a few minutes longer. With a final glance, he left and locked the door behind him. I knew I needed to undress, but sweat broke out all over my body and my clothes stuck to my skin. I couldn't muster the energy when I knew my new form would be bursting out of them in a matter of min—

'ENGH!' I groaned, a growl building in my throat as I let out another verbal cry of agony. At that point I'd usually move myself around on to all fours to ease the shift, but tonight? As I sank down into the foetal position I wondered if I wanted it to hurt. My skin bubbled and boiled as my bones cracked, the noise masked by my screams, which bounced off the walls. I felt my muscles slice themselves apart as they readjusted to accommodate the wolf. All I could do was pant and try to control my breathing as I gave into the relentless agony and let the werewolf have full dominion. The moon was king tonight and the creatures in its kingdom had finally come out to play.

I DIDN'T LEAVE my cell for two full days and three full nights. Usually I'd trudge my way back to the apartment above Phases, get a shower and a few hours sleep, before heading back down. This time though, I didn't trust myself. My wolf might have withdrawn under my skin during the day, but it wasn't leaving me alone. By dawn on day three, Clay had to help me up the stairs of the complex we all lived in together.

He himself had been ravaged by the phases, so it was testament to my dire state that I needed the assist.

'You know,' he said, my arm propped up over his shoulder as I struggled with the keys at my front door, 'I always find the worse my emotions, the worse my wolf.'

Nudging the door open with my foot, I stumbled inside and over the threshold. My eyes swept over the home I hadn't been back to in months, digesting the scene. I hadn't fully understood the ramifications of Lorcan leaving until I looked at the apartment we had once shared. Realising Clay was still there, I thanked him before softly closing the door. I was desperate to be alone with the sight that greeted me. Or, rather, punched me straight in the heart. We hadn't had a whole lot of stuff, but Lorcan's touch had been all around the place – mainly with cooking utensils and ancient books and cases of weapons everywhere. He'd even hung an old scroll on the wall. That was before. Now everything was gone. All of his things were gone. All that remained were my clothes on the IKEA wire rack and my make-up in its usual position at the bathroom sink. I fingered the glass container that had once held both our toothbrushes. Now there was only mine.

My reflection was ghastly, to say the least. Big bags hung under my eyes and I had let the blue dye fade in my hair so much the shade was muted, almost pastel, and my dark roots were at my ears. My locks matched the colour of Seamus' ghost. I showered, and my period arrived just as I was getting ready to stumble to bed – my body deciding to give me one more 'fuck you' just for good measure. Grabbing a heat pack and holding it to my stomach, I downed five whole glasses of water before I collapsed on the bed. I was asleep before I even had a chance to pull the doona over my body.

A persistent, rhythmic buzzing seemed to be coming from my skull and I stirred, trying to work out the source. Eventually I realised I had fallen asleep on my phone and I peeled my cheek from both the pillow and the glass of my screen. Joss's number flashed at me in the darkness and I moaned, blinded by the light. The vibration stopped and the phone powered down, completely out of battery. I hadn't told Joss about Lorcan yet, I realised. With the travel and the transformations, I hadn't even had time to send him a text. Given that my former Custodian had brought everyone up to speed before I even knew what was up, I wondered if Lorcan had already done the job for me. Stretching with a groan as I got out of bed, I dispelled that idea. Joss would have told me straight away, no matter what Lorcan instructed him.

Keeping the lights off, I moved around the apartment, comfortable in the dark. My body was stiff and achy, and I knew laying in the same position for God knows how long probably hadn't helped. Neither had the PMS and I winced through a painful cramp. Turning on a Lykke Li track just loud enough to drown the sounds coming from Heath's place across the hall, I was headed to get something to eat when I noticed that among some of the novelty magnets and band stickers I had collected and stuck to the fridge was a photo. Lorcan had left it there. He'd taken everything he cared about, so it made sense he'd left this behind. It was a picture of the two of us, taken not long after we first moved to Berlin. Clay had captured us mid-conversation, packing up after a night at Phases. It was the evening I had met the twins and, unbeknownst to me, I was only moments away from heading upstairs to fight them as they tried to recruit me to join the Praetorian Guard. I could see the head of the

Rogues, Zillia, smiling at Dolly as she lifted a chair in the background.

I left it where it was and welcomed the white light that poured from the fridge as I opened it, hoping it would burn away my vision. Praising the foresight of my friends – Heath or Yu, I guessed – I was able to cook a massive fry-up with the supplies they had bought for me. I made a mental note to repay them somehow as I left the dishes in the sink and began throwing on layers of clothing in preparation for the Berlin winter – which was in full swing outside, despite the fact it should have been easing by now. The streets were quiet and deserted as I made my way to Mechtilde General. It would still be dark for a few more hours, which I was grateful for. I felt comfortable like this, anonymous and hidden in the night. Well and truly out of visiting hours, I was careful to avoid the night shift nurses as I weaved my way through the bowels of the hospital. At this point I knew the place like my own skin. I was surprised to see a faint glow coming from under Joss's doorway and I peeked around the corner slowly as I entered the room. His head immediately darted up from the other side of his laptop and there was something about the meerkat-esque gesture that made me grin. In fact, just looking at my best friend, curled up in bed with his computer balanced on a knee, made me feel lighter.

'Tom?' he whispered, keeping his voice down as I closed the door behind me.

I practically dived on the bed as I embraced him in a hug, careful not to crush his thin frame.

'Ya wee bawbag, I've missed you so much,' I said, words muffled as my face pressed against his shoulder.

'What are you – I thought you were the night nurse. It's like four in the morning!'

'Aye and why are you up? You should be resting! Getting your beauty sleep.'

'I was reading, thank you very much. Trying to stay the smartest in the room.' He tapped his skull for emphasis and I stifled a chuckle.

'Reading my ass. Only thing you'd be looking at this time of night is porn,' I countered, spinning around the screen to inspect his 'reading' material. 'Oh.'

'Tommi Grayson, if I'm not mistaken you have that "holy shite, I'm wrong and Joss is right" look on your face.'

'You're definitely wrong,' I said, scanning the extensive document. 'Must be the new meds you're on. What the hell is this?'

'Been reading up on rogue werewolves actually, know any?'

'Ha. You just Google this or—'

'What do you think I am, a soggy grape? As if this would be online,' he snorted. 'Askari documents. Tulc got special clearance for me and when you can't sleep ...'

'Lay with werewolves?'

'Ha, that's good. Anyway, screw the boring stuff, how long have you been back? I assumed before the full moon, but I was still expecting it to be a few more days before you were able to leave Lorcan and the others for a visit.'

Something must have passed over my face at the mention of his name. Even in the dim light Joss picked up on it. It took barely more than a few prompts from him before I was spilling everything: the conversation I overheard with Jenica right through to his decision to leave. He sat in silence for a while after I finished, thoughtful, before he reached out and grabbed me. He pulled me towards him until my head found a home in his lap and I let out a deep sigh. Shutting my eyes, I took a long moment to inhale the scent of him, my oldest mate. Up until that point I hadn't realised how much I needed to see him, to be physically comforted by Joss. Usually it was the other way around and I think he was enjoying the role reversal as he stroked my hair.

'You're not a monster,' he said. 'Don't ever let anyone tell you you're a monster.'

I awkwardly nodded, feeling a strong compulsion to cry but quashing it.

'Just because you're not the physical representation of what a hero looks like, that doesn't make you any less a hero. You might appear to be a wee monster three nights of the month and, heck, when you choose to. But that does not maketh a monster.'

'I know. He was trying to justify leaving, come up with an excuse for quitting, and he knew that one would impact me the most. And that's what stings: he knew how much calling me a monster would hurt and he did it anyway. And the lies! Always the lies and half-truths with him.'

'The sodding bampot. You're definitely sure the others knew?'

I thought about it carefully. 'Aye, Clay and Sanjay for sure. The twins? Yeah, definitely. I don't think Yu and Dolly had any idea until we were back and as for Heath . . . Lorcan hated any kind of power he had over him, so I could see him telling Heath at the very last minute as a final way to stick the boot in. Heath already knew what he was up to anyway.'

'Have they said who your new Custodian will be?'

I stirred, lifting my head up to look at his face. 'No, they haven't. I thought the twins might know but they left for their next assignment days ago.'

A whole new set of worries lodged themselves in my brain as I ran through the possibility of having a new Custodian. Would I like them? Would they be human or something else entirely? What if we hated each other and they were hella strict?

'Stop it.'

'Huh?'

'I can see the stress practically pouring out your ears.'

'Heh, no, I've just been so caught up with everything I totally forgot they're going to have to give me someone else. What if I don't like them, Joss? What if they're a massive cunt?'

'What if you get assigned a half-demon or something?' Delight was evident on his face as he entertained the possibility of being exposed to a whole new breed of supernatural.

'Taper down the excitement, will you. This is my fate we're talking about.'

'Sorry, but you know . . . maybe they won't assign anyone at all? If you've proven to the Treize you can survive on your own, they could just assign an Askari to check in on you every now and again.'

'Now there's a pleasant thought. Blergh, later problems for later days. How are ya doing?'

'Good!' he said, life flushing his cheeks as he got excited. 'Like, really good. As soon as this weather clears out, Dr Matthews said we can start looking at a homestay. I personally would like to live with you guys at Phases but the parents—'

'DO! Come and live in the apartment with me! Your parents can live there too, if needed. It's huge and very empty.'

'I'd have my rough days post-chemo, you can handle that?'

'Joss, I've been handling that for years.'

'True. Okay. Quality. Now we just have to learn how to control the weather.'

'Yu would probably know someone who can do that. Are you officially in remission again or is this just a battle that we're winning in the grand war?'

'We're kicking cancer butt, but not enough to get me a remission badge. Yet. Two or three more rounds of chemo, no bone marrow transplant required. Then we'll see where I'm at.'

Joss was looking healthier. He was still bald as all hell, yet his skin looked stronger, if that was a possible way to describe skin. Previously he'd had the pallor of an onion.

I left the hospital feeling better, not about myself but about where things were at in general. Barely five steps out of the building and into the snow, I sensed someone watching me. Spinning around, I was unsurprised to find that it was Heath.

'How was the resourceful little civilian?' he asked, walking towards me. His face was barely exposed between the thick scarf wrapped up to his chin and beanie pulled down practically to his eyebrows.

'Mint,' I said, a genuine smile creeping over my face. 'He seems to be doing *really* well.'

'Fuck cancer.'

'Fuck cancer.' I nodded, by way of agreement. 'You following me or what?'

'Actually, I wondered if you'd be up for some physical exertion.'

'Eh, given the physical exertion I heard coming from your apartment last night I think I'll pass.'

'Ah, Babs. Lovely girl. And no, not that.'

'Then what?'

With a sly grin, he unbuttoned his trench coat and

pulled it wide to reveal a small arsenal of weapons strapped to the inside.

'How do we feel about ghouls?'

'Ghouls . . .' I echoed. 'I've never even seen a ghoul.'

'They look like zombies.'

'I've never seen a zombie.'

'Their faces are all messed up and contorted. Unlike zombies, they move fast. Zombies are also puppets; they have to be controlled by someone and, usually, if you're powerful enough to control a zombie you're not going to waste your time controlling a corpse. You could be hunting down mediums to dismember.'

'Ergh.'

'Ghouls, dear Tommi, you will soon learn are the perfect outlet for pent-up rage and/or spikey emotions. They like the cold, and in European cities during winter, they're plentiful. Just like rats, they need to be exterminated.'

I couldn't help but get caught up in his enthusiasm as he threw me a medieval axe and a Glock.

'Yay, a project!'

6

There were five ghoul nests scattered across Berlin and in the preceding weeks Heath and I had taken them out one by one. I was currently crouched in a sewer pipe that opened up into a cavern underneath the city. This was the last stronghold we had to hit up. I had a skull bandana covering my nose and most of my face, leaving only my eyes exposed. Ghouls smelled incredibly bad, which was ironic given they were blind and a powerful sense of smell was their greatest asset. I didn't want to smell them as much as I didn't want them to smell me. The slightest flash of red caught my eye and I followed the path of a laser pointer down to its source. I was perched twenty or so metres above Heath, who had entered the narrow space from the only other access point: a drain below.

It was almost pitch-black here, which mattered little to me. Not wanting to take any risks with the ghouls, I had transitioned my irises the second Heath and I split up and headed underground. Ghouls were feral creatures that preyed on people unlucky enough to be caught alone by a pack of them. A normal human didn't stand much of a chance, given they usually moved in clusters of three or four. But neither of us were normal humans.

I unfolded my body from the uncomfortable position I had stayed in for the past half an hour – Heath's signal meant that every ghoul in this nest had been accounted for. Time to go a'knockin'. Some fifteen creatures were sleeping below me as I soundlessly stretched my legs from one side of the cavern to the other, bracing against the sides. The narrow space could work both for and against us, but by coming at them from above and below we were doing our utmost to make sure there would be no survivors. I looked down at the slumbering ghouls, all completely naked. They had grey skin that seemed to lubricate itself insuring they were always slimy and gross.

BLAM!

A gunshot rang out, causing me to flinch with pain as the sound ricocheted off the walls of the cavern. Heath managed to take out three more ghouls with single shots as I unsheathed the two short swords strapped to my back and dropped from my vantage point – running the blades down the walls to simultaneously sharpen them and slow my descent. Sparks from the weapons trailed behind me as I landed with a thud and used the motion to swing one sword straight through a lunging ghoul. My blade was so sharp and the creature so thin that with one swift movement I was able to slice it completely in half.

Another ghoul pounced, landing on my back and attempting to go for the jugular. They had razor-sharp teeth that hung on the outside of their mouth like a cursed Anglerfish. Anything could be a meal to them and I would have been if I wasn't quicker. Throwing my full body weight backwards, I felt the ghoul slam against the unforgiving stone and I repeated the movement until I heard its spine and skull crack at the same time as it went limp.

'Having fun yet?!' shouted Heath, who had discarded his gun for an axe to fight in such close quarters. He was grinning, with specks of bright blue blood decorating his face as he slashed and hacked his way through a group of five or more ghouls. He was so cocky and preoccupied that he didn't notice the creature racing down the side of the cavern above him. As two more ran at me in hunched form, I used their backs to launch myself up into the air and decapitate Heath's would-be attacker. My blade hit the cold, smooth stone on the other side as it travelled through flesh and bounced off as I fell downwards. With a quick glance, I realised I was about to land on a group of four who all had their claws extended at me, mouths gnashing in anticipation. Their noses were almost entirely flat, with one large slit across the middle of their face and that was precisely where a dagger landed in one ghoul, who was flung backwards, screeching with the impact.

'Excuse me, fellas,' said Heath, kicking another out of the way as he caught me. His vast frame cradled my body, which seemed tiny in comparison as he held me in his arms.

'You're welcome,' I huffed, as I hurled myself away from him and back into the madness. An arm shot out of the darkness and attached itself to me as a ghoul attempted to drag me towards it. Another came from the side, and I was able to fend him off with the short sword while I concentrated on shifting my other wrist into werewolf form. I was acutely aware of the pressure points and nerve clusters of these creatures, and with a laboured yank I was able to displace its arm from its socket. As far as I could tell they were genderless, their sex indistinguishable from ghoul to ghoul, which raised the question: exactly how did they reproduce? Yeesh, there was an image I never wanted to have again.

Three swift slices down the ghoul's frame and it was over. The handful of remaining creatures began to sense they were doomed and climbed over each other for a hand-hold on the wall. They were trying to escape the way they had come in. One had been successful and was moving towards the opening at a rapid rate.

'Tommi!' called Heath, just as I spotted it.

'On it,' I replied, dropping my swords in favour of the Hunga Mungas at my belt. I took the wall at a run, using the weapons to dig into the cavern surface and propel me forwards. I caught the ghoul just before it escaped, piercing the sole of its foot with the curved blade. Wincing at the sound of its cries, I pulled myself up until I was laying across its back, then placed the weapons on either side of its head and drew them across its throat in quick succession. The body went still as life left it and the ghoul fell backwards. I used one arm to swing myself free before it took me with it. Looking down at my body, I took a moment to be disgusted by the mess I was covered in.

'Next time,' I huffed, hopping down and wiping slime from my hair, can you choose a vaguely less gross hobby?'

One last ghoul had been hiding in the rafters and launched itself at Heath as he stood up properly. Having sensed it, he lunged at my Hunga Mungas, spinning and throwing in one swift movement. The weapon lodged in the ghoul's forehead and the beast screeched as it fell over and died. I hated the sound of the nasty little creatures.

'Nice.' Heath nodded. 'High five?'

His raised hand was covered in grey goo and I laughed, pushing him out of the way. 'Just think of the poor Betty who is going to have those very same hands touching her body later tonight.'

'Poor? Ah, you mean lucky.'

WHEN WE WEREN'T SEEKING violent physical therapy, I was keeping myself busy at the club. Phases was always quieter in the cooler months, but it was still close enough to the city population to attract a steady crowd. The club's supernatural clientele were less affected by the weather than their human counterparts, and from my position behind the bar serving drinks I was able to identify the regulars. With some help from Heath, I was also able to differentiate between the different types of beings, adding species names to the faces I had been unsure about.

'Shifters,' he said, subtly gesturing over his whiskey to a group of four girls dressed in a mix of mod-inspired outfits.

'You sure?' I asked, peering in their direction and looking for any sign that would give away what they *really* were. 'If you told me they were extras in *The Love Witch*, I'd believe you. But shifters?'

'They're ravens. How would you expect them to dress? In feathered cloaks and carrying around Edgar Allan Poe books?'

'Actually? Yeah, a stereotype would be easier to discern from a distance.'

'Not these birds.' He smirked. 'They had a cyberpunk thing going for a while, every few years they switch it up.'

'It appears we're deep into Austin Powers season.'

'Look closer, past the clothes; look at the way they move, their mannerisms.'

I did as he said, noting the somewhat jerky motion of their bodies as they clustered in one corner of Phases. They stuck together, like a flock, their eyes beady and watching the crowd around them.

'If I threw something shiny towards them—'

Heath laughed. 'They would be all over it like ants at a picnic. *Some* stereotypes are true.'

There was a familiar duo I recognised among the crowd, mainly because the first few times I'd seen the guy I thought he was Questlove from The Roots. He *always* had a comb wedged at the front of his hair that corresponded with the shirt he was wearing. Tonight's was pale blue to match cheerful lettering that said: 'Let's have a séance!' while cartoon children hovered around a Ouija board underneath. It was a parody of eighties boardgame boxes and I smiled, recognising the work of artist Steven Rhodes. I was a fan. The woman he was with – *always* with – couldn't have been more different to the geek chic vibe he had going, with her vibrantly coloured hair and big Dominatrix energy.

When they'd first popped up a few weeks back, Yu had grunted in surprise. They hadn't been seen in a while, she'd said. The guy was Hogan, a goblin, and the woman was his personal bodyguard: a demon named Ginger. They had previously run an arcade bar called 1984, something I knew purely through having eavesdropped on other supernaturals talking about how it had unexpectedly shut down.

'They're popping up a lot,' Heath commented, taking a sip of his drink as he tracked my eyeline.

'Is that a good thing or a bad thing?'

He smirked. 'I'll let you know.'

'What about her?' I asked, nodding towards the woman who was making eyes at Heath from the opposite end of the bar.

'Witch. But not a very good one.'

'And how do you know that?'

'Because she's out publicly, by herself, and without the support of her coven. You don't see many witches doing that.'

'They're reclusive,' I agreed.

'Right. That and I had a brief fling with her last year. Brief.'

'Dickin' a Wiccan. I'm not even surprised, Heath.'

'Hey, this is all good "training"—' he made air quotation marks around the word '—for the different kinds of beings you'll see when you have your visitation with Quaid.'

I nodded, hoping that it would be any day now that I'd get the green light from the Treize. I was betting on visitation being a stepping-stone to more visits, then maybe parole of some kind. The kid was barely a teenager and had been locked up without anything resembling a trial due to his part in the activities of my *other* half-brother, Steven Ihi. I felt partially responsible for that. Partially.

'What about him?' Heath questioned, as a lithe man with long dreadlocks sauntered by.

'Arcahnia,' I answered. They were easy to spot. Knowing what I knew now, basically I'd be suspecting every stunning runway model over six foot to be one of the sacred, spider-like creatures.

'Good.'

'And that . . .' I followed Heath's gaze to a gorgeous, Nubian-looking woman. She was stunning, draped in a series of patterned brown scarves that would have looked ridiculous on anyone else. I tried to guess what she could be. An elusive sprite, perhaps? A werewolf? Another shifter?

'That's my dream for the night.'

'You're a dirty reekbeek, Heath. And a cliché,' I called after him as he sculled his drink and made a beeline for his unsuspecting target. I sighed and moved off to attend a waiting patron. I didn't need to watch to see how this went. Every time it played out exactly the same. I would have bet money that within two hours INXS would be playing loudly from the speakers of Heath's apartment in an attempt to drown out very, very loud sex.

With a grin, I saw one of my favourite customers was back: Casper. She had seemed nice enough before, but now after my experience with Seamus I had a newfound fascination with the one-handed medium. She'd been in twice this week and the first time I'd served her at the bar since I returned to Berlin she could tell I had been touched by a ghost. She'd asked to hear the story and I explained in detail. She nodded and listened, yet didn't add a comment or observation. Not once. I kind of liked her for that.

Serving her the usual Midori cocktail, I took a quick glance over my shoulder to see how busy we were. We were a few staff members down so things had been hectic, but it looked like we had a temporary lull in customers. Slicing a lime and grabbing a Corona, I slid on to the stool next to Casper with a deep sigh.

'What's the 411, who are we people-watching tonight?' I said in lieu of a hello.

'Him,' she replied, making the slightest movement with her head in the direction of the man she was scoping.

'The greaser or the hipster?'

'Greaser.'

'That was a test and you passed.'

She laughed, sweeping a strand of long white hair back behind her ear. I watched the man, who actually turned out to be Askari as I saw a flash of the tattoo that marked him on his wrist. He glanced in our direction and the response was immediate: fear. I couldn't be sure who scared him more, me or Casper, but he was *terrified* by one of us.

'I don't know what it is,' she said, as if she hadn't noticed his visceral reaction at all. 'Something about the film *Grease* has ruined me forever. My brother used to say I could never decide who I was more attracted to: Rizzo or Danny.'

'Why choose?'

'That is an attitude I have taken into adulthood.' Casper smiled, casually sipping her cocktail.

We watched as a rowdy group of werewolves danced on a table nearby, the youngest among them doing his best not to topple over the edge. I could see one of the Rogues, Gus, cutting his way through the crowd to yank them back down to the ground. They might have been drunken weres, but few were game enough to test Gus.

'Fucking werewolves,' came the exasperated voice of Yu, who took the seat on Casper's other side. She threw me an apologetic look with a shrug. 'No offence.'

'None taken.'

'Welcome back,' she said, addressing Casper.

'I'm not back. I'm just . . . visiting. On business.'

'You moved?' I asked, feeling like a dickhead for not knowing this.

She nodded, swirling her cocktail in the glass. 'Months ago, when the Treize started shutting down operations in town.'

'Conveniently,' I growled, not at her, but at the frustration I felt over how little help the supernatural government had given us when an undead werewolf pack were eating babies all over the city.

'Please,' Yu scoffed. 'Like it had anything to do with that.'

The two shared a knowing look, smirking at each other, but I barely had a chance to register it before my attention was dragged back to the werewolf party.

'Helluva ruckus for a Wednesday night,' I noted.

'It's a celebration,' said Casper. There was something in the way she said it that made me look at her, watching the group as if she was seeing right *through* them and looking at something else entirely.

'You can tell all that from a table dance?' I asked.

'No,' said Yu, reaching across the bar and pouring herself a vodka cranberry. 'She can tell "all that" because of the years on 'em. That one, the pup? He just survived his pack's coming of age.'

'Hence the table dance.' Casper nodded.

'It's like a werewolf bar mitzvah afterwards,' Yu agreed, sculling half her drink in one gulp. 'If you survive.'

'Yeesh, you're making me grateful for my rogue wolf status.'

Gus was still occupied with the group of werewolves as Clay dashed over.

'Yu, I could really do with a hand at the door if you can spare it? And welcome back, Casper!'

'I'm not back,' she muttered.

He gave her a 'yeah, sure' wink, before quickly diving back into the crowd. Yu rolled her eyes and downed the rest of her drink.

'Men are seagulls,' she grumbled. 'Swoop in, make a lot of noise, crap on everything, and leave again.'

I was still laughing at her comment when someone stumbled up to the bar, looking desperately for service.

'Damn, that's my cue. Sorry to leave you alone,' I said, rising to my feet.

Casper smiled at me, amusement in her eyes. 'That's okay: I'm never alone.'

I couldn't do much but return her smile while trying to ignore the deep sense of unease in my stomach. The rest of the night rolled on as it usually did: Sanjay pumping out the tunes behind the decks in the form of an early Megan Thee Stallion bop and Berlin's supernatural population having a seemingly good time. Clay passed by for a shot of tequila once or twice, mentioning that he had spoken to Zillia and she'd be staying at the retreat a bit longer.

'She reckons she'll be back in a few months,' he added, slamming his shot glass down on the bar.

'How is she?' The unofficial mother of the Rogues had been staying at a Custodians retreat after the revelation that her partner had been, well, an evil douchebag. She had shot him, saving both Joss and my lives. But she had been understandably messed up about it.

'She's good. Sounding better. She asked how the club was going and I told her not to worry, that we've got everything running smoothly. She was pretty surprised about the Lor—'

'I don't want to know what she thought,' I said, holding up a hand to stop Clay. Zillia and Lorcan had been friends for years before I met him. I had no doubt that he had contacted her about the situation. Cramming every second that I wasn't at home with as much activity and interaction as I could was proving to be the best coping mechanism. I did not want Lorcan invading my happy time.

Clay looked apologetic and murmured 'sorry' at me.

'It's fine, it's okay, it's . . . I don't want to bring him here.

The club is packed, people are blootered and happy, I don't want to have to think of his stupid face right now.'

'Stupid-ass face,' said Clay, winking at me. I laughed, pouring him another shot before he raced off to snap partying revellers with the enormous camera strapped around his neck.

~

'SEE, that's not what a dead friend of ours told us, Pete.'

'It's true, I swear! I don't have any! I wouldn't even know where to get 'em!'

'Uh-huh. Tommi, what does your nose tell you?'

Heath had a portly, middle-aged shoemaker held up against the wall of his shop. We'd surprised him just as he was leaving for the night, bag of rat bones in tow. Casper had given me a tip that a ghost 'acquaintance' of hers had come across a man who was trafficking – of all things – vampires. Who on Earth would want the creatures, I had no idea. I sniffed, long and deep. My nose turned my body in the direction of a shelf that had various types of polish and grease stacked along it. I inched closer and the shopkeeper whimpered, giving himself away.

'Warm getting warmer,' I muttered back at them in German.

'Find whatever he's hiding. If it's vampires, Pete, boy are you going to be in trouble. I had the Askari do a bit of digging on you and do you know what they found?'

'I don't kn-know.'

'Yes, you do want to know, because I want to proudly recite my findings. In the past decade alone you've been pinged for illegally exporting body parts *and* underage shape-shifters. If this is offence number three, you could be off to the big house in St Andrews. That's where they keep the real nasties, you know.'

The man was snivelling now as Heath readjusted his hold on him. For all intents and purposes he was a normal guy, just one of the few who had stumbled across the supernatural world and tried to find some way to profit off it. That explained why he was couriering vampires: they weren't the most challenging of creatures. I was running my hand along the wood of the shelving, looking for any sign of a trigger when I found a tiny latch that – once pressed – exposed a hidden pantry. There, sure enough, was a cage full of half a dozen vampires crouched in the dark and munching on fresh rat carcasses. I had never seen a vampire in the flesh before. The closest thing I could compare them to were mangy street cats. Limber and bony, they even hissed at me when I took a step closer. Not for a second did they stop munching on the rats. They chewed them ferociously, much like a dog would a fresh bone, and blood coated their fingertips and lips. The cretins would have barely reached the top of my knees they were that small.

'THEY'RE NOT MINE!'

'Hmmm,' Heath mused. 'It seems some evil mastermind has planted them here just to ensnare you.'

'I SWEAR!

There was a soft knock on the door, and I opened it to let two Askari inside. My face reacted before I could control it as I recognised Jenica. If she was here, did that mean Lorcan was too? She was with an older man I vaguely recalled, and they were wearing thick gloves and carrying sacks to transport the vampires. She must have been back to regular duties after their little 'mission' or whatever.

'Are you sure you want to do that? You could just leave them in their cage,' I said by way of hello.

'The population is so small they need to be catalogued and checked individually,' remarked the elderly gent, one of the few greying Askari I had seen. He looked like a veteran who was ready for anything, but I heard a slight waver in his voice as he called 'Ready!' to Jenica.

Heath returned his attention to Pete. 'I'm going to need to know where they were going, bud. Not that this will make your sentence any easier. It could save you a finger or two, though.'

I waved a dagger in front of his face to demonstrate that my blond friend wasn't joking.

'*NO!* I'll never tell you.'

Heath cast a glance at me, not needing to say a word.

HALF AN HOUR LATER, Pete the shopkeeper was missing a pinky finger, and two Askari were wrestling with unruly vampires as they attempted to bag and tag them. Heath and I stepped out of the shop and into the night air, which was crisp as usual. The sound of smashing glass made me cast a concerned glance back at the shop. Placing a hand on my shoulder, Heath guided me down the step.

'They'll be fine. It's the scent of fresh blood in the air that set them off.'

I looked down at the blade of my skinner knife, which was wet with Pete's fluid. I watched in a far-off way as the blood slid from its tip to splash on the clean, white snow.

'I only wish the twins were here to see this,' he said. 'They *love* vampires.'

'Ew, why?'

'Think of a crazy cat lady. Now extrapolate that by a few hundred years, add a psychic twin sister, and you have some idea. They always wanted one as a pet. Something about a vampire's nasty, spiteful nature amused them.'

'I can see that.'

'It was no ghoul nest but still, a good night's work.'

I couldn't disagree. Once he lost his pinky, Pete was quick to provide us with the name and information of his buyer. A Satanic cult in Brussels intended to sacrifice three virgins to a horde of bloodthirsty vampires in an attempt to resurrect a demon lord. One of the cult's members had helped Pete acquire the vampires at great expense, but that was all wasted now. Lighting a cigarette as we walked, I listened to Heath phone in the information to a PG camp in Brussels.

'Yeah, Count Bachula is transporting them. Will do. Cheerio.' He hung up the phone and answered the question I had before I even asked it. 'Bach is the old guy. He's one of only a few vampire experts and obsessed with them.'

'Again, ew. Why?'

'Beats me,' said Heath, grabbing one of my cigarettes. We stood there for a while, smoking side-by-side in front of a piece of street art that had the words 'MEAT GRINDERS CREW' emblazoned across the bottom of a distorted cartoon face.

'And he's not with her,' Heath muttered, blowing out a cloud of smoke.

'I didn't ask.'

'I know. I'm just telling you, in case you needed to quash any violent tendencies. He's not in the country.'

'Quit chirpsing,' I laughed, kicking snow at Heath.

'Just a little bit of curcuddoch.'

'A bit of what?'

'Eh,' he said, batting a hand. 'Old Scots dialect word,

sometimes I slip up. Means to talk intimately with someone.'

'Curcu-ddo*ck*,' I attempted, butchering his pronunciation.

'Sure,' he chuckled. 'C'mon, you've got bartender duty and I've got bird-watching to do.'

With Zillia and Lorcan both down for the count, Dolly had been forced to hire some new talent at Phases in the form of a civilian bouncer – handpicked by Gus – and two new bartenders. Gus' hire looked strangely similar to him: big and brawny. He was also about as intelligent as a wooden spork. Dolly had been plucking teenage kids from the club since his first night and despite a slap on the wrist, he still didn't seem able to read an ID. I watched as Dolly politely escorted an underage lad and his boyfriend to the door, all the while rolling her eyes at me and mouthing the word 'fuckwit'. The bartenders were good, which was no surprise given Yu hired them and she took no shit.

'Ditch the drink!' I spun around to see Clay grinning at me maniacally from the other side of the bar. Mouthing an explicit rejection at him, I went back to shaking a cocktail. 'Oy! You, the new guy! Take that drink from her hand will you?'

The 'new guy' did as any green staff member would when one of the bosses ordered you to do something. I groaned as he obliged and continued making the cocktail without me.

'There, now you have nothing to do and a song you like is playing for at least another two minutes. Get your blue head on the dance floor with me, *mamacita*.'

Meeting his stare, I knew there was no turning him down. 'Fine!'

I leapt the bar in a single bound and grabbed his hand,

dragging him to the centre of the crowd. A chorus of 'yeeeeeeeeez' rung out behind me as Clay shrieked with joy. He was an intentionally skanky dancer, gripping my torso and stroking a thigh before leaping back and pumping his fists above his head. I laughed, watching him throw himself into the music like he was on a catwalk and voguing perfectly. We had a live act at Phases that light, with Echo Romeo up on stage and purring into the microphone, the crowd eating out of the palm of his hand. Whipping my head around me, it was only a matter of time before I was caught up in it too. A curtain of hair swung as I moved my body, enjoying the carefree sensation of being knocked against others as they thumped with the song. It was a sea of heaving bodies and before I knew it, we were three songs in with no sign of slowing down. It was unbelievably freeing to exert my limbs physically – without a violent end result. I caught a glimpse of Heath, leaning at the bar with Dolly. He was watching me and smiling. I grinned back and was in the process of waving at him to join us when an unexpected odour made me pause.

There. That smell. I caught the faintest scent of something that was eerily familiar to me, but I couldn't pin it. The trace of it was resurrecting a painful memory. There were too many interfering sources for me to get a full-on whiff. Jerking around, I tried to spot who it was coming from using the tracking skills Sanjay had once taught me. I was one hundred per cent sure no one had slipped anything in my drink and yet my skin was buzzing with some unseen force. It was moving further and further from me, and I pushed my way through a group of punks to follow a girl with pink hair whose head was bobbing away from the crowd. I grabbed her by the shoulder of her cut-off denim vest and she spun around to look at me, startled. I didn't know her. The sensation wasn't coming from her.

'Sorry,' I muttered, pushing closer to the exit. I was passing a couple snogging in the corner when the smell hit me again. It was a scent I could never forget. Pausing, I did a full pivot to try and locate its source.

There, staring back at me with equal shock, was my half-sister.

She was thinner than when I'd last seen her, painfully so. Despite being heavily cloaked in a tattered sweater, her collarbones were protruding. Her hair was longer and her face looked slightly dirty. Yet there was no mistaking it was her. My heart pounded against my chest as we each stood our ground, gaping at each other. While she looked just as surprised to see me as I was her, an expression I'm sure I didn't mirror, was terror. With a blur of movement she was gone and barging her way out the door. I blinked for a moment before I took off after her.

Bursting out of Phases and into the neighbouring alley, I could see her speeding off through the snow. She was fast, but I was faster. The few people stupid enough to be out on the street in this kind of weather watched us race after each other, probably wondering what the heck was going on. She didn't hesitate for a moment, dashing across three lanes of traffic and disappearing down a side street.

'Shite,' I cursed, sliding across the bonnet of a car as it slammed its brakes and the driver honked angrily at me. By the time I was across the road she had a decent lead as I pushed on down a grungy lane. I turned a corner and skidded to an abrupt stop at a dead end. Dumpsters faced me on all sides, backed by the sides of towering brick buildings. I spun around to see where she could have gone and spotted an inconspicuous black metal ladder. I craned my neck upwards and saw her frantically scrambling to make it to the top.

With an internal sigh, I began the climb and tried to keep pace without thinking about how flimsy this ladder actually was. The cool metal may as well have been ice as my exposed fingers gripped it, doing their best not to slip on damp spots left by the snow. It felt like an age, but I finally made it to the rooftop.

'Come on, lass!' I shouted in her general direction as her silhouette made a jump from one building to another. Would falling from a great height kill me? I pondered that thought briefly as I dashed across the snowy Berlin landscape, leaping rooftops. I sprinted and soared, airborne for a few seconds at a time before landing on my feet and repeating the process over and over. She took a staircase down to street level and I was relieved once I burst out on to the ground after her. She hadn't gotten far down a narrow alley when I caught her, grabbing her by the arm in a bid to slow her down. She screamed and threw out her limbs to whack me, but I slipped past with ease and pinned her against the wall. 'H-hey,' I puffed. 'Would you wait—' huff '—a second.'

She lashed out and tried to kick me while I threw myself backwards. 'Yo, now, let's not revert to pie kicking, shall we?'

Her forehead creased as she recalled the memory of the first time we'd come into contact and I'd kicked her in the va-jay-jay in an attempt to escape her family. I stayed where I was, keeping my hands raised in front of me as a peace gesture.

'I don't wanna go parkouring all over Berlin after you,' I panted.

Figuring I was less intimidating at a distance, I backed up further to give her the impression she could still make a run for it if she needed. It was here that I was able to take in her appearance fully: from the holey trainers to the stained jeans, it was pretty obvious she had been living on the streets. Where the hell homeless people survived during a Berlin winter was anyone's guess. Tent city, probably. Despite the many signs she had been doing it rough, she still smelled like them: the Ihi pack. My family.

'WHAT DO YOU WANT?!' she spat.

'Me?! What do YOU want? You're the one who came to find me at my club.'

'*Your* club?'

'Well, it's not technically my club but I live and work there.'

'I-I . . . I didn't know. I heard that it was a place where there were rogue werewolves without a pack.'

'Aye, the Rogues. Phases is their haunt. Wait, you didn't come to the club to see me?'

'Fuck no, you're the last person in the world I'd wanna see.'

'It's just a coincidence? Did you want their help?'

'You're not going to attack me?'

'And why would I do that? Huh? I let you go that night at the warehouse when your brother and his band of biker psychopaths had my friends killed. This may come as a shock to you, but you haven't exactly been preoccupying my every thought. I assumed you'd be working your way back to the other Ihi pack members.'

She let out what was a combination of a cry and a laugh. 'I can never go back there.'

I was confused. 'I thought they were your family?'

'And what would you know of it?!'

'Hey, easy there. In this choir that you're preaching to, I'm up front singing the gospel solo.'

She glared at me, still clearly uncertain as to whether I intended to throw her in a cage or punch her in the face. I too was uncertain about whether she was going to try and bite me. More than anything, I just wanted to give her a feed.

'You're skin and bones,' I said to her.

'Try bumming your way from Scotland to here. It's not exactly first class livin'.'

'No doubt. Did you hear about the Rogues on the road? Is that why you came here?'

She nodded. 'Some guys in Edinburgh mentioned it. I wasn't doing anything else and getting out of Scotland seemed like a good idea.'

'Putting distance between me and you, right?'

She nodded again.

'Smart.'

A cloud of warm air issued from her mouth and I noticed that she was shivering slightly. She noticed me looking and tried to hide it.

'Your name's Aruhe, yeah?'

She shrugged. 'I've been changing it from place to place in case they were looking for me—'

'Who? The Praetorian Guard? Or your fam?'

'Both. You too, I guess. I thought maybe you'd reconsider letting me go after . . .'

'Do you know what happened the rest of that night?'

She shook her head.

'Do you want to?'

'I assumed you and your boyfriend killed Steven and Quaid. Maybe one got away.'

'Neither of them got away. Steven ripped my friend Mari's throat out in front of me. I shifted and I killed him. I don't regret it. Quaid was taken into custody by the Treize and PG. He's in a high security supernatural prison back in Scotland.'

She sniffed, and at first I thought it was because she was crying. Indeed, she was. But they didn't look like tears of sorrow. They looked like tears of resolution. I couldn't help but ask the question.

'You sought the Rogues out for help, what do you need? Let me help.'

'Why would you do that?'

'Because . . . because I know what you're going through. Your family can hype it up as this powerful ability all they want and yeah, it can be. But being a werewolf can also *really* suck. It's painful and it's hard and it's scary, and I have no idea how you've managed to do it alone. And despite everything, we're blood. My werewolf genes are the same as yours.'

'Half. We're half-sisters.'

'Can't we be the better half?'

She cracked a smile at that, and I felt like I had gained a little ground. That feeling crumbled beneath my feet as Heath and Yu came sprinting down the alley, fully armed.

'An Ihi.' Heath grinned, skidding to a halt. He made a move towards her and I stepped in front, blocking his path.

'Hold up, lower the bloody handcuffs, Heath.'

'It's the missing Ihi!'

'I'm aware of that. She also has a name: *Aruhe*.'

'Your point?' said Heath, still trying to side-step past me.

I could sense her tensing up behind me and I hoped she was too tired to run again. 'My point is that she's my half-sister.'

He stopped, meeting my eyes. 'No.'

'No what?' I replied.

'You're not taking in strays.'

'Who said anything about taking in strays?'

'I can see right into your bleeding heart, Tommi.'

I turned to face Aruhe, who looked incredibly uncomfortable. I'd say a large part of that had to do with the fact Yu still had a crossbow levelled at her. 'How old are you?' I asked.

'Huh?' She wasn't taking her eyes off that crossbow.

'Your age, Aruhe. What is it?'

'I'm eighteen.'

'Yu, for God's sake would you stop pointing a crossbow at a teenager?'

'He said she was an Ihi,' she defended.

'And so am I,' I retorted. Her eyes flicked to me, and I raised an eyebrow. She begrudgingly dropped the weapon to her side. She kept a hand resting on the gun at her belt though, which looked like a casual gesture. I knew better. That was the place she hid her prized Smith & Wesson revolver if she ever thought she needed it. 'She came to the Rogues for help. So did I. What kind of people would we be if we let her go and spend another night in the cold?'

'You been on the streets?' Yu asked.

She nodded.

Without hesitation, Yu turned to Heath. 'She's coming back with us.'

'Quality. And where's she going to stay?' He was clutching at straws.

'I have one exceedingly empty apartment,' I offered.

'What about that guy?' asked Aruhe.

'What guy,' I muttered.

'Oh.'

Heath looked like he was ready to argue again and I quickly leapt in. 'Look, the least we can do is offer her a shower and a hot meal. We can decide what to do then.

Heck, I'll even continue this debate as we walk back to Phases.'

Aruhe's eyes had lit up at the mention of a hot meal and I nodded at her, gesturing for her to follow us.

'This is a stupid idea,' Heath said.

7

'This is still a stupid idea,' Heath whispered to me, well aware that everyone in the room could hear him, including Aruhe. She looked up from her bowl of mac and cheese and glared. Her hair was damp from a shower and she was in a pair of my tracksuit pants and a jumper, which were both enormous on her. A towel was resting around her shoulders and she was digging into the food I'd had ready when she emerged, clean and dressed. I figured she'd wait until it cooled, but she risked some hardcore tongue burns and plunged right in. She was sitting at the kitchen bench and Heath was standing beside me on the other side of the counter. Dolly and Yu were at the opposite end, talking quietly.

'Mmm-hmm,' I mumbled, turning back to the massive pot and stirring its contents.

'Tommi, you're not understanding me,' he said. 'Think about it: if you let her stay here, what's to say you won't wake with her holding a knife to your throat? *Think* about that for a moment.'

I did. I thought about that sentence. Then I thought

about the crying girl who had been terrified of me that night in the Dundee warehouse. She had disappeared and I never thought I'd see her again. Looking at the teen sitting before me, spooning food into her mouth, I couldn't see anything dangerous about her. Unless I was a piece of cheese-saturated macaroni, she wasn't a threat to me. Clearly she had some ability to defend herself and a resourcefulness I admired, given how long she'd survived out there on her own. Sure, she looked borderline anorexic, but she was otherwise intact. I also felt a sense of sisterhood towards her – literally. Then I thought about James, so desperate to find his brother from across the other side of the world that he'd risked contacting the woman who killed his other sibling. And then, finally, I thought about me. I *was* an Ihi. Mischief demon or whatever he was, Chester Rangi was right about what he told me that day back in Wigtown: I would never be one of them because I was too far removed from it. Yet blood was blood. Aruhe and I had mostly the same lot of it coursing through us.

'I am hearing you,' I replied. 'I am. I value your opinion more than you probably realise. But she's my blood, Heath. It's pure luck that we found each other, and I am *not* leaving her out there to be taken back to New Zealand or locked up by the Treize. Yo,' I said, turning to Aruhe. 'Are you going to slit my throat while I sleep?'

She paused mid-mouthful, shocked by the question. Her mouth was full of food, so she couldn't speak but she shook her head from side-to-side.

'Cross your heart, hope to UTI?'

'I . . . yes? Yes, I promise.'

'See,' I said, turning to Heath. 'No girl is going to risk the pain of a UTI. There's nothing to worry about.' I copied the grin he so often used on me and it wasn't long before I saw the edges of his mouth twitch into a smile.

'I'm watching you,' he said, pointing at Aruhe again. 'You so much as think about harming her and you'll be nothing more than a head mounted on a wall.'

I saw her hand shake slightly as Heath drew himself up to his full height. He left the apartment then, disappearing into his own and I let out a sigh of relief. I served myself a bowl of mac and cheese, adding a generous squirt of Sriracha that I hadn't given Aruhe because I didn't know if she liked spice. Dolly had become the unofficial head of the Rogues now that Zillia was absent and she had been doing a bloody great job. She and Yu separated now, getting to their feet and coming over to Aruhe as I watched and ate..

'If Tommi is happy for you to stay with her,' started Dolly, as I nodded enthusiastically behind her, 'then you can stay here. Until we have a full meeting, which we can't do until the day after tomorrow, you're confined to this room simply because you're an outsider and we can't trust you. Yet. You can have an introduction to the place when we're closed on Sunday.'

'Mean as,' nodded Aruhe, taking a break from eating for the first time. 'I'll do everything you guys say. I'm grateful, honest. I won't stab nobody or nothing.'

I had to stifle a laugh at that last comment and I could see amusement in Yu's eyes too. Dolly kept her cool.

'We'll see you tomorrow,' she replied.

Yu followed her out as Aruhe awkwardly waved.

'Cheers,' she called.

It was just the two of us left alone in my apartment. We glanced at each other, sharing an awkward moment of silence.

'More mac and cheese?' I offered, looking at her empty bowl.

She nodded and I loaded her up again, watching as she devoured her weight in pasta. I wondered if she was going to end up vomiting it back up as her body rejected the sheer volume. She caught me looking at her and slowed her eating until she stopped altogether. We smiled politely at each other, not sure what to say.

'It's a bit weird, ay?' she started.

'Word,' I said, letting out a breathy stream of laughter. 'I've been in weirder situations, but this is up there.'

'Thanks, by the way. For bringing me back here and feeding me. And for not beating me up in the alleyway.'

'I don't think those things necessarily deserve thank yous.'

'Well, uh, thanks anyway.'

The door suddenly swung open and Heath stormed through it, dragging a large mattress. I watched open-mouthed as he pulled it through the apartment and up the wire stairs that led to the second level. He left just as quickly as he entered, before returning once more with clean sheets and a doona. He tossed them on top of the mattress, before dumping the final pillow on the couch downstairs. He strode back over to the kitchen and opened the fridge, grabbing himself a beer. Popping the top on the edge of the bench, he leaned back against the cupboard.

'What?' he said, taking a sip and looking from me to Aruhe. 'If she's going to stay here then she needs somewhere to sleep.'

'Thank y—'

One look from Heath stopped her dead in her tracks. 'I still don't trust you,' he said. 'That's why I'm staying the night.'

I opened my mouth to argue, but Heath *was* the Praetorian Guard's official representative. He might be running some game with pregnant supernaturals and selkies behind their back, but he was appointed by the PG to be *here*. Although he'd become a friend, I couldn't be flippant and undermine his job. I was still treated with suspicion for being vaguely associated with the Ihi pack. What would they think of Aruhe?

'Sure,' I replied, calmly.

Heath looked surprised, if only for a second. 'Good.'

'You can't shag any conquests in here though. This is a skag-free zone.'

'I can deny myself for a night, Tommi. If I have to endure it.'

'Mmm-hmm.'

~

'I'VE LEFT a bunch of clothes in a pile there that might fit you. They're all my smallest stuff because you're tiny, but we can get whatever you have left where you were stay—'

'No. This is great. Thank you.'

'Cool. I'll be downstairs if you need me. Or anything.'

Aruhe nodded, smiling shyly. 'Thanks.'

'Aye.' I lingered longer than I should have, before scampering back down the stairs and flopping next to Heath on the couch.

'I'm down here too,' he shouted to the room. 'Just in case you forgot.'

'Honestly,' I said, shaking my head at him.

'Deterrence is a great defence mechanism.'

'Let me guess: Pict thing?'

'Yes. We used to go into battle naked. The Romans

would come with their shields and their pathetic excuse for an army and we would stand there, waiting, completely bare. Nothing but tattoos adorned our bodies and that was intimidating to them: an army of naked, angry men.'

'Sounds a bit homoerotic.'

He smirked. 'Such notions didn't exist then.'

I took in his appearance: the scruffy blond hair and beard, the long legs stretching off the couch and over the floor. He was wearing long pants and a turtleneck jersey that ran from his neck and down to his wrists. Turtlenecks were sweater foreskins, in my opinion, but it hit me for the first time that I had never seen much of his exposed flesh. Most of the other men switched between T-shirts or – in Clay's case – silver fishnet singlets. Yet Heath remained exceedingly covered up. The question was out of my mouth before I could think it over. 'Do you hide your tattoos?'

He didn't meet my eyes, but nodded as he kept his focus on whatever was playing on the TV.

'Why?'

'People tend to remember someone with very distinctive, blue patterns all over their body. It's easier to blend this way.'

'There's a lot of people tattooed these days, myself included. Do you really think they'd stand out that much?'

'To the folks that mattered, maybe. Beings in our world more than most would be familiar with Pictish marks. The name of our people literally translates to "painted". If it was a civilian or even someone vaguely up on their history, it wouldn't be hard to recognise mine were the real deal. Too many questions would be asked.'

'*All* over your body? What about the women you sleep with, don't they ask questions?'

'Firstly, it's always dark. Secondly, I'm not taking historians to bed.'

'Hmm. Did the tattooing hurt? That was hundreds, maybe thousands, of years ago—'

I watched his expression to see how accurate I was with the date, given that he'd never disclosed how old he actually was. He gave nothing away, only smiled at me, smug.

'—it's not as if they could give you a tube of Bepanthen and send you on ya way.'

'It was needles and hot pricks, but mostly dye. A combination of clay and plant extract that was rich in azurite and malachite. Standard.'

'Says the barbarian,' I teased.

'You know, if you ever want to see my tattoos first-hand —' He made an attempt to pull up his jersey and I jumped to my feet.

'Let me stop you there, Romeo,' I said, averting my eyes and walking away from him.

'Not ready to see a naked man yet?'

I went to laugh but stopped myself as I registered the comment and the truth of it. 'Huh. Not ready to see, not ready to touch, none of it.'

My usual libido had turned into libidon't and I was trying not to admit that it had anything to do with Lorcan leaving, but I couldn't deny the timing of it all. Old me would have willingly tripped on to the next dick to get over any hurt feelings had, yet this was different. Current me felt older and tired and sore in my heart. Looking down at Phases from my window above, I felt Heath's presence at my back.

'Sorry,' he said. 'I didn't mean to stir.'

I raised an eyebrow at him.

'Okay,' he relented. 'Maybe I did. But I didn't mean to hurt you.'

I smiled, patting him on the shoulder as I headed towards my bed. 'Night, Heath.'

'Night.'

He cut the lights and soon the apartment was plunged into darkness. I collapsed on the bed, fully clothed. The couch creaked as Heath squirmed his enormous body on to it. I doubted he would sleep tonight. He wasn't joking when he said he didn't trust Aruhe: he would be watching. And so would I. After my last experience back in Dundee, I had wondered if any Ihi could be trusted. Yet it was only through the passage of time since I first met my blood pack in New Zealand that I had begun to see things as, not necessarily black and white, but grey. James and Simon had shown me kindness in light of a terrible situation. And heck, knowing what I did now about my strength and abilities as a werewolf, locking me up in the hours before my first transformation seemed less like the malicious act I'd thought it was and more a safety precaution. Tommi Grayson back then didn't know what Tommi Grayson knew now. Could Steven have been the exception, rather than the rule? I was quickly realising Aruhe had about as much in common with her dead brother as I did. You can choose your friends. You can't choose your family – especially the supernatural kind.

'I WAS TRYING TO GET A GLASS OF WATER, YOU NUT JOB!'

'Oh yeah? It's funny how the glasses are located conveniently next to the knives.'

'IT'S A KITCHEN!'

Groaning, I lifted my head from the pillow to find Aruhe halfway down the stairs to the landing. Heath was doing an impressive job of blocking her path, as I could barely see her behind him.

'What's going on?' I asked, stumbling to my feet.

'Your house guest is trying to kill you. Again.'

'Huh?'

'It's not true! I just wanted a glass of water and then Phoebus was all up in my grill saying I was going to stab you!'

'What did you just call me?'

She sighed. 'Phoebus. You know, from *The Hunch*—'

'Oh. My. God. Yes, I kind of see it!' I screeched, tilting my head to better examine Heath.

'I have no idea what either of you are talking about. Would you like me to let the fugitive near the sharp objects for a "glass of water", Tommi?' The sarcasm was strong with this one. He even made bunny ears around 'glass of water' to indicate he thought it was a ruse.

'Yes, Heath, come on. Nobody murders anyone before 11 a.m in the morning.'

'Your loss . . . of life,' he muttered.

'Finally, crazy *pākehā*,' said Aruhe, pushing past him with such attitude I was reminded that she was a teenage girl. I watched as she rushed to the kitchen, opening a few cupboards before finding a glass and downing two serves of water. She disappeared to the bathroom and I looked at Heath, who still seemed peeved about the Phoebus comment.

'Do you want me download it for you so you have some context?'

'No,' he said, shaking his head. 'I'm going to leave you here with *her* as punishment.'

With that, he briskly left, picking up the blanket and pillow from the couch and throwing them over his shoulder with such grace I was slightly jealous. Checking my phone, I saw I had a missed call from Joss and a message that said: 'You need to get down to MG, quick. I think I'm getting *the* talk :ob'. I knew what this meant. The doctors were ready to officially tell Joss he had entered into remission. I let out an involuntary squeal, which made Aruhe jump as she returned from the bathroom.

'What is it?' she said, rubbing her face with her hand as she took a few more minutes to wake up.

'My best mate, Joss, is about to be told he's in remission.'

'What's that?'

'He had cancer, a second time for him. He's been here getting treatment and while it looked bad for a while, he has been on the up and up. I need to get to the hospital ASAP.'

She looked uneasy at the statement and I realised it was because she didn't want to be left here, alone. Or worse: under the watchful eye of Heath.

'You're coming with me,' I added, and she immediately looked happier.

'I am? What about being confined to this apartment?'

'Fuck it, this is Joss. He's practically one of us. The Rogues will understand.'

'He's normal and he knows about you? About all this?'

'It's complicated. Get dressed and I'll explain on the way.'

Any concerns the Rogues might have had about Aruhe seemed to have resolved themselves after one relatively peaceful night with her sleeping under our roof. They agreed to let me take her to the hospital to see Joss without an escort, as long as we went straight there and came straight back. Naturally I tossed that rule out the car window as soon as we were down the street. On a drive to source the best burgers in the world – Burgermeister – I gave her a rundown on everything that happened since that night at the warehouse in Dundee. From moving to Berlin and Lorcan resigning, to the Laignach Faelad and accepting the Ireland mission. By the time I finished the tale she had a cheese fry dangling from her lips in shock. I'd learned in the past twenty-four hours that for her to stop eating for any reason was a big deal.

'That's crazy.'

'I knowph,' I said, through a mouthful of cheeseburger.

'No, that's *proper* crazy. That's a lot to happen to a twenty-two-year-old.'

'I'm twenty-four.'

She looked confused. 'Steven said—'

'I've had two birthdays since that shit storm. With everything that has been going on over the past few years, birthdays don't mean as much as they used to.'

'And no one said anything?'

'About what?'

'Your birthdays!'

'Oh, well, Joss has been going through a bunch of stuff and he's usually miles away. I figured none of the others knew and I wasn't going to bring it up. I had a call from my grandparents, but it was always my mum and Mari who made a big deal about that kind of stuff. They're both dead.'

She gulped. 'Sorry.'

'You didn't kill my mum and you didn't kill Mari. I'm beginning to think you didn't even want to be in Dundee in the first place.'

'I didn't. Quaid being the youngest, he was kinda the weakest and Steven was always exploiting that. Plus, we're closest in age so Quaid and I got on better than I did with Steven, or even Simon and James, who treated us like kids.'

'Simon and James seemed . . . reasonable-ish, when I met them. You know, before y'all chained me up.'

She smirked. 'They were really close with pāpā, running the businesses and shit. Trying to follow his example.'

'You miss them,' I said, watching her closely.

'Like crazy,' she whispered, a sadness heavy on her words.

'Then why don't you go home?' I frowned. 'We can get you there saf—'

'I fucked up.'

'I'm sure they'd—'

'You don't understand. You don't understand our pack or our culture.'

I fell silent as her words hit closer to home than I wanted to admit. She took a loud slurp from her drink before continuing.

'When I left, I was sixteen. I wasn't a woman in the pack yet, even though I'd had my first transformation at fourteen. Every werewolf pack around the world has, like, a test that you have to pass, and mine was to happen soon. Dad – Jonah – he'd been preparing me with Wehi.'

'And then I came along.'

She nodded. 'Steven was already on the outs, I don't know what for – the guys had done a good job of keeping it from me but I knew that māmā and the Aunties were pissed. The gang he'd put together, what he tried to do to you . . .'

She trailed off, letting the silence fill the end of that horrific sentence I was grateful she didn't finish.

'That was it for him. The Aunties voted and—'

'Aunties? How many sisters did Jonah or your mum have?'

Aruhe snorted, pinching one of my fries in the process. 'It's not like how you think of it, Caucasian aunties or whatever.'

'Well, I'm completely severed from the Māori part of my heritage so you're gonna have to fill me in here.'

'It's like . . .' Her eyes scanned the surrounding crowd at Burgermeister as she searched for the right word. 'Enforcers, I guess. The alpha is the alpha, but within Māori packs the women are the enforcers and they vote on the rough calls. They're tough chicks and we call them the Aunties.'

'Your mum, Tiaki—'

'She's one. And Simon's mum, Keisha.'

'Not you?'

'Not yet. And now not ever. Like I said, I still had some tests to pass until I was officially of age and then an Auntie, but I got to sit in on the meetings and the votes as part of my training. I heard what they were going to do to Steven.'

'Kill him,' I whispered, my mind triggering something James had mentioned in our correspondence.

'We're strongest as a pack and if there's a poisonous branch, you cut it off. I betrayed the Aunties by warning Steven before they had a chance to carry out the sentence. He might have been messed up, but he was still my brother. I wanted him gone, not dead.'

I shifted uncomfortably, hyper aware of the fact that I had carried out the Aunties' final sentence – unbeknownst to me at the time.

'Anyway, I got what I deserved.'

'What do you mean?' I asked.

'Quaid was there when I told him, and Steven reacted how he always reacted: with violence. We'd already come up with a plan to get him out of the country, but he demanded that I leave New Zealand with him or he was gonna kill Quaid.'

'Did Quaid know this?'

'Maybe, I dunno. Steven had a way of selling the whole thing as this epic adventure to him and by the time we got to Scotland and were stuck with the other werewolves he ran with and the killing started . . . I didn't have the strength to leave him or do anything about it. I'd crossed the Aunties, which was bad enough. I betrayed the pack for Steven, and then I stood by while others paid for it.'

I sighed, long and deep. This was a tricky, twisty situation. I didn't know enough about pack law to offer reassuring words and what I *did* know about the Treize's form of justice was unsettling.

'Do you really think they'd kill you?' I questioned. 'James has been desperate to find out what happened to you and Quaid. It feels genuine, not like a trap.'

'You've spoken to him?'

'Not really. We've emailed a wee bit back and forth. He's the one who told me Quaid had been imprisoned. One of the reasons I signed up to hunt down the Laignach Faelad in Ireland was so I could negotiate some kind of visitation. Release one day, maybe.'

'You're a fucking fool if you ever think they'll let him go.'

I was surprised by the vehemence in her words and looked hard into her stare. My eyes were hers – that was the most obvious physical trait we shared. It's what all the Ihi children and I shared. Her brown eyes looked right back into mine as if they were a perfect mirror of each other.

'Is it weird?' she asked suddenly. 'Looking like us but not really being us?'

'Yes and no,' I answered, fiddling with a discarded chip. 'I've always been brown, so I knew I was different from some of the Scottish kids at school. When mum first told me, I wasn't that old and I didn't really have a desire to find out more until she died. The weird thing is, this part of myself that I know very little about is the dominant half of my genes. It's where the wolf comes from. I've inherited more Māori physical traits than I have anything from my ma's side, yet essentially I'm disconnected from it. Completely.'

'What do you wanna know? I can help you with that.'

I smiled at her. 'Aye, I guess you can, can't you? If you're going to hang around for a while—'

'Where else am I gonna go? I can never go home without expecting punishment.'

'And if you could, would you?'

'In a heartbeat. I miss *my land.* This place has a lot and I've seen cool shit that I never expected to, but . . . I miss it. I miss the way the air feels when you breathe it. I miss the smells. I miss the sounds.'

I bit my lip as I thought. I knew a lot about this family, but I didn't know them well enough to make a call on Aruhe's safety. Thinking about James' emails – the desperation that almost leaped off the screen as he tried to put the pieces of a broken puzzle back together again – that, to me, wasn't someone who would see death as the only solution for his little sister. Then again, his cousin Simon Tianne was the alpha werewolf now. He was the pack leader who had stepped in to fill Jonah Ihi's shoes. Maybe he'd view things differently. This was a lot more than I wanted to handle in that moment.

'Come on,' I said, sliding up from the rickety table we were sitting at. 'Bring the burger with you, we've got a former cancer patient to visit.'

～

'Heeeey, about time you bloody got here,' said Joss, getting up from the bed. 'What took you so—'

He cut himself off when he caught sight of the girl behind me. Joss was quick, and he knew it was out of character for me to bring anyone to a personal occasion as momentous as this – let alone a stranger. Yet as he looked from Aruhe to me and back again, I could see his brain quickly configuring a thesis. Before he could say anything, I grabbed him in a bear hug, squeezing his bones. When I let him go, Aruhe was still standing at the doorway, one arm holding her elbow and looking uncomfortable as all heck. It didn't hit me until then that it would be a very strange situation to walk into.

'Uh, Joss, this is Aruhe I—'

'Aruhe is fine,' she said, rushing forward and shaking his hand.

He shook it slowly and I could see the questions forming on his lips. Joss' parents were in the corner of the room talking quietly among themselves, and I cast a glance in their direction before pulling my best friend close.

'Aruhe is also my half-sister,' I whispered.

'On . . . on your father's side?'

I nodded. I didn't have that many sides to choose from. Giving him the quickest run-down of events as possible, I explained that she would be staying with me for the next while. 'Until we sort out something permanent,' I finished.

'You were there at the warehouse that night, weren't you? You're the one that got away?'

Her mouth popped open and I could tell she was surprised Joss knew all the ins and outs of that evening. Once he had been brought into the know, he'd been pretty rigorous in making me go through everything, detail-by-detail. Whether he'd wanted to try and understand what I was going through or just know all there was about the situation, there wasn't much between us that had been left unspoken. It was good, because I hated keeping secrets from Joss. We'd gone back to the way things were pre-werewolf craziness. I left the two of them together as I went over to speak to Joss' ma and pa. It was only minutes until Dr Matthews and two of his assisting team members came through the door and we assembled oddly around Joss' bed, waiting for the news. Dr Matthews wasn't like the previous doctors Joss had in Scotland, the kind who seemed to always make a conscious effort to be chipper no matter how many awful things they'd seen that day. This guy was always sombre and I imagined his smile would be a frightening thing.

'Hit us, Dr M,' said Joss, beaming at the medical professional.

'As you know, I wanted you all present for some rather significant news with regard to Joss' cancer treatment. We've been seeing a dramatic improvement in his condition over the past few months, which we attributed to a combination of conventional and unconventional treatments over a consistent period. What our most recent data has shown is that it was none of those.'

He took a deep breath, maintaining eye contact with each of us for a moment before he continued.

'There is a phenomenon known as last legs recovery where the body – for some unknown reason – tricks itself into thinking it's healthy. The patient shows remarkable signs of improvement and combined with the effects of a positive attitude, many have thought they were out of the woods, so to speak.'

'What are you saying?' asked Joss' mum Samantha in a stern voice.

Dr Matthews sighed. 'This news is always hard to deliver but . . . I'm sorry. Joss, you don't have long to go. From my calculations no more than a month, but it could be as little as two weeks now that the cancer has finally caught up with your body. We've looked at countless possibilities but it has just spread too far and too fast. At this stage, the most we can do is make you as comfortable as possible for your final transition. Whether you would like to do that here or at home with your family, it's up to you. That's a decision you all need to make together. Again, this is always the hardest news to deliver and I'm terribly sorry. I know how much you were all hoping for a positive outcome.'

You could have cut the silence in the room with a chainsaw. I took a step away from the doctor, positioning myself on the side of the bed. I looked towards Joss, who was staring straight ahead at the white wall in front of him. He was emotionless. His parents began a conversation with Dr Matthews, asking him if there was any way there could have been a mistake and what else could they possibly try? The words 'hospice care' came up. Joss slowly folded himself back onto the bed, legs straight out in front of him.

'Joss,' I started, but he just shook his head at me, not wanting to talk.

Dr Matthews spoke to his parents for a long time. He eventually began to leave, and I rushed out after him.

'Doctor,' I called, catching up with him in the hallway. 'I—'

Honestly, there was nothing as left to say. I'd heard the arguments with Joss' parents, heard the things he had told them, I understood medically there was nothing else to do but . . . I don't know what I needed.

'This is it, Tommi. This is the final stretch.'

I narrowed my eyes at him, looking for any sign of hope.

There wasn't any. 'We've been told that before,' I replied. 'We've been told he's at the end *so* many times—'

'He's not bouncing back from this. There aren't any miracle cures here. No bone marrow or magical elixir from the Gods. This *is* it. You should prepare for goodbye.'

He started to walk away, leaving me shell-shocked and standing there solo. He paused, turning back. 'You know, we offer counselling services to loved ones as well. If you'd like to talk to someone, let me know and it can be arranged.'

I nodded, frozen. I quickly wiped away a tear before I headed back into Joss' hospital room – my heart a whole lot heavier than when I walked through those doors only minutes earlier.

How I managed to drive back to Phases later is anyone's guess. I skidded in the snow more times than I could count and Aruhe's knuckles were white from gripping the dash. In hindsight I shouldn't have driven, but having grown up in Scotland and being used to travelling in this weather, I figured I was better suited to this kind of thing than she was. Aruhe also informed me the only vehicle she knew how to drive was a dirt bike after Simon had banned her from driving his Land Rover when she crashed it at thirteen.

The steps back up to the apartment seemed to stretch on forever. Maybe this was hell? Maybe it was walking endlessly up a set of stairs in a daze of despair? Guns 'n' Roses were blaring from Heath's room. I explained to my half-sister what that meant: he had company.

'Gross,' she muttered. I gave an attempt at a smile, but it must have looked pretty awful because she grimaced in reaction. Casa de depresso was as we had left it and I excused myself to take a shower. Making the water as hot as I could handle it, I stood there motionless while it poured over my body. The end. This was the end for Joss. In a matter of days or, if we were fortunate, a matter of weeks, he would cease to be. That's it. He would go from existing to simply, well, *not*. My mind flashed to Seamus, the ghost boy, and I lost it. I collapsed in a fit of ugly, dry sobs as I imagined Joss in that state. Of course, it wouldn't happen that way. There was nothing sinister about his encroaching death – nothing sinister except the cancer. There had been times when we'd come very close to saying goodbye before, but we had always made it through. Whether it was by the skin of our teeth or flying off the side of a hospital, literally, we had always made it. Always. My own tears mixed with the water as I hugged myself, knowing and trying to accept that this time wouldn't be like the others. It would be the last time.

8

Heath Darkiro was in a toyshop and he had no idea what he was doing there. In fact, he couldn't recall ever being in one before. There had been no such things as 'toyshops' when he was a child. By the time they were invented he'd been a warrior for hundreds of years and, by their very nature, warriors didn't frequent toyshops. But here he was, standing in the action figure aisle at Anna's Toy Factory. Heath looked down his nose at a boy with a mop of blond hair who had just run directly into his legs. The child barely reached past Heath's knee and he stumbled back, surprised.

'Jet!' hissed a flustered-looking father who came scurrying down the aisle after his offspring. The man looked like a librarian and, after taking in Heath's appearance, muttered an apology before picking up the boy and rushing off.

Heath didn't like this place. It was loud, brightly coloured, and there were small people running about everywhere. He secretly didn't mind children, but it seemed as soon as you entered the doors of a toyshop, parents relinquished all disciplinary control. With a wrinkled nose he turned and exited the row of products targeted at energetic brutes and went in search of the person who had dragged him here. He found her standing at the bottom of a huge pyramid of stuffed toys that appeared to be some mistaken monument to cartoon gods.

Tommi Grayson looked about as out of place in the toyshop as Heath felt. She didn't seem to notice. Her black ankle boots led to a pair of skin-tight, red tartan pants that acted as a wink to her Scottish roots. The top half of her was hidden underneath an oversized leather jacket with a black turtleneck underneath. Her fading blue hair was parted to the side and shorter strands that fell out of her high ponytail framed her face. Her hair was unusually straight today compared to her natural waves and it fell sleekly halfway down her back. He noticed all of these details about her and more. He was hyperaware of just *how much* he noticed, and he didn't like it.

Heath watched her with curiosity from a brief distance as she leaned forward, carefully selecting a toy that was a crude version of what an owl might look like. She didn't examine its appearance: instead she brought it to her chest and held it tightly for several seconds. Looking disappointed, she returned it to a spot on the pile and grabbed another – this time an indistinguishable monkey/monster creature. Earlier he had taken Tommi to a Francis Bacon exhibition at the National Gallery of Germany in a bid to cheer her up. Of course, Francis Bacon being Francis Bacon, the nature of the art wasn't exactly cheery. But Heath thought he had succeeded in distracting her to some degree. He'd watched her eyes glaze over as she became lost in the works and the artist's story. He had made her forget, if only for a few hours, and that was enough.

Heath had developed a solid friendship with the young

werewolf, something that was both surprising and deeply annoying. He'd had plans for her before they even met, back when he'd flagged her for Praetorian Guard recruitment in order to measure her response. He knew all the ways she could be useful, given that she straddled two worlds. And among that merry band of rebels slowly, carefully assembling in the shadows, they were worryingly short on soldiers. Prickly witches with superpowered medium spouses? Tick. Impregnated banshees and fulfilled prophecies? Tick and tick. Aquatic messengers and shifty demons? Triple tick. But those who were physically capable of the messy, bloody work he knew was coming? They were lacking. The bonds he'd been building over the past few years were strong in some areas, tenuous in others. Where there were weaknesses, he'd tried to solidify the foundations with favours – traded information, international passage, beneficial introductions – in order to build trust. He'd been making progress, yet he constantly worried it wasn't enough as he juggled a double life between who the Treize thought he was and what he was actually up to.

Time was running out. Ruses didn't last forever and even if he couldn't see it, cracks were forming in his. There were allies sitting on the fence that he knew he could flip if Tommi became involved. It felt like the half of the supernatural world who understood what was really going on was holding its breath and waiting to see what side she would choose. People wanted to fight with her, not against her, just like they had with her father. The catch was that she had *no* idea. He idly thought about the layer of protection that offered Tommi as he leaned up to grab the giraffe toy she was reaching for at the top of the pyramid.

'What on earth are you doing?' he asked, smiling as he

handed it to her. She returned the smile gratefully as she took the toy, bringing it to her chest once more.

'What is life but what we feel?' she said, as she dumped that one as well. He arched an eyebrow, waiting for the explanation that would surely follow.

'Francis Bacon said that. And what I'm doing is a cuddle test.'

She laughed at his expression and the sound made him realise how long it had been since he'd heard her do that.

'I've always had a thing for a good soft toy and I'm in the market for a new one. Let's just say there's nothing worse than one that has no cuddle.'

He looked at the immense pile thoughtfully. 'I don't know, I think being stuck in here for fifteen minutes longer could be worse.'

She smiled, but didn't laugh this time. He wondered how long it would be until he heard it again.

'What about this one?'

He held up an orange, fluffy attempt at recreating a cat with eyes so huge they took up most of the space on the creature's head. Tommi bit her lip and looked from Heath to the cat and back again.

'I'm not really a—'

'Cat person?'

'Orange person. I just don't . . . do it.'

He laughed. 'I don't think they have any wolf soft toys, unfortunately.'

'Look, check out this giraffe. It's fine enough. They've made the mistake of trying to make it look too realistic but get a feel of that.'

Heath reluctantly hugged the animal as she instructed and was surprised at the comfortable softness.

'See? That's a toy stuffed *well*.'

'She's right,' squeaked a small voice from behind Tommi.

They turned to face a wee girl with an elaborate design of braids that clung tightly to her scalp before ending in shiny, yellow beads. The kid couldn't have been more than ten or so and she was short for her age. She was staring at Heath and Tommi intently as if she had been listening to their entire conversation.

'Thank you,' said Tommi, without missing a beat. She took the toy from Heath and handed it to the girl who squeezed it with the focus of a Nobel Prize-winning scientist. Finally, she nodded.

'It's oh-kay. I like them fatter, like . . .' She spotted a blue dolphin and pointed. Heath retrieved it for her and handed it down. Tommi gave him a quick smile before returning to the expertise of their tester.

'This is way fatter,' she said, passing it up to Tommi to try. She did and immediately Heath could tell she agreed with the girl.

'Oh, yeah, you could cuddle the shite out of this one,' she said.

A woman cleared her throat behind them and they turned to see the kid's mother looking at Tommi with a disapproving expression. 'Come on, Tessa,' she said, extending her hand. The girl took one look at her mother's face and relented her newfound friends.

She shrugged and quietly said: 'Bye.'

'Thanks for the help,' Tommi replied.

'Tessa, come on!'

The little girl shuffled off. Just as she was about to disappear around a corner she turned and gave a cheeky smile. Tommi returned it with a discreet wave. She caught Heath grinning as well and shoved the dolphin forcefully into his chest. He took two steps back with surprise, beaming.

'You would make a terrible babysitter,' he said. 'The kids would be drinking shots and cursing by the time they left play group.'

Tommi had the grace to look guilty as she rolled her eyes. 'Aye, I know. I can't censor myself no matter how hard I try, especially around little things. I could do it at the gallery, but maybe I've spent too much time working in a bar?'

'No, it's all you.'

'Ha. Moot point.'

'Are you getting this?'

'The dolphin? No, it's perfect by feel until you look at those creepy, beady eyes. You just know as soon as you leave it in a room unattended something's going to catch on fire.'

A deep, rolling laugh erupted from Heath's belly and he placed the dolphin on the pile with mock caution. A warmth spread in his chest as he caught the look on Tommi's face as she watched him laugh at her joke. It was funny, for someone so distinctly unique and completely her own person she sincerely enjoyed making other people happy. Or was that just friends?

'If we're not buying anything, can we get hell out of here, then? We're the only creeps without children.'

She laughed, taking his arm in hers and dragging him out of Anna's Toy Factory. Heath was stressed, his mind constantly whirring as he juggled multiple identities and jobs, but today had been about trying to cheer up Tommi and it was easy. Despite the fact they should have disliked each other given her romantic entanglements, they'd always gotten along. Now, with Lorcan's abrupt departure, her sickly best friend, and the sudden appearance of her half-sister Aruhe Ihi, he was beginning to feel sympathetic towards her situation.

'What is this hell?' Tommi asked, interrupting his thoughts. She was looking around her with a similar expression of horror to what Heath had felt in the toyshop.

'Pop-up Christmas Market,' he said.

'But ... why?'

'Tourists be spending year-round, what do you want from me?'

They strolled through one of the lines of shoppes, Heath observing her taking in the festive decorations with a glazed expression. They could have taken another route back to Phases, but he'd led her this way because it seemed like a wasted opportunity to be in the vicinity of the markets and not stop.

'You don't strike me as much of a Christmas person,' he noted.

'Meh, I'm not too fussed either way.' She shrugged. 'I like any excuse to hang out and eat too much. The whole Jesus side of it gives me the heebie-jeebies.'

A white and gold decorated crucifix was dangling in front of her from a particularly 'holy' stall and she whacked it out of the way to prove her point. Pausing in front of a stand that sold every type of jam you could imagine, Heath picked up a suspicious looking container of green goo.

'Apple and cinnamon spread,' said the shopkeeper.

'Why's it green?' he asked.

'Green apples.'

'Hmmm.' Heath placed it back down and ushered Tommi away. 'Green apples my ass. That was salmonella in a jar.'

'And I'm the one that didn't strike you as a Christmas person?'

He shrugged. 'It is what it is. My first wife was all about it: honeyed ham, turkey, roast vegetables, the whole lot.'

'Tinsel?'

'She was *all* about it.'

Tommi was quiet for a while, the two of them ducking and weaving between shoppes and clusters of people. She stopped at a stall selling mulled wine – naturally – and bought them a cup each. Snow had stopped falling weeks ago, which was pretty late for winter's grip to last in Berlin, but it was still crisp out. Heath warmed his hands around the cup as he took a sip of the liquid.

'I think I just registered the fact that you said *wife*,' Tommi noted, watching him over the top of her steaming wine. '*First* wife.'

'Aye, there were two. Not all of us are emotional cripples.'

'Pointed jab. How come you never talk about them?'

'No one ever asks. So ask.'

'You said you had two.'

'Yes. Elizabeth and I married in 1894. She died during childbirth.' A coughing sound came from his companion and he turned to see her spluttering wine. He patted her on the back like a consoling parent. 'Calm down, it was quite common back in those days. Childbirth was a fifty-fifty gamble.'

'Your—' *wheeze* '—your baby?'

'Of course.'

'Heath, I had no idea. I'm so sorry. Ugh, I'm such a dickhead. And I thought you'd knocked up a teen back in Galway! I made all those jokes. I hate me, *fook*.'

It had been a long time since anyone had expressed such a sentiment to him or had the need to. He was taken aback by it. A lot had happened in the more than one hundred and twenty years since he had lost both his wife and daughter. He'd had three great loves and countless seat-fillers between that, not all of them women. Yet his memory was as sharp as it ever was as he thought back to Elizabeth: all fiery red hair and a smattering of freckles on her cheeks. Realising he needed to respond, he thanked Tommi. It was a strange moment.

'And the second one?'

Heath smiled at the recollection. 'Uh, Dimity. Marriage was a mistake. She divorced me after six months and then changed her name to Rainbow Lotus in the sixties.' He could tell Tommi wanted to laugh but was being polite. 'Go on, you know you want to.'

'Yo, I'm a girl named Tommi. I can hardly laugh at anyone's name, let alone someone who willingly changed their name to Rainbow Lotus.'

'But you want to.'

'Omigod, SO badly.'

'The thing that always struck me about that, was she went to all the effort to embrace the flower power movement and switch the name, but she never changed her surname. She was Rainbow Lotus Smith.'

Now Tommi did laugh, pressing a hand over her own mouth to stifle the uproarious sound.

'What's funnier,' pressed Heath, 'is that Lorcan was the best man.'

That cut her short. She frowned in confusion and he watched her try to imagine it. 'The ultimate frenemies. Was he at your first one as well?'

'No, he was on rotation at Vankila at the time.'

'Huh. That whole Amos thing really fucked you guys up, yeah?'

Heath narrowed his eyes at the emotions swirling

through his chest as he thought back to the shared friend they'd had, whose death had changed both of their world-views. 'I stand by everything I said. Lorcan leaving the Guard was a knee-jerk reaction to something that happened. Granted, something awful. But it was something none of us had control over. I've known many people who have killed themselves over the centuries, werewolves mostly.'

She flinched at that.

'You can rarely predict it. The happiest person on the surface could be fighting a swirling black cloud inside of them. Being stable on the outside means nothing when you're struggling with something devouring you on the inside.'

'Lo once said that you thought suicide was the coward's way out.'

'Yes. Because if you have any sense of respect and love for the people in your life, you would never leave them to pick up the pieces left after taking your own life. You would never leave them with those questions and that blame.'

He could see her thinking that through and already knew that she disagreed with him before she opened her mouth to speak. 'I *know* we don't experience what were-wolves do. I know that's obstreperous.'

'I – hey, that wasn't what I was going to say at all.'

'No?'

'No. And you will explain to me what the word obstreperous means later. What I was going to say was I never understood why in the great tragedies, killing yourself over your soul mate was the ultimate display of love. I could never kill myself over a man.'

'What about a woman?' He grinned at her.

She snorted. 'I wish. If I had any choice over which

gender I was sexually attracted to, I'd be going with the ladies any day. Sadly, that's out of my control.'

'I thought Joss was gay the first time I met him.'

'WHAT?! Oh my God, I cannot wait to tell him that. Why?'

'I dunno.' Heath shrugged. 'He had a lot of twink sensibilities.'

'How is it that you're over a thousand years old yet can understand and identify queer terminology?'

'Wouldn't you like to know? Live long enough and those "conventions" around love and attraction don't matter so much anymore, Tommi. And a gentlemen never tells his age.'

She smirked, looking up at him as the wind whipped a piece of hair around her face. 'Have you ever been in love with a man?'

'Yes.

'Men?'

'Aye.'

'Clay?'

He let out a roar of laughter. 'No. He's just fun to flirt with.'

They had reached the end of the markets and she turned, staring back at the red and green glowing mass they had just emerged from. Heath was going to ask her if she wanted to go back through, but he already knew the answer. Instead he asked a tougher question.

'What's Aruhe up to today?'

She narrowed her eyes at him. 'Come on, Heath. You don't have to pretend you care. I know you don't like her and you think she's waiting for the perfect moment to throw a toaster in my bathtub.'

'Who said I cared? I simply asked what she's doing. Tracking her movements.'

'She's training with Dolly and Yu, far as I know.'

There was a long pause between them as Tommi, clearly uncomfortable with the subject, was hesitant to add any more information. It was fine. He'd already known the answer to the question before he asked it. But she didn't need to know that.

'I'm not an eejit,' she said, 'I know you hate having her stay with us.'

'I hate it because I know of the danger it brings. I can feel it.'

'What? You have werewolf senses now?'

'Don't lie to me. I know you can feel it too.'

'Frankly, I'm sick of feeling things. I'd stay out here and happily become a werewolf-cicle if it meant I could feel things a little less.'

'That's Aruhe's fault.'

'Oh, come *on*, you can't blame a teenager for everything, Heath,' Tommi chuckled.

'I can and I will. Your feelings are heightened by the two of you being in such close quarters.'

'Mansplain?'

'Most werewolves develop around the same time they hit puberty, thirteen or fourteen. You developed extremely late and a large part of that was to do with your blood pack being in another hemisphere. You were biologically isolated from your dominant genes.'

'Dr Kikuchi told me something like that after I had my first change, that it was being in the vicinity of the Ihi pack that brought out my wolf. It was like our blood had a chemical reaction.'

'Aye, so given that being near your bloodline accelerated

a change in you, that's something you will continue to feel. You do *feel* Aruhe because she's your blood.'

'The buzzing under my skin …?'

'A large reason packs stay together is because they're stronger together, biologically and literally. You'll always be able to sense your blood pack. Many wolves aren't in tune enough to understand what they're feeling, but that's what it is.'

Tommi was quiet for a few moments as she pondered the supernatural science.

'Technically she's still part of the Ihi pack,' he continued, cautious about how much he should say. 'She's on the run but they still have a claim on her. You can't just go off wandering pack-less when you're a pup.'

'I did.'

'Extenuating circumstances. Before you rebut me with "Oh, but the Rogues, Heath! The Rogues!" every one of them was well into their twenties and thirties before they declared themselves "lone" and broke from the pack.' She was grinning at him again and he didn't understand. 'What?'

'Your attempt at my voice is amusing. You do realise I'm not Billy Connolly, though?'

'Arrrgggh, aye.'

A U-Bahn rumbled along a track towards them and Tommi grabbed Heath's arm, pulling him towards the stop.

'We can catch this one and get out of the bloody cold,' she said. They made it in the nick of time, both jumping through the doors as they closed. She let out a puffed breath of relief that mirrored his own as the train continued in the direction of home. They were getting off in four stops, so Tommi didn't make a move to sit. Instead she leaned against one of the closed glass doors and watched the metropolis slowly passing by. Night had properly descended on Berlin now, which at this time of year resembled a model village inside a snow globe sans snow.

'There's this song,' she said, talking to her reflection more than she was Heath. 'It says that "love is watching someone die".'

He thought of Collette, a former flame, and finding what was left of her body on train tracks not far from where they were now. He thought even further back to Elizabeth, of watching her scream and writhe in pain for twelve hours only to disappear forever within an instant. He remembered begging the doctors for help, begging the Treize, but there was nothing they could do. Or so they had said. She was mortal. He understood now that it was a fortuitous thing, in a way, not having two people out there in the world that all his enemies knew he cared about. The Treize would use the people you loved against you; he'd seen it happen. Hell, he'd done the same.

When he opened his mouth to reply, he caught Tommi watching him closely. He hoped she couldn't read anything on his face.

'You're surprisingly wise when you're not flirting or offering to kill people. Is love watching someone die?' she asked.

He thought of Amos, who had been dying without him knowing it. 'I think . . . I think yes, love is watching someone die and knowing that a part of you will die with them. But that's necessary and okay. It's like amputees. It's hard at first to get used to living without a limb, yet they adapt. They learn how to go on and survive and thrive without it.'

'But you never forget that piece is missing.'

'Some days you might. You'd have to ask Casper.'

She turned her attention back to the city.

'How long do you think he has?' he asked.

'The doctors—'

'Not what the doctors said. In your heart, how much longer do you think he has?'

She let out a shuddering breath. 'Things are moving quickly now. You know, when he was getting better, he never got better this fast. It's medically hypocritical that he should be dying this fast. Wanker.'

Without realising he'd done it, Heath rested a hand on the back of her neck. It was a subconscious, comforting gesture and one he hadn't used in a long time.

'Soon. Less than a week but more than a few days. It's happening.

'I'm sorry.'

'When Jakea and Jaira tried to recruit me to the PG – on your advice, might I add – they said there was no point turning down immortality when I practically had no one left. When Joss passes, they'll be right. It should make me feel sick that I'm relieved a friend of mine will die a non-violent death.'

Heath tried to recall the last friend of his that had died a non-violent death. In the end, he felt most forms of death were violent one way or the other. Painful, heartbreaking, and always violent.

9

It was Christmas Eve. Or at least that's what I had decided. The trip to the markets had really burrowed into my subconscious and a few days later I decided we were gonna celebrate Christmas. Now. But first came Christmas Eve, which I was spending with Aruhe and Heath, all three of us drunk and watching *The Nightmare Before Christmas*. Since I was old enough to know what the animated musical was, this had been my tradition – albeit usually alone and actually in December. This year I was murmuring '"What's this? What's *this*?"' to the TV screen, surrounded by candles, alcohol, and an uneasy mix of kinda-family and friends. It was a fire hazard waiting to happen.

'*Another* musical number? I feel like we just got through one!' Aruhe groaned.

'Blasphemy!' I shrieked. Heath had managed to take prime position on the couch and was laying across it horizontally. I whacked his legs, which were resting on my lap, for emphasis. 'This is Ooogie Boogie's Song!'

She hiccupped by way of response. 'I'm not sure if the words you said made any sense or I'm just very drunk.'

'Both,' Heath chuckled, taking a long sip from his glass of whiskey. She watched him through bleary eyes for a full minute before announcing that she 'needed to pee' and stumbling to the bathroom.

I had returned that afternoon from another depressing day at the hospital with Joss. He was sleeping more and more, with only pockets of time where he was awake and lucid. 'You can sleep when you're dead!' was a line he used to taunt me with in an attempt to wake me up. Oh, the irony. The second I left the hospital I knew fake Christmas Eve was going to be a night of getting blootered and drowning my sorrows. Thankfully Heath and Aruhe were more than willing to join me, as everyone else was working at Phases.

'Hey,' Heath said, nudging me with his knee.

'Hey what?' I growled, snapping back to the present. Resting my cheek on the pillow of the couch, I glanced at my friend as he lay there. His facial hair had grown out a little more than he usually let it and I liked the relaxed, comfortable aura it gave him. In my mind, I knew the beer goggles were back as I stared at Heath. Regardless, there was no denying he looked good. Hell, he always looked good.

'Remind me later I have something for you.'

'Something? Like what? Like ... a fake Christmas present?'

'I didn't say that.'

'I'm shook. You got me a fake Christmas present, didn't you? What is it? Is it a weapon? Is it my own spear?'

He laughed, the sound thundering around the room. My heart fluttered in response as I took in the lines that crinkled from his eyes whenever he was happy. 'That's a work utensil, hardly a present.'

My mind snagged on the one present Lorcan had given me: my own machete. Used, but still useful. I'd attached more significance to the gesture and the item than I should have at the time. Looking back on it, I felt a touch idiotic.

'Can I have it now?' I asked, surprising Heath by the look on his face.

'It's not fake Christmas yet. It's fake Christmas Eve.'

'Ha! So it *is* a seasonal present!'

'I'll give it you later, when it's just the two of us.'

My mouth opened in surprise and I felt the tension rise in the room just a little bit. My blood seemingly pumped faster through my veins at the words 'just the two of us' and I desperately wanted to examine what my body was telling me. At precisely that moment the sound of Aruhe throwing up came from the bathroom. Heath and I glanced at each other.

'I think it *is* just gonna be the two of us.' I smiled.

'Fine, ye impatient rascal,' he sighed, getting to his feet and heading for his apartment next door.

'Rascal,' I chuckled, grabbing a towel and a bottle of water as I walked to the bathroom. Placing them next to the toilet bowl Aruhe was hunched over, I held her bangs back off her face as she heaved out the majority of what she'd eaten that day.

'Engh,' she groaned. 'I should have stopped hours ago. Why did I try to keep up with you two?'

I patted her gently on the back. 'We're Scottish, love; ain't no thing. You did your best.'

She tried to laugh but it just brought on a new wave of dry retching. Her body seemed to settle down after one final heave and she leaned her sweaty head against the cool, white ceramic.

'Go.' She waved. 'I'm fine. Just gonna stay here for a

while. And regret my life choices.'

'This is why I can never get a fringe,' I murmured, sweeping the strands of hair off her damp forehead.

'It frames my face,' she slurred.

'Towel and water,' I said, pointing at both items as I took a step backwards. 'We're just in the other room if you need us.'

She nodded and waved me away again. Closing the door behind me, I rejoined Heath on the couch as he sat there expectantly with a silver and blue striped present on his lap. The package even had a shiny, metallic blue bow on top. I smiled, looking at it suspiciously.

'Heath,' I said, aware of the caution in my voice. 'Please tell me this is something normal and not . . . a vampire?'

'Vampires are so hard to wrap,' he replied, straight-faced as he handed me the gift. I flopped down next to him and stared at it for a few solid beats.

'Just open it,' he moaned, seemingly anxious. 'I promise it's not a possessed monkey's paw.'

'See, when you say shite like that,' I started, tearing back the paper as I went. My mouth popped open in a small gesture of surprise as I held the contents. Black, oversized glass eyes were staring back at me at me from a considerably smaller fluffy head. He had bought me a stuffed unicorn with proportions that would have made a Margaret Keane painting look realistic. It was white and incredibly soft, with a silver horn and matching silver hooves. It also looked rather sad. Of course, how it looked was only a small part of it. Hesitantly I brought it to my chest and squeezed. It was perfect. It completely aced the cuddle test. When I finally looked at Heath, he was watching me carefully. I couldn't have read his expression if my life depended on it.

'Heath,' I whispered, surprising him with an attack hug.

He leapt back in shock as I grabbed him, wrapping my arms around his neck. He eventually relaxed into it, but I still had the sense he was expecting me to throw him in to an arm bar at any moment. Closing my eyes, I pressed my face into the groove between his shoulder and neck.

'It's just . . . a toy,' he squeezed out, words muffled in the vast expanse of my hair, which was covering most of his face at this point.

It was stupid, but I couldn't quite explain to him how it was so much more to me than *just* a toy. For most of the past few weeks, I had been struggling to stay afloat. This stupid, bug-eyed unicorn felt like a lifeline. Pulling back, I knew he saw the tears in my eyes and I laughed at myself, hastily wiping them away.

'Aye, but now it's my toy,' I sniffed, inspecting it one more time. He leaned forward, lifting my chin up with his thumb until we were at eye level.

'Tommi—'

Whatever he was about to say was killed in the air as his phone rang out, the tone blaring through the room as he rushed to find where it was coming from.

'Fuck, that's offensively loud.' I winced, unsure if my werewolf hearing was in overdrive or it was just my drunken state.

'It's Metallica. It has to be loud otherwise what's the point?' He grinned at me as he held the phone to his ear. 'What?'

His bemused smile dropped away almost instantly as whoever was on the other end on the phone began speaking to him, the words coming out in a steady, measured pace. I froze, my senses homing in on the person who had called. I would recognise that voice anywhere: Lorcan. Heath gripped the phone with increasing force, rage snapping through his vision like a flash of lightning.

'Do not move him,' he said, the words coming out through gritted teach. 'Or I swear to God—'

Lorcan hung up on his end, leaving Heath blinking away his anger. I rose to my feet, legs suddenly unsteady as I tried to measure the situation. Heath's eyes focused in on me as we both stood there, immobile.

'We need to go,' he said. 'Right now.'

'What about Aruhe?'

'It's better she stays here. They ... don't know about her.'

'The Treize don't know she's here?'

He nodded and I felt my eyebrows rise in surprise. I assumed he'd run off like a good lil' worker bee and told them the *moment* she surfaced. I'd been so caught up with everything happening to Joss that I hadn't bothered to wonder why no other Treize officials had showed up to interview her, at the very least.

Now that I thought about it, it was probably more likely they would have detained her. Heath was supposed to be a company man, but now here was the second *big thing* in just a few months that contradicted that. He'd made a huge show of how much Aruhe wasn't to be trusted, how much we had to keep our eyes on her because she was an Ihi, and yet ... he'd covered up that she was staying with the Rogues. The question of who he had done that for and why tugged at me, but I filed that information away for later.

Without another word, I grabbed a pair of combat boots and threw a trench coat on over the jeans and baggy jumper I'd been wearing. I shouted at Aruhe that we'd be back soon and rushed out the door, barely registering her reply for us to return with food. There was a sense of immediacy to Heath's manner and I didn't question it as we dived into the van and screeched out of the complex faster than we should have. I was still lacing up my boots with my leg outstretched on the dash when I realised where we were going: Mechtilde General.

'Heath—'

'We'll make it there in time,' he snapped.

'In time for what?' I hated hearing the fear in my voice. It was mixed with confusion as to why we were rushing towards Joss and why Lorcan was the cause of it. Screeching to a stop in the car park, Heath was almost immediately out of the car and sprinting towards the oncology ward with me hot on his heels.

The panic I felt rising in my chest took me back to one of the worst nights of my life, when I was speeding towards Mari and Kane in an attempt to save them. Skipping the elevator, Heath slammed through to the stairwell used for fire exits and took the stairs four at a time. When we hit the right level, he dashed into the hall and through the door to Joss' room, only to come to a jarring halt. I ran into his back and would have fallen completely over if he hadn't grabbed my shoulders to steady me.

I could have spent the rest of my life looking over the scene in that room and still never quite understood what I was witnessing.

There were a cluster of nearly a dozen people standing around the bed, with Joss propped up by one of them as he scrawled something on to a piece of parchment. It looked remarkably similar to the blood contract of secrecy that he and Officer Dick Creuzinger had been forced to sign when they first learned about the supernatural world. Lorcan was standing closest to Joss, watching intently, and his was the only face in the room I recognised. An older woman with ebony skin and snow-white hair done up in a bun on the top of her head nodded, clearly pleased with whatever had transpired. Two ghosts hovered at the rear of the room, both dressed in eighties' garb and both preoccupied by Joss' movements.

'What – the fuck – is going on?' I puffed, still breathless from the sprint to get there.

It was then a face I *did* know emerged from the back; someone I hadn't seen since my first unexpected visited to Treize headquarters in Transylvania. I had known him as Chester Rangi, yet it seemed everyone knew him as someone – and something – different. His appearance made my stomach drop even further and I did my best not to overreact.

'Your dear friend Joss is becoming one of us,' he said, palms extended upwards in somewhat of a peace gesture. I wasn't fooled. My eyes darted from Chester to Joss and back again. 'He has signed a contract to join the Custodians . . . forever.'

'WHAT?! That can't be—'

'It is done,' said one of the ghosts, nodding solemnly. 'We can place him in the half-state until the ritual.'

'Ritual?' I screeched, dashing towards my best friend as he let the pen filled with his own blood drop from his hand. He was barely conscious, and I pushed Lorcan out of the way to get to him, catching him as he fell back on to the bed with exhaustion. His eyelids were heavy and I knew what I was seeing when I looked into the glassy depths: death. Death was so, so close.

'Joss, what have they done to you?' I whimpered. He tried to laugh, managing little more than a half-smile as the skin on his sunken face wrapped around his teeth.

'It's okay, Tommi, I wanted this,' he said, voice so weak

the words barely made a sound. 'This is my way of staying around. I can be part of your world now.'

'Joss . . . it's forever. You're trading your life for servitude.'

His eyelids fluttered as he tried to stay conscious. His cold, clammy hand found my own as he attempted to grip it.

'We've all . . . gotta serve something.'

His body went limp in my arms and I looked up, panic etched on my face and tears blinding my vision.

'Is he—'

The older woman was inspecting the contract and she looked up from it to glance at Joss' face, before giving a small shrug.

'He's close, but no. Death hasn't come for him yet. And now it never will.'

I felt Lorcan's hands on my arm as he pulled me away from Joss' body.

'Come on, Tommi,' he murmured, patience in his tone.

'Get off me,' I growled, shaking him free with frustration as I took the steps back from the bed of my own accord. 'There has to be another way! Something else, someone else who can help! Sue! What about Dr Kikuchi? We can ask—'

'Tommi,' Lorcan said, a softness in the way he said my name. 'Dr Kikuchi's . . . well, Sue is dead.'

'*What?!*' I spun to look at Heath, who wouldn't meet my gaze. 'When? How?'

'I know you liked her, I know she was there for you—'

'She saved my life,' I told Lorcan. 'Twice.'

'I know. It was car accident a few days ago. I didn't think to tell you, I was just caught up with all of this.'

'I . . .'

I just saw her, I thought. That's also what I had been about to say before I stopped myself. No one was supposed to know that. That was Heath's and my secret. From the way he continued not to make eye contact, I guessed he was worried I was about to spill in a room full of Treize officials. I wasn't. My chest was rising and falling with everything that was swirling inside, but I swallowed the words down, along with my emotions as I tried to focus on the death that was right in front of me.

'What happens now?' I managed to say.

'We put him into a holding place,' said Chester, nodding at the ghosts nearby as if they were waiting for his command. It seemed they were, both moving towards Joss with purpose. My body made an involuntarily jerk in a bid to protect him, yet I found Heath's arms wrapped around me in a crushing embrace as he yanked me back. I tried to fight against him, but my heart wasn't in it as I watched what was unfolding. Both ghosts seemed to enter Joss' body, his frame arching up before relaxing back down again as the dead disappeared *inside* of my best friend. I clasped a hand over my own mouth in an attempt to stifle a scream. Chester observed with a bored indifference, as if he had seen this a million times before. He probably had.

'Because he's so close to death,' the woman was saying, 'we need to keep him alive until the final rituals are performed and he's officially an immortal Custodian. Once that has happened, death no longer has a grasp.'

The remaining people in the room moved around his bed, packaging Joss up as if he were a mummy ready for transportation.

'Where are you taking him?' I blurted, attempting to rush forward again before Heath held me back.

The older woman looked at me with an amused smile. 'We don't perform the rituals here, dear. He comes back with us to Transylvania.'

'Treize HQ,' I murmured.

'Then with the Custodians in New York,' Lorcan added. My head snapped in his direction and I stared at his face – *really* stared – for the first time. He had a beard forming, but it seemed less intentional and more down to neglect. There were deep bags under his eyes and his hair was longer, touching the base of his shoulders.

'Did you help him? Did you arrange this?'

'Yes,' he said, unashamedly. 'Joss was always smart and when he reached out to become one of us—'

'The Custodians are always short on numbers,' the woman supplied, continuing to instruct others in the removal of Joss' body from the hospital.

'I asked Jakea and Jaira when they wanted me for the PG if there was any way he could be saved and they told me a resounding no.'

'No one gets immortality without a price,' Chester answered, his eyes loaded with meaning. 'You could not have given immortality to Joss without the cost of his service.'

My breath came out in a rushed burst as meaning clicked into place.

'Usually Custodians recruit from within the supernatural community or Askari ranks,' the lady added. 'In only one case, from within the Praetorian Guard itself. I'm assured Joss here is a unique candidate and Lorcan was willing to sponsor his admission, along with several other Askari who agreed.'

'Woman, I don't want your history lessons,' I snapped, the wolf stalking its way to the surface. 'I want my best friend back.'

She seemed to notice the beast was dangerously closer than it should have been and she took a cautious step away from me.

'And you'll have him, for the rest of your mortal life.'

With that, she clicked her fingers and the remaining people in the room carried Joss away. I trailed after them, Heath still restraining me as we shuffled through the hospital seemingly unnoticed by everyone else in it. I glanced at the blank faces of those around us, all moving about their regular activities and completely unaware that one of their patients was being lugged out of the building.

'They can't see or understand a thing,' Chester said, catching my eye. 'Everything will go back to the way it was when we've left and no one will be any wiser.'

'You'll say that he died,' Heath murmured, as if that was the most logical option.

'Of course,' he nodded. 'It's rather convenient death was already on the table. Staging a body's not hard and the parents will be so devastated, they'll want just a small service. Tiny. Private. Minimal exposure.'

'What the hell are you?' I whispered, aware without needing confirmation that this power around us, bewitching the whole hospital, was being wielded by Chester himself.

He flashed me a smile that scared the shit out of me. 'Other.'

When we made it outside, I watched in horror as they loaded Joss into a vehicle.

'Is there anything I can do?' I whispered, more to myself than anyone in particular.

'No,' Heath replied, sounding as defeated as I was. 'Go to the service when it happens. Maintain the lie.'

The words 'why should I?' were on the top of my tongue when Heath answered the question for me.

'It's what Joss would want you to do.'

That sentence felt like a pin piercing me and I was a balloon, deflating hopelessly in front of a crowd. Spinning around until I found Lorcan, I wiggled free of Heath's grip. Eventually he let go, hanging back as I marched towards my former Custodian.

'The last time you and Chester were together, you were trying to kill each other!' I shouted. 'You said he couldn't be trusted and now? You're working together. What the fuck changed?'

'A lot,' Lorcan replied, his voice neutral. Before I could stop myself, I lashed out and punched him. His jaw cracked as my fist connected, sending him flying on his ass. I stood over him, watching as he cradled his face. I expected Heath to run at me, drag me back kicking and screaming. Instead he stayed where he was, watching the scene play out. Chester appeared to be bouncing on his toes with excitement, not quite sure where to glance or what mayhem to encourage. Lorcan eventually got to his feet, his face already swelling from the impact of my hit.

'I suppose I deserved that,' he mumbled, notably keeping himself out of striking range.

'You never cared about Joss in life,' I said, hurt rich in my voice. 'He was just a passenger to you, someone along for the ride. Now you suddenly care enough to help him do this? What are you playing at?'

'He will be able to help countless others now as Custodian.'

'The way you helped me? And I don't care about others, I care about him!'

'What did you expect me to do?' Lorcan shouted back, anger finally sparking in him as he broke the calm exterior. I walked away, my back to him and Chester as the Treize's vehicle idled behind them.

'What you promised,' I muttered, voice barely audible. 'To disappear.'

THE DRIVE back to Phases was ugly. Heath let me sob most of the way, knowing better than to try and console me. I cried so hard my breaths turned into hiccups and the front of my trench was drenched in salty tears. Rage and grief were curdling in me so deep I was physically shaking. We were sitting at a red light when I turned to Heath, desperation seeping through every fibre of my being.

'I need to change,' I said, through gritted teeth.

'Aye, it's that bad? We're ten minutes away from the club—'

'No, Heath. Not a cage. I need to *run*.'

I was gripping his shoulder with such force I felt him flinch under my fingers. I glanced down to see my hand had shifted into a wolf claw that was cutting deep into his arm. I yanked it back, cradling the limb to my chest as I tried to ignore the mild scent of Heath's blood I could taste in the air. With a look over his shoulder and a cursory 'fuck it', the wheels screeched under us as he pulled into a different lane. He'd been driving at a crawl when we left the hospital, both of us still recovering from the shock of everything that had happened, but now he was giving Vin Diesel a run for his money. I could barely talk as I concentrated on staying human. *Inhale and exhale. Inhale and exhale. Inhale and motherfucking exhale.* I imagined my hands doing human things: painting, touching, typing, tearing, slashing . . . crap, I was failing horribly.

'How much longer?' I growled, *literally* growled as my voice failed to resemble a woman's anymore.

'We're close, Viktoriapark.'

'Viktor – ergh . . . it's too public.'

'Not today,' he said, mounting the curb so fast my head hit the roof.

Water from a recent downpour splashed up from the tyres as we skidded to a dramatic halt well inside the park. I didn't stop to tear off my clothes, shifting on the fly did that for me as I burst out of the car. What I had been wearing fell around me in shreds as my paws hit the muddy grass, my body snapping and tearing and reconfiguring in a critical rush to be what it needed to be: the wolf.

I stumbled with the physical exertion of a forced shift outside of the full moon, but it was less than a moment before I was sprinting through the damp bushes of the park. Branches snapped as I cut a mad path, racing in whatever direction I felt like and relishing the sheer exhilaration of being a wild thing.

Heath had been right. Three days of rain had cleared Viktoriapark of any human life and it was truly my playground. My chest burned as I pushed myself faster and faster, my breath coming out in hot puffs as my tongue lolled to the side of my mouth. Eventually I slowed to a jog, letting the warmth in my blood race through my veins with triumph. I stopped once, just long enough to throw my head up towards the sky and let out a piercing howl that sent every bird in a kilometre radius flying to safety.

HEATH WAS inside the car when I emerged from the thick shrubbery an hour later, my fur drenched. He was on the phone to someone and he was angry. No, more than that: he seemed worried.

'What the fuck are you playing at, *demon*?'

I strained, trying to hear the words coming down the

other end of the line, but the car's motor and the distance meant I could only make out half the conversation.

'Yes, ya damn right I would have tried to stop it. I'm not saying death is better but—'

He punched the steering wheel, agitated.

'That's not the same thing! You know they'll use him against her if they can. Ha, you will, will you? Cos I know you, I know how easily you get bored. Cultivating another spy takes *years* and if it's not working to your timeline, the kid's in the wind. And immortal. And trapped.'

Joss. He was talking about my best friend and—

Heath's eyes snapped up, registering that I was back. Damn it, I thought I'd been careful enough that he wouldn't have seen me. His instincts remained sharp as ever and I relented, trotting forward as he rushed to end his phone call. He was out of the vehicle and unbuttoning his winter coat as I began the painful process of transforming back to human form.

By the end of it, I was naked, grunting, and groaning on all fours as the mud around me began to dry on my skin with the heat of my body. The first time Heath and I had met I was nude, covered in blood and my frame weak from a recent forced transformation. It wasn't dissimilar to the situation I found myself in currently and I wondered if there was ever a time when I'd get to choose how and when he'd see me like this.

My limbs were shaky as Heath helped me to my feet, tucking me into his coat as I stumbled back to the car. The warm interior caused me to let out a contented moan as I closed my eyes and relaxed back in the seat. We sat in silence for a long while, the only accompaniment Massive Attack playing through the speakers.

'Thank you,' I whispered. I sensed Heath nodding next to me.

'We can never tell anyone what just happened.'

I opened one eye. He was staring straight ahead and serious.

'The Treize can never find out you just ran through Viktoriapark in wolf form.'

'No one saw me. And it's not the first time I've ran through Berlin as—'

'Aye, but this time *I* let you. Do you understand?'

He met my eyes and I saw the severity of what he was saying hanging in his gaze. Eventually, I gave a wee nod.

'I understand.'

With that, he started the ignition and after some skilful manoeuvring we were back out on the road and driving to Phases. This time, there weren't any unexpected stops.

'There's a mounting list of things we're keeping from the Treize now, isn't there?' I said, focusing on the raindrops hitting the windscreen. 'That favour in Galway, Aruhe, my park run . . . what else, Heath?'

I swivelled in my seat to look at him properly, side-on, and didn't miss the deep creases in his forehead as he frowned.

'A head full of worries,' I murmured. 'Are you in trouble? Am I?'

'You're not,' he answered, 'and I'm not. At least, not yet.'

'Who were you talking to on the phone?'

'Shite, you heard that?'

'Some of it.'

He sighed, shaking his head. 'It doesn't matter now.'

When we arrived at Phases, we both sat in the vehicle for several silent minutes. Then, barefoot, I trekked up the stairs to my apartment. I couldn't shake the image of Joss, seemingly lifeless but still alive as they took away his body to turn him into one of us: a supernatural. My mind kept flashing to the two ghosts plunging into my best friend like he was a sponge. Where did they go from there? What happened to Joss' spirit? I didn't realise I had been standing still at my doorway, frozen, with the keys in my outstretched hand. I spun to Heath, who had let out a deep sigh and was leaning with his back pressed against his own apartment door.

'What will happen to him?' I asked.

'You heard as well as I did. He's being taken to their headquarters where the final transition from human to immortal will take place. It's quite quick, actually.'

'Will it hurt?'

He shrugged. 'Not in the physical sense. In fact, once you've come back you feel great.'

'Back to life?'

'Back to immortal life.'

'Oh. What happened during your—'

'I can't talk about that, none of us can. I also don't know if it's different when you become an immortal Custodian as opposed to—'

'A warrior.'

'Aye.'

I didn't ask whether Heath knew they were planning this: it had been clear from his reaction and his panic that he was just as in the dark as I was.

'Will he be the same?' I questioned.

Heath looked thoughtful for a moment, the question ticking over in his mind. 'Yes and no. He'll still be Joss, the Joss you've known and loved for the past decade. But our experiences change us: they shape us. It will do the same for him, along with full access to the knowledge of what our world is.'

I nodded, only vaguely understanding the ramifications. 'How long until I can see him?'

'It could be weeks, it could be months, it could be . . . years. It all depends on how he takes it.'

'Fuck me,' I whispered, feeling helpless. 'Can . . . Can I help you? Whatever manure you're in—'

He laughed, surprising me. 'Help yourself. Help Aruhe. Save your energy for that. I'm big and ugly enough to look after myself.'

He was rebuffing me, I knew it. I could be trusted to help on some jobs, learn some information, but not everything. It stung. Turning back to my door, my key was inside the lock and I was pushing my way through when Heath called out to me from his own doorway.

'Tommi?'

'Yeah?'

'Merry Christmas.'

'It's fake,' I murmured, letting the door shut behind me.

10

When I woke, I wasn't sure at first what had startled me. It was just after midday and Aruhe appeared to have not moved. She was fast asleep on my bed, having conked out during the middle of watching *Green Street Hooligans*. I'd spent much of last night explaining to her what had happened with Joss, what I'd seen and what I did and didn't understand. She'd only met him once, yet seemed deeply concerned at first. What that emotion actually was, was fear.

'You can't trust them,' she had said, gripping my arm with werewolf force.

'Lorcan and the others? Believe me, I know that.'

'Yes, that asshole, but the Treize also – they can't be trusted.'

'No one with that much power is perfect and they definitely aren't but—'

'Joss is someone you love, right? Someone you care about?'

'Yes, of course. More than anyone else in the world.'

'And now he'll be around forever. They'll be able to use him against you, *forever*.'

Her words mingled with what I had overheard Heath saying on the phone and I was reminded of the weird warning Dr Kikuchi had given me back in Ireland. She'd been making chess analogies, I recalled, and I couldn't help but wonder if Joss was a pawn and his pending immortality was the first move against me. Meanwhile Dr Kikuchi was dead now, in a car accident, killed just like my father.

Those thoughts kept me up long after Aruhe was lightly snoring into the wee hours of the morning.

I'd tried to distract myself with a book: *An Introduction To Pictish Culture*. Whether I was trying to understand Heath better or just scratch a curious itch, I didn't want to think overly about it. I just wanted to read and escape the reality of this fucking awful situation. Unfortunately, besides a warrior woman named Scatha who had an island to herself to train the young, upcoming fighters, I found it very hard to get into. My mind was somewhere else. I'd fallen asleep on the couch, the book balanced awkwardly on my breasts and the pages tickling my face. That wasn't what had stirred me though.

The little light that had made its way through the Berlin sky wasn't doing much to brighten the day and I squinted as I sat upright, elbows resting on my thighs as I hunched over the couch. Scanning the room, there wasn't anything obvious that could be making me feel so uneasy. Rubbing a hand over my face in an attempt to wake the hell up, I pulled on my shoes. My skin felt alive, as if there were bugs crawling just underneath the surface. One of the top windows was open and a gentle breeze flowed through, catching my hair so my ponytail brushed my face. It was then that I caught the scent.

I was sprinting for the door in a second, grabbing a denim jacket and pausing only when I reached the fourth-floor weapons room to grab a Glock, a short sword, and two throwing knives. I loaded the gun as I jogged down the stairs, grateful that I had trusted what my body had been telling me. My blades might have been hidden, but I made no attempt to cloak the Glock as I stepped out of the apartment block and pointed it squarely at the chest of Simon Tianne.

He was shocked, but hid it quickly as a cool, calm exterior snapped into place. He raised his chin a little higher in a proud gesture as he looked at the gun. Simon had been expecting me, I realised, though he hadn't been expecting me to be armed.

'We need to have a conversation,' he said in a crisp New Zealand accent.

'My fists are about to have a conversation with your face.'

'Tommi, I didn't come here to fight.'

I rolled my eyes. 'Now that's what *all* the guys say.'

'I'm here for Aruhe.'

I shifted my aim just slightly and fired a warning shot by way of response.

'How did you know she was here?' I growled.

'She doesn't belong here,' he answered, ignoring my question. 'She needs to come home to her family.'

'The last time I checked, she was worried that if she went home there'd be punishment waiting for her.'

'What Steven did—'

'And why not knock, huh? Why not call first, ask for a chat, instead of lurking out the front of our house threatening to take her somewhere she's probably going to be killed?'

Understanding illuminated Simon's eyes. 'You're close.'

'I'd say by default, given that she doesn't have a whole lot of people to be close to. She has been living on the streets, you know?'

'I do. I've been trying to catch up to her for months. When I heard that she was with you—'

'And who did you hear that from?'

He opened his mouth to reply, but thought better of it. I could see the annoyance on his expression. Simon thought he'd already said too much. He tried again.

'Rumours. Things circulate. Our kind talk. People seem to *know* you. You've made a big impact in a short time.'

'Aye, lay it on, mate,' I snickered, hearing the irregularity of his heartbeat. He was lying. Someone had told him.

'Listen, things aren't like before. Things are changing. We have the opportunity to rewrite history.'

'Using ink instead of blood?'

'Using both, actually. One doesn't work without the other. I know James has reached out to you and we're trying to do this together, rule as family *and* friends. But I'm pack leader now. And I'm here to take our girl home.'

I narrowed my eyes at him, trying to smell the bullshit. 'Why?'

'She's ours.'

'Well, there's a heartfelt sentiment,' I snapped, rolling my eyes.

'She's an Ihi, Tommi. She's of Ihi blood. She belongs with us, ritually and legally.'

'I'm an Ihi too, remember? She's half of my blood too.'

'But you were never part of our pack and you chose to make sure you never would be after what happened. She belongs with her people and with her country.'

'Even if that comes at the cost of her life? Under whatever punishment you see fit to dish out for betraying the vote of the Aunties?'

'I'm not here to argue with you, I'm here to rightfully claim her under pack law and take her back.'

The doors to the loading dock screeched open as Yu and Dolly both emerged into the alleyway. I hadn't even known they were awake, but there they were: loyal as ever, unflinching and running defence. Dolly was carrying a small axe, while her girlfriend was holding a large rifle, which she cocked as she walked. From scent alone I knew it was Heath who slipped out of the door behind me. He raised a crossbow casually, pointing it at our visitor with a grin. Simon raised his arms above his head slowly, looking cautious for the first time.

'I'm not here for trouble, I'm just here for Aruhe,' he said. 'Although I'm flattered by the welcome.'

'And therein lies the trouble,' I said. 'We're quite fond of her.'

'You'd protect her?'

'From a death sentence? Definitely,' replied Dolly, her lips curling slightly as she spoke.

'Wait, you're here for the kid and the kid only? Not Tommi?' asked Heath.

'No. Tommi was never part of the pack. We have no claim on her.'

'Huh,' said Heath, lowering the crossbow and leaning against the door to light a cigarette. 'Very well then.'

'Heath!' I exclaimed.

'What? I thought he was here to try and abduct and murder you like the other brother.'

A snarl from Simon drew my attention away from my blond friend.

'We're NOT like Steven. That curse is dead and gone now.'

'Aye,' replied Heath, looking amused but sounding cold. 'So the Ihi pack has turned a new leaf under the leadership of two halfwits who were raised by the same men who couldn't keep Steven Ihi on a leash? I'd sooner believe Scientology.'

Simon looked momentarily confused and I watched with interest as something passed between them.

'You can't have her,' pressed Yu. 'Aruhe is under our protection and wants nothing to do with you.'

'It's not up to her,' snapped Simon.

'She's over eighteen, she's legally an adult. It's entirely up to her,' I said.

'Actually . . .' Heath started.

The heads of all three of us snapped in his direction. He looked chill: relaxed, even.

'What, Heath?' Yu pressed.

'She technically still belongs to the Ihi pack.'

'She's a human, not a saucepan. She belongs to no one but herself,' I screeched.

'Pack law . . .' whispered Dolly.

'Pack law,' repeated Simon.

'Law? What *pack law*? Packs put the Lucy in Lawless from what I've seen,' I hissed.

'You originated as a lone wolf. You're the exception, not the rule. Aruhe isn't a rogue, never has been. She has a heritage that has a claim on her until she declares other-wise,' said Heath.

'Then let's declare it!' I said.

'It's not as simple as that,' muttered Dolly.

Yu sighed. 'It never is.'

I was peeved. 'Enough with the riddles. Somebody explain this to me, clean and simple.'

'It's like this,' Simon began, stepping closer towards us. 'The Treize might rule werewolves, but pack law existed long before they began enforcing a police state.'

I expected Heath to object to that description, but he was notably silent.

'Packs are bound by blood. Each member is linked by a genetic code more powerful than anything else on this Earth. You never cease being part of the pack you're born into until you spiritually and physically sever contact. Aruhe has done one, but she's not old enough to do the other.'

'Coming of age . . .' I whispered.

'By default, she's still part of the Ihi clan,' said Heath.

'Why isn't she old enough "spiritually"?' I questioned.

'In pack culture, a werewolf doesn't mature until they've completed—'

'No, no, I got this: a magic quest, right?'

'Of course you'd mock it. You have no understanding of what it means to be more than one and part of a *whole*.'

I opened my mouth to argue and paused. I felt like I was part of something bigger living and working and training here with the Rogues. Yet if I wanted to, I could move on within the blink of an eye – nothing tied me here except the people. I hadn't been forced to pass some test in order to become a pack werewolf, because I had no pack.

'It's okay.'

My head jerked around to find the source of the voice. Drawn downstairs by the sound of our argument, Aruhe had stepped out of the complex and on to the street while the rest of us were caught up in disagreement. She was staring at her cousin now, a mix of things playing over her face. There was happiness – she was clearly glad to see him – but there was fear, as she knew what his appearance meant. And mixed among it all, was acceptance. There was a small smile playing over Simon's lips as he looked at her, yet the expression disappeared so quickly I could barely register it.

'It's okay,' she repeated. 'I want to go home.'

'Aruhe, no,' I said, stepping in front of her as she took a step towards Simon. 'You told me yourself there would consequences if you ever went back, that was the whole reason you hadn't!'

'I know.' She shrugged. 'But I can't run from this forever. I need to pay for what I did.'

'Warning your brother? That's a price you're willing to pay for with your life? This isn't fair!'

'That's pack,' came Simon's voice. A feeling returned to me, one I'd experienced less than twenty-four hours earlier. I could only describe it as trying to catch air in my very hands. Another person was slipping away from me and I was powerless to stop it. Or was I?

'Wait,' I mumbled, the cogs kicking into gear in my mind. 'Wait, just ... everybody wait a second.'

I glanced from Heath to Yu, to Dolly and Aruhe, before my eyes eventually landed on Simon.

'Are you authorised to negotiate?' I asked him.

There was a pause, one longer than I expected.

'You're alpha, are you not?' Heath pushed.

Simon glared at him. 'Yes. I have the power to do so, if need be.'

'You've said Aruhe needs to go back for her coming of age ritual, no questions asked. That's what every werewolf from every pack around the world goes through right?'

I glanced at my friends for back-up and they nodded in agreement.

'But she also has to face judgement for disclosing the ruling of the Aunties, when they had decided to execute Steven.'

'Yes,' answered Simon. 'Her interference meant pack justice was never carried out. And we lost two brothers and a sister that night.'

Aruhe flinched under his gaze, but she didn't back down. 'I couldn't let you kill him, I couldn't stand by while that happened – no matter what he did.'

'He's still dead, though, isn't he?' Simon pushed. 'You didn't stop anything. Pack justice always find a way: at our hands or hers.'

He jerked his head in my direction for emphasis.

'Off track,' I snapped, taking a breath in the process. 'What would it take to *ensure* Aruhe wouldn't pay with her life?'

'Tommi—'

I cut Heath off as I held up a hand, desperate for Simon to see how serious I was and offer me a solution. I could sense Dolly and Yu twitching behind me, everyone tense as Simon weighed my question.

'For you to complete ahi hikoi,' he said at last.

'Done,' I replied in an instant, aware that Heath had called out his protests behind me. There was a flash of victory in Simon's eyes and internally I kicked myself, wondering if that's what he had wanted all along.

'Tommi, no! You don't know what this means!' Heath basically shook me by the shoulders as he darted to my side. 'People *die* during the coming of age! People who have grown up with their packs all their lives! It's designed to put werewolves through the ultimate test. You cannot survive this.'

I looked at Aruhe, her mouth was hanging open with

shock and tears were welling in her eyes at what I had just done. If it meant she could go home and have a chance at a life with the family I had inadvertently torn apart? It was worth it. Life rarely gave you an opportunity to make amends, so when it did you had to carpe diem that bitch. And I had *a lot* of sins to amend for.

'Aruhe has to do this, right? Then we can do it together.'

'You can't do it together, it's a solo experience,' Dolly said. 'You would do it on the same night, I suppose, but in a separate area: sacred ground neutral to all packs.'

'Back in Aotearoa,' Simon said.

The last time I had been to New Zealand, I'd had my entire world shaken to its core. I found out everything I knew was lie, I found out my mum was the liar, and I found out I was werewolf. Those truths nearly came with the price of my life. I'd never had a desire to go back there since.

'Fine,' I sighed. 'Just tell me what I have to do.'

'Every pack has their own version,' mumbled Yu, her words quiet with the fear I could sense she was feeling for me. 'The ritual needs the werewolf to spend a night alone on sacred grounds and face the spirits of generations before them so they can reach maturity.'

I looked at Dolly for confirmation and she nodded. 'I did it. It would be different in my blood pack to the experience in yours, but the end result is the same.'

'Māori packs have to walk through the fires of the past,' said Simon.

I gulped. 'Fire?'

'Metaphorical fire,' he added.

'Fine. How many times do I have to say it? I'll walk into your burning ring of metaphorical fire.'

Simon stared at me, not sure if I was joking or serious.

After a solid minute he got the message, taking half a step back before pausing.

'It happens on the next blue moon.'

'What?' Dolly objected. 'That's less than two weeks away!'

'That was when Aruhe was supposed to experience ahi hikoi. She can't miss that window. And if Tommi's going to do it too, neither can she.'

'That's not enough time,' Heath whispered, panic evident in his tone.

Simon frowned at him, seemingly confused as to why the hulking PG warrior should give a damn as to whether I lived or died.

'We'll need to talk,' my half-cousin said, nodding at both Aruhe and I. 'There are things to prepare, travel, customs. I'm staying at the Marriott.'

He placed a piece of paper at my feet. I nodded, but said nothing more.

Heath's hand on my elbow directed me back into the apartment block, with Yu, Aruhe and Dolly filing in behind us. The second the door was closed behind us, I pushed my back against it and let out a gust of air in relief. Dolly looked as shaken as I felt, while Yu's face was reflecting a shade of anger. Heath looked stressed and was running a hand through his beard with agitation. He was the first to speak among our small group.

'When are you going to stop fighting for other people and start fighting for yourself?'

It was less of a question and more of a statement, but it was surprising nonetheless. 'I—'

'This is bad, Tommi. You going back there is bad news. I can't hide this, no one can.'

'I wasn't left with much of a choice.'

'If you think the Treize will be concerned with the two of you living together, that's nothing to how they're going to react when they find out you're *both* going home to complete the pack's initiation ritual.'

'She's only doing it for Aruhe. That's got to count for something,' said Dolly.

'It doesn't matter how you spin this,' Yu agreed. 'Heath's right. They're going to be alarmed. And suspicious.'

'Which means what? They'll stop us from going?' I asked.

'No. They can't be seen to interfere with pack tradition, especially something as old as this: werewolves all over the world would be in uproar. And especially given the treaties with the Outskirt Packs following the conflicts.'

Heath was staring intensely at the doorknob from his position sitting on the stairs, practically muttering to himself. He was dead still as he thought about the situation, hard. Aruhe was quiet, hugging herself as she stood there and watched him too. Finally, he spoke up.

'They'll send me. And others. You'll be given an escort who will keep a close eye on you the entire time you're there.'

'Like bodyguards?' I said, hopefully.

'Like bodyguards who will put you down the second they think you've gone full-Ihi,' corrected Aruhe.

'Jinkies.'

Heath didn't disagree with her. 'You won't stay with the Ihi pack. You'll be under watch twenty-four hours a day the entire time you're there. If it goes wrong—'

'Heath, you're talking crazy,' I said, dropping to my knees in front of him so he was forced to look at me. 'If what Simon says is true, which I don't doubt at this point, they're actively trying to change. There won't be sides. Plus, how hard can it be? I've met a ghost before, I can smoke a pipe with strange herbs, sing kumbaya and go through werewolf puberty just like everyone else has.'

Heath's eyes met mine and it frightened me, only for a second. I steeled myself and put on a brave grin.

'You're still their blood,' he whispered. 'That counts for something. You can't underestimate the sway that can have.'

'I don't and I won't.'

'Tommi,' he said, leaning forward until his face was inches from my own. 'The test is designed to mature a werewolf and integrate them into the pack. The Ihi pack have no control over what the wolf sees or experiences, that's up to the essence of your ancestors. But there's also no guarantee the woman who walks into that forest will be the same woman who walks out.'

'I wasn't,' Dolly murmured.

'If you walk out,' Yu added.

'The Ihi pack have always wanted you in their ranks,' Heath said. 'This could be a ploy to get you not only *back* on their land, but back into the fold: with them rather than against them.'

'What are you saying?' I asked, maintaining Heath's eye contact.

'I'm saying that if you emerge from this wanting to become part of the Ihi clan, the Treize could make me kill you.'

Ignoring the chill that ran through my body, I replied: 'It's a good thing that will positively never happen then, aye?'

Heath looked old as he smiled at me weakly, nodding. 'Aye.'

～

When I dreamed, I dreamed of drowning. In and of itself that was strange, as I'd always been a good swimmer – especially for a Scot. I loved swimming, I loved the water, and now my dreams were full of it. It was as if there was a leak in my very subconscious. I'd be in seemingly normal scenarios – like working behind the bar at Phases or hanging at the apartment with Aruhe – when suddenly the room would fill with water. No matter how hard I tried, I could never get out. I could never break free. I always woke, my chest burning as if I had been struggling for breath in the real world as well as in my dreams. The one time I managed to fight through and break the surface, I found myself floating alone in the ocean. Rain was pelting my face as I floated there, my body rising and falling with the movement of enormous waves the size of buildings. I watched their crests fearfully, but they never broke, they never descended into a towering wall of whitewash. Instead I was left to look around hopelessly for land, help, a ship, any form of a saviour. And nothing ever came. I just stayed there, buoyant and afraid, like fucking Mark Wahlberg at the end of *The Perfect Storm*. That dream was the worst.

When I woke, I was drowning too. I could barely stay afloat amid the myriad of meetings, negotiations, back-and-bloody-forths required to make this deal happen. No one had expected the Treize to just let us prance back to New Zealand and Heath was correct in assuming they would take it very seriously. Yet they were borderline treating it as a threat. Firstly, we couldn't set foot in the country without an escort. The fact that would be led by Heath and a team of his choosing was of little relevance. I was under no illusions as to what that meant. The official line was to provide Aruhe and I with security up until the point the coming of age ritual would take place. The unofficial one – I guessed – was to flex and see if they flinched.

Sitting in the position of being neither fully associated with the Treize nor fully with the Ihi pack, I was given an unusual vantage point. There was *so* much history there: every decision and every comment was loaded with the knowledge of everything that had come before. And me? I had been kept in the dark about so much of it: first by my mother and then by Lorcan. Reasons aside, it felt impossible to navigate a minefield while wearing a blindfold.

The politics of the werewolf-slash-supernatural worlds and where they intersected at least gave me something to think about besides my likely demise. The more I learned about werewolf coming of age rituals, the more terrified I became. Heck, Aruhe had spent much of the last ten years watching her pack go through it – and readying herself – yet even she was in full anxiety mode. Her fears, however, stemmed from not being physically prepared enough: she was spending hours in the training room every day in the lead-up to our departure. I worked with her when I could, but Dolly, Yu and Clay did most of the heavy lifting, running her through weapons, drilling, manoeuvres – all kinds of physical shit that prepared the body but also the mind.

Among all that, I had to attend a funeral. A fake funeral, but I was the only one who knew that. Hell, I'd imagined Joss' death enough times in a bid to mentally prepare myself for that eventuality that it sure as hell felt real to me. As I stood behind Joss' parents, in a tiny chapel, it struck me that in a way this was *real.* Not just because I was watching the two of them cling to each other like a lifeline, knuckles white as their hands gripped tightly, but because Joss was really dead. He was being given a new life and the price of that meant the old one had to die.

It was just the three of us at the service. Heath had wanted to come with me, all of the Rogues had even though they knew the truth. It was a show of support. Yet Joss' folks had wanted a small, intimate affair. There was no body to bury, they had chosen to have him cremated. *Convenient,* I thought. Not that there was any reason to question the death of a terminal cancer patient, but if there was . . . well, now his body couldn't be exhumed. I wondered if the Jabour family always intended on cremation or whether that had been suggested by someone, just a helpful whisper in their ear.

'This way we can take him back home,' Samantha said to me, clutching the urn at her chest.

She meant Dundee. They were going to scatter some of his ashes there in a bigger ceremony with everyone else, so no one had to travel and Joss could be where all his best memories had been, where all his friends were, and his dreams. Then they were going on a trip, something they'd been putting off for years every time he got sick. His ashes would go with them, scattered in places he had never had a chance to visit in life.

'That sounds beautiful,' I mumbled, not knowing what else to say. Joss would end up seeing so much of the world, parts of it his parents would die never knowing existed. Wasn't that the point, in a way? Wasn't that every parents dream, that their child would go on to exceed their wildest expectations? It's what I told myself as I sobbed in the car, playing Joss' favourite band Young Fathers loud enough so I couldn't hear my own cries.

When I finally dragged myself back to the apartment, it was so late even Phases was winding down with stragglers smoking out in the alley. I felt hollow as I trekked up the stairs, not even thinking about it as I turned left instead of right and walked into Heath's apartment rather than my own. Mine was empty, Aruhe somewhere that was else, and I didn't want to be alone. I couldn't. Heath was awake because of course he was, laying on the top of his bed with paperwork spread out in front of him. I guessed it was stuff he didn't want me to see, as he scrambled to sweep everything up as quickly as he could.

'Tommi? How did you get i – '

'Picked the lock,' I answered, not letting him finish as I kicked off my shoes and shrugged out of my jacket. Not slowing down for a moment, I climbed into the side of his bed that wasn't occupied. I pulled the blankets over me and snuggled into the mattress. He had music playing, old folk music, which was how I knew he was alone. It wasn't fuck music. Neither of us spoke for a long while and I had no intention of breaking the silence. He did.

'Do you want to talk about it?'

'No,' I replied, squeezing my eyes shut. I wasn't worried about crying in front of him, it didn't seem possible that any tears could be left inside my body. He kept reading, doing whatever he was doing, and eventually I was able to relax about the idea of him pushing me any further.

By the time he switched the light off, I was already starting to doze as I felt him roll over alongside me. Gently, carefully, he undid my hair from the bun it had been done up in. If I could have purred, I would have as his huge hands worked their way through my scalp, running through my long strands like a human hairbrush. I fell asleep like that, only half waking later and sensing the warm presence of his body wrapped around mine like a protective shield.

In the morning, he was gone. And I needed to keep my head buried in the books. I had an Askari at my disposal and the fact it was Tulc, the girl Joss had been so friendly with, was some comfort. She was quiet and smart and thoughtful, and seemingly had a never-ending collection of overalls: her presence was like having a little part of my best friend there with me, even though he was God knows where going through God knows what.

Tulc helped me source all of the materials I might need, and I was trying to consume everything I could about the werewolf custom. The problem was, they were largely sacred among each pack and therefore the accounts were sketchy. On top of that, everyone's experience was different: it varied from pack to pack, country to country, wolf to wolf.

I could interview a thousand werewolves and analyse what they went through, only to experience something completely different myself. It was infuriating, like studying for a test when you didn't know whether you'd be quizzed on algebra or literature. Slamming one of the thick volumes shut, I hurled it across the room, narrowly missing Heath's head where he lounged on our couch.

'Hey!' He only looked mildly roused.

'I can't do this! I can't handle this!'

'You can handle the Laignach Faelad but you can't handle a few books?'

'No, what I can't handle is vagina dentata.'

He closed his eyes as he raised his hands solemnly in a prayer gesture. 'You had me at vagina.'

'Listen to this,' I said, crawling off the bed to retrieve the book I had just thrown. 'There's actually an account – vague, at best – of a werewolf in Russia in the seventeen hundreds surviving the ritual—'

'That's good.'

'—BUT with obsidian teeth in her vagina.'

Heath looked like Seamus had just floated into the room

and declared his love of the Romans. His face had been drained of all colour.

'That's . . . not right.'

'What am I supposed to make of that, huh? Vagina bloody dentata! What if I come out of this thing with incisors in my ham wallet? I am not okay with that.'

'I think I speak for everyone when I say *none* of us are okay with that.'

'Well?'

'You yourself said that account is vague. It's undeniable some werewolves are changed by surviving the rituals—'

'Physically changed, Heath. If they come out at all, some can be missing limbs, have strange scars, new abilities. Look . . .'

I flicked through the book, desperate to find the page.

'Just twenty years ago in Australia, a juvenile werewolf *survived* but two months later went on to have a mental snap and—'

'Went on a killing spree. I remember the clean-up.' He nodded solemnly. 'You've committed to doing this and you've survived worse. On the bright side, if you make it through this, you'll be better and stronger for it. You can't tell me you haven't read *that* in those books either.'

'IF I survive.'

'Yes, *if*. I won't lie to you. This is serious stuff. Wolves die if they're not worthy. You're coming from the world's most powerful werewolf line and you are, undoubtedly, one of the strongest wolves I've ever seen.'

I shook my head, tired from stressing about what would happen in a matter of days and from spending too many nights trawling through books. Sweeping the hair back off my face, I looked at Heath as he watched me sort through my inner conflicts.

'I don't give a fuck,' I said. 'But if I did, I'd give one to you.'

He stared at me seriously for a few long seconds. His face arched back into his trademark smile as he stood, pulling me with him. 'Come on. I know one last ghoul nest we can annihilate for therapeutic reasons. Leave Berlin in style.'

His mood was infectious, and I wanted so very much to go with him.

'I can't,' I said, sitting back down. 'You know I'd love to, but I can't. There's two days until we're on a plane out of here. Aruhe is downstairs with Sanjay utilising that time. I need to hold up my end of the bargain and make the most of mine with the books. Joss is so much better at this stuff than I am.'

He cocked his head as I spoke. 'All right. I'm going to get sushi for us then.' Pausing at the door, he turned and said to me: 'That was a very mature thing of you to do.'

'Hopefully it gets me spirit points,' I muttered, flipping through dusty pages until I came to a chapter on a Japanese werewolf pack's coming of age ceremony that involved the severed heads of your enemies. Yummy.

11

───────

I was bouncing up and down on the balls of my feet outside of a bustling Berlin café. I should have gone inside ten minutes ago, but I was putting it off. Rubbing my hands together and blowing on them to fight the cold, I kept going back and forth in my head about whether to just walk inside or bail. My mouth watered as the smell of delicious pastries wafted out of the building, daring me to enter.

'Tommi?'

A soft, sweet voice spoke up from behind me. I turned slowly to meet the eyes of Corvossier von Klitzing, better known as Casper. She was draped head-to-toe in purple, with a long velvet coat in a vibrant shade of violet beginning at her neck and sweeping right down to the tips of her pointed black boots. A hand reached up to sweep a strand of hair off her face as it caught in the Berlin breeze and I realised with a start that it was a bionic limb. Usually her right arm was noticeable for what wasn't there – anything below the elbow – but today there was a metallic limb there instead, complete with swirling shapes cut into the exterior and soft, purple lights that glowed from the interior. I'd never seen her wear it before and I was transfixed, wondering if it was rude to gawk but also unable not to.

'Pretty cool, huh?' she said, following my very obvious gaze towards her robotic limb. She shifted the fingers and I watched with fascination as the small gears and pistons moved until she was making the sign of horns.

I laughed. 'Fucking *hardcore*. I've never seen you, uh, wear—'

'Most of the Berlin folks haven't, but I'm growing used to it. What are you doing lurking out the front here?'

'I wouldn't say lurking, I'd say avoiding.'

She smiled, indulging my skirting of terminology. 'Avoiding what?'

I stepped out from the footpath and peered into the café at Simon Tianne, sitting at a table by himself and looking bored.

'Oh,' said Casper, following my gaze. 'Love at first profile picture?'

'What?'

'He had that webglow?'

I gave her a questioning look.

'*Webglow*. Where they look much better on the internet than in real life.'

'Girl, no. This is not an online date. He's my cousin. Half cousin? Half first cousin? Look, I'm certain we're vaguely related somewhere.'

'Oh,' she giggled. 'My mistake. An Ihi or similar then?'

'Are we generally that notorious even a medium from Germany has heard of us?'

'Hmmm,' she said, ignoring my question as she looked at Simon again. As if sensing her gaze, he glanced up and scanned the space until he met her eyes. She smiled, before taking a step back. 'He's very cute. It's a shame you're related.'

'Not really,' I murmured.

'Is this thing you need to discuss so important you're willing to endure discomfort?'

I thought carefully about that. Simon had not only answered my call but agreed to meet me, wave the white flag, blah blah blah be an adult blah. So here I was. Yes, I needed to do this. And I *had* to do this. He was the only person who had the answers to a growing list of questions and – perhaps more importantly – I don't think he liked me enough to sugarcoat the truth. Before I had a chance to reply, Casper lightly grabbed my elbow and dragged me into the café.

'Come,' she said, 'I can see the response in your face without you needing to say it.'

'Are you telepathic now too?' I muttered.

'Don't be silly, there's not a telepath for two hundred miles.'

I gave her a sideways glance as we stepped over the threshold, a series of chimes jingling above us with the door's movement.

'I'll be sitting at that corner table over there,' she said, nodding her head. 'If things get bad or you need an out, signal me.'

'You'll be my back-up?' I grinned at the thought of having someone as powerful as her watching my six.

'Good luck,' she said as she sashayed towards her position with a last-minute pat-pat on my shoulder.

Simon was staring so hard as she moved through the café, he barely noticed as I sat down at the table across from him.

'Hey,' I said, taking a moment to order two doughnuts and a cappuccino from the waitress.

'Hi,' Simon replied absentmindedly, still distracted by Casper as she opened a book and began reading at her table.

'I like your swacket.'

'Swacket?' he asked, subtly sniffing the air. I knew instinctually that he was noting her scent.

'Sweater and a jacket, therefore swacket.'

'Who is that woman you came in with?'

'She's a medium who'll haunt your every waking minute if you don't stop making what you're doing so obvious.'

He looked at me, properly, for the first time since I joined him. 'Friend or foe?'

I considered that. 'Friend.'

'You can never be too sure this close to Treize territory.'

'*Friend*,' I repeated. 'She's the only medium I've met and, all things considered, I'm quite fond of Casper. Leave it, will you?'

'Casper?'

'It's a nickname,' I said, almost missing the recognition in his tone as I paused to thank the waitress who returned with two strawberry doughnuts and my coffee. I listened in pain as Simon attempted to order another drink for himself in shaky Deutsch, the waitress looking almost as confused as his pronunciation.

'*Ein apfelsaft, bitte*,' I said, taking over as he flashed me a look of relief.

'Thank you,' he said, when the waitress had left. 'Or should I say *danke*.'

'There you go, that sounded human.' I grinned.

'It's my first time in Germany and of the five languages I can speak, this is obviously not one of them.'

'Five languages? Bloody hell. I think we can give you a pass for guidebook sentences, you know? Plus, I studied it in school so I had a head start.'

He shrugged, nonchalant. 'James has seven. And that's not the first medium you've met.'

'Oh?' His comment made me pause mid-bite, something I never do.

'Wehi.'

'Your tribal elder? The man who gave me the vision and told y'all I was a werewolf?'

Simon nodded, taking a sip of his freshly arrived apple juice. 'Wehi is our link between past and present ancestors. There's a certain feel to mediums you can sense after a while and there's very few of them left. That's why she interests me – you can practically smell her power. What happened to her hand?'

'Her story to tell, not mine.'

There was a healthy pause as the two of us sat there, digesting the situation. The tension was thicker than a bowl of oatmeal. What I usually did in these instances was make small talk at a ferocious pace and chat meaninglessly until it passed. Somehow I didn't think that strategy would work this time.

'So,' he said, at last. 'We leave in twenty-four hours and I can think of a thousand things you should be doing instead of fidgeting across the table at me.'

'Maybe I enjoy fidgeting.'

'Maybe you enjoy stalling.'

I shrugged, knowing he was right. 'I want you to tell me about the Outskirt Packs.'

'Why?' he asked. I didn't miss the fact that he had visibly stiffened at my question.

'Because I've heard the phrase mentioned no less than a

dozen times over the past few weeks, both in front of me and in secret, and everyone seems to know what the fuck that means except me. It's informing every decision your side and theirs are making.'

'Why not ask your big blond bodyguard?'

Tilting my head, I smiled as I considered that description. 'Triple B, heh, I like it. Firstly, he's not my bodyguard but you already know that. Secondly, I'm asking you because, unlike everyone presently associated with me, you won't hold back from telling the truth just because you think it could hurt my feelings or scare the shite out of me.'

'No kid gloves.'

'Aye,' I said, clicking my fingers to agree.

Running his hands over his face with a deep sigh, for the first time I realised Simon looked tired. Heck, he was looking the way I felt deep in my bones.

'Fucking Outskirt Packs,' he murmured. He took a moment for himself, readjusting his position in the seat. Then as if there was a silent cue, he snapped back into leader mode, looking a world away from the guy I guessed couldn't be much older than thirty.

'They called them the Outskirt Packs because they were on the "outskirts" of what the Treize like to think of as their main territory, Europe, the UK, US, shit like that.'

'The Southern Hemisphere, basically.'

He nodded. 'It included us, some packs from the South Island. Eight or nine from Australia, some from the Solomon Islands, Fiji, Singapore, Tonga, Hawaii, Papua New Guinea and Indonesia. James once told me there was a Yakuza pack involved, but I was never sure if he was joking or not.'

'Bloody hell,' I said, leaning forward with interest. 'To what end?'

'They all wanted the same thing: to go public.'

'Public? As in—'

'Officially come out of the woods.'

'Oh. *Oh*.'

'This was at odds with the Treize's preferred method of keeping everything secret and everyone under their control, like they had for the last millennium. They also wanted to self-govern, like werewolf packs had originally before the Treize came along.'

'When was this?'

'They officially formed in 1993 and it dragged on for five years before they were defeated. My father and Jonah were the primary leaders. I don't think it's a coincidence they're both now dead.'

'I . . . I didn't know, about your dad. I'm sorry.'

He shrugged in attempt to appear more nonchalant than he actually was. 'He was killed when I was seven, right in the middle of the Outskirt Wars. You're not the only one who knows what it's like to grow up without a father.'

'Wait, clear something up for me. Why would any werewolf pack want to go public? Isn't there a huge benefit to the world not knowing we exist?'

'Is there?' he countered.

'Well, yeah, a lack of villagers with flaming torches and pitchforks at your front door for one.'

'People would adjust, they always do. The Treize wouldn't. So much of their power is steeped in fear, in encouraging this idea that the world would be at war with us if they ever found out about supernaturals. The thing is, people knew once. You go back far enough and we're in the history books, living and existing side-by-side with human beings. Scholars mistake that for talk of gods and deities to be worshipped, but they were really talking about us. They were living alongside us.'

The din of the bustling café felt distant and far off as he spoke with an almost evangelical zeal. I sipped my coffee slowly, licking the froth from my lip.

'Think about it: the Egyptians? Anubis? That was *us*. That was a whole civilisation living alongside werewolves in peace for centuries.'

'And then the Treize?'

'And then the Treize. They come with order and organisation, which sounds great. They represent everyone: they build the bridges between the different species. What's not to like about that? They globalise the supernatural community, connecting us all . . . by ruling us all. A few centuries pass, a thousand, and everyone is suddenly comfortable and complacent. They forget what it's like to live without them and they forget what it's like to have their individual liberties. Now humankind forgets us, thinks of us as a myth, the Treize spreads fear about what coming out of the woods could mean, as if there's anything that could really threaten our existence. Supernaturals were here long before humans and we'll be here long afterwards.'

My mouth might have been hanging open, but in that moment I didn't really care. This was just Simon's truth. I'd heard and been told other truths. It would be up to me to reconcile what story was fact and what story was fiction. Maybe the truth was a little bit of both.

'How's that for not treating you like you're wrapped in cotton wool?' he asked, watching as I continued to digest everything he had just said.

'The Outskirt Packs wanted the human world to know what they were.'

'Acknowledgment was just one of the things they

wanted, along with independence from the governing bodies. That was a radical idea to some and ultimately it was an idea that cost the lives of many of our own.'

'You didn't win the right to come out of the woods.'

'Not by a long way,' he said, sadness seeping into his tone. I wasn't sure if was sadness for a lost cause, which I somewhat doubted as it would have been many years after the conflict before he was even old enough to comprehend what that was. No, I suspected the sadness was closely attached to those lost fighting for a 'radical' idea – his father included.

'Your father, Jonah, despite being a fairly decent leader back then, wasn't the best negotiator. When things didn't go the way he wanted, when he got sick of meetings and back-n-forth negotiations with the Treize that went nowhere, Askari began disappearing.'

'He . . . he tried to force their hand? I quizzed.

He nodded. 'He was sick of waiting for the okay to go public, so he started acting out. First it was the odd person being disappeared here or there, which got them nowhere. Then it was giant wolves being spotted in towns, cities. Things got violent as he tried to prove that we existed as quickly as possible.'

'Show don't tell,' I whispered.

'The Aussies believed the Outskirt Packs were geographically so distant from the Treize's main "hunting ground" that they should be self-governing in Asia-Pacific anyway. But the Treize were able to use the disjointed geography to their advantage and quash the resistance, severing their communication with each other. New Zealand was the stronghold and the last packs to be overcome. Jonah realised too late what was on the line and was forced to cut deals with the Treize, which included a stint for himself in

'Vankila.'

'The armed robbery bit,' I added. Simon looked surprised that I knew this. 'When I was trying to find him, whittle down the potential candidates that could be my father, that was something on his record.'

'Three years penance,' Simon said, frowning. 'And then freedom, but not really. Never really.'

'And now they have his son in the exact same position,' I murmured.

'That's Treize justice for you.'

'Quaid,' I said, taking a bite from what was left of my doughnut, thoughtful. 'I cut a deal with the Treize that I would hunt down the rest of the Laignach Faelad if they would grant me visitation and begin processing a parole type situation for him – depending on how the visitation goes.'

Simon looked like I had just told him I was dating a centaur. 'You can do that? You did that?'

'Aye, I did. It hasn't come to fruition yet and Aruhe thinks they'll never let him go. If I live past this New Zealand trip, the next thing on my list is Quaid.'

'You dance a strange line, between us and them.'

'It's like trying to do the Polka on meth . . . I imagine. And I fucking hate the Polka.'

Simon cracked a smile then, a genuine one. I decided to push my luck.

'That's why they're treating this like a grenade about to go off at any moment, isn't it?'

'You going back? Trying to survive the coming of age?' he asked. 'It's a threat to them. The more of us together, the more uncomfortable they'll be. They had us in a good position: Steven dead and they didn't have to do the dirty work, Aruhe AWOL, Quaid locked up, and Jonah off the board.

You were the spanner in the works, but you essentially ended up working for them.'

'Part-time, in my defence,' I snapped. 'And I'm proud of the work I've done. It saved lives.'

'Regardless, look at it from their perspective and then you get some understanding. They carefully shuffled their marker along the gameboard, progressing up the ladder, then it's like they landed on a square with a snake and now they're sliding back down to where they started. Everyone's moving back into position.'

'Aruhe going home, me going with her, the deal for Quaid...'

'Does anyone know you're here? Talking to me? Besides the medium, that is.'

'No, but I didn't try to hide anything. This isn't unusual behaviour for me. If anyone asks I'll tell them the truth: I was here to try and mend a bridge and pick your brains about surviving this coming of age ritual.'

'That's barely the truth, but a good alibi,' he replied, frowning as if something had deeply bothered him about what I said. He opened his mouth to speak then paused, closing his lips like he thought better of it. He looked at me strangely, something forming deep within his brain.

'What? What is it?'

'An alibi,' he murmured, reaching under the table to retrieve something from a backpack he had there. He placed two heavy-looking books on the table – they made a significant thud as they hit the surface. A small cloud of dust billowed out of one of them.

'Gee, you shouldn't have,' I remarked dryly, suppressing a cough. Scanning the spines, my eyebrows jerked up in surprise.

'You've seen these before?' he asked.

'Ah, kinda. I know this book,' I said, fingering the title of the one on top: *The Ancient Ways – Polynesian Principles and Understanding Creation Stories of the Māori People.* 'It was loaned to me once, a while ago. This other one though . . .'

'*Worldwide Ways of the Wolf,*' read Simon.

'That one is new. Who gave this to you?'

'I'm beginning to think you know him. A Māori bro?'

'I don't know if that's his true form, that's how he appears to me but others have said to them he looks like someone . . . else.'

'I was in a secondhand bookstore, tourist crap. And this guy comes up to me and immediately I was surprised because you don't see many Polynesians in this part of the world. He handed me both books and said, 'I think this is what you're looking for, tama'. He didn't even charge me, just handed them off with a wink.'

'Chester,' I mused. 'He told me once his name is Chester Rangi, but that could be just as changeable as the face he presents. After the last time I saw him . . . what is he playing at?'

'Well,' he said, pushing the books across the table at me. 'Alibi.'

I nodded, murmuring my thanks yet still deeply unsettled by Simon's encounter with Chester. Placing the books into my shoulder bag, I was about to say that I should be going when I was pre-empted.

'Someone will be watching you,' he said. 'No one in this café, I made sure of it when I got here, and mediums have little allegiance to anyone but themselves. Someone will be tracking you, following you, to watch what you're doing and where you're going. If the true subject of our conversation is to stay hidden, you should probably leave now.'

'Boy do we need to work on your farewell,' I joked,

draining the last sip of coffee from my mug. 'Thank you for meeting me. And being honest.'

'You should read those,' he said, gesturing at my bag. 'There might be more to them than what we think. This Chester wanted you to have them, for whatever purpose.'

'Aye, but he's mischievous as fuck. I'll pore over them, but there could be no further purpose to it than him hoping I read some Latin in the back and accidentally raise the dead.'

'Mischievous,' Simon repeated, crinkling his nose. 'He did smell . . . strange.'

Getting to my feet, I left some money on the table to pay for my half of the order when I paused. Simon looked like he had something left to say.

'You know how I said the Treize had us in a good position,' he whispered, looking as if he was unsure whether he should keep talking.

'Jonah and Steven dead, Aruhe AWOL, Quaid locked up, me on staff,' I recited. 'And this whole coming of age thing is a huge threat because it could shake that up.'

'There's still a way they could see themselves coming out at an advantage,' he said, meeting my eyes with a hard stare.

'What's that?'

'You dead.'

A cold shudder ran through me and I did my best to suppress it.

'If they can't guarantee you'll stay under their thumb, wiping you out could be just as beneficial. And there's a thousand ways that could happen.'

My voice sounded strange as I spoke. 'No one expects me to survive ahi hikoi anyway, right? It wouldn't raise any eyebrows if I ended up dead.'

'Some of us expect you to survive,' he said, causing my

eyes to meet his. He wasn't bullshitting me; I couldn't sense a lie. 'Just be on your guard, Tommi.'

'Mean Māori, mean,' I said by way of farewell.

His mouth twitched with amusement at the invoking of the memory.

'Mean Māori, mean,' he repeated.

FOR MY LAST night in Berlin I wanted to be busy. As busy as possible, in fact. The busier I was, the easier it was going to be for me to keep my mind off the looming New Zealand trip. Drowning in activities was a coping mechanism I had honed over the years and largely it was dang effective. As I poured and served drinks behind the bar, I watched Clay dancing wildly with Heath to a Stormzy song. Meanwhile, Aruhe was chatting with Yu over a celebratory Fruit Tingle. I could tell Yu was imparting some last-minute advice via her hand gestures. The former PG soldier was a great teacher. She'd turned me into an adequate sniper in a matter of months. Thanks to a combined tutelage – that rewarded my sister with kindness and not beatings – Aruhe had improved steadily too. I felt a little better knowing that Yu was telling her something, because odds were it was something valuable. More importantly, I felt better seeing how intently Aruhe was listening. Heath might say I had more natural ability, but she was a *much* better student. She listened. She paid attention. She didn't argue with her instructors.

Speaking of imparting some wisdom, I spotted Casper at the opposite end of the bar and waved. She calmly nodded in my direction and I made my way over to her, making a Midori cocktail as I went. She was wearing a thin, dark blue top that looked like it was made of some kind of wool. It cloaked her ivory skin – resting on her head in a hood formation and with long sleeves that extended over her wrists. She looked beautiful and somewhat like an aquatic elf, with a robotic limb just to bring things into the current century.

'Heya,' I said, exchanging the green beverage for cash in a smooth gesture that made me feel very cool.

'Good evening, Tommi.'

'Thanks for the other day, I honestly owe you for that. Just having someone else there made me feel a lot better. Comfortable.'

'You're always welcome,' she replied, briefly touching my hand in an affectionate gesture.

I lingered, not sure how I should phrase my question. Turned out, I didn't have to.

'You have something you want to ask.'

'I'm pretty obvious, huh?'

'You're direct, usually. This must be something important given your hesitation.'

'It's not important per se, it's just I don't want to—'

'Ask me something personal?'

'No, I don't want you to feel as if I use you for information.'

'I don't think that.'

'I know what it's like to be used and I've asked you stuff about the ghost world before—'

'Technically I told you and then forced questions.'

'Ah – sure. Okay. Does that mean I get a free pass to ask something?'

She smiled at me, a sweet smile that revealed a gentleness in her I hadn't seen before.

'Tommi Grayson, you have been nothing but lovely and

friendly to me, even before you knew who I was. The fact you stayed lovely and friendly to me after you knew says a lot about you. You have a good soul. You question that part of you too often. Anyone who meets you can see that it beams out of you. Yes, you have darkness in you also. Speaking from personal experience, that can be a powerful gift. Sometimes in life you need to be a shining star or a terrifying warning. You manage to be both.'

My heart pounded against my chest as I let her profound and unexpected words wash over me. 'That . . . I think that might be the nicest and most important thing anyone's ever said to me.'

'You're welcome.' She smiled and sipped her drink. 'Now, what is your question?'

'I'm leaving tomorrow. Aruhe and I are going to New Zealand to do this coming of age type deal.'

Casper squinted at Aruhe, considering her. 'She is related to you. A sister, perhaps?'

'Aye. Half.'

'And you're returning to your homeland.'

'We both have to complete ahi hikoi. We'll confront the spirits of our ancestors and they will test us in whatever way they see fit. I guess my question isn't specific exactly, but rather do you have any over-arching advice for dealing with powerful mystical entities?'

'Hmmm. Have you spoken to Heath?'

'Over and over again and he has been helpful but – wait, you two know each other?'

I followed the path of her eyes to where he was with Clay, moving through the heaving crowd of people. He was so tall and broad that he couldn't help but stand out from the masses, with folks parting to let him through and others throwing back an appreciative glance. The muscles in his forearms strained against the fabric of his long-sleeved shirt as he slapped Clay on the back and I let out a sigh, eyes moving downwards towards to his butt. If God was a baker, they'd given that man the whole loaf.

'Heath is . . . an old friend. And not in the way you're thinking.'

I raised my hands in a truce gesture. 'No judgement here, girl.'

Casper chuckled. 'With a body like that, he could certainly throw you around.'

I grunted appreciatively. 'Take control, take charge'

'I imagine that's the appeal. But no, my type leans towards the more . . .'

'Feminine?' I said, smiling suggestively.

'Australian,' she replied. 'Let's just say I owe Heath a great debt and leave it at that. As for your question, Māori people have a high respect for their dead. They've always had a very advanced understanding of ghosts. Of course, they don't call them that.'

'No,' I agreed. 'It's the spiritual power or essence of a person.'

'Yes. I suspect you won't be dealing with much of that though. Spirits and ghosts are different. *True* spirits are on a higher plain of being than ghosts. Ghosts are more consumed with self. Spirits are much more powerful and older. They're tied not to their human existence, but to the rituals and beliefs of their people. They will remember what it's like to walk on this earth. You cannot fight them or reason with them, so do not waste your time. They deal in character traits and emotions.'

'Like a metal detector?' I suggested. 'They pick up the power or defining elements of an object – what makes it metal – but not specifically what it is.'

'Yes. Precisely. The spirits will work out the things that define you, whether that's jealousy or bravery or love or greed or courage or passion or virtue. The tests they will throw at you will naturally bring these to light. Let them. Once you enter their domain they will see all. You cannot hide from them.'

Three songs passed before I was able to speak in response to Casper's information and even then, it was just a few guttural sounds before the word 'quality' emerged from my mouth.

'I don't envy you,' she said. 'Yet do not underestimate your gifts, Tommi Grayson. You are more than a werewolf. You have more compassion than most, which is a sweeping generalisation but also an accurate one. I have no doubt you can survive this.'

She paused then, tilting her head and turning as if she was listening to someone. There was no one there, at least no one that I could see.

'You enter that land alone,' she said, finally. 'But you do not walk alone.'

I narrowed my eyes as I sifted through the meaning of her words. 'Okay . . . I'll take all the invisible accompaniment I can get, so long as I live through this.'

'And Tommi?'

'Aye?'

'Do not bargain with spirits. Do not make a deal or negotiate, it will give them power over a world they need to leave behind.'

Frowning, I nodded in agreement as I took a sip from the beer I grabbed across the bar. 'Whatever you say, you're the expert.'

'That I am. Oh! And I've been told to tell you not to be alarmed by the cannibalism.'

Beer seemed to spurt out of my nose and mouth at that comment. I attracted the disgusted looks of a few patrons as they passed by. Coughing and spluttering, I choked out: 'What?!'

'The cannibalism. It was popular among werewolf packs all over the world in the beginning, most likely including yours.'

'I just thought it was mentioned in the books as, like, a metaphor,' I whispered, sounding hollow.

'Yes, it was. It was also factually accurate and essential to survival. Werewolves hunted and ate humans as prey. If I was a spirit and looking for a way to unsettle you and expose raw nerves, then I may throw you a cannibal flashback or two.'

''Kay.'

'Just something to keep in mind.'

'Mental. Bloody mental, this is.'

By the time I stumbled over to serve an enthusiastic (and pinging) lad in an outfit that would have given Clay a run for his money, I was feeling nauseous at the thought of having to witness any kind of cannibalism. Spiritual or otherwise, that shit was reserved strictly for Neil Marshall movies. It was only after I'd served the drink that Casper's comment nagged at me. She'd been told to tell me about that? By who? I spun around to ask her, but her seat was empty. She was gone.

'Hey!' Aruhe practically shouted in my ear and made me jump.

'Ah! Um, hey.'

'What's up with you? You look like you saw a ghost.'

'No, won't be seeing any of those until a few days' time I hope.'

She giggled and I sensed it was to do with the sugary

cocktails running through her system. 'I had a chat to the new guy . . .'

I looked over my shoulder at said man. He had neon-red hair sticking out in tiny twists. 'Yeah?'

'And he's going to close for you tonight.'

'Really? That's nice. That's nice, Jörg!'

He nodded by way of response.

'Now you're free to have a bit of dance. With me. And the others. Well, whoever is around.'

I was still doing my best to shake the image of cannibalism from my mind, but I tried to return her enthusiasm by ditching the dishcloth and leaping the bar immediately. 'You twisted my arm.'

'Pfft, like I could,' she said, grabbing my limb and doing a fairly good job of twisting it as we weaved our way through the throng of bodies to the centre of the dancefloor towards Heath and Clay. Sanjay was behind the decks but as the song transitioned into a classic Run-DMC track, I met his eyes and gave him a mock salute. Dolly and Yu were dancing together, Yu cradling Dolly's hips from behind in a way that made me think of them as cute. My lethal lesbian friends were behaving 'cute'. I chuckled and threw myself into the song. Aruhe had plunged into it long before me and I prayed that although we had the same genes, our dancing talent wasn't similar.

'It looks somewhat like an animal in pain, doesn't it?' Heath whispered in my ear as we watched the eighteen-year old move.

'It's cruel she gets to dance like that and still look so young,' I replied. 'Like, science fiction young.'

He laughed.

'And hey,' I said, spinning around to face him. 'We can't all be as skilful as you Fred Astaire.'

'Come 'ere.' Heath yanked me towards him and attempted a faux tap routine. I cackled, throwing my head back and trying to imitate him. It wasn't long before Aruhe too pulled me to her side as we jumped and threw our hands up in the air, relishing the last few moments we had of carelessness in one of my favourite bars in one of my favourite cities with some of my favourite people in the world.

~

'YOU'RE GOING to regret this in the morning.'

'It's already morning, Heath.'

'You're going to regret this mid-morning.'

'I'm sure I read somewhere that it was good to be tired before a long-distance flight, that way you sleep more on the plane.'

'Sounds fake, but okay.'

'Besides, my nipples are already regretting this. It's so cold up here I think they're about to snap off.'

'Good, yes, a topic I enjoy: nipples.'

I laughed as I rubbed my gloved hands together. 'Cigarette, please.'

He lit one between his lips and handed it to me. I inhaled, savouring the tang and the warmth as it filled my lungs. 'I'm giving these up. If I make it through this, I'm giving them up.'

'Sure, kid.'

'Sure, kid? Sure, kid as in "sure, kid, you'll make it through this" or "sure, kid, you're going to give up"?'

'Does it matter?'

'To me? Quite.'

'Aye, I'm sure you'll make it through this, kid. I'm not sure you'll quit though.'

'I've done it before.'

'And yet, here we are.'

'Here we are,' I said, exhaling as I looked out over the dark rooftops of Berlin before us. Phases was just kicking out the last of its patrons before closing shop and I could hear merry shouts from below. The Fernsehturm stood tall in the distance, winking – always winking. I wondered where Joss was, what he was doing, what he was thinking. I pondered over the smallest things about him. What did he look like right now? Would his hair still grow? I missed my best friend so much I thought a crack would physically split down my person.

'Since it is our last night,' I started. 'Shouldn't you be making the most of Berlin's most eligible bachelors?'

He smirked. 'I am Berlin's most eligible bachelor.'

I made a gagging noise to let him know what I thought of that and his smirk became a full-on grin, teeth and all.

'And I'll have you know I haven't spent time in the company of a "skag" as you call them for almost two weeks now.'

'All right, in my defence I said "skag" as a term of endearment and I don't begrudge any sexually active woman for getting hers: I'm just bitter and jealous. But oh my God, are you okay? How are you coping? Is this Heath or backed up willy I'm speaking to?'

'Jokes? That's all I get? At the very least I was hoping for a congratulatory blow job.'

I laughed in spite of myself.

'The last "skag" I had in my bed, was you.'

That stopped my laughter. I could feel him looking at me, but I didn't want to meet that gaze. I was a coward.

'All right, that's enough pseudo sex jokes. I don't want to corrupt Aruhe if she has the misfortune to overhear us.'

'You don't think she's a vir—'

'No. I'm sure she's had sex, probably more times than I want to know about. Small country towns and all that, you make your own fun.'

'She could be having sex right now.'

'Can we not? Last I checked she was getting into bed, which is where I should be.'

Heath laughed. 'I enjoy making you squirm.'

'Yeah, well, watch me squirm my way down the side of this building to catch what little shut-eye I can before this crap begins.'

'Night.'

'Night,' I said, lowering myself over the roof edge. Heath was still standing there looking at the sky when I paused. 'Hey.'

'Hmm?'

'Thank you.'

'For what?'

'I know I take the piss, but I really mean it when I say thank you. I'm not gonna get into specifics. You know.'

'You're welcome.'

I nodded and ducked my head down as I negotiated the building's brickwork. My last image was of Heath serious but smiling as the breeze rustled his golden hair.

12

'Whelp, this is it,' I said, extending my arms to Clay. He knocked them away and pulled me into a crushing hug that attempted to leave an impression of my face on his broad chest.

'I'll see you soon, ya crazy Scot,' he replied, sniffing.

'Guaranteed, you fabulous creature.'

'Mami, you know it. And you too, Tommi Jnr.'

Aruhe blushed as Clay gave her an all-encompassing embrace. We were standing in the loading dock of Phases, under the apartment, saying our goodbyes before the three of us trekked to the airport. It was strange to see all of the Rogues assembled like that – minus Zillia – and I was feeling oddly sentimental. Gus had given us a pat on the shoulder, which was as much of a farewell as we were going to get from him. Dolly had given me a half-hug and I watched her now as she brought Aruhe in for a proper one, holding her at arm's length and whispering something to her. As a former runaway herself, Dolly had really taken my sister under her wing. It had showed me a different side of her: the one Yu got to see.

'Cute, aren't they?'

'Getting clucky, Yu?'

'Maybe. I never really thought about kids in the Guard but once I gave up immortality, my body clock started ticking again.'

'If you guys did have a bub, who would carry it?'

'Are you kidding? Me, of course. Dolly would want to rip the thing out the moment her belly started to swell.'

'You'd do that? Carry a child for her?'

'I gave up immortality for her.'

I turned, examining Yu's face closely as she kept her eyes focused on my sister and her partner. She shrugged.

'I planned on telling you eventually. It's one of those things only a handful of people know and they don't speak about. And you knew I gave up immortality for something—'

'I just thought you might have been over their bullshit.'

'That too.'

'You gave up immortality for love,' I repeated, getting swept up in the romantic notion of it.

'The way I see it, I didn't give up anything.'

'That's beautiful.'

Sanjay had showed up and I watched him awkwardly chat with Heath for a moment.

'You girls are going to be okay,' said Yu.

I didn't reply.

'You will.'

'Shut up and give me a cuddle.'

We gave each other a strong, genuine embrace and I rested my head on her shoulder before pulling away.

'Thank you,' I said, 'for teaching me how to potentially assassinate a political leader from a safe distance. And for just being a friend.'

She smiled, tugging the ends of my hair that hung down my back in messy waves.

'Thank you, Tommi Grayson. You really livened things up around here.'

'Yeah, because Phases was such a chill place before that.'

Sanjay was waiting for me as I separated from Yu and we embraced briefly, ending in a slick handshake.

'So,' he said, 'this is goodbye then, for a while.'

'You keep those decks funky fresh, Sanjay.'

He chuckled as I picked up my bags and threw them into the car waiting for us. As Heath spoke to the driver, I bundled into the back with Aruhe. She shivered involuntarily through the burgundy trench she was wearing and adjusted the knit cap on her head.

'You can't wait, can you?' I asked, recognising nervous excitement when I saw it.

'I'm scared, but pumped-as.' She grinned. 'I miss the air: I can't wait to *breathe* it in.'

Looking out the window as Berlin sped by, I didn't really care about breathing in New Zealand air. More than anything, I was just hoping to still be breathing a week from now.

WITH THE TREIZE when you fly, you fly private. Not only was it quicker, and they could keep an eye on us by footing the bill, but it meant you avoided all those pesky questions from customs about why you were travelling from one country to another with a small armoury. Plus, if a member of your party happened to be a guy whose skin shimmered under certain light, that was going to attract plenty of attention in economy.

One of the perks of existing for an eternity seemed to be the number of assets you could acquire: for the Treize that included a stable of private jets. It had started sprinkling with rain by the time we walked on to the tarmac and I squinted as a cool breeze pinched my face. The plane was sitting there patiently, with lights illuminating the windows from the inside. The passenger door was open and the staircase leading into the interior was slick with water as Aruhe trudged up it.

'After you,' said Heath, performing a mock bow.

'Yeah, yeah, yeah,' I replied, looking up as raindrops splattered on my cheeks.

Placing his hand on the small of my back, Heath nodded in the direction I needed to go.

'Up.'

The inside of the cabin was warm and dry, two things that endeared it to me straight away. The plane's occupants on the other hand ... they all had a certain air about them that ranged from scary to supremely 'don't fuck with me'. They were bodyguards for hire and I didn't expect to recognise any of them. Yet as I scanned their faces, I had to hide the flash of surprise I felt inside as I made eye contact with a woman I recognised from Phases. It was the rockabilly babe, Ginger, who had been muscle for the goblin at 1984. I glanced away just as quickly, hoping that my face didn't give away that I recognised her. Thankfully there was someone else to focus on: Simon, sitting at the very back and looking extremely uncomfortable. I understood the expression of pain plastered on his face. He was in a confined space surrounded by enemies and would be for the next twenty hours. Man was on edge. Aruhe made her way down the aisle with confidence and plonked herself in the seat next to him. Heath and I took the duo of seats on the other side of the aisle to them. I thought I was being subtle by giving Heath the window seat in an attempt to make sure there was as much distance between him and Simon as possible. He threw me a sideways glance with a smirk that let me know he knew exactly what I was doing.

The other guests on the flight, including Ginger, were Heath's acquisitions. There were ten in total, half of them freelancers and half Praetorian Guard. They all looked as different in appearance as the next, with even a dwarf among them: a muscly looking chick with a thick, black braid. The man with shimmery skin drew my eyes immediately as it was rare to see such an outward display of the supernatural in this type of crew: usually the aim was to blend.

I was uncertain what the formal form of greeting was when you faced people whose mission could be to kill you and make it look like an accident, so I said nothing. Heath had exchange hellos with a man and woman at the front of the plane as he made his way down the aisle, trading a smooth hand gesture and speaking a few quiet words to them. He nodded at Ginger, and she nodded back. The knowledge of everything Simon had said to me over coffee was playing heavily on my mind as I scanned the faces on the plane.

If things didn't go the way the Treize wanted, I wondered which one of the people here would take care of it. Aruhe was already consumed in a movie and fidgeting with the controls on the headrest when I turned to look at Simon. He was watching me as if he knew exactly what I was thinking. He glanced away when Heath returned and flopped down next to me with a relaxed grunt. The plane's engine rumbled in preparation for take-off and I couldn't quell the discomfort caught in my throat. I was quiet, unnaturally so for me, and when the motor was loud enough to drown out most of the chatter in the cabin Heath leaned across and whispered in my ear.

'Every single person on this team was hired personally by me,' he said, his breath tickling my neck as he spoke.

I stiffened, my eyes widening with his implied meaning. Turning to him, his face was barely a centimetre away from my own as I judged what I saw there. He held my gaze, unflinching and hard. I opened my mouth to respond and he gave his head the smallest shake, as if saying 'not here'. He turned to look out the window as the plane took off, the scenery whipping by at frantic speed as I continued to watch him.

STAYING up late the night before had been a smart move on my part as I spent the first ten hours conked out entirely. Aruhe woke me when we stopped at some off-the-radar airport to refuel before the final leg of the flight. The two of us stepped out on to the tarmac to stretch for a few minutes and get some fresh air. The humidity was suffocating and for the first time in months I was able to shed some layers outdoors.

'My God it feels good to be in just a tank top and jeans. Oh! I'm even slightly sweating! Quality.'

'Where are we?' asked Aruhe through a yawn.

I squinted, trying to look for some kind of identifiable landmark or clue. It was a private airfield, that much was obvious, but besides two small illuminated buildings at the end of the runway, there was nothing else to see. A Treize outpost of some kind, I guessed. I knew they had them all over the world, not just in cities but in rural areas too. Off the grid. It was night and blackness stretched as far as the eye could see. Raising my head to the sky, I enjoyed a few minutes getting lost in the vastness of the stars. There were no city lights to detract from the brightness: only white, twinkling eyes on a canvas of endless noir.

'I dunno,' I said, finally. 'Indonesia, maybe..'

'You could tell that just from the stars?'

'Sure. You can see the word "Treize outpost" written out just over there.'

I watched Aruhe grimace as she tried to find the non-existent letters and fought the urge to laugh.

'I don't see – ah. You bitch.'

Giggling, I ducked a swipe from her and leapt back a few paces. 'Aw come on, is that all you got then?'

'Want more, do ya?'

'We've got the time, may as well,' I said, gesturing at her with my fingers.

Aruhe lunged forward, throwing a dummy punch to test my reflexes. I dodged it easily and she grinned. Dropping to all fours she tried to sweep my legs out from under me – a favourite trick of mine – but I leapt off the ground quickly and somersaulted backwards. We mucked around like that for a while: grunting and puffing with the exercise as we played cat and mouse. Or Big Bad Wolf versus Slightly Less Big Bad Wolf.

She had improved since living and training with the Rogues and it showed: she was a smarter fighter and more controlled. It ended with me poised on top of her, leaning over and laughing. Her own cackle joined my own and I extended an arm to pull her up. A slow clapping cut us off. We turned to find a cluster of six of the assigned guards watching us from the steps of the plane. Ginger seemed to be enjoying the spectacle the most and her eyes flashed momentarily – I swear, actually fucking flashed – as she blinked.

'Um . . .' Aruhe performed an awkward courtesy and I tipped an invisible hat. One of them – a tall, thin Norwegian-looking man – nodded at us before heading back on to the plane. The others soon followed and Aruhe and I were left standing there oddly, the stars of a performance we hadn't known we were part of. I ran a hand through my hair as I tied it back up into a bun.

'That was interesting,' I said.

'Could've been worse.'

'Aye?'

'I was kinda expecting your ex to be part of the crew,' she whispered.

'Who? Lorcan?'

She nodded.

'Why would you think that?'

'He always seems to show up at the worst times, you know? And especially now that you're getting things back on track, I thought this was the exact kind of moment he'd pick to show up—'

'And throw a spanner in the works.'

'Yeah.'

'We're on a trip to New Zealand to face our estranged relatives and complete a task neither of us are that keen to do. My best friend is Lord knows where doing Lord knows what and I had to attend his fake funeral. I wouldn't exactly say my life is on track. Actually, it frightens me that you think this is what an *on track* version of my life looks like.'

'You quit smoking though.'

'For all of twenty-four hours so far. And hey, how'd you know?'

'Heath told me. He said I was to dob on you if you tried to bum a smoke off someone.'

'Tricksy hobbit.'

'How did you do it?'

'Quit?'

'No, cope with the whole Lorcan thing?'

'That. I don't know if even Urban Dictionary could be loose enough with the word "cope" to apply it to how I got through the Lorcan thing. I mean, everything I gave him he took like a thief: my trust, my body, my belief. And a huge part of that is on me, because you fall into the dicksand and just get blinded, you know?'

'You're not an egg, he is ridiculously hot. Those cheek-bones, ooft'

I laughed, kind of surprised to learn we had the same taste. 'It was the *Speed* thing: relationships based on intense experiences never work. And there was the guilt, which was a weird thing to grapple with among all of that.'

'Guilt? What did you have to be guilty about?'

I let out a shaky breath. 'Shite, I haven't told anyone this.'

'Not even Heath?'

'Especially not Heath. He and Lorcan have history. Literally. They've been historic together and come out the other side not the biggest fans of each other. When I say I felt guilty, it's because I kept having this incredibly selfish thought. I wished he'd died. Not in a vengeful way, like, I wanted a piano to drop on his head the second he said he didn't want to be in my life anymore. Not that signs weren't there: he had been distancing himself for months and I kept thinking that we could fix it, that if I just stayed steady and constant we could heal it. But you can't. I couldn't. I just wished that he'd died with me never knowing that he stopped caring about me. I felt sick knowing that I would have preferred for him to go out in battle and that be the end of our story rather than the simple fact he got *over* it. It would have been easier to grieve him had he died. I would have got on with my life a lot more easily and carried this perfect version of him that I thought existed with me forever.'

When I finished, Aruhe was staring at me, fascinated.

'I sound like the worst human on earth, don't I? Yikes, why did you make me tell you this?'

'No, no,' she said, grabbing my shoulder. 'I was just thinking, I don't know if I'll ever love someone that badly.'

'Ergh. You don't want to. It makes a dunderhead outta you.'

'A what? Be less Scottish, please.'

'An idiot, fool, doober. Some sisterly advice? Stay complacent as long as you can because those epic loves pop out of nowhere and you never see 'em coming.'

'And they never have a happy ending?'

'Not that I've experienced, but I feel the whole werewolf thing can be counted as an extenuating circumstance in the relationship stakes.'

'OY! You two! If you're finished razzling we've got a plane to catch.' Heath was dangling out of the doorway and gesturing at us.

'C'mon, we better head,' I said, linking Aruhe's arm in my own as we made our way back.

THE REMAINDER of the flight wasn't spent unconscious, at least on my behalf. I watched a movie with Heath: *Predator*, his favourite (most likely because of the high body count and gore), then switched over to going through the books Chester-by-way-of-Simon had given me. I wasn't sure what I was looking for anymore, my eyes were barely registering the words, but at least I felt like I was doing *something*. An hour before we were set to touch down, I grabbed a change of clothes and headed for the bathroom. Brushing my teeth, pulling my hair into shape, slapping on some deodorant, I realised I was trying to make myself presentable for impending doom. I laughed then, lightly and to myself, shaking my head as I splashed water on to my face. Taking several deep, long breaths, I planted my hands on either side of the basin for stability as I stared into the mirror.

Barefoot and in nothing more than my jeans and a black bra, I glared hard at the woman before me. What would be left of her if I survived this? More importantly, what would be left if I didn't? Fear was etched into every line of my face and it was something I knew I would have to make a conscious effort to mask over the next few days. Sometimes though, I just wanted the luxury of being the scared little girl I felt that I was on the inside.

There was a soft knock on the door and I glanced up. There were two bathrooms on this one, small, plane, and I wondered who could possibly need mine when there was likely another free at the front of the aircraft. Sniffing away my frustration, I slid open the door to find Heath standing there. I barely had a moment to register his appearance before he was pushing his way into the tiny space and locking the door behind him.

'Heath, what—'

He silenced my protests with a hand over my mouth, moving the two of us further into the compartment. His frame took up so much of the room I pushed myself back until I was sitting on the edge of the basin so we'd both fit.

He raised his free hand to his lips and made a shushing gesture. I nodded to show him I understood and he removed his hand from my mouth. My chest was rising and falling with the shock of his sudden appearance and I placed a hand on my heart to measure the beats. It was only then that he seemed to notice I was hardly dressed.

'What?' I hissed, willing his eyes to my face with the tone. 'It's not like you haven't seen me naked before.'

'That bra is . . . doing great things for you.'

I buried a smile I felt unfurling deep inside.

'Heath?' I snapped and he seemed to click back into the present. 'What the fuck are you doing in here?'

'The Askari and Praetorian Guard that are meeting us at the airfield.'

'Aye?'

'Don't trust them. The only people you can trust are on this plane.'

'What—'

'I handpicked these ten people. The team I asked for on the ground are not the team that will be picking us up.'

'Heath—'

'I know what Simon told you back in Berlin. He's right.'

'How could you possibly know that?'

He stared at me, blinking as if waiting for me to catch up. I mentally slapped myself.

'Casper,' I groaned. 'She said you two were . . . acquainted. You had her spy on me?'

'No, she did it of her own accord. She likes you, for some reason.'

'Well, I'm likeable so—'

'Listen to me,' he said, gripping my shoulders as he leaned forwards. Goosebumps sprung up on my body as his flesh connected with mine and I tried to push it away.

'I'm going to do everything I can to protect you either side of this ritual, but I need you to take precautions as well. Follow your gut: if something doesn't feel right, then it probably isn't. The Ihi pack will be watching out for Aruhe and they have the advantage of being strongest on their home turf. There's no one looking out for you, so you need to be smart.'

'Except for you, right?'

''Course.' He smirked, the genuine concern that had been pouring from him a second earlier was replaced with warmth. 'I'm one very strong, well-equipped, skilled man—'

'Okay, okay, I get it.'

'But I'm still one man. The beings on this plane will be watching, but many won't expect suspicious activity from within PG ranks. They don't know about it and won't be looking for it. They're alert and ready for anything, but they could still . . . miss something.'

'That's why you hired freelancers,' I whispered, understanding the mix properly now. 'People who owed you favours as well, like Ginger.'

'I trust the people in the air with us, but they still don't need to hear this conversation.'

'Hence the secrecy?' I replied, gesturing around the cubicle.

He nodded. I let out a sigh, rubbing my face with frustration. Heath was watching me closely, measuring my response and reaction.

'And I thought surviving a werewolf hazing was going to be my biggest problem.' My voice sounded as deflated as I felt.

'I suspect that relying on you dying in ahi hikoi is a back-up plan.'

'What the fuck did I ever do to the Treize, Heath? I even

worked for the cunts.'

'It's not "you" so much as what you represent.'

'And what's that?'

'A way out of the woods.'

I stared at Heath hard, drinking him in like a tall, Scottish glass of milk. My body raced ahead before my mind had a chance to catch up. I grabbed the front of his shirt and pulled him roughly towards me. The last thing I saw were his eyebrows arching in surprise as I pressed my mouth to his in a searing kiss.

Thankfully it took less than a second for him to catch up and return the gesture full throttle. It was open-mouthed and passionate as our tongues hungrily found each other. I gripped his jaw, my fingers running through his beard as my other hand twisted his shirt around my fist, yanking him closer and closer to me. His hands ran up the length of my jeans before he spread my legs and hitched them around his waist so our bodies were pressed together. I poured into him everything I had been feeling but hadn't said out loud – all my fear, all my panic, all my anxiety – into one physical act. His fingers weaved their way through my hair and, with a tug, he yanked my bun loose until my locks fell down my back. I don't think I had ever kissed someone so desperately and it felt as if we were both fighting to find a way under each other's skin.

The plane jerked in a sudden sideways motion as it hit an air pocket and we were thrown apart, Heath hitting the opposite wall of the cubicle. As he stumbled to regain his footing, I took a shuddering gulp of air. Wide-eyed and open-mouthed, we both stared at each other for several long moments as we regained our bearings.

Running a hand through his own hair, he pulled it up into a man-bun on the top of his head and straightened his clothing. I was still sitting on the basin, somewhat in shock, as he glanced at me one more time and quickly exited the bathroom. He closed the door behind him and I followed his movements with my werewolf senses as he sat back down in his seat and let out a shaky breath. I remained where I was for a while, minutes, maybe, just sitting on the basin of the tiny plane bathroom going over what had just happened and trying to quell the fire he had ignited in me with his touch, his tongue, his kiss.

I touched my lips with my fingers, gently smiling to myself. A voice over the intercom told us we needed to prepare for landing. Hopping up, I hurried through the rest of what I wanted to do and grabbed my things. I nudged my way out of the cubicle and took my seat next to Heath. Tucking away my belongings, I closed my eyes and pressed my back into the soft cushioning as the plane began its gentle descent. There were worse things waiting for me on the ground and soon what had happened ten minutes earlier felt like a decade ago as my mind got swamped with worries once again.

I HAD NEVER ENTERTAINED the idea of becoming Prime Minister, but as I stepped off that plane in Auckland I got a fairly good idea of what that would feel like. There were four non-descript black vehicles waiting on the tarmac of the private airfield with a line of PG and Askari standing at attention besides them. It looked like a very posh, very prim funeral procession with everyone dressed in varying shades of black, grey, khaki and navy blue.

'Gee, it's almost like they're trying to prove something,' Simon whispered just loud enough so that I could hear. I smiled in spite of myself, taking the last few steps with a hop until I was standing besides Aruhe. As Heath went out with his team to speak to the company awaiting us, I realised that myself, Aruhe and Simon had subconsciously clustered together as a group.

'I could do with a cigarette about now,' I grumbled.

'Simon, you're not to give her one under any circumstances,' Aruhe said, not looking at me as her eyes watched those gathered before us carefully. 'She quit.'

I opened my mouth to rebut her, but fell silent as Heath approached our trio, noticing as he made a few quick gestures with his hands. The team that had been with us on the plane seemed to know what this meant as they split themselves up into small groups that would ride in each of the cars.

'Simon, you ride with Tommi in the second car,' Heath said as he continued to march in our direction. 'Aruhe will ride with me in the third.'

'Not a chance,' Simon replied, triggering a deep sigh out of Heath as he closed his eyes and pinched the bridge of his nose with frustration.

'Just do it,' Heath moaned. 'It's barely a three-hour drive and then you're the boss.'

'From the second you set foot in my country, I was the boss,' Simon answered, coolly. His eyes moved to the left of our group and I followed where he was looking. Five women of the toughest looking women I had ever seen were strutting across the tarmac towards us, seemingly oblivious to the reaction they were causing among the gathered PG and Askari. Simon walked away to greet them and I felt Aruhe stiffen beside me.

'The Aunties?' I asked her.

She nodded, lips pressed in a tight line. My bargain

meant no one could hurt her and she was safe from any form of punishment, but that didn't mean she wasn't scared. Simon was talking to the women in te reo and I looked to my half-sister to see if she could follow what he was saying.

'He's assigning them to us,' she murmured. 'Just like Heath did.'

'This could actually work out nicely,' Heath said, his mind busy with the possibilities. A smile twitched at the corner of his mouth and I wondered what he was up to. Before Simon joined us with the Aunties, he embraced with an older woman, their foreheads and noses pressed together for barely more than a few seconds.

'That's his mum, Keisha,' Aruhe told him.

'Good to know,' I replied, watching as the women joined us. There was something about Keisha that I couldn't quite place, yet it made me unable to look away from her. She met my gaze for a moment and my skin did that buzzing thing it seemed to always do now when surrounded by my blood pack. I was the first to break eye contact.

It appeared there was no physical type to what made you an acceptable candidate as an Ihi pack enforcer. The women were different ages, different heights, different weights, yet all of them carried the same distinct gravitas: it was the kind that said, without saying it, 'fuck with us and we'll end you'. I think I was developing a crush on all five of them.

'They ride with us too,' Simon told Heath, the women very subtly placing themselves in and around him and Aruhe. Me? I don't think they were so concerned about protecting, which was fair enough. 'If you thought I was going to be comfortable with security by your people and your people alone, you were severely mistaken.'

'Eh.' Heath shrugged. 'More the merrier.'

Heath gestured for us to follow him and we all moved to

the waiting vehicles as a group. The PG that had been assembled on the ground were working hard to throw off a calm vibe, but I didn't miss several carefully placing their hands near weapons I knew they must have on them. The Askari just looked outright pissed at this unannounced arrival.

'Change of plans,' Heath called, waving at us and the Aunties. 'Few of you will be walking. We've got some players from the home team here that are gonna need a lift.'

'This is not what we discussed,' a frazzled man said, rushing forward until he was standing practically on Heath's toes. 'No one was even supposed to know when we were arriving.'

'That, I believe, was your job. And yet, look at this hospitable greeting party!'

The Askari guy glanced at the Auntie nearest him, who practically growled by way of response. He jumped.

'If you think we don't know about every wee move you make on every wee inch of our land, you're mistaken,' Keisha said, her voice calm and measured.

'T-there are set protocols—'

'That we are adapting,' Heath snapped, waving at those of us waiting as he opened a car door. 'Come on!'

We filed into the vehicles, with Simon jumping in alongside me and following the order Heath had laid out less than five minutes earlier. An argument was still raging outside but, like most things, it was one Heath was winning.

'This isn't what was approved from higher up.'

'Aye, well, if you're content to get into a physical altercation with the ruling packs less than one hundred metres into the journey then I'm quite happy to let you explain that to the higher ups as well.'

'We had orders—'

'So do they, clearly. Yet unlike you, I'm not willing to spill blood over someone's desire to carpool.'

There was a little more snapping back and forth, but it was a losing battle for the Askari who had taken command. I watched with satisfaction as Heath dived into the car with Aruhe behind us, and left the frazzled man stuttering out a final sentence to thin air. As the vehicles started forward, I couldn't help but notice that not a single person who had been on the plane with us was left with the group standing behind on the tarmac.

Waking with a jolt, I realised I must have fallen at the start of the trip to the Ihi pack property just outside of Rotorua. Simon had been discussing whatever local pack the Aunties had negotiated with to enter their territory and meet us at the Treize airfield, but he fell quiet as I fully roused to attention. Rubbing the sleep from my eyes, I glanced at the scenery passing outside the window.

'How far away are we?' I asked.

'Twenty minutes.'

I grunted in reply, falling quiet as the car descended into silence. The day after tomorrow – the *day* of ahi hikoi – we would rise at dawn and drive some six hours from Rotorua to Wellington. Then we'd jump on a ferry to travel three hours to the port of Picton on the South Island, where we'd be on neutral territory: sacred werewolf grounds protected for hundreds of years specifically for this purpose. It was where all New Zealand werewolf packs went to perform their coming of age rites and where I would perform mine . . . or die trying. But first, there were customs to be upheld among the Ihi pack and on Ihi land. Needing to keep my hands busy, I worked my hair into two tight braids. For whatever reason that gave me some sense of confidence that stayed with me right up until we pulled up at their house. The car stopped a small distance away and we had a one-hundred metre walk to the front gate.

I hung towards the back of the group as Simon, Aruhe, the Aunties, and Heath's crew of bodyguards began the procession towards the property. Simon was at the front of the group and marching with confidence: he was their leader and he had returned home with one of the pack's beloved daughters. Suddenly a cold, creeping fear spread through my body as the memories of my first and last visit came flooding back. Spinning on my heel, I walked face-first into Heath's chest.

'Oh God, oh God, oh God, oh fuck, what have I done? Is it too late to go back? Oh God,' I blurted.

'What's happening?' asked one of the bodyguards.

'You okay?' queried Aruhe.

'She's fine,' said Heath. 'Give us a moment.'

I heard their footsteps retreat as they moved on and I tried to calm my breathing. 'Ohgodgodgodgodfuckshite-godchrist.'

'Tommi,' he said, grabbing both of my wrists that had been resting on his chest.

'Mothermarythiswasabadide—'

'TOMMI.'

He shook me slightly and my head lolled up to look at him. He whacked me with my own wrists lightly on the cheek.

'Stop hitting yourself.'

I blanked. Did he really just do that? He whacked the other side of my face with my arm.

'Stop hitting yourself.'

'I – what are you doing?' I protested, yanking myself free. 'What are *you* doing?'

'I'm . . .' I thought about it. 'I'm acting like a child.'

'Good. Me too.'

Confused, I titled my head to see if he was serious. He smiled, slow and wide. I laughed at the ridiculousness of the situation.

'Can we go and get this over with now? Or do we need to freak out some more?' Heath asked.

The laughter was a release of nervous energy and I breathed deeply for a moment. Nodding, I moved back towards the others

'Aye. Let's do this.'

As we walked, Heath leant down and whispered in my ear. 'You might be experiencing inner turmoil, but you're the most powerful werewolf this pack has seen in a generation. Make sure they know it.'

My skin burned at his words and I resisted the urge to peer at him. I knew what I would see there: Heath, looking serious but always with a hint of amusement. Always. He'd told me what I needed to hear, and I held my head a little higher as I pushed through the annoyingly screechy gate that marked the beginning of the Ihi property. There was a line of people waiting for us, some in traditional dress and some not. They were positioned on either side of the path and holding wooden bowls. Our personal bodyguards parted like a curtain, revealing Aruhe and me standing next to each other. I knew how this worked. This was a welcoming ceremony that was little more than a few songs and customary words to be muttered among a select crowd. But it was important. I glanced at Aruhe and she looked as nervous as I felt. I squeezed her hand quickly and gave her a small smile.

13

'Here goes,' I said, beginning down the path.

Aruhe kept in step with me and neither of us responded as the pack members and elders began singing a traditional song. They threw herbs and dried leaves down like confetti as we walked. A silver-haired woman splashed a liquid on us with a leaf. Smoke was issuing from the end of a collection of twigs that two young boys were holding and they waved them dramatically, like sage sticks.

When we got to the end of the line, Simon was waiting, surrounded by his pack. They were in a combination of traditional and modern clothing. All of the men were shirt-less, with their chests and tattoos exposed proudly, while the women had their long hair out and flowing over the shoulders in way that looked like a smoky cloud descending down the mountain ranges of their bodies. They were wearing black and white patterned skirts with a texture that I resisted the urge to reach out and stroke. Some of the older men had facial moko, a few of the women too, but most of the pack's younger members were absent of the tattoos.

Instead they had some of the same symbols painted on their faces in tribal patterns.

I recognised the elder Wehi among those staring at us, along with the Aunties from earlier who had worked their way into the crowd. There were other ladies I didn't know, and they wore woven red and white headpieces. The matriarch of the Ihi pack – my father Jonah's widow, Tiaki – stood out from the crowd like there was no one else present. Her eyes bore right into my soul. I frowned slightly, trying to cover my expression as soon as I did it. There was something different about her. She looked the same as I remembered: beautiful and deadly, her lips coloured black with moko that spilled down her chin. Yet I could sense something . . . else. It was a vibe that I had picked up from Keisha too and I wondered what my senses were trying to tell me.

Simon was leaning on a taiaha – a traditional fighting staff – and he lifted it slightly before slamming it into the ground where it embedded in the dirt. He threw his legs apart and let out a terrifying yell. Slapping his chest with force, he walked towards me while shouting in te reo. Dolly had told me to expect a display of challenge from the pack leader: she had been physically forced to fight her father in an exhibition match the day before her ritual in Germany. It was supposed to test the bravery of the newcomer. I prayed I wouldn't have to do that here, as Simon continued to lead the others and I watched for any clue of what we were expected to do next.

As the commander, he was the most animated of all as he continued to cry out – the Aunties answering his calls with their own. I didn't know enough of my native language to understand what they were saying, but I sensed Aruhe was following along. He moved closer and closer to me until he was practically hovering in front of my face. And then it ended. He held the iconic pose of his people: tongue out and exposed, eyes wide and body ready for battle. It was beautiful and it was *boss*. Everything in my being told me to turn around and run, yet I held my ground. I could not afford to flinch for a second. I held his stare with the same intensity he was trying to project at me.

Eventually he relaxed his face and took a step back. I wanted to breathe a sigh of relief, but stopped myself. Whether consciously or not, Aruhe was leaning slightly forward, as if drawn to the power pulsing from her pack. Simon extended his hand, with the palm facing upwards. I was spared having to ask what the heck I was supposed to do with it when a boy no older than ten sprinted up to him. He placed a single, green fern in his hand and Simon nodded at the boy before bowing his head slightly. The kid scampered back to his place in line with a grin and Simon turned his eyes towards me, extending his hand and offering the fern. I knew what this meant. The presentation of a fern frond was a gesture of peace. We had passed the initial test and were 'welcome' among the Ihi pack.

'Tēnā koe,' I said, repeating the phrase Aruhe had taught me that meant thank you. Carefully I took the fern.

Simon walked backwards until he was standing with the rest of his pack.

'Now begins the welcoming feast,' he said. 'You are invited to dine and sing with us.'

I wanted to say that I wasn't much of a singer. I wanted to add that I had lost my appetite the moment I touched down in this place and that I was unsure which direction I should be looking for an attack: at the Trieze, at the Ihi pack, or within my own cluster of bodyguards? I wanted to say a lot of things. Instead, I nodded politely.

The assembled party scattered to socialise with each

other and prepare the food. I looked to Aruhe for the first time and saw that her face seemed younger somehow. She looked like she was home. This would never be the same home for her as it had once been, yet she seemed willing to be here none the less. We'd never discussed what would happen after the coming of age – there was so much riding on whether we both even made it. But if she survived, she'd have the freedom to do what she wanted, go where she wanted, and be who she wanted.

Surviving the ritual meant she could liberate herself from her blood pack if she wanted or – alternatively – embed herself in it. Watching as people spilled around us, I genuinely had no idea what she would choose. Could she move past the fact that we were only here because they had alluded to a scythe swinging above her neck? If it had been me, I didn't know if I could. But I was petty that way.

The welcoming feast was strangely just like a regular barbecue, except with more people. Older ladies were fussing over pieces of fish roasting on stones, while small children chased each other between the legs of their parents. There was a large number of dogs running around, of all different breeds, yet they remained well-behaved and didn't snatch any piece of meat that wasn't handed to them. In fact, there was something eerie about how well-trained they were and I wondered for the first time if being a werewolf meant you had some control over lesser breeds. I added a mental post-it note to that thought as something to follow up if I didn't die in the next few days. The PG posse didn't mingle with anyone, but they subtly moved through the party as sun set.

Aruhe and I were required to stay for the meal, and we stuck together like glue, as if the ever-present threat was something tangible. There was a log beside one of the open fires and we found ourselves perched on it. As I looked around, trying to soak everything in but also stay aware of my surroundings, Aruhe's gaze kept flicking back to a cluster of people sitting together on the opposite side of the flames. There was something different about them, I noted, as they seemed apart from everyone else. All of them were dressed in plain, black clothing that was deceptively fancy and not dissimilar to what you'd wear to church on a Sunday. Untouched plates of food sat in front of them as they remained there, not talking to each other or anyone else.

'Who are they?' I murmured.

'No one,' she said quickly, realising that I had noticed her interest. 'Just pack members.'

Aruhe looked away, fidgeting with the hem of her pants. She must have sensed my eyes burning into her as she glanced back at my expectant expression. With a sigh, she leaned forwards.

'They're the whānau of people who didn't make it.'

'Didn't make it?'

She looked at me hard, unblinking, for several moments. My eyes widened in shock as I registered what she meant.

'As in, didn't *survive* the coming of age?'

Aruhe nodded, casting a nervous look at the bunch.

'Jesus fucking Christ,' I breathed.

'You knew that people died during this.'

'Aye, of course – it has been plaguing my every thought. I didn't think the relatives of those killed would have to come to something like this, though.'

'It's the same for every pack,' she said. 'Each year, all living members of your blood pack need to be present for the rituals. Regardless of the pain.'

I spared a thought for the group, my heart panging at

how hard it must be to show up every twelve months and go through the motions of something that killed your son, your daughter, your brother or your sister.

The rest of the Ihi pack flitted around them, occasionally placing a hand on a shoulder or whispering something quietly in an ear. They were fussing, obviously aware of how tough it must be just to remain there and wallow in grief. Once, their own family members had sat where we sat, afraid but also hopeful at the prospect of becoming a fully mature wolf. Except they hadn't made it that far. One of the men looked up suddenly, as if sensing exactly what I was thinking. He stared through the fire at me, his eyes and every line on his face marked with the grief unique to losing a loved one. I broke away first, glancing down at my feet as I felt him continue to gaze at me with misery.

Aruhe and my conversation died away, neither of us even moving for a good hour before Wehi shuffled over towards us. He paused a few metres away and Aruhe slowly got up, sensing a conversation. She walked over to him and he placed his wrinkled arm around her affectionately. They stood there, talking to each other quietly. He told her she had grown and asked her where she had been and what she had seen. He kept it light. He didn't mention Steven. He didn't mention me. He didn't mention the Aunties. She seemed to enjoy the small talk.

Wehi was the icebreaker as, once he and Aruhe had a conversation, more members of her extended family and pack came up to speak to her. Her brother James was the first to embrace her, and afterwards he gave me a small nod. He didn't attempt to come my way or provide me with company as I sat there alone on the log. I think we both sensed it wasn't the time or the place for it. I wondered if there ever would be. He had reached out to me before, albeit digitally, but in person there was just simply too much water that had passed under that bridge.

I could tell Heath was keeping me in his line of sight from wherever he was lurking, but I appreciated him leaving me to just stare at the fire, hypnotised. We hadn't spoken about the moment on the plane and I was curious as to who would bring it up first. I didn't think it would be me. It had been such a fast and furious burst of passion, I honestly didn't know what was left to be said. More importantly, I didn't really know where that left us. I shook my head gently to make myself stop pondering those questions, however nice a distraction they were from everything else that was going on. Someone offered me food at one point – one of the women with the headpieces – and I shook my head, smiling as I declined. Truthfully, I wasn't hungry. I felt a presence behind me, not an ominous one, and I casually turned to see who it was. Keisha had a plate in one hand and a beer in the other. She was watching me from a few steps away.

'Can I join you?' she asked in her raspy monotone.

'Aye, sure,' I replied, surprised.

She plopped herself down on the log, leaving a space between us that could have fit two more people. Safety from a distance, I guessed.

'How you finding this so far?' she asked casually, biting a juicy piece of fish off her fork.

'Foreign.'

'You've been doin' some studying of your own, I'd wager.' She nodded, not pausing as she ate. 'Aruhe has been catching you up on werewolf customs.'

'Something like that. She didn't prepare me for the intensity of that welcome though,' I said, letting out a breath and releasing a burst of nervous energy I'd been holding.

'The boys,' she remarked, with the briefest of eye rolls. 'That was Simon's idea. He has so much sense, that kid, but he can be stubborn.'

'Having to make continuous compromises with the Treize about all this probably hasn't helped cure that.'

'You said it, sis.'

'Sis,' I said, rolling the word around in my mouth. 'You seem remarkably good about this whole thing, having me here after . . .'

'You killed Steven? Well.' She shrugged. 'We made our peace with his death the moment we voted. There are some here who think his end should have come at the hands of an Ihi and, in my mind, it did.'

I cast her a sideways glance, watching as she ate. 'He was your nephew.'

'We may be monsters, but we don't raise 'em. He was my blood, but he was also a curse on this pack from the moment he was born. There's no reason Steven turned out the way he was, Tiaki and Jonah did everything right. Raised him just like all the others: *right*. Sometimes there are those born with a blackness on their soul that never goes away and can't be fixed.'

'Aye, I think I've met a few of them.'

'More than your fair share, for this world. And yet you're still standing.'

'Luck.' I smiled, not able to shake the feeling that I was being weighed up in some way.

'You do yourself a dishonour with lies like that. I've known for a long time the power in this pack comes from the women and not the men who think they're in control. It's nice to see that expand further down the tree, whether you're with or against us.'

If it was possible for my eyeballs to fall out of my skull

with shock and roll into the fire, they would have. Keisha smirked as she sipped her beer, taking in my befuddled expression.

'For the record,' I started, 'I was never with or against anyone. I was Team Tommi, playing in a rigged game.'

'Fate had bigger plans.'

'Maybe. Or maybe it would have always ended up the way it did, thanks to the web of lies and half-truths.'

She looked thoughtful at that comment, tilting her head as she stared into the flickering flames of the bonfire.

'Sometimes I forget what it must be like to be you, stumbling in the dark,' she murmured.

'Fuck you,' I said with a laugh, catching the surprise in her expression as she chuckled too.

'What I mean, muzzi girl, is we're born knowing who we are: we understand where we fit in the pack, who came before us, where our power comes from and why. We know our mountain. You've got none of that. All things considered, you've done pretty well.'

'The jury's still out. This all might be for nought if I don't live through ahi hikoi.'

Aruhe's laugh drew my attention and I watched her as she reacted to a younger kid's animated retelling of some family story. She was happy, genuinely happy, even with our coming of age so close I could practically taste it.

'Well, not nothing,' I noted. Keisha's eyes followed my gaze until she too was caught up in watching Aruhe interact with the pack.

'You did a good thing, bargaining for her safety as you did.'

I didn't reply. I wanted to say 'I shouldn't have had to', but I had found myself enjoying this comfortable impasse with undoubtedly one of the most powerful Aunties in the

Ihi pack. I didn't want conflict, for once. Simon joined his cousin then, passing her a cob of corn smeared in butter and I smiled as she wolfed it down.

'You've raised a leader,' I said, watching the kind of respect he commanded from those around him. At first Keisha seemed confused, then her face glowed with the compliment as she realised what I meant.

'It's because I knew what I didn't want him to be,' she said. 'When he got old enough, he knew it too.'

She paused a beat, before continuing. 'There's a power in knowing what you are. All werewolves are monsters and when you embrace that, you overcome it. I'm a proud monster. You seem like one too.'

We sat there in easy silence for a long while, the party carrying on around us. Across the other side of the fire a hearty man was pelting out a tune on the guitar and I felt my foot subconsciously tapping along to the music.

'You're doing a good job of not looking too uncomfortable,' she noted.

'It takes practice.'

'It does, but look at me,' she said with a flourish. 'You would have no idea this entire time all I've been thinking about is slitting the throats of every single Praetorian Guard soldier in our midst and mounting their heads on sticks for *all* of the Treize to see.'

My back stiffened as I spun to face her. She had her eyes trained on the guy with the guitar, her body swaying in time with the rhythm as people had begun to sing along. An easy smile had been plastered on her face, but for the first time now I looked deeper. There was barely contained rage in her eyes and it was familiar to me: it was the very same rage I felt stirring within myself almost constantly.

'You mask and you bear what you cannot stand,' I

murmured, glancing back at the crowd and the PG that were moving through it.

I wondered if they had any idea how much danger they were in. Given how seriously the Treize were taking all this, I wagered they had some clue. I caught a glimpse of Heath's hulking figure on the other side of the fire and felt a pinch in my chest.

'Spare the blond one, will ya,' I said, trying to keep my tone jovial.

'We'll see,' she replied, her voice as light and joking as my own while an entirely different conversation took place underneath. Keisha got to her feet suddenly, wiping the fish oil from her hands. She patted me on the shoulder as she walked past.

'Good ta meet you, Tommi. I've heard interesting things.'

Hours later, we were driven back to where the Treize had arranged for us to stay. It was a huge house about half an hour away from the Ihi property. They had told us we'd be staying off-site to keep us safe until the coming of age, which I had agreed to. Yet I also wondered whether it was so they could keep a closer eye on us and make sure we were distanced from the very people we could form a close allegiance with. As Aruhe went indoors with the rest of the bodyguards, I stayed sitting in the car with Heath, frozen to my seat.

'That was ... weird,' I managed to say.

'Did you expect it to be any different?'

'No, that's almost exactly how I imagined it would go. Right up until the point I got a kind-of-endorsement from Simon's mum. Or maybe it was a threat? It's hard to tell. Am I an eejit?'

'Yes, always,' he answered, dodging my attempts to whack him hard on the shoulder.

'Listen,' he laughed. 'Maybe you should believe Simon when he says they're trying a new path.'

'I got the impression he's sharing the load with James.'

'Sharing the load or diverting attention from the real puppet master? That's the question. From what the Askari have told me, and what I've been able to read up on their family case file, those two have been thick as thieves since they were in nappies.'

'That can only be a good thing for the pack, right?'

'The pack isn't your concern.'

'No, they're *a* concern. They're not usually *my* concern. Yet here we are.'

'Freezing in a car in the middle of bloody Rotorua,' said Heath, his finger inching towards the door handle. 'I'm going in, and since I'm tasked with watching you, I'm begging you to come indoors also.'

'Begging, are we?' I said, leaning across flirtatiously. I watched a flicker of something in his eyes as he registered my tone.

'Begging,' Heath repeated, his voice coming out so low it was almost a growl.

His hand reached up, resting on the curve of my neck. I desperately wanted him to pull me forwards and on to his body, but he seemed content running his warm fingers up until they were entwined in my hair. His eyes never left mine and I heard the ragged sound of my own breathing. Slowly, I unclicked my seatbelt and shifted my frame, but his other hand stopped me – holding me in place. Heath gave the slightest shake of his head before his eyes flicked to look at something behind me. I swivelled around and sighed as I caught a glimpse of a PG figure coming into view walking the perimeter. Reluctantly, I willed myself out of the car and what had *almost* been. The only saving grace was that if I was bummed about it, Heath seemed doubly so as we walked past and he grunted a non-verbal reply to the guard who asked him how his night was.

The house was, quite frankly, a dump. It had obviously been chosen for strategic reasons and not aesthetic ones. When I walked through the door, Aruhe was tapping the edge of a shag pile rug with her toe just to check rats didn't emerge from it.

'So this is . . . gross,' she muttered.

'We're only here for a few days,' said Heath, dumping a bag on the living room floor. 'We're on the road to Picton day after tomorrow.'

'This isn't even half as bad as that dive we stayed at in Dublin,' I said to him, trying very hard to look on the bright side of things.

'That was a crypt, Tommi. We were sleeping in a two hundred-year-old crypt.'

'It had atmosphere.' I shrugged.

I HAD disturbing dreams that night. Dreams of being chased by glowing orbs and branches lashing at my body. It was only when I woke up that I realised it may have been a nightmare about my first transformation on this very same land. Somehow it had felt new though. Impending. I shook off the feeling and went back to sleep, ignoring the light peeking through the windows and snoozing for another hour or two before Aruhe came and woke me up.

'One of the guards said I should check on you in case you were dead. He said it wasn't healthy to sleep that long.'

'Yeah, well, he's a bodyguard. What would he know about sleep?' I murmured as I kicked back the blankets.

'Has anyone ever told you ya have a body like Gina Carano?'

'I have literally no idea who that is.'

'MMA fighter? *Haywire*? Baby Yoda's mate?'

'Girl, it is so early – don't test me.'

'It's afternoon. And we haven't got anything to do anyway. The greeting is over and there aren't any more rituals until the morning of ahi hikoi.'

'Mint. Tomorrow. What have you been doing in the meantime?'

'Watching *Rick and Morty*,' she said. 'And training with Heath.'

'Heath trained with you?'

'I was surprised too! I was eating cereal in front of the TV and he was all "Come on, aye, up ya gett".'

'That's a terrible attempt at his voice.'

There was a subtle knock on the bedroom door and Aruhe and I shouted 'COME IN!' in unison. The subject of our conversation stuck his head into the room and I was sure he had heard us talking about him. Heath's face was strangely ashen.

'There's a phone call for you, Tommi.'

'For me? Who could be—' I stopped myself as my blood pumped frantically. Leaping to my feet, I pushed past him and sprinted into the kitchen where his phone was resting on the bench. I didn't hesitate for a second as I held it to my ear and screamed my best friend's name down the speaker. My knees felt like they were about to give out from underneath me as Joss replied.

'Tommi! My God, you're in New Zealand?'

My words caught in my throat at how exactly like Joss he sounded. Except stronger. In just seven words he sounded stronger than I had heard him in a long time. I tried to formulate a reply as I battled the urge to choke up.

'Hello? Tom? You there?'

'I'm here,' I said, clearing my throat. 'Just trying not to go all *Beaches* on you.'

There was a long pause on the other end as he attempted to hold it together too. 'You big sook,' he sniffed.

I laughed. 'Joss, I just . . . I wasn't sure if I'd ever speak to you again.'

'What! Are you crazy? One of the whole reasons I wanted to be a Custodian was so I could be around you all the time. I can help you out with stuff, officially.'

'You were doing that before. You're one of them now, Joss. You have orders. You have eternity.'

'Hey! *You're* one of them. At least I chose this.'

'Oh, so we're getting catty now?'

'Meow.'

'Hiss hiss etcetera. How are you, though? Are you good? Are you safe? Are you hurt?'

'Settle down, maw. I'm fine. The procedures and ceremony . . . we rushed through a lot of it since I was on my last legs and all. I don't remember much. Then I woke up in the recovery bay, which was weirdly like a pool of noodles. But I have a shiny new necklace and a life, Tommi. I'm alive!'

My mind tracked back to the time Lorcan explained the philosophical difference between the Praetorian Guard and the Custodians. Immortality was a reward for the soldiers, but for the Custodians it was a choice and those that chose it wore a silver necklace adorned with the Egyptian ankh.

'I'm glad.'

'You don't seem glad,' replied Joss, sounding uncertain.

'I am. When the PG tried to recruit me, I said the only

way I'd sign on the dotted line was if they could save you. Believe me, Joss, you alive and well means everything to me. I just . . . I never wanted this for you. Immortality. You're their eternal servant now. The Treize is your number one priority for the rest of all time. Me, family, friends, a life of your own, a career: that's all second fiddle to your mission with them. I wanted you alive, but I wanted your freedom more.'

'That part of it was something I thought about really carefully, Tommi. Like, I know I was doped up on painkillers for a big chunk of the decision-making process, but this was worth it for me. If signing up to the Custodians meant I wouldn't die, what's to baulk at?'

'And he helped you with all this,' I said, scrunching up my face with frustration. 'Didn't he?'

There was a pause on the other end of the phone.

'Joss?'

'Aye, I'm sorry for going behind your back with that, but Lorcan was the only person I knew with enough sway in the Custodians to broker the deal.'

I sighed, the phone pressing into my cheek as I leaned against the door. 'I get it, I'm not mad, Joss. At you, anyway. I just never wanted this life for you.'

'You wanted to keep me as your one, normal friend,' Joss stated, no trace of bitterness in his voice. 'But if I wanted to be normal, I wouldn't have befriended you, would I?'

I let out an angry breath and laughed. 'If I remember correctly, I befriended you.'

'Technicality.'

'I'm sorry, Joss. Can you not hate me for it? The wanting to keep you wrapped up in cotton wool and protected from the world?'

'I couldn't hate you if I tried. More importantly, you'll be pleased to know things are going well here. I'm learning fast and Lorcan reckons I could be out with him in the field soon.'

I flinched with the knowledge that Lo was there with him, seeing Joss through all of this and guiding him when I couldn't be there.

'Obviously I'm going to request to be assigned to you and maybe Aruhe if she's still sticking around. You've got to make it through the coming of age though.'

'You're the supernatural psychologist now, any book wisdom you can impart?'

'Oh yeah, let me just pull something out of my ass from the how-many days since I've been doing this, ya wanker.'

I snorted.

'Besides, I think the Rogues were probably more useful than I could be. And anything I've read up on, you probably have too. I am surprised you're back there though, that you'd even put yourself near them.'

'It's not—' I cut myself off. I was about to say I wasn't doing this for me. At the core of it I wasn't. At the same time, I had to take ownership of the decision I'd made. 'I cut a deal. Whatever punishment the Aunties were going to dish out for Aruhe's betrayal would be off the table if I came back with her and attempted it too.'

'That deal's not contingent on your survival, is it?'

'Nope. I'm just like Evel Knievel.'

'You're getting points for the attempt,' he chuckled, finishing the joke. 'Ah, but I know you, Tommi Janice Grayson. That's right, I'm bringing out the middle name shaming here, *Janice*. You hate bullies. You always have. You hate seeing people smaller than you get left behind or picked on. You're in some serious shit now because of it, but don't underestimate the power of doing the right thing. I don't really know this lass. You're putting yourself out there on a limb for her and I hope it pays off. Just be careful.'

'Bloody right. Where are you, anyway? It sounds quiet there.'

'It's night. You know I can't tell you where I am.'

'Don't be a gobshite, why not? I've been to the Treize HQ for goodness sake, why can't you dish a little dishy? Custodian base camp is New York, so are you in NYC?'

'You've been to the Trei— huh? Okay, give me a wee second,' said Joss, responding to someone on his end. 'Listen, I have to go. I just wanted to speak to you before tomorrow night.'

'Aye, thanks. It's amazing to hear your voice and cop some verbal abuse. When will I get speak to you again? Or see you?'

He sighed, but his voice sounded hopeful. 'Soon, I'm thinking. I'm hoping. I— *all right*. Tom, I gotta bail.'

'Joss, can—'

'I'll speak to you soon. Be careful. I love you, ya bampot.'

'Jo—'

The line went dead. My mouth was still open with the farewell I had been trying to form. I looked at the phone in my hand to see if there was a return number. The screen was entirely blank. I scrolled through the phone only to find the incoming call hadn't registered at all. Freakin' Treize bullshit. I turned to see Heath standing at the entrance to the room. Aruhe was peering around him from further back in the hall.

'How was it?' he asked.

'Good. He was good. I needed that. I didn't realise how much.'

I looked up at the ceiling to avoid crying. A noise behind me signalled that one of the bodyguards had joined us and I suddenly became very aware of the fact I had sprinted out of bed in nothing more than a skimpy pair of undies and a singlet top.

'I need to get dressed,' I blurted, dashing past Heath and Aruhe and into our temporary room. I pressed my back against the door as I shut it, breathing out. This house felt suffocating. The people, the mortality, all of it. I needed to be somewhere that was else.

A shredded pair of denim hot pants, blue kicks, white shirt and a leather jacket was my uniform of choice and it was on me in less than a few seconds. Slipping some cash into my back pocket, I silently wedged open the window and peeked out. I caught the back of one of our bodyguards as she disappeared around the corner on perimeter patrol. Not wasting a moment, I leaped out of the window and landed on the soft lawn. Before you could say 'prison break' I was over the wooden fence and sprinting down the road.

It was exhilarating to have the room to just run again. I sprinted hard for at least eight hundred metres, fully aware of how fast I had become. Slowing down into a more comfortable jog, I took a second to enjoy the movement and the wind whipping back my hair. Time was of no consequence as I vaguely noted the changing scenery on my route. Using my sense of smell, I worked my way towards the centre of town, but it still felt like a long while before I reached it. Dampness from a light sprinkle of rain mixed with my sweat and I relished the cool shower as it increased in heaviness. Moving through the suburban streets, I paused at the car park of a seedy-looking pub. Fit as I was, my urge to keep running was overcome by my urge to drink.

14

I t had been three hours since Tommi had gone missing and Heath had done as much as he could to keep anyone from thinking this was out of the ordinary. The house was filled with members of his own team – who he trusted – and members of the ground team – who he implicitly did not. Although he'd managed to make sure his people were in closest concentration around the room Tommi and Aruhe were staying in, he was still on edge. And now, Tommi was AWOL. He'd tried to give her space after the phone call as she was clearly upset, but when Aruhe caught his eye an hour later he knew something was up.

'What?' he asked, following her to the girls' shared room and closing the door behind them.

'Tommi's gone,' Aruhe whispered, her voice laced with panic.

'Gone? What do you mean *gone*?'

'She's not here, I've looked everywhere and—'

Heath held up a hand to silence her as he glanced down at the small pile of possessions Tommi had brought with her on this trip. He moved to the only exit from the room –

the window – and examined the frame there, before ducking back inside.

'She's fine,' he said.

'How do you know?'

'Because her favourite leather jacket and runners are gone.'

'Which means what? If one of the PG took her and she was wearing those—'

'She does this,' he interrupted. 'You don't know because you haven't been around long enough, but when she's upset or can't deal, she runs.'

'Runs . . . runs away? From me?'

'Not you, pup: from this house. She needs breathing room and it's best we give her that.'

Aruhe looked confused.

'I never said it was rational, it's just a cycle.'

Heath cast a cursory glance out the window, thinking about his options.

'Fook, here's what we're gonna do: say nothing. If anyone asks where Tommi or I am, say that you saw the pair of us leave together. If they ask where, just make up something cool and vague so people will believe I said it.'

'And what are you going to do?'

'Go look for her. If they think we're together and that we *left* together, then they won't push it. But if she's on her own—'

'They'll hunt her down.'

'Interesting choice of words,' he remarked, watching the younger werewolf as she thought about his plan. 'We clear?'

'Crystal. How should I get in touch?'

'You don't. We should be back in a few hours.'

He was halfway out the window when he paused, his body stuck between leaving and going.

'Aruhe?'

'Hmm?'

'Try and stay in this room, if you can. Don't find yourself anywhere in the house where you don't recognise the face of someone who was on the plane with us.'

She nodded, nervously biting her lip as a reflex. He couldn't waste any more time here when the bigger issue was out there. He knew he was betting on the best-case scenario: Tommi, alone but unprotected as she desperately tried to escape from her problems for a few hours. Sure, he didn't really like the best-case scenario. But he wouldn't even entertain the worst-case scenario.

Several hours later, Heath was still on the trail and drenched as he navigated his way through the surrounding streets. Unlike Tommi, he couldn't use scent to track what he was trying to find. He had only guessed that she had headed south – away from the house – because that part of town had more pubs. He knew that's where he'd find her in the same way that he knew she was Scottish down to her soul.

Given that no one was on his tail, they must have bought the story Aruhe had fed them. After bouncing from dive bar to cocktail lounge, he was feeling hopeful as he strolled through the car park of The Leaping Deer. His optimism stemmed largely from the fact there was a row of motorcycles parked out the front and he had passed two drunks brawling by the laneway. If there was any kind of joint Tommi would have been drawn to, it was this hole.

Pushing through the swinging doors, he ignored the pointed glances. He was used to them at this point: Heath was a physically intimidating man who drew passing interest. It made it hard to blend, but in this place – as he passed men taller, wider, thicker and meaner than him – the looks didn't last as long, the reactions weren't as shocked. In this pub, he actually came close to fitting in.

Scanning the room for a mass of pastel-blue hair, he paused when he saw something else entirely. There, at the opposite end of the room, was the woman he had been looking for . . . along with a group of six other people, all dancing on top of the bar. She was drunk: off her face, in fact, and he breathed an inward sigh of relief. Tommi knew in part how dangerous the situation in New Zealand was, but she clearly didn't understand the full scope of it. It meant that she could let her guard down enough to look almost happy, if you didn't know her. Heath did. He knew she was hurting and doing everything she could to try and forget about it. Heck, it was his coping mechanism too.

As he cut his way through the crowd of people, he had a chance to admire her sloppy attempt at dance moves as she swayed and sashayed to the Dave Dobbyn song they were all belting at the top of their lungs. One of the group was obviously keen on her and slipped his hand on to her thigh as they danced. Heath chuckled as she very naturally, very casually, bent the man's fingers backwards and stayed moving to the rhythm. His cries were muffled by the awful singing and he disappeared into the crowd, yelling and clutching at his limb.

'That seemed a tad heavy-handed,' Heath called up to her once he reached the base of the bar. She froze, recognising his voice instantly. He did his utmost not to react at the look that washed over her face as she glanced down at him. It was testament to how blootered she was that Tommi hadn't registered his scent the moment he walked in.

'HEATH!' she screamed, seemingly ecstatic. 'It's you! Here! Making a good joke!'

She launched herself off the bar at him and he caught

her easily. It was a display of his own strength in a way, as Tommi might not have been tall but she definitely wasn't little. The shorts she was wearing could barely contain her and that was a big part of the appeal to him. She was thick, she was strong, and her body – even in human form – looked like the weapon it was. Through the material of her shirt he could feel the muscles in her stomach as if they were desperate to burst through. He caught the gaze of a woman across the bar who was frowning as she watched him drop Tommi slowly to the ground in what would have been a notable display of grit for a regular human man. Heath wasn't one and Tommi was even further from that centre. He needed to get them out of here, before they created any more of a scene.

'Aye, I'm here. And you're a fucking nightmare, I'll tell you that.'

She had the grace to look guilty as she looked up at him with eyes he knew had got, and would continue to get, him in trouble.

'Come on,' he groaned, grabbing her by the hand and pulling her towards the door. They passed the man from earlier who was trying to explain what had happened to a buddy of his by throwing up his fingers and trying to wiggle them. Tommi ducked her head, using Heath's body as a shield so she remained out of his sight.

'I see you're making friends,' he remarked.

'Whatever you wear, wherever you go, yes means yes, and no means no,' she chanted, unapologetic. 'And *please*, nothing was broken.'

He cast her a glance, his face breaking into a genuine smile. 'What I'm saying is, maybe his fingers should have been.'

She returned his grin, albeit sheepishly, and they paused

at the exit as Heath swiped two shots from the table next to them, downing them quickly, while their occupants remained completely unaware. Grabbing an unopened water bottle in one final gesture, they broke out of the pub and into the fresh air outside. She let out a breath, blinking as she took in the night around them. The rain had eased up slightly so that it was now nothing more than the occasional pitter-patter.

'Huh,' she said, looking around. 'It's dark.'

'That happened some time between when you ran from the house and when you ended up in this shithole.'

There was a long beat as he watched her watch him. He was doing his best not to think about the little frayed edges of her shorts and how they might feel brushing against his fingertips.

'What?' he asked.

'You what,' she countered.

'*What?*'

'This would be the moment you yell at me, Heath. You should be yelling at me.'

'For running out?'

'Bloody exactly.'

'It's just what you do,' he said, nonchalant. 'I knew I'd find you eventually.'

'You did?'

''Course. The way you deal is by bolting. Now drink this.'

He shoved the water bottle at her and she stumbled slightly. He watched her take a tentative sip of the water before throwing the whole thing back in thirsty gulps. She finished it in a few seconds and was crunching the plastic under her fingers. Heath jerked his head in the direction of the side of the pub where he had seen the two men scuffling earlier. There was little sign of their fight now, besides an errant tooth laying in a puddle at the entrance to the lane. She followed him around the corner until they had privacy.

'What I'm pissed about—'

'Oh boy, here we go.'

'—is you know how much danger you're in, from both sides. We don't know who's a greater threat to you at the moment – the Treize or the Ihi pack – until someone shows their hand. That could have been tonight, that could have been *while* you were shitfaced, unprotected, and by yourself.'

'Heath—' Her words died as she blinked, catching the second water bottle he threw at her. 'Where did that come from? How many more do you have shoved down your pants?'

'Just drink it, will you? You don't want to be going into the coming of age with a hangover.'

'Aye, that's why I've been going one drink, one glass of water, one drink, one glass of water. Also, these.' She pulled a packet of aspirin out of her back pocket and waved it at him.

'That's great.' He sighed. 'How can you have enough foresight to take aspirin but not take *me* with you? I love to get drunk! It's one of my top three favourite things to do! We could have done it together and I would have felt a wee bit better with the knowledge that if someone tried to start shite, there'd be two of us and not one of you.'

The rain had picked up again and it was getting heavier, with water droplets making triumphant splashes around them as they spoke. He was doing his best not to focus on how the weather was making her white shirt cling to her body. He was focusing on the situation at hand, really.

Heath watched her open her mouth – no doubt a witty

reply on the tip of her tongue – when she paused, evidently seeing something in his face. She took a step towards him and he resisted the desire to take one backwards, curious to see where this would go. When she closed what little distance there was between them, he felt like he was holding his breath.

'Heath,' she said, her voice barely more than a whisper. She reached up and placed a hand on the side of his face, holding his gaze to hers. 'You're scared for me.'

'I'm terrified for you.' The words had rushed out of his lips before he had a chance to even consider them and he felt momentarily betrayed. When her other hand cupped his face, he couldn't help but close his eyes with the relief of her nearness.

'You're so brave and cocky, I didn't think anything could scare you.'

'The coward dies a thousand deaths, the brave man but once,' he muttered.

'I'm no man, Heath. And bravery has many resting places.'

His eyes flew open and he pinned her with his stare. She was even closer to him now, somehow. He hadn't even sensed her move.

'I'm scared because it's hard for me to fight what I cannot see,' he explained. 'I can anticipate a threat, but when there's *so* many I'm petrified that I'm going to miss something and it's going to get through . . . to you.'

She looked up and read him carefully as he spoke, her dark-brown eyes warm beneath her eyelashes as they fluttered. Heath liked to think he had a good mask that could snap down whenever he wanted, yet from their first encounter – when she had sized him up in a matter of seconds – he'd found it rarely worked with her.

'Which is why you're scared right now.' She nodded with understanding. 'You think that if you do miss something, at least I'm capable enough to protect myself. Except tonight I'm not. I'm drunk.'

'And vulnerable.'

'I wouldn't say that.'

He saw it signalled a mile off, yet he didn't do anything to stop it. In fact, Heath leaned in to meet her kiss despite more than a millennium of judgement telling him he shouldn't. The first time she had kissed him it had been all flame and heat and desperation. He had loved it and he almost expected that now, given her inhibitions were lower. When Tommi's lips met his, however, and her tongue gently pressed inside his mouth, he was surprised by how gentle she was.

Pulling her body tighter to his, every kiss danced on his mouth like he was on drugs. She moved slowly, as if savouring what he was giving back to her. This didn't feel like a physical knee-jerk reaction from Tommi: it felt like she was pouring her heart out. And he was willing to drink in whatever she served him.

Taking a few uneasy steps backwards, unwilling to separate, he pushed them both up against the laneway wall. He arched over her, protecting her somewhat from the rain as it continued to beat against his back. Water snaked down the side of his face and into his hair as they continued to kiss each other, rain eventually mixing into the momentum of their lips. She didn't pause for a second, her eyelashes tickling his cheeks. He whispered her name and she kissed him deeper in response that, in and of itself, was her own answer. He pulled back slowly to say something else and she peered up at him. Something moved deep inside Heath as he saw the flush of her skin and the way she watched him.

'There's—'

She frowned, causing him to pause. She sensed it a moment before he did and he began to spin around when something sliced at his chest. He was overwhelmed with sharp agony for a moment, letting out a grunt as he glanced down. Ah, just a dagger. Someone had been aiming for his heart when Tommi's reaction had caused him to move off target. Yanking the blade out of his flesh, he turned to get a full look at his attacker who was dressed in jeans and a grey hoodie. Their face was hidden from him, but he could tell just from the way they moved that it was a woman.

'HEATH!'

Tommi shouted from behind him as another dagger flew directly at his right eye. He caught it in a flash, just inches from his face, and tossed it back at the woman in one smooth gesture. It clipped her shoulder and a small screech informed him it made contact. He was about to do a whole lot more than that as he surged forward, pulling himself up to his full six-foot-six height and storming at her. He was almost there when a blue flash darted in front of him, wiping out his target in a swift tackle and knocking her to the ground. Heath watched, stunned for a moment, as Tommi and the woman rolled across the wet ground in a clash of teeth and knives and claws.

'THE OTHER ONE,' she called, managing to strangle out a sentence during the fight. 'Watch the other one!'

Heath dropped to his feet with a speed that would have surprised most people given his bulk. Although he might have been tall, he was also quick and he used that to his advantage as someone lunged at him from behind. The assailant stumbled as the sword they had thrown their weight behind plunged through thin air. Heath pulled his own weapon from his coat and used the Bowie knife to slash through the Achilles tendons of his attacker. A man let out a guttural yell of pain and fell forwards, dropping to his knees. Heath rolled out of the way and propelled himself upwards, wedging the man's neck perfectly in the space between his elbow and bicep. Gripping his wrist to lock in the position, Heath twisted his shoulders and hips using his all his strength until a loud crack rang out. The sound seemed to echo off the walls of the lane as the man slumped down, neck well and truly broken.

Heath looked up, letting the dead body fall to the ground in front of him as he measured Tommi's situation in a split second. His own victory had taken barely more than a few breaths, whereas hers was proving messier. The woman seemed to be armed with an endless supply of daggers, which Tommi had utilised and turned back on their wielder. Bleeding and desperate, the attacker was attempting to crawl away to freedom while Tommi recovered from a swift kick to the gut. As he made his way towards them, she glanced up and met Heath's gaze.

'Don't you dare,' she said, pointing squarely at his chest from her position on the ground. He paused where he stood, raising his hands in surrender. With a groan, she sprinted after the woman, catching her by the ankles and dragging her backwards. He blinked, always amazed at how quickly she was able to access her inner wolf as she raised a clawed werewolf hand above her head.

'WAIT!' he called out, but it was too late as Tommi brought her limb down in one deadly movement. She held her assailant's head by a clump of red hair as blood sprayed out of the woman's throat in a frantic gush. Panting, Tommi let the now-dead woman slide to the concrete as blood continued to pool around them.

'What did you want me to wait for?' she puffed as Heath approached.

'So we could question her.'

'Here?' Tommi looked around. 'It's so public. Where could we take her that wouldn't attract attention? She strikes me as a screamer.'

'He wasn't.'

Tommi glanced at the corpse crumpled at Heath's feet. He saw the wolf dancing beneath her eyes, brought closer to the surface than it usually was due to the bloodshed. As if fully comprehending the situation for the first time, Tommi grimaced like she was in pain and dropped her head into her hands.

'Fuck,' she whispered. 'I shouldn't have killed her.'

'They didn't leave us much choice, Tommi. We should worry about that later. Right now, we need to move these bodies. It's a miracle no one has seen us. Yet.'

'Sure.' Tommi nodded, pausing for a moment as she swept the area with her werewolf senses. 'We need to hurry. A group of three just left the pub for a smoke.'

The man had been big, but Heath was bigger and with a hefty tug he threw the dead guy over his shoulder. Heading for the opposite end of the lane, Tommi followed by dragging the woman along behind her with both arms. Usually he would be worried about the blood trail, but it was so dark drunk punters weren't going to notice. The heavens had also chosen that exact moment to open up, helping wash away what little crime scene there was.

'Here,' he said, pointing to a collection of garbage bags that were stacked on top of each other. 'Lay them down.'

Tommi looked a little sick, but did as he ordered. As she stepped back from the bodies and dusted her hands, Heath moved forward. Blinking away the rain that was trickling over his face, he crouched down to inspect both of their faces carefully.

'You know 'em?'

'Her, yes.'

'Let me guess, Praetorian Guard?'

'Aye, she was at the airport with the greeting party. Cassandra is her name. Was her name.'

'That's why I recognised her scent. She was one of theirs stationed at the house. *Motherfuckers.*'

Heath pulled up the sleeve of the man's jacket to reveal the marking there. It was the tattoo of the Askari, an ancient symbol for wood: the foundation on which something great could be built. The notion amused him in their current scenario.

'Askari?' she asked, uncertainty in her voice.

'Him I know only by reputation: Gustav Rein. Former Askari recruited by the PG once they learned he was a part-time boxer. Or was it wrestler? Ah, who gives a shite.'

Heath stepped back from the corpses and piled the surrounding garbage bags on top of them so that soon the only things visible were the remnants of rotting food and the odd beer bottle.

'A perfect crime,' Tommi scoffed. 'How long until you think they're discovered?'

'There's not a lot of garbage around, so bin day is still some time away: the other side of the weekend, maybe. If this weather keeps up, we might get lucky and they're not found for a week.'

'Isn't this, er, proof? Or something?'

'Proof of what?' Heath snorted.

'That the PG are out to *get me* or whatever.'

His world had crumbled around him years ago and yet, he felt sorry for her naivety in that moment. 'All this proves is that we killed two members of the Praetorian Guard for . . . what reason? We wiped them out too efficiently, we have nothing to prove our side of the story: self-defence.'

'Fuck. Fuck, fuck, fuck. I'm not interested in these people! Why come after me? I'm not interested in the Treize.'

'Ah, but the Treize is very interested in you.'

Heath frowned, looking at the pile of garbage so hard he felt like he was visibly penetrating through to the bodies underneath. He couldn't be certain these Praetorian Guard soldiers were actually here for Tommi: it was just as likely they were here for him. Every mole worked with an invisible clock ticking down alongside them. He had hoped his clock would tick a little longer, giving the allies more time to do everything they needed to do, giving Sadie more time to deliver the triplets safely. And change all of their fates, hopefully.

But Aruhe's unexpected arrival, and Tommi agreeing to participate in ahi hikoi, had forced him to take risks he wouldn't have otherwise. It had meant his invisible clock had ticked a little bit faster, yet he couldn't stop himself. From the team of freelancers he'd hired as their personal bodyguards to the scene at the Treize airfield, he knew his actions were creating doubts where there had been none previously. He'd had 'doubts' about the Treize once, too. Then he'd had proof: lots of it, bloody and not open to interpretation.

He opened his mouth and not for the first time, he braced himself to tell her everything. He wanted to unburden himself of this knowledge, of *all* of these secrets, and fates he was juggling. He wanted to share what he knew with Tommi, partially so she could help him, but also so he wouldn't feel quite as alone in all of this. It had been decades since he last felt that way.

As the rain trickled down the back of his shirt, he closed his mouth. Tommi could die during ahi hikoi. If she was to survive, all of her concentration and focus needed to be on that, no matter what the cost.

'We need to get out of here,' Tommi was saying, her shirt soaked right through so that her bra was visible underneath. Her hair was so wet she was able to slick it off her face in one gesture. 'The smokers have gone back in; we should leave, Heath. In case there are more of them.'

The words were barely out of her mouth before she spun around, crouching over as she vomited. He took a step towards her, concerned, but she held up a hand to stop him.

'Just stay right there,' she choked.

Heath watched her body heave with exertion as it rejected all the events of the past few minutes. Finally, she straightened up and let out a shuddering breath. He wasn't sure if the illness had been brought on by the alcohol, the Treize ramifications, or the knowledge that she had just killed someone. After all, it might have been in self-defence, but Cassandra wasn't a ghoul or a vampire or a member of the Laighnach Faelad. She had been human.

'You okay?' he said quietly, Tommi answering him with a small nod. She made for the lane entrance but he grabbed her arm, tugging her in the opposite direction.

'Not that way. We walk home, the long way, lose any potential tail we might have or—'

'Give ourselves an opportunity to bite it off.'

He smiled. 'Precisely.'

'The question is, how did they find me? I didn't even know where I was going until I got here, so if they were following me . . .'

'They followed me, they must have. Or they had a scout tell them where you were. The timing was too perfect. I don't think they would—'

'Heath!'

'What?' he stopped, suddenly poised and ready to fight at the alarm in her tone. 'Where?'

'You're bleeding,' she said, batting away his raised fist as she crossed the space between them. Her fingers touched a spot on his chest that made him flinch. He looked down to see his blood snaking over her fingers as she examined the wound.

'The dagger.'

'The rain is making it look worse than it is, the blood is spreading in water. Still, I think you're going to need stitches.'

'Gah, when we're back at the house. I can do it in the mirror.'

He went to push past her when she nudged him back.

'Wait, just . . .' She looked around for something, before staring down at herself. With a swift gesture, she ripped her T-shirt in half until most of her midriff was exposed.

'What are you—'

'Shut the fuck up.'

He obeyed, for once, staying quiet and very, very still as she reached under his shirt and made a temporary bandage to cover his wound with the material of her own. She looked unhappy with the end result. Heath more than anything was trying not to think about how it felt to have her hands on his body. That's not where his mind needed to be. They had an hour walk back to the house and literally anything – and anyone – could be waiting for a moment of inattention like he had in the laneway.

'That will do,' she grumbled.

'All right, let's move.'

'You okay?' she asked, looking up at him. 'Are you in pain?'

He huffed, looking out at the darkness and what lay ahead of them. 'I'm fine.'

'You know,' she said, the two of them beginning to move. 'This is how we met: blood and bodies in an alley.'

'What dreams are made of.' He smirked.

The walk back to the house was tense, with both of them on alert for any threat coming from any direction. They wouldn't be caught off-guard again. Tommi used every sensory advantage she had to scan ahead while Heath focused on what was behind them. At some point he handed her a gun from within his coat, he himself still armed with his Bowie knife and a few other tricks up his sleeve (quite literally). The rain continued to beat down heavily, their breaths coming out in small steam clouds as they moved as quickly and quietly as they could. The walk home was silent. When Heath noticed Tommi shivering, he wordlessly handed her his coat. He cast her a look that begged her not to refuse and she didn't.

When the light of the house illuminated both of their faces, he felt something like relief because although they mightn't be completely out of danger, at least they were somewhere where the numbers were stacked a little more closely in his favour. It was just past 10 p.m when they crossed the threshold. He knew some of his people would still be awake and alert. He knew Ginger would be watching and he was grateful for it. No doubt some of the Praetorian Guard would be too.

They crept down the hall that led to Tommi and Aruhe's shared bedroom and paused when they got to the door. The light was off and from the faint snoring he could hear on the other side, Aruhe was already asleep. They both stood there, still and relieved for a moment. Heath glanced behind him to where his room was.

'I should . . .' he started, nodding in the direction of where he intended to go.

'Stitches.'

'Aye.'

Tommi glanced down at her sneakers, which were wet enough for a small patch of moisture to be forming on the carpet beneath her.

'You should get some sleep,' Heath whispered, watching her. 'We leave early in the morning.'

'That we do.'

With a hand on the door handle, she murmured good night to him and he mumbled something back. He clutched the makeshift bandage she had applied and winced as he made his way to his bedroom. He hoped it was just the pain from the wound in his chest.

15

Pressing my damp forehead against the door, I listened to Heath's footsteps as they faded down the hall. It wasn't until I heard the click of his door closing that I slowly turned around, scanning the room for my bag and dry clothes. Aruhe was spread-eagle across her bed, arms and toes dangling off the side as she stayed in a deep sleep. She didn't even stir as I moved through the room, peeling off Heath's coat followed by my own sopping garments. I didn't do much more than leave them in a pile at the foot of my bed as I snatched a towel and headed for a shower in the bathroom down the hall. I set the water hotter than Mt Vesuvius in an attempt to regain feeling in my limbs, my hair sticking to my back as I stood there.

I'd killed someone, and perhaps the thing that frightened me most was that with every passing second I was feeling less and less horrible about it. Sure, we could have questioned that woman, but at the end of it we still would have had to execute her. This was my life now; had been for a long time, in fact.

Scrubbing my body clean, I noted that I had nothing

more than a few scrapes on my knee from our tussle with the would-be assassins in the laneway. Suddenly, it wasn't the fight I was thinking about. It wasn't even the body disposal.

It was that fucking kiss.

It was a sign of how absent my mind was as I returned to my room that I only sensed there was someone coming around the corner when I was a few steps away from the door and wrapped in a towel. I tensed, quickly reminding myself that if this wasn't one of Heath's people then I was in danger. My chest deflated with relief as Ginger appeared on the other side, Victory Rolls in her hair disgustingly perfect for this time of evening. I gave her a small smile, which she returned.

'You two are back earlier than I expected,' she said.

'Big day tomorrow,' I replied. 'Good night.'

She murmured something similar and I slipped inside my room once more, brushing the knots out of my hair as I stood there naked in the dark. Aruhe hadn't moved positions. I dried my ends with the towel, pulled on underwear and a four-sizes-too-big shirt, then collapsed on to my own bed, my hair fanning out around me like a halo.

Something pressed into my back and I squirmed to pull the object out from under me. The huge glass eyes of the unicorn soft toy stared back at me and I was glad I had decided to bring it on the trip. For luck, I reasoned, tucking it under my arm with a smile. As I stared at the ceiling, my mind ticked over as the quiet house slept around us. I tried closing my eyes, but they flew back open in less than a few seconds. Despite my best intentions, I was wide-awake. And my mind would . . . not . . . stop.

I was thinking about everything: my first time in this country, my half-sister asleep next to me, the consequences of our actions, Joss becoming a Custodian, the Treize and the sticky web they had built around themselves, the people I had killed, Heath's mouth, the first ghost I saw, the pull of the full moon, and the reality that this time tomorrow I would be midway through the werewolf coming of age. Or I would be dead.

I sat up, kicking the covers off and springing from the bed. I paused at the door and used my werewolf senses to scent or hear if there was anyone nearby. With a careful creak, I slipped from my room once again and walked down the hall.

Heath's door was unlocked, as I knew it would be, and his room was completely dark as I entered. The only light was coming from the bathroom where the door to his en suite was slightly ajar.

He was standing in front of the mirror with damp hair and nothing more than a towel wrapped around his waist, blood oozing down the right side of his chest where the dagger had found its mark. He had a needle in his hand and thread was running from it back to the wound as he paused in the stitching process. He let out a long breath and hunched over the sink, the muscles in his back rippling as he put weight on the basin.

He didn't know I was there and I revelled in the sensation of being unseen by him. My eyes were drawn immediately to the blue tattoos that covered so much of his body. For the first time I got to see his Pictish markings in all their glory, the blue tribal patterns wrapping around his torso and snaking their way up his chest and down his limbs. There was one that decorated his collarbone like an elaborate necklace, which morphed into two others as they rolled their way across his shoulders. I got a fair idea of just how far down his tattoos went as the towel hung on hips, defying gravity. I had studied the history books for clues about Pictish culture and Heath's nature but this . . . this was unlike anything a sketch could capture. My fingers itched to trace the patterns.

Pushing the door further ajar, I stepped into the bathroom and his head flew up. Alarm faded from his face almost immediately as he registered that it was me. Straightening, he remained still as I closed the distance between us and picked up the needle that was dangling from the thread in his chest. Wiping away some of the blood with a nearby hand towel, I examined the flesh with careful fingers as I closed the wound. I felt his eyes burning into me as I worked, his gaze lingering over my body as I stood there.

'Have you ever stitched anyone up before?' he asked, voice hoarse.

'No, but I figure this is just like Home Ec.'

'Home Ec?'

'Home Economics, where they teach you to sew and shit.'

'And you were good at that?'

'I thought it was a patriarchal construct of a class. Barely scraped by with a C.'

He smiled at that and I cast a quick glance upwards to confirm it.

'This, however, might be my finest work.'

I finished the last stitch, clipping the thread with scissors and tying the excess in a neat knot. In the end, he only needed six stiches, and I cleaned the wound with disinfectant. He didn't even flinch when I knew for a fact it must have been stinging like a motherfucker. Pressing a small adhesive bandage over the area, I noticed that goosebumps had extended across his skin. It gave his tattoos an interesting ripple effect and I couldn't help but follow it upwards with the tips of my fingers. Whatever skin my fingernails ran over, the goosebumps followed and I risked a glance back up at Heath. What I saw in his eyes scared the living shit out of me.

'Why are you here, Tommi?' He asked the question innocently enough, but it was hard to focus as his hands ran up the length of my arms causing their own reaction.

'Because,' I gulped. 'If this is the last night I have, I want to have it with you.'

The words were barely out of my mouth as he leaned forwards, planting a deep kiss on my lips. It was the kind that consumed you, body and soul, and I returned it as I felt the fire in my chest spread to other parts of my body.

My kisses got faster, more desperate, but he was able to keep up as we clutched hungrily at each other. His lips kissed their way from my mouth and down my jawline until he found the weak spot at my neck. I let out a small moan as he made contact and his body responded, his hardness pressed against my stomach. I ripped the towel from his waist and in a second he had my shirt up, over my head, and off. His hands ran over my bare breasts and I knew the moment his mouth covered my nipple that it was over. Gripping the back of his head for dear life as he sucked and licked, I let him push me up on to the basin as he continued to preoccupy himself with my most obvious assets. But Heath was nothing if not a multi-tasker. As his lips softly and sweetly kissed my nipples until they hardened in his mouth, he slid my panties off and down my thighs in one smooth gesture. Breathless, I watched him do it and felt a primal longing. He caught my gaze, his lips returning to mine for a second.

'Do you want this?' he asked, the words barely audible between kisses.

'Yes,' I breathed. 'I want this.'

'Do you want me?'

'I want you, Heath,' I replied, whispering my answer almost directly into his left ear. Lunging upwards, my tongue darted out as I sucked gently on his earlobe and gave him a wee nip. I felt his body shudder against me and I smiled, pleased with the result. The time for play was over and he lifted me to him, my back arching and my head resting against the mirror as Heath parted my legs. He stroked me, sighing with appreciation at how wet I was, how wet I was for *him,* and his touch drove me wild.

Heath filled me in one long, careful movement: cautious at first, to see if I could take all of him. He was holding back. And I wanted everything he had to give. Bracing my hips, my fingernails dug into his ass as I pulled him deeper and he let out a cry. Locked together in the most intimate pose imaginable, I clung to him as we both began to move. I thought he was the only one making noise at first, but I must have been louder than I realised as he covered my mouth with his hand.

'Ssshhh,' he puffed. 'This house is full.'

I parted my lips just enough to suck his index finger and he looked simultaneously furious and pleased with me. His eyes soon fluttered shut as we increased momentum, our bodies moving in sync. My fingernails dug lines down his back as I clawed towards climax and gritted my teeth. My body was dripping with the need to feel every morsel of the man that made Heath who he was, every part of me stretching to absorb him. The sensation was indescribable: that longing and patience and tension finally had an outlet as we gripped each other as tight as we could and tried to stifle our screams. The bed was just on the other side of the door, yet we never made it that far. He took me right there on the basin and then again, once more on the tiled floor.

~

WHEN I WOKE, it was like regaining consciousness inside a dream. You have that hazy sense of everything being better here somehow, yet you know the harsh reality of actual life is one alarm clock tone away. I hadn't thought I would sleep a wink at all the night before the coming of age ritual, but Heath had seen to the opposite. When we'd eventually made it to the bed, there was little time for anything but collapsing into a deep coma. However, I mustn't have slept for more than a few hours, because when I woke it was still dark. Heath was awake, his hands resting behind his head in a relaxed posture as he stared into darkness. His eyes moved in my direction as I lifted my head, brushing hair out of my field of vision as I fully came to. I had been across the other side of the bed, flat on my stomach, and as an almost subconscious gesture he reached out to me. I squirmed over to him, finding a comfortable place wedged between his chest and his biceps as he tucked an arm around my waist.

We were both naked and I felt no shame in it as our limbs wrapped back around each other. Only being in werewolf form felt as natural as this moment did to me right then. Sometimes, no matter how much you like a person, no matter how much you feel for them, your bodies just aren't compatible. Try as you might, you can't reach that place where you know what it's like to feel a deep, honey-burn start inside you until it washes over your limbs like a wave. It prickles down your legs and tingles until you can't feel your toes anymore. Time freezes. Heath and I would never have a problem finding that place, I realised.

'How long until I have to be up?' I murmured, not wanting a real answer.

'An hour and a half.'

My body stiffened as I digested that reality. There was no going back now. No quitting. The time was nearly upon me. He sensed my discomfort, his grip tightening around me as we lay there. I too was staring into the darkness now, captivated by whatever nothingness had kept him awake. With a start, I realised it most likely was a choice: he had stayed awake to make sure nothing like what happened in the laneway would happen again. I felt a pang in my chest with this knowledge. Whether or not I had come to his room last night, Heath would have stayed up and kept guard just to make sure I was safe.

'I'm glad that, if this is my last night, I spent it with you,' I whispered, placing a kiss on his hard chest.

Heath angled himself so he could look at me properly, and I tried to avoid his gaze but he gripped my chin and held me there. Usually there was so much warmth between us, so much humour and laughter, even when things were really bad. There was no joy in his face now as he watched me, his fingers stroking my cheek. His thumb wiped a lone tear from the hollow under my eye and I hated the fear I was showing.

'Only a fool would be unafraid, Tommi. There's no shame in being scared.'

Leaning forward, he kissed me just the once: slow and soft. As he pulled back, I tucked a strand of his golden hair behind his ears. I was trying to pore over every detail of his face, every line and wrinkle and perfect imperfection I'd need to take with me if I was going to make it through today.

'Stop looking at me like I'm going to disappear.' He smiled.

'Aye, it's not you who might disappear.'

'Tom, I know this won't be easy, but you have to know you can surv—'

'Heath,' I snapped, cutting him off.

'Mmm?'

'We have an hour and half, probably an hour and twenty minutes now. I don't want to use those minutes for a pep talk.'

As I leaned back down to kiss him, the wetness of my tears pressed against his cheek. He rolled over until he was on top of me, this time leisurely exploring every part of me the way I had consumed every part of him just hours earlier. It felt like there was no inch of me he didn't claim, but this time the hunger was different. As we built our own castle in between the covers of his bed, I realised what it was. Last night we had fucked each other's brains out. That morning, we made love.

THE ROAD ahead was empty as the black bitumen stretched out like a coarse snake disappearing into even more blackness. The sun wouldn't rise for another few hours yet and I felt sleep tugging at my eyelids. I'd been back in my bedroom and dressing for the day's travel when Aruhe had woken that morning, unaware that I hadn't been sleeping in the bed next to her. She was only concerned with me: how I was and how I was felling after my 'mental vacay' as she called it.

Heath was already outside and waiting for us in the cold when we left the house. A brief yawn was the only clue he hadn't slept a wink. As we filed into one of the cars we'd be using to drive down the North Island, he gave me a flicker of a smile. With a beanie tugged so far down over my face that my eyelashes brushed the edges, I jumped into the passenger seat next to him and Aruhe slid into the backseat. She was dozing within twenty minutes of our journey and I was staring out the window at nothing, just the occasional passing light, while Heath strummed his fingers on the steering wheel to the beat of T. Rex. We were on a winding, narrow stretch when our surrounds seemed to open up around us. The night sky was reflected back in the surface of a massive lake that seemed to span forever and my mind snagged on a memory.

'Are we passing Lake Taupo?'

'Bringing back memories for you?' Heath replied, by way of response.

I sat up a little straighter in my seat as I made out the looming figure of Motutaiko Island off the coastline. It was strange passing this spot – this *exact* spot – where I had come alone, in pain, and with a deep sense of hopelessness. The memories rushed through my mind just like the setting as Lake Taupo passed by the car window in a blur. The physical pain of my first transformations, everything I had suffered, speeding out to the island believing that I wouldn't see morning and Lorcan, with his complicated introduction into my life. I stretched my legs out, resting them on the dashboard and tugged my beanie over my eyes.

'Tommi?' Heath asked, observing my long silence.

'I'm going to sleep,' I mumbled.

～

I awoke some hours later, long after sunrise. We stopped in a tiny town called Hunterville for a toilet break and I took a detour on the way back to the cars as I spotted a butcher. It was early and they had only just opened, but I bought enough prime cuts to have the man beaming over the counter at me.

'Now, miss, you'll have to refrigerate that quickly with all the meat you've got there. I hope you haven't got far to go?'

'Never fear.' I smiled, grabbing my change. 'I guarantee these will be in hungry, happy mouths within the hour.'

'Have a choice day.' He waved as I left the store, swinging the bag of raw meat in one hand. Aruhe was stretching by the car as the bodyguards lingered nearby, watching but trying not to look like they were.

'What's that?' she asked.

'Travelling snack.'

'Oh yum!' She rifled through the bag until I heard a sharp 'Eeek!'

'Tommi, it's raw as!'

'Hey, I'm a medium-rare kinda girl usually but today we're going to need this.'

'Yeah, yeah, I know. I just never liked eating bloody meat except during the—'

'Full moon?'

She smiled. 'Word.'

Heath and I had agreed to swap over, so he could relax while I took on driving duties. I was just about to settle myself behind the steering wheel when I sniffed a delicious scent. I leapt out of the car and laughed with glee as I spotted him walking towards us with three huge coffee cups. From the biggest one – which I knew must be for me – the tang of a long, black coffee was radiating.

'I was pooched but thank the werewolf Lords, you found coffee, Heath Darkiro!' I screamed, sprinting full pace at him. His cheesy grin wavered at my reception, and he held the coffee cup above his head to avoid my grasp.

'GIMME!' I huffed, launching myself at him in a combination of a hug and a straddle. I tried to climb up his frame to reach the cup, but he just held it higher and attempted to swat me away. He leaned forward in a bid to throw me off but I merely clung to his body tighter with my legs. Heath poked me in a particularly ticklish spot on my side and I yelped, letting go. We were both laughing as I took a few steps back, bumping into the hood of the car.

'Now, do you want this coffee?' he asked through puffs.

'And how!' I exclaimed.

'Then play nice.'

I straightened up and placed my hands behind my back. Never one to come off as innocent, I did my best attempt at batting eyelashes. 'Please, Heath, our Fearless Leader of the Caffeinated Army.'

'Very well.' He smirked, handing me the cup.

'OhmigodthankZorggetitinme.' I groaned appreciatively as the dark liquid I needed so badly hit my lips. It had four sugars, exactly how I liked it.

'If I'd known that's all it would take . . .' he whispered, as I playfully kicked the back of his legs, tripping him slightly. I noticed for the first time that we had an audience. Our bodyguards and the PG had all been watching closely as we fooled around, standing there silently and stoically. Ignoring them, I headed to the driver's side and jumped behind the wheel. I cast a look at Aruhe in the rearview mirror and she raised an eyebrow at me as she sipped her own coffee. I quickly diverted my eyes back to the road and started the car, keen to be moving again and away from this awkward situation.

We reached Wellington by early afternoon and drove the cars on to an Interislander ferry. 'Ferry' was actually a deceptive term, because the dang thing looked more like a cruise ship. Any floating transportation that is big enough to have its own movie theatre and a playground inside officially renounces the 'ferry' title. Scottish ferries? Many were barely above sea level and you were lucky if your seat didn't have old gum pressed under it. Now *that* was a ferry.

It was a solid three-hour journey across the Cook Strait to Picton and we all made our way up to one of the cosy indoor passenger decks. Aruhe spread herself out across three seats, with her head resting on my lap. Heath took the seat across from me and dropped a collection of junk food on to the small wooden table beneath us.

'No,' I said, shaking my head.

'Who are you and what have you done with the rogue wolf I used to know? There are three different types of confectionary here that are likely to give you cancer. Your favourite types!'

'Heath, I appreciate it but no.' I glanced around quickly before continuing. 'I just spent the past drive chewing my way through raw and bloody meat. I'm now about to spend the next few hours trying not to hurl as we sit on a giant, sodding boat that will be rocking backwards and forwards in the sea. Oh yeah, and any last-minute nerves I might have about travelling to my death.'

Silence stretched out between us while regular passengers moved around the ferry, chatting and happily oblivious to the fact that this could be my last afternoon. Ever.

'I'm sorry,' I said, rushing an apology as I got up and carefully placing Aruhe's head on the chair instead of my lap. I pushed my way past a gaggle of loud school kids who were milling about by the staircase that led to the outdoor deck at the top of the ship. Pulling open the cabin door, my face was smacked with an ice-cold wind and my ponytail lashed my face like a whip. It felt like relief, like nature slapping me to my senses. There were only two or three people up there, with the chilly conditions too much for most passengers. I steadied myself against the cool metal of the ferry as it rocked with the motion of the sea. There was no one at the back of the boat and I sighed with release as I leaned over the railing. It had stopped raining, but the clouds maintained their hold with the sun unable to sneak through the army of grey and white. It looked like a storm was hovering over Wellington in the distance as I watched it and its surrounding hills get smaller and smaller as we sailed farther away.

This was it. No more stalling. Ahi hikoi was happening, whether I was one hundred per cent prepared for it or not. I found myself staring hard at the turning, twisting white foam trailing behind the ferry as it churned the blue waters on its journey forward. No more running away. No more stupidity. No more immaturity. I had killed people, I had nearly been killed, and I had seen people I loved killed. And here I stood, on the other side of it all with the tang of sea salt on my tongue. I was Tommi Grayson. I was a werewolf. I was the daughter of Tilly Grayson and Jonah Ihi. One of my parents was a wonderful, albeit flawed, woman and the other was a werewolf I'd never know. Both were dead. But I was not alone. I had a half-sister I was actually fond of. I had a best friend who was going to live forever. I had a posse of supernatural pals who were just as terrifying and powerful as I was. It was a comfort to know that if I made it through this, there was still all of that waiting for me on the other side. And then there was Heath.

Two long, lean arms dangled over the railing next to me and I pulled my eyes away from being entranced by the spinning foam. It was him, naturally, and he had relieved Ginger who had been quietly observing me from a few feet back. Watching him perched in a position mirroring my own as he looked out over the ocean expanding between us and the shore, it struck me again how physically intimidating he could be. He was a solid, hulking mass and for the most part – until he put it to good use – he seemed oblivious to it, moving around the rest of us like we were tiny ant people. Last night he had also shown me a gentleness I hadn't expected and hadn't realised I so desperately needed. There was a lot to unpack about him: a lot more than he liked people to know there was.

'Do you think,' I said, after some time, 'that last night, this morning, would have happened if we both weren't terrified about the outcome of ahi hikoi?'

He didn't look at me as he thought about the question, keeping his eyes on the ocean instead.

'I honestly don't know. I haven't thought about it like that.'

My gaze moved from his face to the vast waters, with a few islands popping up in my periphery now. It wasn't too late to just jump off the side of this ferry and swim for it, I thought, looking down at the drop and the chilly ocean waiting for me below.

'And you shouldn't either,' he said.

'Shouldn't what?'

'Think about that. Think about us. It should be the furthest thing from your mind right now. Every bit of your focus should be on making it through this ritual.'

I saw the seriousness in his gaze, the sincerity there, and the genuine concern.

'Please make it through this,' Heath said softly.

He unfolded his body from leaning on the railing until he was at full height. I straightened too, staring directly at him and the knowledge and wisdom that lay behind his eyes. He pulled me towards him and I pressed my face to his chest, savouring the scent of him. I devoured every note and tried to commit the sound of his heartbeat to memory. Gripping me tightly, he absentmindedly stroked my hair as we remained in that position for what felt like an age, inching ever closer to the final destination.

16

Picton was beautiful. It looked like it could have been a seaside village in Greece rather than New Zealand, with its tiny community carved into the bay and protected by massive, green hills. I hoped I'd have more time to explore it later on. For the meantime, I had to settle with the glimpses I was able to get as we left the boat. Driving the cars off the dock, we were forced to brake suddenly as a kid chased his ball bouncing in front of three lanes of traffic. His panicked father was in hot pursuit, jerking the kid back to the sidewalk by his arm while shouting something about 'protecting him' when I felt a drop in my stomach. My head snapped to look at Heath and, sensing my gaze, he peered back at me. A confused frown crossed his features for a moment until I mouthed the word 'protection'.

The Treize had everyone staying at a hotel on the waterfront and on the drive there, Heath took a slight detour, waving the other cars around us and assuring them everything was fine.

'Why are we stopping?' Aruhe asked, as we pulled up to a series of shops.

'I gotta grab aspirin real quick,' I said, sliding out of the car. 'Stress headache.'

'Wait here,' Heath told her, locking the doors behind him as he followed me. Throwing a glance over my shoulder as we entered the pharmacy, he looked as nervous as I felt.

'How the fuck did we forget to use protection?' I hissed. 'I feel like such an idiot.'

'Ease up on yerself, it happens. We got caught up in the moment—'

'There were *a lot* of moments.'

'Aye.' He smiled.

'Heath, I have never had unprotected sex in my life. This shite stresses me out!'

'Well, if it gives you peace of mind I'm perfectly clean and healthy. The PG make us have regular STD check-ups and mine was last month. I haven't been with anyone except y—'

I stopped him, placing my fingertips to his mouth to prevent him from talking as we queued for service.

'I love you for including that information and I will be grateful later, but right now I'm more concerned about whether this pharmacy has MAPs on hand.'

'MAPs?'

'Morning After Pill.'

'God bless this century,' he said, a look of relief washing over his face. 'And that will work? I usually have condoms in my wallet but—'

'Yes, if taken within three days of having unprotected sex.'

'What magic. In my day it was all IUDs made of silkworm and unreliable herbs.'

'I can't speak for the herbs, but IUDs are out. Anything that physically stays in my body would get mangled during transformation. Wait, what did you think I was coming in here for?'

'I had no idea, I was just following you to avoid panicking.'

I laughed, a quick burst, and it ended almost instantly as the chemist asked me what I was after. I told her and she gave Heath a probing look, before her eyes flicked back to me.

'How long has it been?' she asked.

'Uh,' I replied, quickly doing the math in my head, 'twelve hours, give or take.'

'Take these then,' she said, handing me the pack. 'See a doctor if your period is more than a week late.'

'Let's bloody hope not.'

Grabbing a bottle of water as well, I paid and popped the pills right there in the pharmacy.

'Crisis averted?' he asked.

'I'll let you know when I'm riding the crimson wave. On the bright side though, if I die tonight at least I won't have to worry about being pregnant.'

A man gave us a funny look as we made our way out of the store and back to the car, clearly having overheard me. He could cast me strange glances all he wanted, but technically I was right.

'Is motherhood not something you've ever wanted?' Heath asked.

Usually a question like that coming from someone I had slept with in the last twenty-four hours would have me moving interstate and changing my number. But Heath broached the question with an inquisitive tone, as if he was more interested in my answer than impregnating me at the next available opportunity.

'Honestly, I hadn't really thought about it until . . .'

'Until?'

'Kids weren't on my agenda growing up. I figured one day, maybe, sure; with the right person. But that future seemed on the other side of a lot of things I wanted to do first and *very* far off. It's different now.'

'How so?'

'I'm a werewolf, Heath. I know how strong the gene is. It gets passed down no matter what, from either the father or mother. It doesn't matter if only one of your parents has it, the end result is the same. I've never been treated like "half" a werewolf and I haven't seen anyone else treated that way either. But this . . . lycanthropy? It's a curse. I wouldn't wish it upon anyone. The power and the possibilities are hyped up by a lot of people, but there's the pain. Fuck, *such* pain. And all the baggage that comes with it, like what Aruhe and I are about to walk into right now. I couldn't knowingly bring someone into this world when I understand everything they would have to face.'

Heath looked thoughtful as he unlocked the car with a beep of a button, an amused expression dancing on his features.

'What?' I pushed, slipping back into the passenger seat and feeling ten times lighter.

'How old are you?'

'You know how old I am.'

'Aye, twenty-five in two months' time.'

'What does that have to do with it?' I blinked. I thought he'd just say twenty-four, not acknowledge that he knew exactly when my birthday was.

'Nothing.' He smiled. 'Nothing at all.'

'Where's the aspirin?' Aruhe asked.

'Sold out,' Heath replied, quicker than I could formulate a response.

'Got water instead,' I answered, waving the bottle.

She sighed, looking annoyed as she crossed her hands over her chest. The agitation she was feeling was for what was coming: I knew because I felt it too.

'Welp,' she murmured. 'Onwards and upwards then. I guess.'

THEY LEFT Aruhe and I to ourselves in a room so we would have time to shower and get ready. When she returned from the bathroom I was already dressed and doing a once over of my outfit. I checked that I felt as equipped as possible.

We weren't allowed to take weapons in with us and Heath had warned me against trying to sneak any in, adding that we would be searched thoroughly beforehand. That was fine. I could be my own weapon.

In a pair of plain joggers, full-length exercise tights, a thermal T-shirt and a loose hoodie, I was as comfortable as I could be. We didn't know what we would need once we stepped into the woods. I assumed we'd be wolfing out at some point so whatever we were wearing seemed kind of useless. On the flip side, practical clothes that we could fight in seemed like a solid back-up. In a legit eighties' throwback, I was wearing a bum-bag that was stocked with a dozen hydration and energy gels in colourful sachets. We couldn't exactly take a snack pack with us, so this was the next best thing. Aruhe was in a matching olive-green tracksuit, the word Hine splashed across the front in big, white writing. She had snaked my beanie and was wearing it so low that it almost hid the ends of her thick, black hair entirely. I looked at my own hair and made a move to throw it up into a bun when Aruhe grabbed my shoulders and forced me down on to the edge of the bed.

'Here,' she said, hopping behind me on her knees and grabbing a hairbrush. 'I'll braid it for you.'

'Thank you. I didn't know you could.'

'Yeah. Saves you having to do it. It's long as, Tommi.'

'I know, I need to sort that out . . . after.'

'Are you gonna keep the colour? You've got inches of regrowth now and the blue is kinda white.'

'Not sure. I'm usually pretty on it with the dye, but I just haven't found the energy to give a shit lately.'

'You could change it. Go pink?'

'Maybe.'

'Or dark green. Pounamu.'

'Huh.'

A comfortable silence descended as she tugged and pulled my hair into one thick braid that wrapped around the left side of my head and a thinner one on my right. They joined into an impressive plait at the base of my neck. This would be the last time Aruhe and I would be alone before the coming of age. In under an hour we would be surrounded by the Ihi pack as they completed the final preparations. And then we'd be on our own.

'Are you nervous?' she asked, as if reading my thoughts.

I thought about that, long and hard. No point in lying.

'Yes. It feels like there's a pack of pterodactyls swarming in my tummy.'

She laughed, a burst of uneasy energy. 'Me too. I just want this to be over already.'

The second I felt her twist the hairband around the end of my plait I turned to face her.

'It will be. It's gonna be tough, we know that. I know there's a lot of people who think we can't do this. That's useful. Let them underestimate us.'

I leaned forward, holding her in a deep hug. She returned it, resting her head on my shoulder in a subtle gesture. Someone cleared their throat at the door and we let go to see Heath patiently standing there. It soothed something deep inside me to see his silhouette in the doorway.

'Hey, Heath!' said Aruhe, almost excitedly.

'Pup. You girls ready?'

We looked at each other for a quick moment, with Aruhe giving the smallest 'here goes nothing' shrug of her shoulders.

'Fuck yes,' I replied, both getting to our feet.

The drive was short and striking. I had headphones on and was listening to Pharoahe Monch to get myself 'in the zone' or whatever professional athletes called it. Aruhe and I were in the backseat of the car, with one of the bodyguards wedged between us and Heath driving. The sacred, protected grounds used solely for werewolf packs' coming of age rituals were rushing past the window as the light slowly faded. The ground was invisible beneath branches of dead trees that were so grey they almost appeared white. Thousands upon thousands of them stretched out as far as the eye could see, with their dry branches reaching up towards the sky like ghostly hands. The plain was bordered by the road on one side and surrounded by thick, dark forest from every other angle. The trees were so massive and so close together they seemed to block out all light from penetrating the forest floor. The tree trunks were indistinguishable from the black forest inside. It was foreboding.

We pulled off the main road and down a barely visible route that saw dirt flying up from beneath the tyres as we sped along it. There were two men waiting at a large metal gate that had the words 'STRICTLY NO ENTRY: PRIVATE PROPERTY' emblazoned across the front of it. There was a long fence spanning in either direction and wrapped in barbed wire for added effect. They nodded at us as we passed through, parking among a group of two dozen or so other vehicles.

'All this for us; it's kinda nice,' I said, trying to quash my nerves.

Aruhe said nothing: she'd seen this before; she'd been here before and watched her family members do the same thing we were about to attempt.

Wehi was dressed in traditional garb and waiting for us under an old, wooden archway. He flicked water on Aruhe and me as we passed through. Keisha was standing by his side and gave me a wink. Besides a large, greenstone tiki hanging at her neck, she was dressed in standard clothing. There were three children no older than eight by her side and they ran along next to my sister and me excitedly.

'Aruhe, Aruhe!' chanted the oldest, a boy.

She subtly waved before telling him to scoot off, 'ya egg'. Heath stuck close to us as we walked over to where a large gathering of people had assembled. The remainder of the bodyguards trailed behind and spread out as discreetly as they could among the Ihi pack. It turned out Wehi was the only person in the entire family who had felt the need to dress up as the others were in jumpers and cargo pants and scarves and jackets and boots: practical clothing for the weather conditions. Tiaki Ihi was sitting on a log as far from us as she could. Despite being in front of a fire, she had her arms wrapped around herself as if she was cold. Keisha joined her and they exchanged a few brief words. Simon came over to greet us officially. I noticed how James came with him and they stood together side-by-side, presenting a united front.

'Welcome,' said Simon.

I nodded while Aruhe mumbled something that sounded vaguely like 'thank you' and held her head high. If she was as nervous as I was, it wasn't showing.

'It's good to see you,' said James, sincerity dripping from his words and expression. 'Both of you.'

'As much as I'd like to say the same, given the circumstances . . .' I trailed off.

He smiled, understanding. 'Do you want to have a seat? There are only two things left to do before we get underway.'

Aruhe and I were made to sit on separate sides of the fire so as not to mix werewolf auras or something, I wasn't clear on the specifics. There were five songs sung by the crowd of people while Wehi chanted under his breath. I bit my tongue to try and repress my nervous energy when I caught Heath's expression from across the other side of the group. He quickly looked away and I saw the faintest smile tugging at his lips. When Simon extended a hand to me, I looked at it suspiciously, but eventually took it. He pulled me to my feet and I glanced around the group, who had now fallen silent after the series of songs.

'What now?' I asked.

'Moko.'

My hands automatically went to my face as I traced the smooth, un-tattooed skin there. Simon actually chuckled at the panicked look I must have expressed. James saw the exchange between us and rushed over.

'No, not on your face, Tommi. You will only have three arrows tattooed on the side of your hand, like this.'

James held out his own so I could inspect the markings.

They looked less like arrows and more like three small Vs spaced out along the base of the index finger. The skin was slightly raised there where the flesh had healed from being chiselled away. Aruhe had known this was coming and she looked somewhat comfortable with the idea. I tried to mimic her calmness as I shrugged. Tattoos were natural to me.

A massive bull of a man made his way towards us with a tray of utensils that made me gulp.

'Aruhe should go first,' I said, concerned that if I made it look too painful she'd feel worse about the whole thing.

She smiled bravely and sat down, unnecessarily pulling up the sleeve of her tracksuit. I joined her for moral support. I knew how it worked: one man chiselled away the skin in the shape of the tattoo while the other injected the ink into the wound. It was not a pleasant process and Aruhe was doing her best to not look at the equipment.

'This your first tattoo?' I asked.

She nodded. 'How many is this for you?'

'Fourth.'

'The arrows are to let the spirits know the direction you're heading,' said Tiaki, taking a seat on Aruhe's other side. It was the closest I had seen mother and daughter get to each other since we arrived. 'It's a good luck omen too, so they know you're passing through and they're not tempted to keep you.'

'Wahoo,' I joked.

'You ready?' asked the butch man, chisel and needle hovering over Aruhe's brown skin. She nodded. And so it began. She was doing well, biting her lip and staying quiet for the first two minutes or so.

'Ow,' she whispered, finally cracking.

When the man told her she was done, Aruhe jumped up

from the chair looking relieved and sore. There were tears resting in the hollows under her eyes that threatened to dribble over her cheeks and she quickly wiped them. Trading places, I squeezed her thigh as she sat next to me.

'You did good.'

She was examining the three marks closely and smiled at me.

'Next time we'll get you something cute with it too, like a butterfly.'

Aruhe grinned. 'I wouldn't mind that.'

I scrunched up my nose. 'It's not very metal.'

'Oy, you ready for this sis?'

I met the look of my would-be tattooer. 'Make it quick, please.'

Less than ten minutes later, I was looking down at the angry red skin of my own hand. A slither of blood was oozing from one of the cuts and I wiped it away. Our accelerated werewolf healing would see these scabbing over in a matter of hours. Soon Aruhe and I were standing at the edge of the woods, facing in separate directions. It was almost time. The sun was minutes from setting completely and the shadows had grown long. The entire Ihi clan was gathered behind us a hundred metres away, clustered in a group as they waited for the ritual to begin. I cast a look back, not to them, but to Heath who was standing at the front of the pack with his arms crossed, Ginger on his left. Most of the people there were chatting among themselves and if any of them were looking at anyone, it was at Aruhe. She was their daughter. I was just an inconvenient tourist. But Heath's eyes were focused on me. I met his expression. For once he didn't look amused. He didn't wink or smirk at me. He simmered, offering only the slightest head nod. It was the biggest sign of support he could offer in the present company. I returned it.

Simon came to stand beside me, while James joined Aruhe.

'You ready?' he asked.

'I'm getting rather sick of people asking me that,' I huffed.

He chuckled. 'I know, I'm sorry. I remember how nervous I was before mine and people kept driving me insane with well-wishes.'

'You've done this. Any tips?'

'Don't die,' he replied, straight-faced.

'Gee, that's helpful.'

He sighed. 'Listen, I'm sorry.'

I looked at him to see if he genuinely meant it. He did.

'The past few years haven't been easy, for me or the pack. From the moment Jonah died, it just seemed like everything got insane. I know you were surprised to see me in Berlin and believe me, you were the last person I thought Aruhe would run to. We're her family and I thought she'd come to us first.'

'Hey, I was surprised to see Aruhe in Berlin too, and she was surprised to see me, it was a surprise mecca all around.'

'I want to apologise. I know we haven't been the easiest people to deal with over the past few weeks. I don't blame you for Steven and Quaid, I truly don't. But they were also my brothers, not blood b—'

'I know.'

'They're gone forever to me now. Leadership, being a pack leader, it seems to come naturally to you, but this was never my design. My mum is more of a people person anyway. I . . .' He took a deep sigh then. 'When this over, if—'

'I survive?' I offered and he looked grave as he nodded. 'I know my odds are fifty-fifty at best.'

'*If* you survive,' he repeated, mirroring my own words. 'I want the possibility that we could work together. More than just polite smiles over coffee and negotiations. Is asking to be friends too much?'

'Asking for me to be alive might be too much,' I chuckled, nervously. 'No, I think it would be just enough. I think that would be great. For me, it was always James and you that showed the most kindness in an otherwise unkind shit storm. To see how you two are trying to work together and lead, it gives me hope, Simon. I want to believe you guys can do it. I also want to believe we can move past everything and if friendship is what waits on the other side, then that would be great.'

'Really?' he asked, seeming surprised by my admission.

'Really. I know how much has happened since the day we first met; blows and barbs have been exchanged, but I'm willing to move past it if you are.'

'I am.'

'Good.'

'I'm trying to do the best I can with this pack, and that means we're not always going to see eye-to-eye, but I am trying. We both are.'

'Everyone's a hero in their story.'

'Maybe you can be part of our story.'

I frowned, catching the hidden meaning in his words. 'Part of that story or part of the pack?'

'I guess the coming of age will decide that for us,' he said, with a sly smile.

I opened my mouth to say something more, but this wasn't the time. I needed to have my head in the game and not be concerned about the Ihi pack's ulterior motives for getting me in this spot. I filed away the thought for later.

'I'm glad we had this opportunity to talk.'

'Aye, before my forthcoming death.'

'Sure,' he said, smirking. 'I have to go. The Treize won't be able to pull any shit when you're in there. It's my job to make sure they don't try to pull anything out here.'

Something must have crossed my face as he hesitated, looking at me closely.

'What?' he asked.

'Nothing,' I answered, shaking my head.

'Something happened . . . didn't it?' He let out an angry breath that almost sounded like a laugh. 'I warned you, I knew you had a target on your back. I knew they would do this.'

'Hey,' I said, gripping his forearm. 'This isn't a conversation for now. Point is, they failed, and I'm fine. Heath and I took care of it.'

'*Heath.*' The way he said his name surprised me. There was something in it, something about the tone . . .

'If I survive this, we can both fill you in,' I said, trying to stay focused but the fingers of my mind just grazing at the thread of something. 'In the meantime—'

I jerked my head at the dark forest for emphasis.

He nodded, getting my message. 'Wehi will announce when it begins. Here. You need to chew this then spit it out.'

I looked suspiciously at what appeared to be green mushrooms resting in the palm of his hand.

'Calm down, you don't have to smoke a hallucinogenic herb. This just helps you go into an enhanced state.'

'Goodie,' I said, placing them in my mouth and crunching. He was only a few steps away when I hesitated, calling out his name. 'Simon, if I don't . . . will you look after Aruhe if she ends up on her own?'

'We're family. She'll never be alone, I promise.'

'Thank you.'

'Kia ora.'

'Kia ora.'

Faint drumming began from the gathered crowd and I returned to stare at the black forest before me. As instructed, I spat out the herbs with a thought that this was as close as I would probably ever get to experimenting with hard drugs. Wehi's voice spoke up behind us, but I didn't watch him. Instead I kept my eyes focused on the destination in front of me.

'Aruhe Ihi and Tommi Grayson. On this night of the blue moon you will both begin the coming of age rituals sacred to our kind. Werewolves the world over have done what you're about to attempt and will continue to do so for decades after you. Your journey will start here and the path is unknown, but you must have faith to continue the course. If you survive until sunrise tomorrow, you will have passed the ancient test of all werewolf people. Turn your face to the sun and the shadows will fall behind you.'

The drumming intensified and a soft chorus began as the witnesses started singing a traditional song under their breath. This was it. No chance to turn back now. Time to woman up.

'Begin.'

17

I should have shifted by now. That's all I could keep thinking as I walked further and further into the darkness of the woods. I should have shifted by now. It was completely black by this point, and although the tree branches were thick enough to block out the night sky, I knew the moon would be sitting high and pretty among the stars. I could feel the urge to change pulsing beneath my skin, which was usually all it took – sometimes less. So why hadn't I shifted?

The moon was full and inescapable yet somehow I had walked into what could only be described as a werewolf dead zone. It's like my inner wolf was getting no reception on the grounds of ahi hikoi. What else could I do but keep walking?

Aruhe and I had been sent in opposite directions and given no other instructions except keep moving. That's what I did. I walked, and I walked, and I walked for what felt like hours but could have very well been minutes. I had no concept of time in this place.

I downed three of the energy gels I'd brought, counting

the number that was left. They tasted like scented mois-turiser. Every tree trunk I passed looked the same, every log I stepped over identical to the last, every twig sounded similar as it snapped beneath my feet. I was just alone and walking through this long, infinite, black wood.

There was a wolf howl in the distance and I halted, spinning on the spot to try and evaluate where the sound came from. Nothing. It quickly faded and I was left in silence again. I had no idea where it had come from because it sounded like it appeared from all around me. A second howl confirmed it, the noise like an invisible swarm of bugs as it echoed and pinged off the forest. A third howl sounded closer, much closer, and I searched for the source of the cries. A fourth cry, then a fifth, and then suddenly they were non-stop.

My werewolf hearing intensified the sound as howl after howl cried out through the night, so loud that I dropped to my knees and attempted to cover my ears. It didn't seem to work, nothing could drown out the sound. My eyes twitched at the volume as the howls overlapped each other until it was an impenetrable wall of noise. I had to get away from the racket.

I turned to sprint and tripped over a massive log I hadn't seen. I struggled on all fours before I picked myself up and wiped my hands free of the dirt that had lodged on them – and ran. It seemed the faster I sprinted the louder the noises got, but I didn't stop, I couldn't. Focusing on what was in front of me I increased my speed as I dodged tree trunks and jumped logs as they appeared.

The forest was getting thicker as branches lashed at me, scratching my face and body. They tore at my clothes and my jumper until I realised they weren't actually branches, but hands. Thin, black, spindly digits were stretching from the trees and trying to grab onto me. I yelped, smacking them away and attempted to run faster. It felt impossible, with the trees growing closer and closer together the further I ran.

A hand caught a firm grip of my hoodie and tried to drag me down. I shrugged out of the jumper and sprinted away. The spaces between the massive tree trunks was tiny now as I oushed uphill. The howls seemed to be right on my neck as I squeezed between the trees in a desperate bid to escape them. The harsh bark tore at my shirt and I felt the skin along my stomach graze as I pushed through the gap.

It was the last space I was able to make it through as I was suddenly faced with an impenetrable wall of wood. I tried to go back, but the gaps between the trees were quickly closing and I was too late. I rushed along, trying to find a way out of the coffin I was trapped in, banging on the wood and pounding to find a weakness. It was impenetrable, just like the wall of howls, and I dropped to my knees again as the sound became insufferable. Covering my ears had no effect, but I did it anyway in a bid to protect my head and myself as I curled into the smallest ball I could manage.

Over time the noise receded, decibel by decibel, until my ears were left ringing. I lifted my head, drawing my body up into a sitting position and was shocked to find myself in some kind of hut. The wooden wall of trees now made up the arching roof of the structure, which had a small circle cut out in the middle of it. I could see the clear night sky through it, with stars twinkling against the inky blue background.

A fire in the middle of the space spontaneously roared to life and I leapt back. Red and orange flames licked the air as smoke poured through the opening in the roof and into the evening. A low growl came from the other side of the fire and I looked closely through the flames.

I saw two red, glowing eyes emerge from the darkness as an enormous black wolf slowly crept forward. There were no entries or exits to the enclosed space that I was sitting in. Yet I was not afraid. I was a wolf. Other wolves did not frighten me. The creature carefully paced around the flames, never once taking its eyes off me. As it came to a halt inches from my own face, it was obvious from its size that this was a werewolf. There was a person behind those ruby eyes that seemed to penetrate my soul. A voice rang out and although its snout didn't move, I was certain the words were coming from the wolf.

'You are a murderer,' it said.

I had no response. I had murdered people. In self-defence and in the heat of battle, sure, but dead was dead. I felt there was little justification I could offer a mystical, telepathic werewolf. So, I said nothing.

'A murderer is condemned to death,' it continued, eyes moving over me as if it was reading my very thoughts. 'You have three options.'

Somehow I didn't think 'no, nope, and hell no' would be classified as suitable options.

'You can choose to meet your end in one of three rooms. The first room is full of raging fire.'

As if to prove a point, the flames intensified in heat and height as the existing space mimicked the inferno I could be stepping into.

'The second room is full of the fiercest warriors who have ever lived. They are waiting to reclaim your soul.'

I gulped.

'The third room is full of werewolves that haven't eaten in two years.'

'There's no . . . uh, option D?' I asked.

The wolf growled by way of response, revealing a set of pristine white fangs dripping with saliva.

'You must choose.'

'Okay, okay,' I whispered, sweat forming on the back of my neck as I tried to make a decision. Fire was out. I couldn't think of a more painful and agonising death. As for the room of warriors, if I was sentenced to die I would like those who loved me to know I didn't go down without a fight. I would be going to my death, certainly. As for the ravenous werewolves, perhaps I would have time to shift? Could I assert my dominance before they attempted to tear me apart? After all, human flesh would be irresistible to any beast if it hadn't eaten for . . . wait. No creature could survive two years without food. Nothing could. It was a trick.

'The wolves,' I said, speaking up. 'I choose the room full of wolves.'

'You do not get a second choice,' replied the beast.

'The wolves,' I repeated, trying to sound confident.

Within a split second the fire and the wolf disappeared and I was once more plunged into darkness. I opened my eyes, worried about what I would see next. The hut had vanished too, and I was now crouched in an open field of ash. No, not just ash: ash and skeletons. The bones of hundreds of wolves surrounded me everywhere I looked. Standing up, I tried to spin around but all I could see was skeleton upon skeleton.

So, this is what it looks like if you haven't eaten for two years, I thought.

There was a faint grey light coming from somewhere and it illuminated the bones. A light breeze blew the ash over the fragments as if it were sand and I tried to inch forward. There was a rough crack beneath my foot and I realised I had crushed a skull with my step. I paused, reversing my movements so I was exactly where I started. Swivelling on the spot, I could see there was no escape. This was a field of corpses and I was stuck at the centre of it.

'Bleak, isn't it?'

'Yeesh, that's an understatement,' I muttered, brushing more ash off a bone to expose what had once been the spine.

'You'll end up here one day.'

'Inevitably.'

'You're tied to them now, all werewolves past and present. I guess that's my fault.'

'It's no one's fault, ma,' I muttered. 'Mum?'

For the first time in the conversation, I realised who I had been subconsciously talking to. My mother. My dead mother was standing before me, except she wasn't really standing. She wasn't floating or hovering or even walking. She just was. The last time I had seen her she was lying on a cold, silver slab in the Edinburgh morgue. Her body had been black and blue and bloated from drowning in the flash flood that had swept her car off the road.

Here though, projected before me, she looked just as she always looked. She was even wearing one of her favourite outfits: a pair of dress jeans with this pink, knitted sweater that had tiny costume jewels sewn into the cuffs. My mother loved pink.

'Is it you, ma? Is this actually your ghost or . . . or is it them?'

She smiled and shrugged. 'I can't tell you that, dear.'

'No. Of course you can't.'

I drank her in, every inch of the woman I missed so much every day that I had just gotten used to living with the gaping hole she had once filled. Even her hair – which she

always wore out no matter what activity she was doing –
appeared the way it usually did, the tips brushing her shoulders as it swayed in the breeze.

My mother and I actually didn't look that much alike. I
had her chin and a certain way that I carried myself, but
everything else had been inherited from my father's genes,
including his dark brown, almost black hair. My mother's
locks were a natural honey-blonde colour that, growing up,
I'd envied until I was able to convince her to take me to the
hairdresser when I was fourteen. I'd begged her for months
to let me get highlights and she finally relented, saying that I
could get 'foils and foils only, young lady'.

The result was hideous, with what I had envisioned as
light streaks through my hair like J.Lo looking more like
yellow skunk tracks when the hairdresser was done. I'd
been so upset, I wore a hat for two months and tried to hide
the disaster with braids. My mum had told me it was just
hair, that I shouldn't get so caught up about it, and she
would love me no matter what my locks looked like. That
was a good thing, because just over a year later I came home
with blue hair after spending the night at Joss' and getting
him to help me do it.

'You're not one of them, you know,' she said, snapping
me out of my memories. 'You're not one of the Ihi pack.'

'No,' I replied, my smile dropping. 'But I'm not exactly
just a Grayson, am I?'

'You'll have to choose, one or the other.'

'Why?'

'It's just the way it is, Tommi.'

'No.'

'What do you mean "*No*"? Listen to me when I talk to
you, I'm your mother!'

'You're not my mother.'

'Excuse me?'

'You heard me. You dress like my mother, you look like my mother, you're my projection of the physical version of my mother. But you are not her.'

My mother, or the spirit that was pretending to be her, smiled. That smile grew wider until she was laughing a deep, rumbling laugh. 'What gave it away?' she asked.

'Everything,' I replied.

'Fine. You still have to choose though.'

'No. I do not.'

'And what makes you different?'

'All of it. I can't choose to be a Grayson and I can't choose to be an Ihi, because I'm neither and I'm both. I'm not defined by one bloodline. I define myself.'

The spirit continued smiling at me. 'Very well.'

My mother sprinted at me then, catching me off-guard as she launched herself through the air and we toppled to the ground. I felt a blow connect to my side and knew without even having to hear the crack that at least one, maybe two, of my ribs had broken. Trying to push past the pain, I watched as her head morphed entirely into a wolf's, looking monstrous as it sat atop her body.

Her jaws gnashed at me as she attempted to rip my throat out. It took all my strength to hold her at arm's length and to keep her away from my neck. Her teeth were piercing my skin, but as long as I kept the bites away from anywhere vital, I figured I could survive this. My inner wolf was itching to emerge for the first time that evening and I craved the release. My hands were gripping the forearms of the thing that was my mother and they shifted into full were-wolf claws, ripping her skin as they elongated into deadly limbs.

With a triumphant grunt I threw her off, launching her

backwards through the air until she crashed on to a pile of wolf bones, sending ashes flying up around her in a smoky cloud. I sprang to my feet, wasting no time as I ripped my own clothes off so I could phase freely.

'Enough of this,' I hissed, kicking my shoes free.

Shaking my arms, I let out my own growl as I huffed with the concentration needed to bring on the transformation. It came easily to me, my wolf relishing the opportunity to be released on one of the few nights it owned each month. My muscles made a snapping sound as my bones popped in and out of place. My skin stretched and tore as the beast within me punctured through, demanding its freedom.

My side screamed as my injury ripped apart and then back together. The spirit of my mother had shifted completely too and she wasn't alone. A whole pack of werewolves were now surrounding me. My focus was solely on her as I sprinted headfirst at the creature. My teeth sank into her grey fur and she let out a pained howl as I pulled her down beneath my paws. She lashed at me wildly, but I ignored the cuts her claws inflicted. I wanted this creature gone, out of the skin and memory of my mother. She squirmed free but I pounced on her rear, dragging her back.

The other wolves did nothing, just watched as the scene played out. They barked and howled as I asserted my dominance, finally sinking my teeth into the juicy artery near her neck. Yet instead of delivering the killing blow, I paused my bite. It took incredible self-control to keep my fangs hovering only millimetres away from death. The wolf under me was whimpering, pleading, and I held her there for several long moments. I saw her close her eyes as she prepared for the end. Judging from the silence that penetrated the pack, they were shocked as I released her. She was stunned too, whining into a position of submission before me. With her eyes downcast, blood leaked from several wounds as I growled at her one more time.

Her form shifted then, rapidly getting smaller and smaller and smaller until it was a tiny injured wolf pup sitting before me. I reached out to stroke it, surprised to find my arm had shifted back to human form without me even noticing. I stared at the scratched, bleeding, brown skin in front of me with shock as I wiggled my fingers. The puppy yelped, directing my attention back to its hurt form.

'Oh, hey there, wee fella,' I whispered, scooping up the animal in my arms. I stood to my full height, patting the puppy as I moved, and noticed that I was completely naked. The wolf cub's tongue leapt out from its mouth as it licked my chin and I giggled at the sensation. It was then that I became aware I was being watched.

As I spun around, the dozens of wolves that had witnessed the fight had become a crowd of Māori men, women and children. They were all watching me, holding everything from spears to each other's hands. My nakedness didn't seem to bother them, and I barely even registered it as my eyes swept the faces of people who were unmistakably my ancestors. Yet they weren't alone: they made up only the first line of beings surrounding me. The longer I looked, the more the faces changed.

These others weren't related to me genetically, they couldn't be: they were every age, every gender, every body type, and every race spanning an endless sea of bodies before me. There were some with skin so white it looked like flour, others with illuminated blue eyes, and a man with a shock of red hair that perfectly matched the freckles on his skin. Werewolves. These were the werewolves that had come before me from every country and time period my puny mind could perceive. I felt their presence weigh heavy on my soul as I stood there, floored, for a long time. The puppy continued to snuggle into my body as I muttered the words: 'What now?'

A man who I guessed was in his mid-forties broke the line and stepped out of the group. His chest was broad and muscular, his face deeply lined with wrinkles that seemed to speak more of a wisdom than of years.

'These are your people,' he said.

I bit my tongue as I resisted the urge to say 'no shit'. Sarcasm wouldn't help anyone here.

'Not just the Ihi pack. All the tribes, every generation, every pack, every werewolf is here before you. We are one, you see.'

I looked around the group – this time *really* looked – and picked up more of the obvious differences, the varying shades of skin and plethora of shapes. Yet they all had one unmistakable trait I shared: a defiant look in their eyes.

'You can access the power of all of us, if you want to. If you need it, there are generations behind you to help you lead.'

'Lead what?' I asked.

He fell silent and said nothing, gesturing that I should follow him. I did. The bones of starved werewolves were nothing but twigs that cracked beneath our feet now. I looked behind me to see the people were following behind us silently, moving as one. The wolf cub in my arms was now fast asleep, its tongue lolling adorably from its mouth. We walked for what seemed like ages. Unlike before when I was uncertain whether time was a trick of my mind, I had a feeling that this was genuine perception. Even my legs ached as we pressed on in silence.

'To lead is to be alone,' said the man as we moved slowly

up a hill. 'It will be lonely, and you will be alone. But you must remember: you are not.'

He came to a sudden halt and I paused with him.

'You must remember us, Tommi Grayson. A leader is nothing without their pack. You have chosen not to be one or the other. You are kathurungi, but you also are not.'

'Wherever you go, there you are,' I whispered, only half-joking.

He didn't seem to hear me.

'We leave you now. You must go on alone.'

'Goodbye.'

'Remember us.'

I looked at his deep, dark eyes as he spoke. I said nothing, but he seemed to understand that I wouldn't be leaving behind their memory anytime soon. He extended his arms and I handed him the wolf pup, reluctant at first, but understanding that I was going somewhere it could not follow. It didn't wake from its slumber.

I picked my way through the black forest alone, this time not afraid of the darkness but embracing it. The faint sound of the branches and leaves rustling in the breeze was my only company and I didn't mind it. My thoughts felt like they were my own, yet with each step I took something foreign seemed to seep into my brain. My body continued to move forward, limping, but my vision was overcome with a scene that was entirely different to the place I knew I was in.

It was Wehi and he was painting swirling symbols in black ink on an enormous piece of hardboard. He looked calm and relaxed, sitting in some kind of workshop with half-finished carvings and tools laying around him. There were sketches hanging on the walls of work to be completed, with notes jotted in the margins. Somehow, I knew those carvings would remain unfinished. This was

Jonah's space and Wehi was among the artefacts of a man who was no longer there.

He was also entirely oblivious to the dark figure that was standing a few inches behind him. His body stiffened as he became aware of the presence, which I now recognised to be a ghost. I watched as Wehi turned to face the broad figure and they began conversing. The words came out silent and I tried to read the tribal elder's lips, missing most of it but able to distinguish the phrase Wehi repeated back at the man with a surprised expression: 'She's here?'

They exchanged a few more sentences before the ghost faded before me. Wehi sat by himself for several long moments before getting up and grabbing a small piece of paper from a pile as he sat down in front of the workshop's lone computer. He typed away, surprising me with his competence on the technological device. He paused and looked at the screen before him: it was an address; an address I recognised. Slowly he wrote down the URL for the *White Pages* website onto the paper, pausing as he waited for the ink to dry.

My breath caught in my throat as I recognised the font, the paper, the everything. The whole scene dissolved like the ghost and I wanted it desperately to stay. But my mind was mine once more.

The forest path blocked by a figure I hadn't noticed. An older woman was staring intently at me. A dark curtain of hair seemed to pour from her scalp and descend the length of her body in frizzy waves. She was draped in animal furs and sitting atop what could only be described as a throne of some description. She held her head high, with dignity and authority. It was then that I knew without any doubt that she was a great leader of our people. A queen.

'This is your last test, Tommi Grayson,' she said, her

voice booming through the space between us. I nodded, readying my body as I prepared to fight her or whatever invisible forces she had lying in wait. Instead, she just continued to talk.

'I can be half without getting thinner. I can shine with no fire. I can be hidden but never taken. I can stay dry while moving the ocean.'

'A riddle?' I questioned.

She ignored me and asked her own. 'What am I?'

Great. A riddle. I wasn't Edward fucking Ngyma. I was consistently terrible at riddles and had no patience for puzzles. But this wasn't maths, this was my personal quest. If I was being asked to solve a riddle, the answer would be something relevant to *me*. My only child mantra was finally coming into play. Half without getting thinner could be a piece of paper, folded, but it couldn't shine, and it definitely couldn't stay dry while moving the ocean. The wind? The wind could move the ocean, you could hide from it indoors, but the first two descriptors didn't fit.

'Ouch!' I yelped, clutching my chest as it was slashed with a silver blade. The man wielding it leapt back into the shadows and I glared at him. Not the subtlest way to tell me to hurry up. I grabbed my collarbone, feeling the fluid seep through my fingers, which were already covered in other small cuts and abrasions. This was a deeper wound though, and I applied as much pressure as I could. I was struck again, this time on my calf and by another man I hadn't seen.

'Give me a minute!' I screeched, trying to ignore the pain as another wound was opened up on my back. Death by a thousand cuts, unless I could solve this. A fourth cut was inflicted on my left wrist, dangerously close to the vein, and it struck me for the first time that I was going to be killed if I couldn't solve this. I clutched at the cut, trying to stem the blood flow that streaked towards my crescent moon tattoo. As I bled over the black spherical shape, my mind snagged on the obvious right in front of me.

'Half without getting thinner . . . something that shines without a fire,' I mumbled, trying to maintain my focus and not be overcome by fear. 'Hidden but never taken . . .'

There was nothing more relevant or powerful to me than the moon. As a werewolf and a woman, it controlled two of the most important phases of my life. Another man appeared from the blackness and came at me with a blade, this time heading for a spot I would be less likely to recover from: my heart.

'THE MOON!' I shouted, seconds before he made contact. His weapon hovered just inches from my olive, sweaty skin. My chest was rising and falling rapidly.

'The moon is half without getting thinner. It shines without fire *and* can be hidden by clouds or the earth. It moves the ocean tides. It's the moon,' I repeated.

The woman nodded, once, solemnly, before getting up from her throne and walking towards me. I involuntarily flinched, worried that I was wrong and she was there to deliver a final cut. Instead she held out her hand to me, slowly unfurling her finger to reveal a necklace sitting on her palm. It was a complicated symbol that resembled a dagger made out of a beautiful, luminescent greenstone. A single black cord was tied around it. I took the necklace without a word, slipping it over my head and ignoring the pangs of my various injuries.

'This is the messenger between the gods and the mortals,' she said. 'It will protect you against evil.'

'Then it's going to be a busy little token,' I replied.

She smiled, before walking past me and back in the

direction of the ancient tribes. The men with blades trailed after her, not giving me a second look. I was surprised that she was leaving and I turned to watch her go as her furs dragged behind her like a bridal train over the forest floor.

'Hey! You just gonna cut and run?' I shouted. 'Where are you going?'

She ignored me, not even looking behind her.

'HEY! What the hell am I supposed to do now? Hey!'

I dropped to my knees, exhausted and entirely spent of all hope. My body issued a whimper that sounded unlike myself, but as warm tears dripped on to my cheeks I knew where it had come from. Everything hurt. Injuries that I had tried to put away and push through came surging to the front of my consciousness: the cuts, the broken ribs, the bites, the blood loss. I crouched down, protecting myself for a while until I heard a lone bird whistle.

Strange. I hadn't heard any wildlife this entire time and I looked up to track the sound. It was then that I noticed the forest was no longer black, but a slightly lighter shade. I watched it for several more long moments as the tree trunks continued to grow paler and paler. The sun was rising. I had survived. I had no idea where I was, but there seemed to be only one way to go and that was in the opposite direction of the spirits.

Stumbling to my feet, I sniffed and inched down the slight slope I was at the top of. For the first time I realised I was thirsty and starving, my bum-bag having been ripped from me hours earlier – or was it days? I gripped my bleeding wrist as I ploughed on, walking in the direction I hoped was right.

'Hey, where are you going, girl?'

A figure materialised in front of me and I recognised it immediately as a ghost. Although pale and made up of blue hues just like Seamus had been, this one was an adult male with long, luscious hair. I limped past him, ignoring his questions as he continued to chatter with me.

'Naw, don't be like that, sis. Come, stay a while. Doesn't even have to be long, just slow yourself down a bit.'

I was moving pretty fast, probably faster than I should have been with the injuries I was sporting. I did slow, just a little, and he seemed pleased with that. Another ghost joined him, this time a woman.

'Oh, you are *wild*. What's your name?'

'Tommi,' I grunted.

'Tommi! Well, that's original. Say, there was someone looking for a Tommi, wasn't there? Who was that?'

'A Mari,' replied the man.

'Mari?' I questioned, coming to a halt. 'Where? Where is she?'

'I know, I know,' supplied a third ghost, a child not much younger than twelve. 'She's back where you came from.'

'Scotland?'

'No, silly,' the kid giggled. 'There.'

I spun, following the direction she pointed until I was facing the dark forest I had just stumbled from.

'That's where ... I just came from there.'

'That's where she is, her and a guy she hangs with,' the woman answered. 'Come on, it will just be a quick visit.'

'I'll show you the way,' the man replied.

'You can come right back here and bleed,' the child agreed.

It felt as if there was a physical cavity opening up in my chest as I thought of Mari, thought about how much I would give literally just to see her roll her eyes and laugh at one of my jokes. Heck, I'd happily give up a few digits just to chat shite over a plate of her spaghetti bolognaise. The last

time I saw her flashed into my memory: me trying desperately to stop the flow pouring from the artery at her neck
and staring at the ribbons of torn flesh. The fear in her eyes
and the bubbles of blood forming at the corners of her
mouth . . . I could hear a murmur of voices not too far away,
probably just on the other side of the trees. I was almost
back to where I started the coming of age ritual, what was
another few minutes? Everything would be over with soon.

'Come on.' The woman smiled, extending her hand until
I felt a physical tug against my own. Huh, I didn't know
ghosts could do that. I took a step in her direction, nodding
to myself. Another step followed and soon I was trailing
after them, inching away from what was likely the end of my
ritual but already feeling much better about it. Suddenly
there was a flash of blinding light and I staggered back, my
hand and the ghost's breaking apart with the interruption. I
blinked, my eyesight adjusting until I recognised the form of
Chester Rangi.

'Tommi, turn back around and keep going,' he ordered.
There was a power in his voice that seemed to ripple out
with the command.

'Ch-Chester?' I stuttered. 'Are you dead?'

'She was just coming for a little—'

The male ghost's words died in the air as Chester turned
to him, eyes flashing.

'DO NOT TEST ME, FOOL! I sent your brother on and I
can do the same to you.'

All three of the ghosts dimmed at Chester's words,
which vibrated through my skeleton.

'Do. Not. Test. Me. She does not belong to you, does
she?'

'No,' whispered the child, sounding as meek as she
looked.

'Then let her go on to the land of the living. There are others who need her.'

The ghosts glanced at each other before slowly slinking away into the trees. I sensed they remained there, watching us both. Chester turned back to me then, nonplussed.

'Tommi,' he said. 'Don't you have somewhere to be?'

'Aye, I . . .'

'Then I suggest you be there. I'll see you soon.'

Moving on in the direction I had been heading, towards the voices, I cast one last look over my shoulder. Chester was still there, following behind me, like a silent guardian making sure I wasn't tempted to turn around. As his eyes met mine, he gave me a wink.

My body gave an involuntary shudder as I lurched forwards, stumbling and limping and running in bursts when I could. As the trees began to thin, I sighed with relief as I picked up the scent of those I knew. I clenched the greenstone of the necklace the woman had given me in my fist, which was now slick with blood. When I finally broke free of the tree line, everyone fell silent as they caught a look at me. I had no doubt I appeared to have been on the losing end of a fight. Despite the fact that I had 'won', it certainly didn't feel that way to me.

'Tommi!' Heath sprinted up, his face a mix of concern and relief. His shining, gold head was the best thing I had ever seen as he rushed forward. I collapsed when he embraced me in a hug. His arms gripped me with such force that it kept me standing. I closed my eyes for several long seconds as I savoured the warmth and safety I felt within his grip. He rested his chin on the top of my head and he whispered to me.

'It's over, Tommi, it's over. You did it.'

'Pop a bottle,' I slurred, my own voice sounding drunk as I mumbled the words with exhaustion.

'You did it. I'm so proud of you.'

'Heh.' I smiled, inching my face up until I was looking up at him.

'Aye, you heard me. Proud.' He looked like he wanted to say something else, but my blood must have leaked on to his body as he looked at his now sticky hands. 'You're . . .'

Something changed in his face and I felt his eyes running over my injuries. Aruhe rushed forward, a blanket wrapped around her shoulders. Her face was alive with joy and excitement. Besides a lone cut down the side of her face, she looked otherwise unharmed and I smiled at her. My half-sister's own smile faltered as she drew closer, her eyes filling with the same panic I had seen in Heath's. My legs chose that moment to give out and Heath was pulled downwards with me, catching the full weight of my body before I hit the ground.

'Tommi?' Aruhe asked, worry drenching every syllable.

'Hey, wee sssi . . .'

I couldn't finish the sentence as my eyelids grew heavy and my vision narrowed to black. Still awake but unable to see, I felt Heath lift me up into his arms. *Good,* I thought, as my body jostled with movement when he broke into an uneasy run. *He's taking me to the Paranormal Practitioners that are on standby, my clever Heath.*

'She needs a doctor!'

'I know,' he huffed in response to Aruhe's panic.

'Heath, they're all over there.'

'Aye, I *know.*'

We came to a stop and I heard voices around me, their scents mingling in with other things I was struggling to feel and register.

'Please,' came Heath's cry, desperate. 'She needs help. She needs *your* help.'

There was a long pause during which I wondered what was happening, as if I were listening to everything from a far-off place not attached to my body. A hand touched my skin as Heath held me in his arms, the pain of my various wounds buzzing back to life.

'Place her down here,' came Tiaki's voice. 'We'll help.'

Those words were the last thing I heard as I fell, unsure whether Heath was placing me down or we were both spiralling. I let out a small cry of panic as all sense of gravity left me, but the fear was short-lived as darkness once again truly – and utterly – took over.

18

'Aw, there's a bloody tear in my baffies,' said Mari, holding up her foot for my inspection. There was, indeed, a hole in her favourite slippers, which were shaped like enormous novelty hot dogs. Her immaculately painted toenail was sticking out the end, the purple gloss shining brightly in the light.

'They're on the verge of grotty,' I noted, glancing up for a moment before returning to the pages of my book. She whacked the volume in my hand so that it jerked forward, dinking me in the face.

'Oy!' I snarled.

'Pay me some attention! We haven't seen each other in ages! Since I got here you've been buried in that book on a fucking American president.'

'How *dare* you,' I said, mock-outraged. 'Firstly, I only started reading because you said you were on deadline and needed a few hours.'

'Aye, but—'

'Secondly, this is a biography of Alexander "young,

scrappy and hungry" Hamilton, who was never an American president.'

'If this is part of your grand scheme to make me see that freakin' musical on the West End again then—'

'*Thirdly,*' I pressed, grinning at the glimmer of frustration that crossed Mari's features. 'It hasn't been ages since we saw each other! We hung out just last—'

I couldn't finish the sentence, frowning as I tried to find the passage of time in my head that would tell me if we'd been hanging out just last week or last month. We were definitely seeing less of each other these days, I knew that, but I couldn't quite place my finger on why. Mari seemed to know what I was thinking, as if she could read the guilt in my face. I was certainly the guilty party, I could tell. She smiled at me, the gesture bringing a flush to her cheeks that I loved as the rose colour beneath the surface spread out with the pale, alabaster shade of her skin.

'I'm just teasing you,' she said, tucking a strand of her black hair back behind her ear and into alignment with the rest of her bob. 'Anyway, we've got more important things to do.'

'Like this next chapter— OY!'

Mari snatched the book from my clutches and sprung from the couch, cleverly keeping the coffee table between herself and me.

'Mariposa Bronberg,' I said, beaming as she flinched at the sound of her full name.

'I'll give this back, look, I'll even place it right down here, *if* you let me show you something cool first.'

I watched her hand carefully as she laid the book down where she promised. 'You got me. What do you wanna show me and do I need to get changed?'

'No, you look great. Come as is,' she said, gesturing for me to follow her through our old apartment.

'Damn, you have amazing gams.' I titled my head and admired her long, lean legs in the jeans she was wearing.

'Bless your heart, sweet baby angel,' she laughed, nervous. Mari always struggled to handle a compliment. She opened our front door and I followed her out into a huge hall that seemed to stretch on endlessly. She was moving forwards with confidence, her feet even making a shuffling sound in the slippers as she walked. I was staring around, open-mouthed as I craned my neck to look up at the ceiling far, far above me.

'Is this where the ghosts wanted me to meet you?' I asked, my own steps echoing along with my words.

'Hmm? Oh, no. Chester was right showing up when he did, they weren't leading you to me.'

'Weird.'

'Some ghosts will do anything to cling on to the living. Spirits are even worse. You have to be careful not to invite them, Tommi.'

'Why's that?'

'Because they'll *consume* you, if they can. Especially after the coming of age, you're more attuned to them now.'

My next question drifted away like a dandelion clock on the breeze as Mari brought us to a stop at the base of an enormous stone staircase with hundreds of steps stretching towards a place I couldn't see. The steps felt odd in this setting. They were old and fitted within the expanse of the hall we'd just marched through, yet they didn't mesh with the rest of this place. The walls had been rendered smooth, with lamps built in every few metres so the space was well lit. There was a clear effort to make this area look modern, but I had the distinct impression I was sitting inside a very,

very old castle. I expanded my senses, attempting to pick up any smell or scent I could use to give me more information yet there was . . . nothing. I couldn't smell a thing. Scent was completely gone to me in this place.

'The hell is this?' I whispered. I paused for a moment, hoping that I wasn't actually *in* hell. Given I wasn't surrounded by ten-foot-tall versions of Mel Gibson though, that seemed unlikely. The silence was astounding in that it was complete and absolute. As I trudged my way up the stairs after Mari, I heard the faintest whisper coming from the top. Wary but curious, I continued my path as I strained to hear the words.

There was something in the pitch, something that connected to me in a primal way. When I reached the landing, I was left with two options: left or right. Mari had positioned herself to the left, but the whispers were coming from the right. I felt my body naturally angle itself in that direction. I wanted to follow those whispers directly to their source.

'It appeared and they lived there. On three occasions she gave a greyhound puppy to one of the Fhinn who asked her for it—'

Immediately I stopped leaning towards the whispers, my body jerking back with a severe reaction. I knew this story, every Scottish child knew it: *The Daughter Of King Under-Waves*. This had been my favourite folktale growing up, and my mother had read it to me over and over and over again as I demanded it before bed. And it was my mother's voice I heard now: my dead mother.

'Diarmaid angrily said that she wouldn't have done it if she recalled what he had rescued her from—'

It was here, her exact voice speaking at her exact pace with her exact inflictions over the same words in the same parts.

'He begged her forgiveness but on the third time, despite his apology, she and the castle vanished.'

'Ma,' I whispered, frozen to the spot and desperate to hear her continue this stale story. My foot inched forward down the right corridor when another voice joined the fray.

'Under the sea! Under the sea he goes the swick!'

'Tommi, we're getting to it.'

'A wee bit faster, just a wee bit, please – the blood bit is next!.'

My mother sighed with exasperation, as she always had when a smaller version of me had urged her to hurry up to the most exciting – and gruesome – part of the tale. A few more steps down the corridor and I could see a door sitting open, a subtle bluish light sneaking out of the space.

It was my nightlight, I knew that as sure as I knew anything. A sorry attempt at a lava lamp, I'd seen the bobbing blue thing in a charity store and, despite my mum's warnings that it was a fire hazard, she had eventually relented. It had sat next to my bed for years in our old house, right up until I moved out. My hand extended towards the doorway, reaching for the past that was no longer mine. This was a just a memory, yet instinctively I knew it could be mine if I just—

'Tommi.'

Mari's cold white hand clasped around my own. I met her eyes with a pained look, one that I knew she understood.

'That's not for you just yet,' she said, tugging me down the left corridor.

I gulped, trying to swallow both the tears and swell of emotion I felt bubbling up inside me. Hand-in-hand, I let Mari lead me further and further away from the sound of my mother's voice. My steps felt louder and more powerful the further they took me from the room, even though it seemed as if deep down in my core that was the wrong thing to do. It hurt me, but I trusted my friend.

'Where are we going?' I asked.

'To meet some friends of mine.' Mari grinned. 'They're belters, you're gonna love 'em.'

'Whatever you say,' I murmured, remembering with discomfort the last time she'd made that promise and taken me along to an interview she was doing with a Loch Ness truther.

As we moved down the corridor, we passed other things that I wouldn't have minded pausing at. Door after door was just slightly ajar, giving me a hint of what was inside. The first had the sounds of the Arctic Monkeys billowing out of it as Mari and I danced our way through a whole album in the bare lounge room of our old apartment. That was the day we had moved in.

The second was an obscure birthday, I couldn't be sure which, but I had a *Powerpuff Girls*-themed party and my grandfather was singing the theme song at the top of his lungs.

The third was my mother's wedding, the words *'I do'* following me as I sprinted past the door and through trails of other suffocating memories. My cries of sexual climax bellowed from another, Mari's excited whispers about a guy named Kane that she had crossed paths with, my grandparents' anniversary, one particularly wild night of debauchery, the day Joss went into remission, making out with a lad whose name I'd forgotten in the empty chemistry labs at high school . . . it all flowed through and over me as we drove forward.

I think if I'd been on my own, I would've stopped: I couldn't have helped it. Yet with Mari by my side and setting an unwavering pace, I carried on. The corridor was coming to an end and there was a door wide open at the end of it, the only door where silence greeted me on the other side. Dragging me through as quickly as she could and slamming the door behind us, Mari let out a relieved sigh.

It's her.

Is it her?

Mari said she could find her.

Yes, it's her. I thought I was the blind one?

Their voices all rushed at me, talking and chatting and bickering and overlapping but never out loud. I cringed as they penetrated my skull, the croak of three old ladies bouncing around in my brain like a ping-pong ball on acid.

Quiet.

Sssssshhhh.

You shush, look what you're doing to her.

And that's no good.

No good, no good at all.

Well, quiet then.

Yes, quiet.

Like someone had clicked their finger, the chorus died away and I was left with silence. Resounding, penetrating silence, that slapped me back to the present. I lifted my head, my fingers retracting from my scalp where I had been attempting to hold the voices at bay. This was no precious memory that I was bathed in, this was no hallmark moment of mine. I was standing before three tiny women who looked so old that if I sneezed they might blow over with the gust. They were the sole occupants of the space, which was completely grey and dull except for one enormous arched window – the only source of light in the room. My eyes cut back to the faces of the ladies as I moved closer, Mari at my back. They had thin, wispy hair so long it brushed the floor like cobwebs. Huddled together, they were perfectly still except for their hands, which were moving constantly as if they were typing into the air. Dressed in maroon velvet robes that looked from another time, what the women looked like on the outside was nothing compared to what was on the inside.

I could feel their power. They looked as if they were peering right through me. The smallest smiles played on their lips, but their mouths were so small I wasn't sure if that's what I was actually seeing. The sister two of the women bookended was blind, her grey eyes looking out into a world that didn't look back at her. Yet I had the distinct impression she saw more than was physically possible as her head followed my movements.

I am blind, dear. It's not a trick.

My breath caught as she plucked the thoughts right out of my head.

'I-I'm sorry, I didn't mean to accuse you,' I stammered. Mari giggled behind me.

You know who we are?

The sister on the right asked me the question, her lips never moving as she spoke.

'Yes; you're the Three.'

We're not telepathic.

The third had answered my question before I'd even finished forming it in my head.

Usually the only heads we're in are our own.

'Then how—'

There are special avenues open to us when it comes to the dead or . . .

in-between.

We've been waiting for you.

Almost twenty-five years, in fact.

'Waiting for me? Why? What have you seen?'

The future.
The past.
The present.
'You saw this?' I asked, gesturing to myself and Mari.
No, but . . .
We made it come to be—
All the same.
Mari cleared her throat.
With some help, of course.
Yes, thank you, Mari.
Very helpful.
'You're welcome,' Mari replied, taking a bow. 'I did say you'd like her.'
Very much.
Lots of friends you have, on the other side.
Enemies, too.
Yes, yes. Best be careful of those.

'What . . . what do you want from me?' I asked, regretting my tone as soon as I heard it. I felt power roll off them immediately and I flinched. It was laughter, though. They cackled at my comment like witches around a cauldron.

Straight to the point.
Pushy, I like it.
I like what she promises.
I frowned. 'And what's that?'
Freedom.
For us.
You're our liberator.
'Me? I liberate you from being all-seeing, all-knowing? I think that's almost a backhanded compliment.'
We've spent so many lives trapped here.
Living only in our visions.

Our taste of the outer world has been through viewing other people's destinies.

We've forgotten what it's like to experience.

To live.

We miss it. We miss Ireland.

Galway.

The river; the water always moving so fast . . .

'Galway,' I said, a memory coming back to me of a task, a place, a girl who needed help. 'I've been there, with Heath, I've—'

Oh, Heaf!

We love Heaf.

So important, so vital.

Never would have seen.

Never would have guessed.

Pretty Pict.

There was a knock against the door Mari had been so keen to drag me through and I turned, the noise distracting me.

'Sorry,' Mari grimaced. 'I told a friend to meet me here. Well, technically *they* did.'

Always late.

Never punctual, that Creeper.

Busy, we must forgive him for being busy.

What could be more important than this?

Many things, so many things to watch.

So many things to spy.

As the sisters bickered among themselves, a man entered through the door Mari held open. He was tall, statuesque, and *stunning*. I had never seen him before, yet I had the weirdest sense of déjà vu as I examined his facial features and the glorious colour of his copper hair that seem to glint in non-existent sunlight.

'I know, I know,' he huffed. 'I'm tardy. But there is a lot happening down there, you wouldn't believe – ah, well, maybe you would.'

He spoke with a musical German accent and from the way his eyes pored over me, I could tell this man knew who I was.

'You know me?' I asked, aware that under normal circumstances such a question was brash and, in many ways, rude.

These were not normal circumstances.

'I do,' he replied. 'Although you don't know me. We haven't been formally introduced, as yet: I'm Barastin Von Klitzing. Most people call me Creeper.'

My mouth popped open, his last name *and* the nickname filling the gaps for me. His uncanny resemblance to Casper did the rest.

'You're . . . Casper and Creeper. I've heard of you. You're her brother.'

'Twin dead brother,' Mari corrected.

'Present!' he chirped. 'And I gotta say, your whole thing you have going on? I *love* it.'

'Whole . . . thing?' I tossed Mari a look.

She shrugged. 'Grunge girl who takes no prisoners but low-key has a heart of gold.'

Barastin nodded enthusiastically. 'Love. It.'

He's here to help us.

To meet you.

To witness.

The Three explained one after the other, Barastin watching me with an intelligent gaze.

'You'll be seeing more of me,' he affirmed. 'This seemed as good a time as any to make the introductions.'

'It's important to have ghost friends.' Mari smiled.

'I have you,' I replied.

Her smile faltered somewhat, and it was sad to watch. 'I can't stay, Tommi. This is temporary. Creeper can be places that I can't, when this is all over.'

I wanted to ask when 'what' was 'all over', but the sister were quicker than I was at anticipating my own needs.

Yes, we want freedom.

'And I suppose the Treize are reluctant to let go of their biggest asset,' I murmured. 'The one thing that gives them a pre-emptive advantage over everyone else?'

Reluctant, yesss.

Foolish, even.

Forgetful, they are.

We did get them here, but we can take that back.

With what little power we have.

I glanced at Mari and she smiled and gave me a shrug. 'Don't look at me, I'm not clued-in on their plan. They just asked me to guide you.'

'What do you want me to do?'

Just a little thing.

Tiny, really.

But we have to show you . . .

The three women moved forward all at once in what was an excessively creepy physical act. They gathered around what looked like a sundial positioned in the middle of the room. What I thought was a hard, flat surface shimmered as I approached and realised it was actually some type of fluid. Not a liquid exactly, but thick: almost like see-through slime. I reached out my index finger to touch it when my hand was slapped away by one of the sisters.

Not for you, dear. Not for any of us.

It is for looking.

Not touching.

'My bad,' I mumbled, still staring at the strange surface and unable to tear my eyes away. 'Oh my Glob . . .'

What was once clear was now reshaping itself to show me an image: a moving image. Hands, no, werewolf claws were stretching out of a row of cages as they attempted to grip something, anything. Beyond the metal bars were the desperate eyes of the humans behind the monsters – many of them still in their people skin, others having shifted in part. It looked wrong. There were other things, though, other monsters as the view moved deeper and down into the depths of this place; things that couldn't be restrained by cages. Glass walls and supernaturals confined behind them. A huge demon with horns curling on his head drew a smiley face on the transparent surface, his terrifying appearance contradicting the cute gesture illustrated in dripping goo. A light was pulsing, throwing the view in and out of focus. A figure marched along the barrier between creatures, jumping slightly as a fully transformed arachnia threw itself forwards and was hurtled back, all eight limbs flailing in the air.

It's difficult for you to see it clearly.

But we do.

And we know.

'What the fuck am I looking at?'

'They can't tell you,' Barastin said, speaking up from behind me. 'They can only show you.'

You must find a way to help them.

'Them? Who are they? *Where* are they? And how can I help them?'

You'll know.

'I literally couldn't know less if I was blindfolded and in the middle of a Stanley Kubrick movie.'

You help them.

It helps us.

When the time comes.

Shaking my head, I took an uneasy step back from them as the scene continued to play. The light from the images illuminated the faces of the Three as they too continued to stare, entranced.

Something very bad is happening.

They're doing very bad things to your kind.

And all kind.

'Okay, great, what am I? Werewolf Moses? How am I supposed to lead all supernaturals through a desert for forty years when I don't even know where I'm leading them from! That was an arachnia I saw, a super powerful, super scary, spider-human hybrid and it was *imprisoned* in a *cell*. And the biggest demon I've ever seen! How am *I* supposed to help something, somethings, a thousand times more powerful than myself? And what can I even do for you, at the end of all that?'

Nothing, dear.

We're dying.

Not much left to do.

For us, anyway.

'You're dying?' I hissed. I mean, none of them exactly projected a picture of health, but still. 'What the hell do you need me to liberate you for, then?'

We'll liberate ourselves.

The power will pass to the next.

The otherworld sisters.

The babies, so beautiful they'll be.

So fat.

Shame we'll never get a chance to see . . .

Yes, but leaving is more important.

Change the balance, permanently.

Nothing is permanent.

For a while, then.

For good.

Yes, yes, for good.

Mari and Barastin were standing side-by-side, watching the proceedings, while I felt like I was spinning out with David Lynch on an acid trip. The Three, naturally, could tell exactly how I was feeling.

Absolute power corrupts.

Absolutely.

We don't like it.

Not one bit.

'So, you're intervening?' I asked. 'Wait, nah, you want me to intervene on your behalf. While you all die.'

Mari chuckled. 'Less intervening and more like meddling, with these old biddies.'

I turned to face my friend – the easy smile that rested on her face seemed in stark contrast to the horror I knew was etched into mine.

'How can you handle this with such lightheartedness? Can't you see I have no idea what to do? I have no idea what you all want from me!'

'I'm sorry, Tom,' she replied, genuinely. 'But it's hard for me to care about things I can't impact from over here. And we're out of time.'

'What? Out of ti—'

The floor beneath me shook with a tremendous shudder and I shrieked, trying to grab the nearest wall for support. There was nothing even close to me to hold on to, so I dropped on to all fours as the very structure around us shuddered like it was paper.

'WHAT IS THIS IS?' I screamed. Barastin was standing perfectly still, unmoved by the force of nature that was bringing the roof down around us. Mari smiled at me once more, something meaningful penetrating her gaze as she watched me crouched there.

'Earthquake,' she said.

With that, she disappeared as a huge chunk of the roof fell in front of us. I screamed for her, hell, I even screamed for the Three as the entire place collapsed on me in giant chunks of jagged, concrete rubble.

19

It was hard to tell what was a dream, what was a nightmare, and what was reality after that. It felt like I was trying to swim through oil, my subconscious gagging on the fumes and the taste as it entered my mouth. Yet trying not to move – just staying afloat – was worse, and I was overwhelmed with an even deeper sinking feeling. At some point, I felt a pull: I can't explain it any better than it was as if I were a paperclip and someone had a giant, mystical magnet, and I was yanked in its direction. It seemed easy to let myself go with it, so I did.

Soon, I was hearing voices. If I could have cried, I would have at the sheer relief of hearing human words coming from human mouths and not something I was imagining. Scents followed soon after but so too, unfortunately, did the pain. Nothing is quite comparable to the full moon but this wasn't that. It was smaller things, numerous things, that were pinching at me here, and pulling at me there.

I couldn't say when I regained a full sense of my body, but eventually I could feel the soft cotton sheets. I could feel the hard press of the mattress beneath my spine. I could feel the itch and irritation of my skin as it fought to heal itself. I could feel that I wasn't alone in the room.

It was probably another massive chunk of time before I attempted to move, and even then, it wasn't more than a finger.

'Did you see that?'

'See what?'

'I think her hand just – there! It did it again!'

'You're right! She's coming to!'

'Aruhe, you should get Simon.

'Nah, I'll get the alpha and wake Wehi.'

There was a scurrying of feet and a door opening and closing, followed by repeated motions. Suddenly I was left alone. Good. That's how I wanted it. I tried opening my eyes and it pained me to admit how much effort that took. Blinking, I could barely make out the ceiling above me as my pupils adjusted to actually being in use.

Jesus, how long had I been out? And what kind of shape was I in? There was the slightest sound of someone exhaling, as if relieved, and I froze. I'd thought I was by myself. I willed my senses to kick themselves into gear and tell me who was inching towards the edge of my bed.

'Joss,' I croaked, my mouth feeling dry and stale.

He smiled, the smallest of smiles, and let out another relieved breath.

'I've been waiting for you to say that.'

My best friend had a calm exterior, but his eyes were scanning my face feverishly. He was still pale, but I guessed that was something that would never change. The most obvious difference in his appearance was how much healthier he looked. His eyes were sparkling, there was colour in his cheeks, his ginger hair had already grown back and even his freckles appeared brighter somehow. My eyes were drawn to the metal that glinted on the necklace he was wearing: the infinity symbol. He was truly an immortal now.

'You look *so* good,' I whispered, the words feeling like they were strangled out of me.

He smiled as if he knew it. 'I wish I could say the same to you.'

'Where am I?' I asked, wincing as I tried to sit up. Joss reached out a hand and placed it gently on my shoulder.

'Don't move,' he said. 'Don't exert yourself too much.'

'All right, *dad*,' I whinged, settling back down. 'What's going on, Joss?'

'Aruhe will be back in a second and she'll explain everything.'

'I'm not asking Aruhe, I'm asking you.'

He hesitated, as if weighing up his options, before he shrugged. 'Fuck it, we're in a house full of werewolves. Anything I tell you they're gonna be able to hear if they're listening.'

'May as well give me the primer.'

'Are you sure you're up for this?' He smiled. 'I don't want to overwhelm you.'

'Bloody get to it. But start with how you're here and not in Custodian school, will you?'

'This *is* technically Custodian school,' he said. 'This is my first bit of field experience. Lorcan's more of a train-on-the-go kinda teacher.'

'I remember.'

Silence fell between us as Joss stared at me once more, seemingly in a daze. I was desperate to know what was so interesting to him and opened my mouth to ask, but he cut me off.

'He's not here.'

'Okay.'

'He's on the North Island.'

'And where are we?'

'On the South Island. We're in a safehouse in Christchurch.'

'Who's safehouse? The Treize or—'

'The Ihi pack. These people have resources, Tommi, Jesus. I mean, I knew they were powerful from what you told me, but shite. Once you have the full historical context and can see the scope of their assets . . .'

I had viewed glimpses of this, largely from things that Aruhe had referred to or something as simple as seeing Simon in what had looked like an expensive, tailored suit the first time I met him. But Joss no doubt had access to financial records I couldn't even fathom in his new role, and if he was impressed, there was reason to be. The Ihi family had bounced back and built themselves up after the Outskirt Wars in a way that concerned the Treize enough they kept record of it. I packaged that information away for later, not sure what the hell to do with it in the present moment.

'What did they do to you?' I whispered.

'The Ihi pack? Nothing! They've been great, they've taken really good care of m—'

'No, Joss. The Treize. The Custodians. Lorcan. Whoever the fuck took you where you needed to go.'

'Oh,' he said, eyes widening with understanding. 'That.'

'Aye, "that" casually turning immortal thing. I want details, damn it. Not a rushed voicemail.'

'It wasn't what you're thinking, there was no drinking of blood or anal probing.'

'Anal probing?'

'You know what I mean. The last thing I remember was

seeing you at the hospital, which was hazy to me anyway, and then I woke up.'

'Where?'

He gave me a pointed look.

'Right. Super Secret. Got it.'

'It was like . . . waking up from a really, really long nap.'

'Then what happened?'

'I woke up slowly. It was like every minute I was awake, things became clearer and more acute. Don't get me wrong, I don't feel any different. It's just been so long since I haven't been *dying* that even feeling healthy seems like having superpowers.'

I didn't have anything to say to that. He seemed so happy, so light, and yet . . . I couldn't shake the image of his parents at the memorial service. I couldn't shake the old photo of him, smiling, that had been framed and set next to the ceremonial urn. I couldn't shake the videos Poc had sent me from Dundee as all our old friends gathered and toasted in Joss' honour.

Yet Joss had got what he wanted. This was not what I wanted for him, a life of immortal servitude. But it was what my best friend had desired more than anything, maybe even before he found out his cancer was terminal, right back when he first learned about our world. My eyes scanned his face as he watched me, patient, and I saw that he was happy – truly happy. That counted for everything.

'What are you, then, a proper Custodian?' I asked.

He snorted. 'Maybe in a few years. Right now, I'm Lorcan's apprentice.'

'Just don't shag him, that's when things started to screw up for us.'

'Duly noted.' Joss grinned.

'Then one day you'll be my Custodian.'

'That is, if you're not joining the Ihi pack.'

'I'm not!' I blurted. 'Joss that's so—'

'I know. But listen, we won't be alone for much longer and there's something else I need to tell you.'

'What?' I asked, frowning slightly at his expression.

'Aruhe was never in danger.'

'What do you mean?'

'The threats against her? The "repercussions" she'd have to face from the Ihi pack for telling Steven about the Aunties' ruling? They didn't exist, Tommi. It was all a ploy to get you back here to New Zealand.'

My throat felt dry as I tried to gulp. 'For what purpose?'

'I haven't worked that out, yet, but I think they wanted you to complete the coming of age because it would increase the odds that one day you might join their pack.'

'Why does everyone keep thinking that?'

Joss let out a long, deep whistle. 'They studied you, Tommi. They know compassion is your weakness.'

'It's not a weakness,' I snapped. Heath had said basically the same thing to me enough times that it stung.

Joss threw me a look. 'The Ihi pack knew that once you met Aruhe, once you befriended her, you couldn't let someone vulnerable face a fate like that.'

'Did she know?'

'Aruhe? No. I don't think so. Although I think she's about to.'

I titled my head to listen as a rush of voices came towards us from down a hall. There was the sound of feet pounding up stairs and more doors opening and shutting as they came closer. With a bang and a thud, suddenly the bedroom I was in was a lot fuller as Tiaki, Aruhe, and Wehi surged into the space.

'Omigod howareyou areyouokay areyou inpainwhatcanwedo?' my sister said, the words coming out in a continuous rush of energy. Moving my lips, I tried to answer but my first attempt was a failure.

Her breath caught as she looked my face. 'Tommi, your eyes—'

'Give her some space, kid,' Tiaki murmured, gently pulling her daughter to her side as Wehi took over the inspection. It seemed to take forever and he lifted up each of my eyelids, lingering on my right eye for longer than the left. Finally the old man sat down on the bed next to me, placing a hand to my forehead and gauging my temperature.

'Are you back?' he asked, finally. Every time I'd encountered him, this man had used his words sparingly.

'You tell me,' I replied.

A smile twitched at the corner of his lips. He threw Tiaki a glance and she let out a relieved breath.

'Simon is bringing water and soup,' Wehi said, getting up and placing himself next to Joss in one of several chairs that had been arranged around my bedside. Tiaki filled another, while Aruhe helped me into a sitting position and arranged pillows at my back. I winced, my stomach still sore and winced again when I saw what I was dressed in.

'What is—'

'Highlanders jersey.' Aruhe smiled, clocking my confusion. 'They're a Super 15 team. We're Hurricanes fans, but this was all that was laying around.'

'Legit everything you just said to me could have been in another language.'

'Rugby,' Tiaki supplied. 'And you have two broken ribs.'

'That all the damage?'

'No. Some scars that won't heal, a few that will, twenty or so stitches that are due to come out, and the after-effects of exhaustion and dehydration.'

'Oh.'

'That's not why you're in this bed, though,' Joss added.

I raised an eyebrow at him. I thought he was about speak up when Wehi's voice filled his place.

'Your body survived the coming of age, barely,' he said. 'But your mind was another matter. Here.'

The old man passed me a small, cracked mirror no bigger than my palm. My hand shook slightly as I took it, holding it up to my face. I had a second to register my reflection before the mirror slipped from my grip in shock. Fumbling through the blankets for it, I quickly held it back to my face, and digested what I saw there. My skin was pale and I looked sickly, but most of the small cuts I'd sustained in ahi hikoi had healed now.

It was my eyes that frightened me. My left eye looked as it always did: a dark-brown iris blinking back at me. My right eye, however, had changed: the iris was completely grey. It looked like storm clouds had taken over where the old colour used to be and the effect was . . . unsettling. Holding the mirror further back so I could take in more of my face, I tried to adjust to the reflection staring back at me. Suddenly I knew what Joss had been looking at earlier.

'Is it permanent?' I asked, unable to look away from the one brown eye, one pale grey that blinked back at me.

'Yes,' said Wehi, gently taking the mirror from my hand. 'You have been scarred by spirits. That eye is testament to how close you came to never making it back.'

'I'll . . . I'll carry it for the rest of my life?'

'Yes.'

'We could get coloured contacts,' Aruhe suggested, rubbing her eyes as if she was tired. 'Even it out.'

'It doesn't matter,' I said, shaking my head. 'It's just an eye colour, I can still see. How long have I been here?'

Joss nodded. 'You've been out for a week.'

'A WEEK?!'

A knock came from the other side of the door and Simon entered with soup and water.

'Hey, how you doing?' He smiled.

'I feel like I've woken up in an alternate dimension.'

I noted the rumbling that came from my stomach when I caught a whiff of the food.

'Well, this dimension has food, so—'

He paused, taking in my appearance.

'Whoa, Tommi, your eye! That's … new.'

'Soon everyone will want one,' I murmured, reaching towards the bowl.

'Slowly, wahine,' Tiaki snapped. 'Slowly or you're going to be throwing it right back up.'

'How about I eat, slowly, and somebody break down what the hell is going on, quickly.'

It was less soup and more of a meat broth, which was glorious, and I slurped at a steady pace as the Ihi pack members began talking. Simon did a lot of it, but Aruhe and Tiaki jumped in to provide further details at various points. I had spent more time with Keisha than Tiaki, so it was interesting listening to the matriarch talk – especially noting how and when she chose to. Wehi stayed completely silent, just watching me with a heavy gaze as I processed the information.

Long story short: I died. At least for a wee bit. It was hard to tell if I had fully expired or just been on the brink, but for almost a full five days I had been teetering on that knife's edge. Wehi had not left my bedside, working day and night to help my spirit survive and come back from *wherever* it was I had been. Once I had made it past the fifth day, he thought I'd turned a corner: something had changed. I was improving in increments and he hoped that within a few more days I might regain consciousness. He was right.

The physical injuries I'd gained in the coming of age hadn't helped, though – weaker body, weaker mind – but they had been tended to during my many moments of unconsciousness. With the werewolf healing factor, my body was repairing itself, but not as quickly as anyone would have liked (and not as quickly as it usually did). There were the marks that wouldn't heal, Simon noted, as they weren't physical wounds. Glancing down at my body, my eyes ran over the new scars that would make up part of me now: the grizzled flesh from a few wolf bites and, most evidently, the long lines from the slices of daggers. The skin on my collarbone and back itched as I looked at the one running up the inside of my forearm. In the grand scheme of things, I had my life. I could live with my scars.

Aruhe had survived the coming of age ritual rather seamlessly, emerging from the woods hours before I had. Besides some serious fatigue, she had been otherwise unharmed, and I thought about what Joss had shared earlier. Aruhe had never been in any real danger, at least not from her family. Her scars had all healed.

I, on the flip side, had barely made it before the sunrise deadline. And when I did, and Heath got a full look at my condition, he'd known there was nothing the Paranormal Practitioners on standby could do. I'd needed the help of my people and he'd gone against protocol to deliver me to them. If I survived the coming of age, there had been strict instructions: I was to go back under the protection of the Treize and the Praetorian Guard that had been with us since we landed. Heath had openly disobeyed that order.

'We didn't have time to get you back to our land,' Simon

said. 'And our safehouse had everything we needed, so we got here as fast as we could.'

'Plus it had the added benefit of the Treize not knowing it existed,' Tiaki muttered.

'They have no idea where we are?'

'Nope.' She smirked. 'There was so much commotion afterwards, it gave us the opportunity to slip away. They would have expected us to head north.'

'James and my mum ran interference while we headed south,' Simon added.

'If the Treize don't know where we are, then how is Joss here?'

'Lorcan followed the main party and told me to stay on the South Island just in case there were any leads we needed to chase up here.'

'And Joss,' Tiaki said, unable to hide her annoyance. 'Followed Aruhe.'

'I couldn't even scent that I was being followed!' she protested.

'No,' I agreed, inhaling deeply. 'He smells different, not at all like himself. I couldn't tell I was alone in the room with him before.'

'See?!' Aruhe said, spinning to face her mother.

'You're a wolf, girl. You don't run around this world following *only* your nose.'

'Anyway,' Joss said, subtly rolling his eyes so that only I noticed. 'They took me hostage at first—'

'Hostage!' I shrieked, as Joss batted away my alarm.

'—but once they established I was only following them to see how you were, they let me stay.'

'We thought you were going to die,' Simon said, taking the now-empty bowl from me. 'Seemed cruel to deprive a loved one from being by your side.'

I met his gaze and he glanced away, not wanting me to see whatever was lingering behind the look.

'Where do Lorcan and the Treize believe you are?' I asked Joss.

'Still chasing up possible sightings of you. They think I only arrived in Christchurch yesterday, the rest of the time I've been "on the road". To be honest, I feel like they just wanted me out of their hair for a few days while they focused on trying to find out what happened to you.'

'The Ihi property is locked down and closed to anyone who isn't pack right now,' Tiaki said. 'We're behaving as if you're there and in dire condition. That's what they think too.'

'You're very good at playing these games,' I said, watching her face as she digested the real meaning behind my words. Aruhe picked up on my intent and frowned, glancing from her mother to me and back again. Joss was correct: she had no idea what they had been playing at.

'You have to be,' Tiaki said, after a long pause. 'It's the only way to survive in this world and protect the ones you love. I think you're learning that.'

My mouth went dry as I clutched at a thought that whipped through the front of my mind at lightning speed.

'Where is Heath?' I asked. I was surrounded by people who cared about me, each in their own way, and he should have been among them. Silence descended on the room as they all glanced nervously at each other. My stomach dropped as I took in their expressions.

'Well—'

'Where *is* he?' I repeated.

'He, kind of, went postal,' my sister mumbled.

'Postal?'

'There was a pushy Askari who tried to intervene when

he handed you off to us,' Simon said. My mind flashed back to the guy at the airport.

'Aye, I know the one.'

'He was trying to drag you back over to them and Heath punched him. Knocked him out. One hit.' The admiration was thick in Simon's voice.

'It took six PG to drag Heath off him,' Aruhe added. 'They arrested him.'

'ARRESTED him? Where is he?'

'We don't know, exactly,' Simon said. 'He's in PG custody and he's still on the island, that's all we can ascertain.'

Glancing down at my lap, I felt sick and it had nothing to with my stomach actually having something in it. Running my hands through my hair, my skin suddenly felt hot as if my very blood was boiling.

'They fucking *arrested* him,' I growled. 'I'm going to kill them; I'm going to kill them all.'

'He's not our concern right now,' Tiaki said, doing her best to hide the pleasure that washed over her face as I made my threats.

'No, he's *my* concern,' I snapped, throwing my legs over the side of the bed.

'Whoa, slowly now,' Joss pleaded, reaching out a hand to still me. I brushed it away.

'And do you have anything to say?' I asked Wehi. 'You're just sitting here, looking at me?'

'I'm watching,' said the old man.

'For what?'

'To see if it's you who came back.'

'As opposed to?'

'Something else.'

I sighed, letting out a breathy laugh. 'God, I didn't think I could wake up to something worse than a week of nightmares about earthquakes and the ghosts of dead friends. Given my life, I should've known better.'

'Earthquakes?' said Tiaki, glancing at Wehi and her nephew. I watched the exchange between them with interest.

'What? What did I miss?'

'There have been three earthquakes in Christchurch,' Joss whispered. 'All minor, but all in the last week.'

My heart thudded against my chest. My body was still weak, and I willed it to get stronger every second that I was conscious, simply because I needed it to. I was alive. I wasn't stuck in that awful purgatory state I was before. I was surrounded by allies. But I didn't *feel* safe. Looking over the nervous faces gathered in the room with me, I could tell I wasn't the only one.

'You probably want a shower,' Tiaki said, getting to her feet. Her movement acted as some kind of invisible signal for the rest of the group, who all murmured in agreement and shuffled to standing.

'No,' I replied. 'What I want is to have a proper discussion. Everything on the table.'

The widow of my dead father, the father I never knew but inherited *so much* from, returned my stare. I did my best to hold it.

'After,' she said. 'You're barely staying upright.'

I had a snappy reply on the tip of my tongue and I bit it back, knowing she was spot-on. A small look of triumph flashed over her face.

'Aruhe will help you,' she said, as everyone else filed out of the room one by one, including Joss, until it was just my sister and I left behind.

'So,' she said, smiling gently as she threw out her hands

like a shrug. 'A shower has to be better than a sponge bath, right?'

'Has that . . . has that been what I've been getting?' I asked, glancing down at my body and realising that somehow I must have gotten tidied up after ahi hikoi.

'Don't look so horrified, yeesh. It was either mā or me. We're all werewolves anyway. At some point, everyone is bound to see each other naked.'

'You're right,' I sighed.

'Always am,' she chirped, carefully helping me to my feet. My vision swam for a second before I was able to steady myself and the space around me returned to normal. If there was any room in my brain for being humiliated as she helped prop my naked body up under a stream of water, I didn't feel it. In actual fact, it was nice to be taken care of. I closed my eyes and enjoyed the sensation as she towel-dried my hair.

'Thank you, for all this,' I murmured.

'All what? A shower?'

'Don't be a dick. You know.'

'Heh. I'd do it anyway but I just feel . . . bad.'

'You feel bad? For what?'

'You wouldn't be hurt like this if it wasn't for me. You risked your life to save mine. And for what?'

I spun around to face her. 'You heard what Joss said?'

She nodded.

'You hid it so well.'

'I'm not the only one who can hide things. Tommi, they tricked you.'

'Aye, they tricked you too.'

'I guess. They had their reasons but . . .'

'It's not fun being played,' I said, with understanding. 'No matter who's playing you.'

She smiled, glancing down at my bare torso. 'That's a pretty hectic tattoo. How long did that take?'

'Four hours or something,' I remarked, looking at the Día de Muertos-inspired skulls that wrapped around my ribcage and down my body with a spread of black and red roses.

'Where are the others?'

'There's a wee splatter of paint here,' I said, showing her the tattoo on the inside of my bicep. 'Then just the crescent moon on my wrist, which you've seen.'

'And now the arrows.'

'Them too.' I held out the side of my hand to inspect the small markings there and Aruhe pressed her own against mine.

'What are your plans after this?' I asked. 'Travel the world, be your own boss, see some cool shite?'

'Actually . . .'

'What?' I pushed, picking up that she was nervous to tell me something.

'I'm going to stay here. With the pack.'

'Oh. Um, that's—'

'I know that's probably not what you expected me to do after everything that happened, but you and I walk different paths.'

'That we do.'

'And this is where I belong. That's what they did all this for: to get me back here. Now that I'm here, well, I want to stay.'

'I get it,' I said, cupping her face with my own two hands. 'I really do. And hey, near-death aside, I'm so glad that you got to find your own home after all – even if it was the very same one you left.'

She smiled, hurriedly wiping an errant tear before it

trickled any further down her face. 'You should probably take a look at the damage, you know.'

I let out a shuddering sigh. I had been avoiding turning around and facing the mirror for this exact reason. She sensed my hesitation.

'Just get it over with.'

Steeling myself, I spun and planted my feet firmly as I copped a full eye load of Tommi Grayson post-werewolf-coming-of-age. Aruhe was peering out from behind me as I gazed, my ribs on one side of my body still purple and black as they continued to heal. I looked at the scars and the bites, mostly stretching over my arms and my collarbone and my back. Wearing a singlet from now on was going to get me stares. My new and unusual iris looked back at me, the overall effect of having one grey and one brown eye something that was going to take a while to adjust to. There were still a few cuts pulled together with black stitches, the stiff thread sticking straight out from my body.

'Those ones will heal, Wehi reckons,' Aruhe said, pointing out a few on my chest. 'The others not so much.'

'Meh,' I shrugged. 'Goes with what I've already got, I guess.'

'And don't forget this,' she said, pressing a small object into my palm.

I looked down at the tiki that was resting there, the black cord entwined within my fingers. Aruhe had her own memento dangling at the hollow of her neck.

'Yours is different,' I noted.

'Pikorua,' she said, following the path of my eyes. 'They told me it symbolises the eternal emerging paths in life and the bond between two people. Love, loyalty, and friendship.'

'Is that what your spirit told you?'

She nodded.

'Was it a woman?'

'No, a boy. Like, a really young boy, not much older than ten.'

'Creepy.'

'Creepy *as*.'

'So, sisterhood, huh?'

She beamed. 'Do you know what yours means?'

'It's supposed to ward off evil spirits.'

She stroked the shape as it sat in my hand. 'The tail of a fish, the body of a human, and the head of a bird. This will protect you against great evil, Tommi. I guess it already has been.'

Helping me into clothes, Aruhe led me back to the room where Wehi was waiting to pluck out the last few stitches I had in my body. Afterwards, I felt my eyelids getting heavier and heavier as I lay on the bed, chatting with Aruhe about stupid shit. I'm not sure who said the last word, but I slipped seamlessly into a deep, dreamless sleep that felt the way I imagine heaven feels.

20

When I stirred again, it was dark. I was alone in the same room I had first woken up in but now rich smells of pork had brought me out of my slumber. Slowly, I slipped from the bed, waiting on the edge until the nausea passed, then I dressed as I listened to soft sounds of chatter and cutlery clinking together. They were coming from inside the house and I let my nose tell me where to go. My bare feet padded along the carpet and down the hall taking it slow until I arrived in the kitchen. The only person surprised by my appearance was Joss, who looked up from a weathered manuscript he had been absorbed in.

'Tommi.' He smiled. 'You're up. How are you?'

'Hungry,' I answered, easing myself down on to a stool next to Aruhe who had a plate ready for me stacked with vegetables and a bread roll overflowing with chunks of steaming pork and crackling. The room fell into a peaceful hush as the sounds of eating took over any possibility for discussion. Four werewolves could eat a lot. More importantly, they didn't like to be disturbed while they did it. It felt like a long time before I leaned back from my plate, fully sated and satisfied. Wiping my mouth with a paper towel, Simon slid a bottle labelled L&P across the table to me. It contained a fizzy liquid and I sniffed it suspiciously before taking a sip.

'It's not alcoholic,' I noted, while Joss chuckled from his seat.

'No, Tommi,' Simon replied. 'Weirdly, I didn't think giving you alcohol the first day your body returned to the living was the best idea.'

'You don't know her that well,' Joss muttered.

'Listen,' I said, placing my hands flat on the table before me. 'No more putting this off, no more dancing around it. We need to get everything out in the open, right the fuck now.'

'What are you talking about?' Wehi asked.

I glanced at Joss, who tried to give me the smallest shake of his head. I ignored him.

'I'm talking about lying to get me here,' I growled. 'I'm talking about putting both Aruhe and my lives in danger just to get us back on home soil.'

'She would have always had to complete the coming of age,' Tiaki said. 'With or without you.'

'You made me think she was going to be punished; executed even,' I said, spinning to Simon. 'You made *her* think that.'

'She had to believe she was, so you'd believe it too,' Tiaki murmured. 'Aruhe's not a great liar.'

'I'm sorry,' Simon said, first to me and then to his cousin. 'I'm truly sorry, but it's what we had to do. We're stronger when we're all together.'

'I nearly died, Simon! I wasn't strong enough to make it through like Aruhe was.'

'But you did,' Wehi countered, his voice quiet compared to Simon's authority. 'And here we are, all sitting around the table sharing kai like whānau. Could you have ever imagined this after the first time we met you?'

'I . . .'

The answer was no. This reality would have been science fiction to me then. Now, it wasn't so strange. A series of slow, careful steps had led us here and I would have been lying if I said I wasn't grateful for it.

'It was my idea,' Tiaki said, pushing back her stool so that it made a scraping noise as she stood up. 'Well, Keisha's as well. We were the ones who came up with the plan of how we could bring not only one Ihi back, but two.'

She was a short woman, but when she stood to her full height there was something about her that made me unable to tear my eyes away.

'We're stronger together,' Simon repeated. 'And we need to be strong now more than ever, Tommi.'

'What do you mean?' Joss said, hunching forward with interest. Simon looked as if he didn't want to speak any further with an outsider in the room.

'Please,' my best friend huffed. 'I've been lying for days about where I am and what I've seen to keep the Treize off the scent. If they find out, it's treason. My life is on the line for you lot, I've done more than enough to earn your trust.'

'It's about more than trust, boy,' Tiaki said. 'There are some things you can't un-know. Paths you can't un-tread. You crave knowledge more than anything, but are you ready for the consequences?'

I watched the look that passed between Tiaki and Wehi: it was significant. It was weighted. The eyes of every wolf in the room flicked to my best friend. They were watching him, and I couldn't help but watch them in return. He was the only human among us, even if he wasn't quite that, and in that moment the difference felt stark.

'Joss,' I started. 'Give us a minute.'

His lips were already parted to plead his case with the Ihi pack when I spoke and he looked up with surprise.

'Tommi,' he huffed. 'I need to—'

'Stay alive,' I snapped. 'That's why you signed up to the Treize in the first place, I get that. You wanted to stay alive and be a part of this world. I couldn't stop you from doing it. I couldn't stop you from putting your neck on the line and risking what you've risked just to be here, in this room with us. But I can stop you from hearing whatever Simon is about to say, especially if it means putting you in further danger.'

'It will,' Wehi said softly.

'I've already been to your fake funeral,' I said, landing the killing blow. 'I don't wanna attend your real one.'

'Fine,' Joss replied, clearly annoyed. He pushed his chair back as he got to his feet, rolling up the manuscript he had been reading and tucking it under his arm. He walked towards the hallway I had come from, pausing in the doorway and looking back at me.

'I can't help you if I don't know what kind of trouble you're in.'

'Hey, *I* don't even know what kind of trouble I'm in.'

He smirked, glancing at the rest of the wolves. 'That goes for all of you.'

He left, gently shutting the door behind him, and the four of us that remained were silent as we listened to his footsteps journey further into the house and away from us.

'He's out of earshot,' I sighed. 'Now, for the love of God, start talking. I hate leaving him in the dark about anything.'

Simon shrugged. 'What happened to you before ahi hikoi, are you sure that was the Treize?'

All eyes swivelled in the room to fixate on my face.

'I didn't know about this!' Aruhe exclaimed.

'Nobody knew except Heath and I,' I said, my heart panging as I said his name. 'The night before the ritual, two assassins were sent to kill us. Or kill me, I think, but Heath was there too, and perhaps they didn't expect that. They were PG, and Heath recognised one of them as being from the security detail that met us at the airport. When it was over, we returned to the house and acted like nothing had happened. That way the Treize would think we were still ignorant about the fact they had sent someone to kill me and they wouldn't know precisely *what* had happened to their operatives.'

'What *did* happen to their operatives?' Aruhe asked.

I ran my finger across my throat.

'You killed them?'

Wehi was nodding appreciatively and Simon clicked his tongue with approval. This was how werewolves took care of business.

'They weren't there to kill you,' Tiaki said, frowning. 'They were there to kill the Pict.'

'Heath?' Aruhe and I said in unison, glancing at each other.

'That makes no sense,' I pressed. 'Why on earth would they try to kill . . .'

My sentence fell away as I thought back to the 'favour' I had done for him in Galway. He had sworn me to secrecy and he had been up to *something*. Dr Kikuchi was dead now and an attempt had been made on Heath's life. Hell, I had nearly died myself in the coming of age rituals. Those three things couldn't be a coincidence and my mind leapt to Ginger, wherever she was. I hoped she was on her guard, because by now she must know something or someone was coming. Even worse, I fretted about the safety of the pregnant girl: so young and in so much peril. If she was still alive, she'd be close to delivery and in more danger than ever.

'Whatever you're thinking of right now,' Tiaki said, 'whatever comment he made or warning he gave you, I can assure you that's just the tip of the iceberg.'

I gulped, eyes darting from her face to Wehi's and Simon's and then my half-sister. 'Better give me the whole fucking snow cone, then.'

'My husband's death wasn't an accident. The "car crash" that took his life? The timing? It was all too convenient.'

'Jonah was about to come out of the woods,' Wehi said.

'I know that term,' I murmured, frowning. 'It's what the Outskirt Packs were fighting for, right? The opportunity to be public, to self-govern.'

'Among other things,' the old man continued. 'But we tried with force the first time round and were not effective. We learned a lot though, so did Jonah. What we couldn't do with power, we could do with politics. The day of his death, he was due to speak in front of parliament about prison reform and youth incarceration rates among our people. Not only would he have had an audience among the most powerful minds in Aotearoa, but parliament is televised. Live.'

My mouth hung open as I tried to catch up, Aruhe next to me just as shocked. It was obvious she was learning this all at the same time I was.

'He was going to shift in front of everyone,' Wehi whispered. 'Then shift back, showing all how in control he was and how safe they actually were. He was going to show rather than tell the world what we were, what we *are*. There would be no going back after that.'

'Idiot,' Tiaki snapped. 'He would have forced a decision upon all of us without any warning.'

I glanced over at her. 'I take it you didn't know?'

'Of course, I didn't know! He knew I would've stopped him. Only two people knew: Wehi and Jonah. It was their grand plan.'

'Someone else knew,' Wehi replied. 'Because he never made it to parliament. He was killed en route, which was highly effective as not only did it end our plans, it threw the Ihi pack into chaos.'

'How . . .' Aruhe croaked. 'How long have you all known this?'

Her eyes were brimming with tears, but her fists were clenched. Simon reached across the table, taking her hand in his. It took some work, but eventually he was able to loosen her grip until his fingers were entwined with hers.

'I learned about it after Tommi killed Steven, so did our mums,' he said. 'Officially, anyway. All of the Aunties suspected foul play, Keisha even suspected—'

'Enough,' Tiaki snapped, cutting him off.

'No, mā,' Aruhe replied. 'I can't take any more secrets, from anyone. Dad was *murdered* and I'm only just learning this now? Who did Keisha suspect?'

'Steven,' I answered, reading it on the woman's face. Her glare was deadly as it cut back to me, but I could sense I was right. 'Keisha thinks Steven killed his own father.'

'That's ridiculous,' Aruhe muttered.

'You were always blinded by your love for him,' Simon muttered.

'No, I wasn't. He wasn't *evil* for evil's sake—'

I cleared my throat. 'Sorry to disagree, but there's no retroactively making him a good guy. He tried to rape me, he dragged you *and* Quaid into the crosshairs, he killed countless innocent people, and he murdered my two dear friends right in front of me. He was a brother, a son, a cousin, I understand. But he was also inherently not . . . good.'

'She's right,' Wehi agreed, the words causing me to blink in shock. 'It's likely he was paid to assassinate Jonah by the Treize themselves, or someone working as a cover for them: money and mana were great motivators for him. It wouldn't have been hard to get in his ear, to tell him that if his father was out of the way he could be let back into the pack, that the opportunity would present itself for him to take over as leader.'

'It would never have happened,' Simon snorted. 'But I see how you could make him believe that.'

'It's pointless either way,' Tiaki growled, slapping her hands down on the table. 'This is done with. The past is the past. The son is not the father. The daughter is not the mother. The child is *not* the parent.'

Her words hung there for several beats, weighing on me as heavily as I'm sure they did everyone else in the room. I looked down at my hands, lacing my fingers together as I thought about all the blood that was on them.

'Jonah never knew who killed him,' Wehi said quietly, breaking the silence. 'We may never know either. Whether it was from the inside or the outside, it ultimately doesn't matter now. What matters is what's to come.'

My mind flashed back to something I had seen, something during the coming of age: him writing down the address that would eventually lead me to the Ihi pack and my first transformation as a werewolf. Not to mention the ghost who had given it to him. *Jonah never knew who killed him.*

'How did you know Jonah was killed, Wehi?' I asked. 'Besides the timing of it all, I'm assuming you're the one who broke the news to the rest of the pack when the moment was right that this wasn't all some "accident"?'

'Yes.'

'How did you know?'

'Jonah told me.'

I sucked in a stream of air through my teeth, leaning back as he dropped that bombshell. I had to close my eyes, just to steady myself. Every pack – whether they were Swedish or South African – had someone like him who could communicate more freely with ancestors past and present. That didn't mean they had his power – after all, Simon had said Wehi was a medium not that different to Casper – but they had a variation of it. Jonah's ghost had known when I arrived in New Zealand all those years ago. He'd told Wehi and that old, unassuming, and deeply powerful man had dropped the bait that would eventually lead me to my blood pack.

I took a big breath in and a shaky one out. When I opened my eyes, I almost expected the ghost of Jonah to be standing behind him. But he wasn't. Tiaki, Aruhe, Simon, they were all used to this communication between the living and the dead, even if they couldn't do it themselves. Their ancestors were a present force. Meanwhile I was trying not to have a seizure at the thought of my dead father's ghost orchestrating a meet-cute.

'Aye,' I said, voice sounding as unnerved as I felt. 'Now more than ever I understand that the line between the living and the dead is not a solid one.'

'Good,' Tiaki replied. 'Because we've been exploiting it for months.'

'We,' I breathed, knowing without it needing to be said who she meant.

'We?' Aruhe asked. 'As in . . .'

'Heath,' Tiaki finished.

'You knew,' I said, looking up at Simon. 'That day you showed up at Phases, demanding Aruhe come home with you, Heath and you shared a look. You knew each other. I thought I was going nuts, imagining it, but—'

'We didn't know each other,' he corrected. 'We'd never met. But we knew *of* each other. Who do you think passed on the tip to us that Aruhe was with you?'

I pushed my chair back as I leapt to my feet.

'He didn't know that it was a ruse to get you back to New Zealand,' Simon continued. 'He did everything he could to stop that and he truly believed – like Aruhe did – that she would be punished by the Aunties. But he also had an agreement with Tiaki.'

I spun to face her. 'Which was?!'

'That I would help protect a group of fugitives here, in Aotearoa, if he would feed us any information about my children. In Aruhe's case, it meant any details on her where-abouts: locations, rumours, whatever there was. You were very good at staying hidden, my girl. I'm proud of you.'

There was a touching mother-daughter moment going on behind me, but I couldn't focus on it as I moved to the kitchen and began pacing.

'JOSS!' I screamed, calling for him at the top of my lungs. 'JOSSSSS!'

His footsteps echoed down the hall, my best friend wasting no time at being beckoned back into the fold. Simon and Tiaki were both already protesting his return as he burst through the door, eyes lit with excitement. I held up a hand to silence them, noting that it was shaking just a little.

'*No,*' I said, the words sounding deadly out of my own mouth. 'Just no.'

There was the smallest twitch of amusement on Wehi's lips, but otherwise they remained still.

'You want to find Heath,' Aruhe said, an impish smile creeping into the corners of her mouth.

'And you,' I snapped, pointing directly at Joss. 'Are going to tell me where to start.'

'I don't know where he is, Tommi,' my best friend said, honestly. I could sense a lie and Joss would never lie to me the way I once had lied to him. 'I just know the status of his situation from what Lorcan told me.'

'Go on then, ya bampot.'

'It's not good. They took him into custody after the coming of age and most of us thought that would only be a temporary thing, but they're holding him indefinitely.'

'Indefinitely?'

Joss shrugged. 'He broke the rules. I mean, he's kind of known for it, but never so publicly.'

If only you knew, I thought. I peered over at Tiaki and she gave me the smallest shrug of her shoulders.

'If you want the details of the web, you have to ask the spider,' she said.

'So, you'll tell me nothing about the specifics of what he's into?'

'I can tell you some, but he designed it this way: each faction knows about their piece, very few know about the entire whole. Maybe Heath, the medium, the witch, the ghost . . . I couldn't say who else. We're not making the same mistakes we did last time.'

'Faction?' Joss said, verbalising the word that scared me the most.

Simon shifted to view him more clearly. 'For the record, speak on anything said or heard in this house and I will know it. You'll be dead before the information even has a chance to travel up the grapevine.'

'Simon!' Aruhe snapped, stepping protectively in front of Joss as my friend blanched at the threat. 'He has as much to lose now as all of us – his life! He won't say anything, right, Joss?'

He nodded, but didn't look like he could properly speak.

'Why not just kill him?' I asked, trying to keep everyone focused. 'If Heath is such a thorn in their side, why not kill him like they do everyone else who is apparently a problem to them?

'Say someone might think he has a use,' Tiaki murmured. 'That there's information he could divulge.'

'Then he'll die,' I said, sure as I was of anything. 'He'll be tortured to death before he betrays the people he cares about.'

Tiaki nodded. 'He might also be handy leverage to keep somebody else in line.'

All eyes were on me then, following the direction of her stare and the intent of her words.

'I . . . but, I didn't think anyone knew about . . . us.'

'There's an us? When did this happen?' Joss screeched, almost leaping at me. Looking around the room, he cleared his throat before taking a step back. 'Clearly not the most pressing issue at hand.'

'They don't have to know that you too are "whatever",' Aruhe said. 'Just like they knew you cared about Joss, the Treize must know you care for Heath and that's enough.'

'Or at least they know he cares openly for you,' Tiaki mused. 'And they're betting on you not hanging him out to dry.'

'How did you know he was still on the South Island?' I asked Simon. 'Could he still be in Picton?'

'No, we had the Frankton pack search the town top to bottom and there's no trace of him. We have people watching the airports and the docks. They do have him, but they haven't left with him yet.'

Joss rapped his knuckles on the table. 'Only members of the Praetorian Guard would know where he's being held.'

'That's not exactly accurate,' Wehi whispered, glancing up from where he had been staring fixedly at the table in front of him. His old, dark eyes burned into mine and for the first time, I felt the possibility of hope.

21

Christchurch looked much the way I expected it to as we drove into the city with the breaking of dawn. It was a sprawl of grey and brown buildings as far as the eye could see, with snow-capped mountains lining the outer perimeter like stoic watchmen guarding the town. Joss was in the passenger seat giving Simon directions as he drove us towards our destination in what Tiaki called 'the most common car in New Zealand'—a Ford Ranger. The vehicle hadn't been cleaned in a while and had a few scratches near the bonnet, all things that were supposed to help us blend in. Though at half past five in the morning, we didn't really need the assistance: the roads were practically empty.

It was a risk leaving the safehouse. For one, since they had arrived there in the dead of night with an unconscious me in tow, no one had set foot out the door. An ally had stocked the place with enough food to last a month according to Aruhe, and the Ihi family kept every safehouse equipped with medical supplies, weapons, spare clothes and anything else they could possibly need. After all, that was the whole point. We all knew the pack's carefully laid diversion would be in jeopardy the second I decided to go outside. More than that, if Joss was spotted with Simon or me, he would face the same fate as Heath. It was crucial that we stayed unnoticed and under the radar. And soon, underground.

Wehi had a friend, he said, someone he had known since he was a child when his mother had introduced them the same way he was about to introduce us. They were based in Christchurch, and if anyone knew where Heath would be, it would be them.

'I'm sorry, a *what*?' I had repeated at the time, my voice reaching a dangerously high octave.

'An earth demon,' Wehi repeated.

'Really?' Joss asked, curiosity drowning his tone. 'Living here in the city?'

'Yes,' the old man repeated. 'They can reach out and locate anyone on any square surface of land that they inhabit.'

'They could tell me where Heath is?' I grinned. 'Then what are we waiting for?'

It turned out, quite a few things. Joss descended on Wehi with enthusiasm, peppering him with questions on what an earth demon was really like and comparing that to the extensive reading he had done on the subject. My best friend was insistent on coming, regardless of the danger he could put himself in or the possibility of blowing his cover with the Treize.

Wehi eventually retreated to a quiet section of the house, saying that he needed to 'make contact' about our arrival. I assumed that didn't mean sending a casual DM, but something of the supernatural variety. The Ihi pack were not going to let Joss and I venture out unprotected, and

Simon became the third and final member of our expedition.

Once that was decided, Tiaki had ordered her nephew and me to follow her. We did so obediently, and I was able to get my first proper look at the interior of the house. Put simply, it looked like a lumberjack's version of a mansion: everything was built from timber, including a huge ceiling that angled up into a sharp point. Hanging from its centre was a macabre chandelier made entirely from antlers. Lights were embedded within, giving it a practical purpose besides something that screamed 'I can and will kill things for ornamental reasons'. The house wasn't so modern or flashy that it would draw attention from the outside, I later learned. Rather, it fitted perfectly into the middle-class section of suburbia it was trying to exist within.

She led us into a clean but kitsch bathroom that resembled something the Brady Bunch would have adored. Tiaki closed the door behind her, then pressed three ornamental tiles – a flower design, a duck and seashell – hard into wall.

'Very *Demolition Man*,' I murmured, and Simon snorted with appreciation.

The tiles sank backwards and there was a mechanical pop as the bathtub drew back like the top on a convertible to reveal a small ladder leading down. Fluorescent lights blinked on and illuminated the interior as we headed into the depths. I took the climb slowly, each movement hurting as my body protested any form of activity after spending a week horizontal. Simon helped me down the last rung and I turned around to register what I was looking at.

Rows and rows of weapons were displayed on the walls, all locked behind various cages with each requiring a pin code to open.

Blinking, I moved through the aisles with an open

mouth as I took in every implement that could kill you. The Ihi pack favoured guns, I realised, with everything from a .22 Ruger to high-powered assault weapons. This told me they liked to keep their enemies at a safe distance, but there was another case filled to the brim with a variety of knives. There was a machete that caught my eye, but nothing that usually met my killing implement preferences: no short swords, no throwing knives, no Hunga Mungas. Tiaki had come to a stop in front a wall used to display dozens of fighting tools I hadn't seen before, many of which looked like small paddles made out of everything from whalebone to greenstone.

'Patu onewa,' she said, jerking her head towards one of the weapons. 'That's what our ancestors would have taken into battle.'

'Simon's never been the leader of the Ihi pack, has he?' I asked, voice barely more than a whisper. I sensed him stiffen behind me.

'Not for a second,' Tiaki answered.

'I thought there was a bait and switch, but between he and James. Not you.'

'Our last alpha led for nearly twenty years and then died, rather conveniently, in a car accident we now know was a cover-up. Jonah was a proud man, a brave man: he was also foolish. He was never afraid to rattle cages and make himself a target. This time, we won't make it so easy for them.'

'So Simon takes all the heat, all the danger, while you're the real person calling the shots?'

She smiled at him, warmth emanating from her every cell as she looked at the wolf.

'Keisha raised her son right: he understood what he was

getting into. Insisted upon it, in fact. He just wants to keep his mā and his pack safe.'

He squeezed her hand in response. 'We all want more than that, now. Besides, it would take a lot for them to successfully kill me.'

'This is pack business,' Tiaki said, returning to look at me. 'Nobody knows this information outside of nga Ihi so if you're not joining us—'

'I'm not,' I blurted, rushing to clarify. 'No way. Not this pack or any pack. No offence. I think I'm built to be a solitary wolf.'

She shrugged, as if this was exactly what she had expected me to stay. 'Then our shell game remains secret.'

Tiaki spoke with authority: she sounded like a leader. It wasn't dissimilar to Keisha or the rest of the Aunties. So much pressure came with leadership and Tiaki knew that every call she made could end up costing someone their life.

'To be fair, the ginger knows,' Simon whispered.

'Joss? He does? Before me?'

'He's too smart for his own good, that one,' she grumbled. 'I think he worked it out on day two of staying with us.'

'Classic Joss.'

'Go on then, pick your poison,' she pushed, as my eyes ran over the killing utensils in front of us and my brain hoped that I wouldn't have to use any of them. Nervousness churned in my stomach but right alongside it was my monstrous side. The beast was excited, come what may.

As we joined the others, Wehi was handing Joss a small bag and when I asked what was in it all he'd say was 'payment'. Our earth demon contact expected us just before six in the morning, leaving me enough time for one more nap before getting changed into clothes more appropriate for what lay ahead.

'Does this look like Scotland to you?' Joss asked, tugging me away from my recollections and pointing at a battered church we drove past.

'A lil' bit,' I admitted, eyes sliding over the city's outer streets. The signs of the brutal toll the earthquakes had had were all around us, both loud and subtle. In some places it was nothing more than a small pile of rubble where a house's concrete fence used to be. In others, a whole school building had been cordoned off with construction tape and warning signs stamped around the property.

When we pulled to a stop, it was in front of what looked like one of those ruined locations. We followed Joss as he ducked through a hole in the wire fence, crossing the construction site with purpose infused in him by Wehi (who had clearly given him very detailed and specific instructions). I watched Simon take in our surrounds, inspecting the signs of the company building on this land as we moved through and navigated around massive piles of dirt.

'S'all fake, obviously,' Joss said, as if sensing Simon's question.

'I was gonna say, Ihi and Sons have been in the construction business for over a decade now and I've never heard of—'

'Dirty McDirt and Co?' I read, chuckling to myself. 'That's actually pretty great.'

'I didn't know earth demons had a sense of humour,' Simon noted, trailing after Joss who turned a corner around another massive mound of dirt. He seemed completely at ease with the fact that a spiral staircase had opened up in the ground in front of him, jogging down the stairs with Simon close behind.

Taking a breath, I shrugged and followed the lads. The very stairs themselves seemed to be made out of hardened dirt and I caught myself twice nearly slipping off their edge. Rock walls expanded out from us and we entered a massive cavern. The whole place was illuminated by candlelight; warm tones etched into everything as I tracked the roots of trees that seemed to hold the entire structure together. My nostrils twitched with the overwhelming scent of ammonia and fresh dirt.

'Oh, it's my guests! How rude of me,' a voice called out, almost in a sing-song fashion. 'Take a seat, I'll be out in a jiffy.'

Apparently, I wasn't the only one who had never been in the home of an earth demon, as Simon's mouth was hanging open while he took it all in. There was a wall made up almost entirely of television screens, each with something different playing on it. An inch of dirt was caked between every monitor in a strange juxtaposition of nature and technology. I threw a look at Joss, hoping to see some of my own discomfort mirrored in his expression. Yet my best friend looked calm. And confident. His chin was raised ever so slightly as he waited, seemingly relaxed as he anticipated the entrance of our host. This was him at work, I realised. This was Joss in job mode. I had no idea what kind of creatures he'd encountered at the Custodians' base, but in his new life he'd have to get used to dealing with beings very far from human. Watching him with interest, it appeared he already was.

'All right, all right,' came the voice, this time with a physical presence attached to it. 'My apologies, I had something to attend to.'

Sashaying out of one of the cavern's dark corners was someone unlike anything I had ever seen before. I was unable to tell if they were a man or a woman; they seemed somewhere in between. *Elevated* beyond classification. They moved like the ground was liquid, bouncing and surging towards us with thick roots trailing behind like tentacles. The demon was wider than all three of us put together, and its skin looked as if it was covered in a fine, red dust. The earth demon's eyes widened with delight when it saw Joss, a fine shriek emitting from its lips.

'Darling!' it said, arms extending. 'You must be the sweet strawberry Wehi told me about, give me a kiss.'

Joss hesitated for less than a fraction – something only I would have noticed knowing him so well – before swooping in and planting a kiss on each cheek.

'It's lovely to meet you, Gaea, I'm Joss Jabour.'

'Even prettier in person,' the demon said, smacking their lips appreciatively.

'And this is Simon Ihi, leader of the Ihi pack.'

'Helloooo! You're quite a snack too, aren't you?'

'Uh, thanks?' Simon murmured awkwardly.

'That's a compliment,' I chuckled, elbowing him in the stomach. 'Don't be so hetero about it.'

My comment was met with a tinkling laugh as the earth demon moved forward, reaching out to stroke the skin of my hand.

'And you must be Tommi Grayson. Of course, I've heard all about you.'

'You have?' I asked, surprised as they moved even closer to me. I couldn't help but take a deep sniff as the soothing, fresh dirt smell increased exponentially.

'Ah, you werewolves always love that,' Gaea said. 'It's geosmin, an organic chemical generated from the bacteria in dirt.'

'Eau de fresh dirt.'

'Heh, exactly! Oh, Joss, I like her. She's witty!'

Spinning back around to face me, they pointed a long, spindly finger at my face. 'You can stay.'

'Much obliged.' I smiled.

'And you can stay,' they said, switching to Simon. 'Because you're pretty and unassuming about it.'

'Thank you,' he replied, lips twitching. 'I'm honoured.'

'Am I the first earth demon any of you have met?'

'Yes, actually,' Joss answered. 'I had no idea there even was one based on the South Island.'

'One? Ha! There are dozens, you sweet summer child. We love the earth here and the connection the people have to it. I'm the only one who has stuck around Christchurch this millennium though. I like the excitement! The earth is so unpredictable in this city, always up to something.'

'That's what brings us here,' I said, trying to lead the conversation back on track. 'We were hoping you could locate someone for us.'

'Ooooh, what fun. Who are you looking for and where should I start?'

'He's on the South Island somewhere, we don't know where, and he's being held by the Praetorian Guard. His name is Heath Darkiro.'

'HEAF!'

I paused. That was the second time someone had called him that in my presence and the memory of my maybe dream, maybe hallucination with the Three surged through the fog of my brain.

'Tall, blond, and Scottish?' Simon asked, sounding uncertain.

'Heaf,' Gaea repeated, clapping their hands together with delight. 'She knows who I'm talking about, don't you, love?'

Joss and Simon both looked at me with surprise. 'I . . . I've heard that name before.'

'When?' Joss pushed.

'Later,' I hissed, as Gaea continued their strut down memory lane.

'We met back when I was a lot thinner and when he . . . gah, Picts. He has always been edible.'

'All true,' I murmured, glancing down to avoid meeting the gazes now levelled at me.

'My old flame, my dear friend, what kind of trouble has he gotten himself into this time?'

'He has been arrested on charges of treason,' said Joss. 'But it's a trumped-up excuse, they're just looking for a reason to hold—'

'*Treason*, shush, will you? You think I care? I've been here since long before the Treize stamped their flag in the ground, I care nothing of their "charges". My poor baby though. Will they execute him?'

'We don't think so, at least not yet. We think—'

'Joss,' Simon said, cutting him off.

Gaea watched the two men as they engaged in a silent stare-off. Delight danced in the demon's eyes before they cut back to me. Gaea mouthed 'men'.

'They want to use him as a bargaining chip to influence Tommi,' Joss said at last, as steam almost literally poured out of Simon's ears. 'Wehi said you can tell when someone is lying to you, so we need to be forthright.'

'That I can, that I can. Rest assured, the Treize don't bother with me or my kind anymore. We're beneath them, literally.'

Their booming laugh echoed through the cavern.

'Usually I would require an increased payment to keep your secrets, but I'm not a barbarian. I remember when

Heaf and I actually *knew* barbarians, so don't crease your precious forehead. My very kissable lips are sealed.'

Moving across the space, I followed the path of Gaea's impressive body with my eyes until they came to a dead stop.

'And I'll find your man,' they said, going completely still as their eyelids fluttered closed. Several moments passed in silence before Gaea stirred, their mouth twitching as they made a 'huh' sound. They swivelled on the spot so that a small cloud of dust was left in their wake, and I tracked their course with interest as worms surfaced from beneath the ground as they moved across it.

Gaea made a humming noise, their hands flitting over a column of shelves that seemed to house thousands of rolled up pieces of paper. Some looked like ancient parchment while others were the bright blue often associated with more recent blueprints. I had no idea how you would tell which was the right one, yet Gaea easily plucked a roll of yellowing paper from among the masses.

'This is what you want,' they said, carefully rolling it out on a wide wooden bench nearby. We crowded around it, looking at the plethora of black lines that crossed over and intersected with each other, seemingly at random.

'Hope y'all know what you're looking at,' I mumbled. 'Because this looks like another language to me.'

'It's old building schematics,' Simon said.

'The good news is Heaf is being held here in Christchurch,' Gaea said, holding up a finger to pause any excited sounds that may have escaped my mouth. 'The bad news is he's being held here, at the Christchurch Centre For Contagious Disease Research.'

The warm lighting around us suddenly increased in brightness so we could read the plans better.

'And it used to be known as Augustus Asylum before the Treize bought it and took over the property after World War II. The asylum was shut down for malpractice, of course.'

'Of course.' I shrugged. 'Asylums either get shut down for malpractice or turned into a horror movie set.'

'There were certainly some horrible things going on inside it,' Gaea mused. 'Now it's used as one of the Treize's New Zealand outposts. It's two floors, with the top storey shared by Askari, Custodians and Paranormal Practitioners who have a small medical bay. The ground floor is barracks, I guess you could say, for visiting colleagues. The Praetorian Guard use the basement level below that, which has a series of cells: including one holding Heaf.'

'I didn't know prisoners were held there,' Joss whispered.

'They're not supposed to be,' Simon growled. 'But look at this place, we'll never get in there.'

Gaea clicked their tongue with impatience, tapping the blueprints with a long finger. 'This tunnel here is secret. No one knows about it and it was constructed as a way for the orderlies to ferry bodies from the asylum to the cemetery without anyone finding out.'

'That could be our way in,' I mused.

'Come on,' Joss said. 'How could they *not* know about it?'

'Because these are the last existing structural blueprints,' Gaea beamed. 'And there's no one left alive to tell them the tunnel is there, except for me.'

'If the tunnel is still standing,' Simon countered. 'Any number of earthquakes could have brought it down by now, especially if no one knows it exists. It could have fallen into disrepair.'

'It's still open,' Gaea replied. 'The entrance is through

the Symbolis Family Crypt, which has a headless angel standing guard.'

I glanced at the earth demon. 'I hope you mean the cement kind.'

'I do,' they said, reaching down to grab a much newer set of blueprints. Gaea lay them side-by-side next to the old ones. 'These are what they have registered with the city council. As you'll note, only two floors are accounted for – both above ground.'

'It's as if the floors below don't exist,' I muttered. 'Or they want people to forget that they did.'

'And people have. I, however, am not people and this blueprint is the last record of what the building actually looks like *beneath.*'

I sighed, leaning back against one of the dirt walls and crossing my arms as I looked at the problem before us.

'The tunnel is our way in, but it's only our way out if we manage to get to Heath and release him undetected. How many people could be in that building at any one time?'

'It's a transient job,' Joss supplied. 'There could be ten people in there or a few hundred, but if he's being held on a floor no one is supposed to know exists then there mightn't be that many staff.'

'What you need is a distraction,' Gaea purred, leaning forward to rest their chin on their hands like Shirley Temple. Dimples formed on their round, plump cheeks as they smiled.

'Is there something you had in mind?' I asked.

'How about an earthquake—'

'What?' Simon choked.

'Just a small one,' Gaea continued. 'Itsy bitsy, really. Contained to a very specific part of the building.'

I grinned. 'Very specifically away from where we need to be?'

'Naturally,' they replied, batting their eyelashes. 'Aftershocks happen all the time, after all.'

Turning to Joss, I could see him thinking it through.

'You can't be anywhere near this,' I said. 'The car has tinted windows and shit. You drop us off at this cemetery and you stay there until we return, never once stepping out of the vehicle.'

'I know.' He nodded. 'No one will have an opportunity to see my face.'

'And if you get weird vibes or think we've been caught, you motor, Joss. Don't wait around, get out of there and get back to whatever story you're supposed to be following.'

'What about our faces?' Simon asked. 'They could have cameras down there, other prisoners who could recognise us. Even if we get Heath out—'

His words fell away as he was hit in the face with a ball of pink material. Spluttering to regain his composure, Simon pulled the items away and held them up so we could all see what Gaea had thrown at him.

'What are these?' he asked.

'Balaclavas,' they said, matter-of-factly.

'Why are they fluoro pink?'

'Why would they be any other colour?' Gaea countered.

'These will do, thank you, Gaea,' I said, snatching mine from Simon's hand. I gave both our outfits a once-over, grateful that Simon and I were dressed in indistinguishable garments of black.

'Then we should go soon,' Joss remarked, glancing down at his watch. 'The closer we get to eight o'clock and regular business hours, the harder this will be and it's already ten past six.'

'How will you know when to—'

Gaea batted a hand, cutting me off. 'I'm an earth demon, love. I can track anything that moves along me. I'll know when.'

'Aye,' I said, exhaling. Before I could think twice about it, I gave the demon a hug. They seemed startled at first, before chuckling with glee. As I pulled away, they clutched my arm with wince-inducing strength.

'Heaf's not used to being the damsel in distress, so I'm intrigued to see how this goes. Promise me one thing, will you?'

'Sure.'

'When you get our Heaf back, bring him for a visit. I haven't seen his smiling face in a decade.'

I laughed. 'I promise. I'm sure he'll be desperate to see you after all that you've done.'

'It has been a pleasure,' Joss added. 'A true honour meeting one of your kind.'

'Gosh, you're making the mites blush. Lovely to meet you too, cutie.'

Joss slipped something discreetly into Gaea's hand, but the movement was so quick I almost missed it. Simon nodded a farewell to the earth demon, thanking them profusely before we followed Joss out the way we came. When we emerged on the surface, the early morning air seemed unbelievably fresh as I breathed it in.

'That was one of the strangest experiences of my life,' Simon said, dusting loose granules of dirt off his shoulder.

'What did you give them?' I asked Joss, curious about the price of our transaction.

'It's disrespectful to deal with an earth demon and not pay.'

'The price?' I pressed.

'A dozen pearls,' he said, smiling at my shocked reaction. 'Wehi said precious stones mean little to them, as they're a result of their very existence. Pearls, on the other hand, don't form inside the earth. They're a completely foreign and hypnotising object to earth demons, Gaea especially.'

The fact Wehi had had pearls on hand seemed like the least weird thing in what had been an increasingly weird year. We piled into the car as Simon pelted across the city, going as fast as he could while remaining inconspicuous. He knew exactly where the cemetery was, and while he focused on getting there, I selected a handful of weapons for each of us.

When I looked up, gravestones were flying by the window and I caught a glimpse of an elaborate iron fence as we drew closer. Slowing down and switching off the lights, Simon rolled through the entrance of Aldershot Old Cemetery. The property looked like it extended for kilometres in each direction, which I knew was accurate from glancing at both the map and blueprints. At the northern end was the Symbolis Family Crypt, looming large among a line of other family crypts that distinguished the more affluent graves. There was a large stone wall signalling the official end of the cemetery's property and the start of the asylum's. I couldn't see what was over the other side, but my insides churned like they knew something bad was coming. Simon pulled to a stop and we sat in the car for several moments.

'How long should I wait for?' Joss asked.

'Until seven thirty,' Simon answered.

'That doesn't leave you long.'

'If we're in there for more than fifteen minutes, we're going to have bigger issues than the deadline.'

Simon unclipped his seatbelt, signalling that it was time for us to leave.

'On yer bike,' Joss said, as close to a farewell as we could spare. Simon and I climbed out of the car and tooled up. The day was going to be an overcast one thankfully, but it was still getting lighter every minute as the clocked ticked further into the am.

'What are we about to get ourselves into, cuz?'

'Heroic shite?' I offered. 'A rescue mission?'

He chuckled, rolling his neck and shaking out his muscles as he did so. 'It's almost a shame our aim isn't to leave a body count, cos there are some scores I wouldn't mind settling in that building.'

'Well,' I said, strapping a machete to a sheath at my thigh and tucking extra ammo under the strap of my bra. 'If you're a good boy this time, then I might just let you have a massacre of your very own on the next trip. As a treat.'

He smirked, following me as we jumped a small, ornamental fence that surrounded the family's crypt and came to a stop in front of a structure that would have looked like nothing more than a rundown, overgrown greenhouse during broad daylight. Vines and bushes had grown over the building and formed a thick layer of shrubbery over the years.

'This is it, right? This is where they brought out the bodies after the live lobotomies?'

'No more lobotomy talk, Simon.'

Someone obviously once had intentions for this place, as they had tried to cover the entrance to the tunnel but they'd given up halfway through. Everything had been left to rot. The door was boarded up, but it didn't take more than a few well-placed kicks for me to dislodge the rotting wood. A strong stench of decaying earth washed over us as air escaped from the enclosed space and I heard Simon cough and take a step back.

I braced my senses, closing my eyes and soaking in the many smells that wafted up from below, careful to place everything and make note of anything that could be a warning of what was to come. I strained my hearing, pushing myself as far as I could to try and decipher threats from within the darkness. Nothing. I opened my eyes, taking in the narrow set of concrete steps and unstable railing where it led down into the abandoned tunnel.

My irises shifted by instinct now, warping from human to wolf so seamlessly I barely had to blink as the path before me was illuminated. The route was divided by a rusted old banister that was slick with moisture and moss, lest I be tempted to touch it for added support. There were old fragments of glass that crunched under my boots as I inched down, step-by-step. I had a Glock loaded and extended in front of me, just in case there were surprises waiting around the next corner as we came to the bottom of the decline.

'Suns out, guns out,' Simon whispered.

We made our way along what had once been a platform, broken tiles sticking up at odd ends beneath our feet. The occasional beer bottle rolled away with our movement as someone's foot brushed it, remnants of a celebration once held in this prime abandoned location. The floor was slippery with moisture: everything in here was damp, even the very air felt wet when you breathed. A rhythmic drip-drip-drip was our soundtrack as we moved through.

We followed a rusty track going in only one direction and I jumped soundlessly down to the bottom level. The last few metres of the platform ran alongside us at eye-height before we were truly in a deep, dank tunnel. The ceiling was higher than any tunnel I had ever seen, extending in a curved shape some hundred metres above our heads like a Gothic cathedral.

My eyes scanned the roof carefully, making sure we hadn't overlooked anything simply because it was out of our line of sight. The ceiling was a black, moving mass where thousands of bats hung from it: wriggling and writhing against each other. Their squeaks had been louder when we first entered, but they died down now as we prowled beneath them. They sensed predators and fell quiet as we passed.

'We're officially in the Bat Cave,' I muttered.

The tunnel was getting narrower and we were forced into single file as the path beneath us disappeared altogether. Any sign of the intended purpose of this space became invisible beneath weeds and loose stones that made up the sorry excuse for a floor. There was even a period briefly where the ceiling opened up, exposing the morning sky to us through bars that crisscrossed above.

'We must be at sewer level now,' Simon suggested. 'You can smell it.'

He was right. The unmistakable stink of shit, piss, waste, and things rotting wafted up as the tunnel slopped downwards and we disappeared under the roof again.

'God, that's rank,' I coughed, my eyes watering with the intensity of the smell. The trail's downward slope became more extreme as we neared the end of the tunnel, just like we'd seen it would on the blueprints. Water pooled at my toes as the ground sank lower and soon I was knee-deep in it. There was only one more bend in the tunnel before we'd ascend a small set of stone stairs, but the water was getting deeper and deeper. The path had been flooded for some time and moss had grown from the water level and up the walls in thick, clotted clumps. Probably the result of another earthquake, I thought, before internally cursing myself for thinking about an earthquake while I was underground.

Please have our back, Gaea, I thought. The water was freezing and stagnant, the stench so thick it was almost bitter on the tongue. We were deep in it and my lack of height was not helping as the liquid was now just under my armpits. It made it difficult to get to any of my weapons easily and I had my arms raised at an odd angle to make sure my gun didn't get wet. Given that Simon was built like a Hemsworth brother, he was faring a little better.

In the darkness, the liquid looked black – almost inky – and small ripples pushed out from my body. I could see the stairs a mere fifty metres in front of us as they led out of the water and to a rusted old door that would bring us up underneath the secret cells. I kept scanning the surface of the water and told myself not to panic. I increased my pace anyway and only felt relief once one of the concrete steps was solid beneath my feet. My body was heavier as I pulled myself on to the ledge, water streaming from all of my garments.

'Here, Pussy Riot,' Simon whispered.

Crouching down so he could fit as well, I wordlessly took the pink balaclava Simon handed me and pulled it over my face. Taking extra time to make sure all of my braided hair was tucked in, I strained to hear what was on the other side of the door. Simon held up five fingers to indicate that he could sense five other beings. I nodded and waited for our distraction to come through. The first shudder nearly sent a yelp of fear from my mouth. I bit my tongue to prevent any noise and gripped Simon's shoulder for dear life.

22

———

The world felt violent as it shook around us, a deafening growl curdling up from deep within the earth. I squeezed my eyes shut as specks of dirt, dust and heck knows what else dislodged themselves from the structure and fell in a shower around us. We were experiencing the mildest effects, I reminded myself. Everywhere else would be feeling this much, much worse. The vibrations eventually died away, leaving Simon and me to listen to shouts and orders being issued from the other side of the door. There was a small rumble far off in the distance and I knew that something big had collapsed, even if I couldn't necessarily see it.

'Good job, Gaea,' I whispered, getting to my feet. Steadying myself on the door, I cast Simon a sideways glance.

'There's no quiet way to do this,' he said.

'Then let's not be quiet.'

With a nod of his head, we both silently counted to three before kicking the door in unison. It made a metallic screech that only got louder as we repeated the motion four more times. Finally – on the fifth go – the door flew from its hinges and landed with a clutter on the ground. We stepped inside a small, dank room that housed several old barrels, some discarded medical equipment, and even an old gurney with rusted handrails.

'Where's the entry' Simon asked, his eyes scanning the solid brick walls around us.

'It must have been walled up years ago,' I replied, noting that there was practically no light in the space, save for the tiniest glow coming from above us. I craned my next upwards and let out a puff of air.

'What?'

'The only way through, is up,' I said, pointing at the steel vent above us.

'We've come out directly under the Praetorian Guard cells,' he noted, reaching up and lacing his fingers through the grating. 'No wonder Gaea was confident nobody knew this tunnel existed: no one knows this *level* exists.'

I watched his muscles strain as he pulled against the structure. His hands had morphed from human to wolf and the longer he flexed, the more the transformation spread down Simon's limbs from his claws to his shoulders. I ducked a spray of concrete as he yanked the grate free from the ceiling with a triumphant grunt.

'Can you fit through here?' I asked, placing a foot in the cradle he had made for me with his hands. Hoisting myself up into the space, I shifted just enough so that my claws got a firm grip on the damp walls, then I pressed my legs into the sharp corners and slowly inched my way up.

'You should worry less about me and more about the Pict.'

'He'll fit,' I replied, not wanting to admit that he had a point. 'He has to.'

It was only ten metres or so we had to navigate vertically before my head gently bumped the steel grate at the other end. Looking down, I watched Simon drop to a crouch before he sprung into the space with superhuman agility and scrambled to get a grip. Waiting until he was a few inches below the heel of my foot, I used his prowess as inspiration to throw my full body weight upwards into the grate above me. My frame was still trying to heal itself from the coming of age and didn't take kindly to me putting it through this kind of strain so soon afterwards. Yet it worked and I dislodge the steel covering and pull myself up and on to the floor of the PG's holding cells. The earthquake had done the trick, with the bodies we had heard moving about freely in here earlier having vacated to more pressing areas of the building: all except for one, unlucky rookie. I almost felt sorry for him as I reached my hand down into the shaft and hauled Simon up behind me with a groan. No member of the Praetorian Guard was a pushover and this lad probably had centuries on me, but it was hard to take him seriously as his mouth hung open with shock as two intruders hidden behind pink balaclavas climbed out of a hole in the floor shortly after an earthquake.

'What the hell . . .'

He took a few uncertain steps towards us as his mind tried to digest what he was seeing and I seized that opportunity. Staying low to the ground, I sprinted across on all fours and yanked his ankles with both of my hands. He didn't even have time to let out a yelp as his head connected with the floor and he was knocked out cold.

'Sorry, mate,' I whispered. Patting him down, I found and unhooked a keychain from inside his pant pocket and held it in the air triumphantly. I could hear Simon busy around me, ripping down every camera he could see in the room. I had been hoping that Gaea's interference would take them out of operation, but we couldn't be sure. We also didn't know if we'd be able to see every monitoring device clearly, so had agreed not to use names in a bid to disguise our identity.

'Woman,' Simon called and I spun around. There were only half a dozen cells in this room, with the rest of the level closed off behind doors that looked sturdy and alarmed. Not that they would be expecting anyone to escape, mind you. The floor was white and tiled, giving the place a sinister cleanliness that I didn't like, especially when I noticed small drains positioned every few metres – including in the cells. There was a steady trickle of water mixed with blood snaking its way into one of them and my eyes followed its path to the source.

My breath caught as I took in Heath's appearance. His arms hung above him on either side, held in place by manacles that had bitten into the flesh enough that blood was streaking down his wrists. His blond hair was covering his face in thick clumps where the blood had coagulated. He was naked, with no garment to cover the damage they had done to his body: cuts and burns and deep abrasions that marked his skin like the Pictish tattoos. His old scars had been hidden under new ones and I realised a deep, primal growl was radiating from within my body.

Heath's head twitched at the sound, slightly shaking from side-to-side as if he was trying to wake from a nightmare. Eventually, his shoulders stiffened as he realised whatever he was imagining was *actually* real and I saw his blue eyes peer out from under the curtain of his matted locks. It seemed to take a moment for him to process the scene – from my sopping wet clothes to the pink balaclava –

and when he finished giving me a once over, his mouth twitched up into a lazy smile.

'Hey babe,' he breathed, the words barely audible.

There was a mechanical clank as Simon unlocked the cell door and began working on Heath's hands. I hadn't even noticed my cousin slip the keys from my clenched fist. Snapping out of it, I leapt into action and caught Heath just as his body dropped from the wall.

'Hey there, big fella,' I whispered, using every muscle I'd been building up over the past few years to support his body as it rested on my shoulders. Simon went to slip himself under Heath's other side, but I shooed him away.

'Keep an eye on what's ahead of us,' I grunted.

We took it one unsteady step at a time, our pace quickening as Heath slowly regained momentum and got used to the feeling of solid ground under his feet. He nuzzled his head against the curvature of my neck, as if looking for the Tommi he knew and remembered, but finding only the tough cotton of my balaclava. It didn't seem to matter to him though, as he let out a contented sigh.

'Tha gaol agam ort,' he murmured so quietly I wasn't even sure Simon picked it up.

We came to a stop at the gaping hole in the floor we had crawled out of. If possible, it somehow appeared to have gotten wider and I noticed tiny cracks and fissures extending out from the source. Simon noticed it too and gave me a quizzical look. *Gaea.*

'I'll go first.' He shrugged. 'Send him down after me.'

I nodded, watching as Simon planted his two feet together and leapt forward. He dropped down like he was moving on an invisible elevator and I heard him land perfectly at the bottom. Heath unlinked himself from my body, preparing for his own descent.

'I wouldn't advise that,' I said, awed by Simon's display of werewolf dexterity. With a start, I realised that Heath was actually shuffling away from me and towards the secure doors that kept the prison locked off from the rest of the building.

'What are you—'

'Only take a minute,' he replied, coming to a stop in front of a bank of computers and screens that looked as if they monitored the cellblock.

'We don't have a minute,' I hissed.

'What's taking so long?' Simon shouted.

'Nothing,' Heath called, limping back towards me as quickly as he could. He was gripping something in his hand and passed it to me, pressing it into my palm.

'Put this somewhere safe, will you?'

He was missing a pinky finger and that's what I noticed first, rage coursing through me at the idea of them taking *and keeping* any part of him. Then I glanced down at what looked like a USB of some description. Quickly tearing off a piece of material from my shirt, I wrapped it delicately and tucked it into my bra. When I was done, I blinked. Heath was gone. There was a sharp whistle and I jerked my head to look down into the shaft. He was already halfway to the bottom, taking it slowly one inch at a time until he found the space that opened up below. Simon helped him to a standing position as I scuttled my way after them, still hurting too much to be able to do anything impressive like my comrade had.

'Where to now?' Heath asked, looking around the dank room until his eyes focused on where we had kicked the door free. 'Oh.'

'Hope you don't mind getting wet,' Simon huffed, leading the way off the platform and into the murky water.

We weren't moving slow or quietly this time; we were trying to get out of there as quickly as we could. The noisy splashing covered the sound of a small gasp that escaped my lips, my grip loosening on Heath's arm as he moved ahead of me. Hovering directly in front of me in the tunnel was the ghost of a woman dressed in a tattered hospital gown. The vision of her shuddered slightly as my cousin marched right through, completely unaware of her presence. I stayed frozen on the spot, unable to move as she looked backed at me.

'Tommi,' Heath said, having realised that I stopped. 'What is it?'

'I-I . . . nothing,' I replied, swallowing the fear I felt and pushing forward. 'It's nothing.'

He reached backwards, holding out his hand for me to take. I blinked as another ghost appeared, this one an old man who was missing both his arms. His mouth was twisted in a permanent grimace that looked like a scream. I entwined my fingers in Heath's, the water and his blood making our grip slippery as he tightened his hand around mine. He yanked me forward, towards the ghosts and eventually through them.

My thighs burned with the exercise and inwardly I felt relief as the ground underneath us sloped upwards, signalling that we were nearly back on dry land. My feet stumbled with the change of terrain and Heath steadied me. I gave him a grateful smile, willing myself not to turn around and look at the dead who were watching us. I couldn't be certain, but I felt like the number of ghosts had doubled since I passed them: the bluish glow from their bodies having brightened exponentially.

I used the extra light to guide Heath from the tunnel, steering him out behind Simon until we burst from the

Symbolis Family Crypt and into the early morning air. Heath dropped to his knees with relief, his body sinking into the grass as he closed his eyes for a moment and took several deep breaths. The Ford Ranger was waiting exactly where we left it and the headlights flashed on and off quickly, indicating that Joss was safe and waiting for us behind the wheel.

'Let's move,' sighed Simon, before suddenly we *all* started to do just that. In fact, the whole cemetery began moving as the ground shook beneath our feet.

'It's another earthquake,' I said, having to shout to be heard over the grumble of the earth. There was a crunching sound coming from far off and I watched one of the nearby tombstones crack down the centre and collapse on to the ground. A cloud of dust exploded from the crypt behind us, sending dirt and debris flying like disgusting confetti.

Without needing to say a word, we all sprinted for the car, which Joss already had idling as Heath and I dived in the back and Simon in the front. With an impressive bit of defensive driving I hadn't known he was capable of, Joss revved the engine and whipped the vehicle around in one swift movement, gravel spraying up behind us. Heath and I stared through the back window as we accelerated out of the cemetery, leaving the unsteady earth in the rear-view. He turned to me, a half-smile decorating his battered face.

'I see you met Gaea,' he laughed.

'They just collapsed the tunnel behind us!' Simon said, surprise and delight mirrored in his tone. 'I'm gonna kiss the next earth demon I see!'

'They'd probably like that,' Joss replied.

I pulled a blanket out from under the seat in front of me and wrapped Heath in it like a huge, Scottish burrito. Yanking the balaclava off my face, I watched as his smile grew larger and larger as he drank me in. The grin faltered for a second and I realised he had just noticed my eye. I couldn't read his expression as he reached out for me, holding my face in his hands for what felt like minutes.

'Like my new look?' I asked, jokingly, yet feeling strangely vulnerable in his presence.

He smiled, almost sadly. 'I adore it, lass.'

He leaned forward and kissed me, like it had been the lifeline he had was waiting for this past week. Holding him close, I didn't care what Simon and Joss thought or what they were seeing as I transferred every bit of love I had into returning the movement of Heath's lips. The car rocked backwards and forwards as we moved through Christchurch, driving closer and closer to safety. Yet it didn't seem to matter now that I had him back with us, back with me, where he belonged.

SIMON HAD Joss ditch the car in a dodgy part of town, telling him to leave the windows down and the keys in the ignition. Heath hotwired a beaten-up ute that looked like no one had loved it in a long time, with Joss and I squeezing into the tiny space behind the cab while the larger among us took the proper seats.

'Are you sure this is a good idea?' Joss asked. 'Just leaving the Ford Ranger behind like that?'

'Bro.' Simon smiled. 'It will be gone within the hour. Max.'

'Aye, but what if they can track it back to you or the Ihi pack?' I questioned.

Heath scoffed, chuckling to himself. Simon cast him a sideways look and they both burst out laughing as we joined the main throng of commuter traffic. I glanced at Joss – whose face was painfully wedged between my feet – he looked as puzzled as I was about the joke we clearly hadn't gotten.

'Please,' Simon said, breathless. 'We've been staying ahead of the Treize for a while now, Tommi. We know what we're doing.'

Given what I'd seen so far, I knew he was right. The Ihi pack had been around for a long time and with every mistake they'd made – every battle they'd lost or werewolf they'd said goodbye to – they had learned. The Ihi pack had adapted and evolved until they'd finally become the threat the Treize had feared so much. By trying to destroy them, the supernatural organisation had ended up *making* them.

'What are you smiling about?' Heath asked, catching the wee grin that was playing on my face in the rear-view mirror.

I met his gaze, my smile getting wider. 'Nothing.'

Aruhe was waiting and the second we pulled into the long driveway, a steel gate rolling shut behind us, my sister had the garage door folding back down to hide the car from view. Most of the house was hidden from the casual passer-by thanks to a looming row of hedges, which bordered the property along with a Gothic fence. It wasn't quite creepy enough to be 'that' spooky house on the residential street where it sat, but it was probably enough to keep neighbourhood kids away.

'Jesus Christ!' Aruhe exclaimed, as I helped Heath from the passenger's side. 'You look fucked, what did they do to you?'

'Nice to see you too, pup.'

'Get the door, will ya,' I hissed. She obliged, awkwardly

watching as someone she was used to seeing physically strong was reduced to a state of weakness.

'Where did that heap come from?' Tiaki said, appearing from the lounge and catching a glimpse of the ute.

'Thought it was best to switch,' Simon said, embracing her briefly. 'The rego sticker was two months overdue, no one is going to report it nicked.'

'I'm just glad you're safe,' she said, sounding less like the pack leader I now knew her to be and more like a worried aunt. Carefully lowering Heath on to a table in the kitchen that had been prepped for his arrival, I felt a deep relief at the sterilised needles, stitching, bandages and raft of medical supplies I saw assembled there. Standing back to fully look him over, I felt Wehi's presence at my side.

'Where do we start?' the old man whispered. At first, I thought he was overwhelmed by the sheer state of the injuries. It wasn't until I glanced at his face – serious and ready – that I realised he was asking Heath to tell him what was the priority.

'The cuts on my lower abdomen are deep, deeper than they should have gone, and I think they've cut into the muscle.'

Wehi nodded, moving towards the needle and thread.

'He's missing a finger on his left hand,' I said, feeling helpless.

'S'all right, love.' Heath grinned. 'I'm right-handed anyway.'

'Clean him off first,' Tiaki barked at me, pointing to a tap attachment that ran from the kitchen. 'Wash him down with that hose there, don't worry about the water.'

I ran the stream over my hand until it was warm – not hot – and slowly poured it over Heath's body. There was an anti-bacterial liquid soap that Aruhe handed me and I apologised as I worked up a lather. I knew it would sting. He winced only occasionally, particularly when I moved the hose to the cuts hidden under his hair and tried to get rid of the dried blood there.

'You got tetanus?' Heath asked when I was done, climbing into a pair of jocks Simon tossed him along with a towel. The werewolf pointed it out to him and I let out a small gasp as Heath grabbed it, removing the cap with his teeth and plunging the syringe into a gash across his shoulder. He flinched, barely, before dropping the needle to the ground.

'Tommi, do you know how to cauterize a wound?' he asked me.

'Hot bit goes on flesh,' I murmured, meeting his gaze. 'Pain ensues.'

'I need you to do it.'

'Um ... '

He held his left hand forward, the one that was missing a finger. 'They kept the digit, I won't be getting it back anytime soon and the tissue is already dead. This is the quickest way to seal the wound.'

I hesitated, gripping his wrist tightly with my two hands as I held him still. There was a slight tremble running through him, I could feel it.

'If you don't think you can do it Tommi – ' Simon started to say, before Heath cut him off.

'I've watched her dismember a werewolf with an axe, she can do it.' He turned his gaze back to me, tone softening. 'Please.'

He wanted me to do it. For whatever reason he needed it to be *me* rather than anyone else in the room. I didn't want to cause him pain, but I nodded and extended my hand. The handle of a small knife was placed in to it, the end of the blade already hot as a I felt the heat near my skin.

'Five seconds, hold it on for five seconds,' Wehi was saying as I moved it closer.

'Keep your eyes on me,' I told Heath, willing him to be brave.

'Where else would they be?' he smirked, but it was strained as he steeled himself.

Simon placed something in front of his face, telling him to bite down and Heath did so just as the blade made contact with his skin. He held stiller than I could have ever imagined anyone being able to as a singeing sound mixed with the scent of burning flesh. In my head I counted, pulling away the instant I reached the fifth second.

'GARGH!' Heath cried, spitting out what Simon had given him and sagging against me as I held him, his skin slick with sweat. He was shaking and I pressed a kiss on to his shoulder, followed by another, and another, while whispering that he was so brave. Because he was *so* brave. Wehi gently moved me out of the way as he began working on wrapping and treating the newly cauterized wound.

Passing the knife to Simon, I stepped away for a moment. Retreating deeper into the kitchen, I searched until I found a bottle of whiskey. Taking a quick swig for myself, I returned to the group. Wordlessly, I handed Heath the bottle and a handful of painkillers. He gave me a grateful look, his face pale and drained as Tiaki and Wehi continued working on multiple areas at once.

'Will you explain how I do this?' I asked Tiaki, gently taking his red and swollen wrist from her.

'It's not broken, just sprained maybe. So we want to place the splint underneath, yes, that's it. Then we bandage around his wrist, tight but not too tight so we can allow room for swelling.'

'It's kind of like wrapping a present,' I noted, as she moved away to work on tidying up several cuts.

'Except there's no treat inside' Heath said, his voice tense with discomfort. I met his gaze and he gave me a cheeky grin.

'I don't know about that,' I whispered, pointedly looking back down at his wrist.

'Were there any problems getting him out?' Wehi asked, not even sparing a moment to glance away from needlework.

'No,' Simon said. 'Gaea was very . . . helpful.'

'If by "helpful" you mean told us exactly where he was and created a casual earthquake as a diversion,' Joss scoffed.

'Like I said, *helpful.*'

'I was wondering how you found me,' Heath mused, looking at Simon and Joss thoughtfully. 'Go on then. Walk me through what's been going on in the outside world. I need the distraction.'

Arhue carried the burden of talking, with Simon seemingly too tired to do anything more than nod and grunt in key parts. Heath listened carefully and looked pleased when it was mentioned that most of the Treize – including Lorcan – thought we were all in lockdown at the Ihi property in Rotorua. That expression expanded when he heard Joss was feeding them misinformation as he continued his own 'search' on the South Island.

His jubilation didn't last for long and he darkened when Aruhe got to explaining why it was important to keep them focused north when we were all south, specifically me being stuck in an in-between state. I finished wrapping his wrist and placed it gently against his body, tying it in a thin cotton sling that was handed to me. It felt like Heath's eyes were drilling into mine and eventually I met his gaze. He was looking at me, just *me*, as I was and as I existed. Then his focus shifted to my eye, his forehead burrowing into a frown.

'You did the right thing,' Tiaki said, breaking the silence that had descended on the room. 'They would not have been able to save her. In two to three days, she would have slipped away forever. This was pack business.'

'I know,' he said, still not looking away from me. 'I was confident in my choice then and I'm confident in it now.'

He reached up his bandaged left hand, cupping my face in it, and I closed my eyes for a moment to let out a contented sigh.

'But it's not without consequences,' Heath continued.

'There's no way they can tie us to your breakout,' Simon snapped. 'No way in hell. Our faces were covered, the tunnel is destroyed and the car's gone even if they tracked us that far. I'd say most of the other evidence is too, including the cameras.'

'Gaea is thorough,' Heath agreed. 'And they can't solely place it on them either: there's more than one earth demon on the South Island. Earth demons are connected to everything, they'll be ten steps ahead of any Treize counter-measures.'

I nodded. 'They said the Treize had forgotten about their kind, ignored them.'

'But we haven't,' said Wehi, rinsing blood from his hands in a small bowl. 'This is our land and it's a living thing. We remain connected to it and all those who dwell within it.'

'Am I done?' Heath asked, slowly inching himself off the table. Tiaki prowled around him twice, inspecting the damage and the areas we had tried to repair.

'For now,' she said. 'You'll have to move carefully for the next week, like her.'

She jerked her head in my direction and I took a small bow to demonstrate my obedience.

'Moving either of you is out of the question,' she continued.

'No,' he replied. 'We need to get off the South Island and back to the North as soon as possible. There can't be any extra focus or attention here. Christchurch is too cl—'

He stopped himself, shaking his head.

'Too close to what?' Joss asked.

'Whatever they were torturing him for,' I answered, arms crossed as Heath cast me a sideways glance. 'Whatever needs "factions" working together. Whatever is big enough that I was pulled into a spiritual Skype meeting with the Three, Casper's ghost brother, and Mari. Whatever requires secrets worth risking multiple lives over. Like Dr Kikuchi's.'

Joss's mouth opened and shut several times as he tried to process everything I had just said. Even Aruhe was blinking rapidly, making noises from her throat like she was about to say something and then repeatedly changing her mind. Tiaki, Simon, and Wehi were all silent: they knew what this 'whatever' was. So did Heath, who was watching me cautiously.

'Sue's not dead,' he said, speaking up. It was honestly the last thing I had expected him to say.

'She—'

'We staged her death,' Heath continued, cutting me off. 'Hers and her wife's. We made it look like something the Treize would do, so they would constantly be searching internally to see exactly who had given the order. In the meantime, it gave us enough of a window to make sure both women were safe, away, and somewhere they could be of use.'

'When ... when was this?' I stammered.

'Not long after I needed you as muscle in Galway.'

'Should they all be hearing this?' Tiaki asked, glancing pointedly at Joss.

'They know enough,' Wehi answered, as if deciding for the room. 'Everyone has pieces, the time has come to assemble them.'

Heath nodded at the old man. 'Get the ghost, will you? If we're going to do this, we should *do* this.'

For a moment, I thought he meant my father. I had never met him, never even come close, and I had only a second to panic before a different ghost appeared.

'Barastin,' I whispered, Casper's brother materialising just seconds after Wehi had closed his eyes and looked briefly like he was meditating.

'How do you do?' He smiled, amused as several yelps came from the lips of those gathered. 'I have to say, Tommi, you've looked better. You too, Heath.'

'Not now, Creeper,' Heath responded, rolling his eyes as he turned to me. 'This the ghost you saw on your, uh, spiritual Skype meeting or whatever you called it?'

'Aye.'

'Right. For everyone else in the room not acquainted – Aruhe, Joss, Simon – this is Barastin Von Klitzing, twin brother of Corvossier, affectionately known as Creeper and Casper. He's also, quite clearly, dead.'

'Mā, you . . . you know him?' Aruhe asked, blinking as she stepped towards Barastin's otherworldly form.

'He has been our liaison for the past few months,' she said, as if it were the most normal thing in the world. 'Wehi and Creeper have known each other ... longer.'

The old man nodded discreetly, while Barastin's eyes twinkled as he stared at me.

'So.' He beamed. 'I see you haven't caught them up on everything you saw.'

'I wasn't sure *I* saw what I saw, frankly.'

'Oh, you did. And if these are your chosen allies, it's time to dish.'

My eyes swept over the face of my best friend, over Tiaki and Wehi in one corner, Simon and Aruhe in another, then Heath, who had honestly never looked worse. His hands were shaking slightly as he lifted the whiskey bottle to his lips, a dribble of alcohol escaping out of the side of his mouth. He wiped it with the back of his hand, before eventually returning my stare.

I did indeed 'dish', recounting everything I had seen and heard while I had hovered in that in-between place between life and death. Joss took a seat somewhere during all of that, Mari's cameo being a lot for him to handle. I understood that feeling. When I was done, I excused myself for just a moment before returning with an oversized woollen jumper that I passed to Heath. I had to help him into it, there were too many injuries external and internal for him to move freely. He didn't grumble about it though: he just took the assistance without a word and then leaned into me as he remained sitting on the table, blanket wrapped around his nether regions.

'The Three are dying,' Joss mumbled, as if he couldn't believe it.

'Technically right now they're just sick,' Barastin corrected. 'Gravely ill, actually. But in a few months' time, they'll let themselves die. Despite everything the Treize is doing to try and sustain them.'

'They're doing terrible things to your kind,' I recited. 'And others.'

'And then what?' my best friend questioned, slumping back in his chair. 'The Three die and then ... what?'

'The Three die,' Heath repeated. 'And then we strike.'

My head jerked around to look at him, noting the clench of his jaw and the way his pulse was thrumming hard enough that I could see it through the skin of his neck.

'Who is we?' Joss asked, flummoxed.

'Factions,' I murmured, more than one thing finally clicking into place for me. 'God, I'm such a fucking idiot. I feel like I've been playing catch-up this entire time and now that I'm caught up—'

'Dizzying, isn't it?' Barastin chirped.

'It's an uprising,' I said, letting the words echo around the room. I didn't need to see the looks on Tiaki and Wehi and Simon's faces to confirm it. As soon as it was said out loud, I knew it to be true. All the secrets, all the stakes, all the interconnectedness between beings who should have absolutely no business with each other, that's what *this* was.

'Honestly,' Barastin said, pointing his finger between Aruhe and Joss. 'You two are doing great impressions of the shocked-face emoji right now. You know, the—'

He mimicked the face, hands slapped on either of his cheeks and mouth wide open.

'I love it,' he finished, with a grin.

'They wanted you to know,' Heath said, looking at me. 'The Three pulled you to that place, had Mari do it so you would know it was true. I've been trying to keep you safe, trying to do everything in my power not to get you mixed up in this, but all of that was futile because they clearly want you knee-deep in the danger with us.'

'Good,' I growled. 'I'm useful! I can be of use! I'm a

soldier, how many times have you said it? And I survived the coming of age with this Terminator eye upgrade, let me help. Do not do this alone. Do not keep me in the dark.'

I wasn't quite shouting, but I was forceful. Even though it was Heath's face I was hovering just inches away from, I wasn't speaking only to him: I was speaking to Tiaki, to Wehi, to Simon, to the power players of the Ihi pack, and to the ghost, naturally, and whoever he represented. Heath's left hand reached out, stroking the length of my neck tenderly as he stared deep into my very being.

'But you see so well in the dark,' he whispered.

I pressed my forehead against his, gently resting our skin against skin. '*Please.*'

He pecked me, lips barely brushing against the flesh of mine, but it was a Ross River Fever kiss. It sent fire into my bones.

'Aye.'

23

At some point, somebody asked what was being hidden on the South Island. I assumed it was Joss, because honestly that's the kind of smart question he would ask. But I couldn't be certain. Once the werewolf was out of the metaphorical bag and everyone got talking, they didn't stop. Turns out the 'what' was actually a 'who'.

'You've met her,' Heath said. 'Sweet, quiet, and pregnant.'

'The Galway girl?' I spun to face Barastin – who had already started humming the tune – and clicked my fingers at him. *'Don't.'*

He raised his hands in surrender.

'Her name is Sadie Burke,' Heath continued. 'She's a banshee, and any day now she's about to give birth to—'

'Triplets,' I finished. I had heard their wee heartbeats. He nodded.

'Here? On the South Island?' Aruhe questioned. 'Why?'

'Because it's the last place the Treize would look,' Tiaki explained. 'And she's under our protection.'

She frowned. 'Why is the Ihi pack protecting a pregnant banshee?'

'Not the Ihi pack, girl, or, not *just* the Ihi pack: all were-wolves in Aotearoa.'

'Oceania, actually,' Wehi murmured.

Joss was on his feet, walking slowly around the room as he peeled a mandarin and shoved the slices aggressively into his mouth.

'The Three are about to die,' he mused. 'And a banshee is about to give birth to *three* children. This reeks of prophecy.'

Barastin made a wavy gesture with his hands. 'Kind of yes, kind of no. It's inevitable, this cycle. Life. Death. All of it. The Three see so much and they're tired. They're ready to leave, and if they do, there must be another force of similar power in their place.'

The otherworld sisters, I thought to myself, the Three's words sweeping through my skull like a cool breeze. *We'll liberate ourselves. The power will pass to the next.*

'The Three are banshees?' Aruhe asked. 'I never knew that.'

'Very few do,' Barastin replied. 'Considering how few banshees there are and how little we know about them as a species.'

'Three banshees.' Joss smirked, brushing over their conversation. 'That's why you want to strike then, right? When Sadie's daughters are born, the Three die and the Treize lose any predicative powers they have.'

'They haven't predicted anything fresh in a long time,' Heath said. 'Not since Tommi prowled on to the scene.'

'Me?' I blanched.

Heath pressed on. 'And yes, when the babies are born they lose their biggest advantage. That's why they're so desperate to keep the Three alive, cos once those old broads are toast they'll be at their weakest.'

It seemed as if everyone in the room held their breath for several beats, the full magnitude of what this meant – what was happening – being felt.

'We need to get off the South Island,' Heath reiterated. 'My escape is going to be noticed: that's a major Treize outpost that was destroyed, thanks to Gaea. We can't afford to have their eye focused this close to Sadie when they don't know the babies exist. We need to keep it that way.'

'Where is she?' Joss asked, as Heath's head snapped in his direction. No words were exchanged, but it was clear from the death-stare generated at my best friend that no answers would be forthcoming.

'Uh, r-right,' Joss gulped. 'So when are we moving?'

'Within the hour—'

'No,' I snapped, cutting Heath off.

'Excuse me?' He looked shocked.

'I know you're used to making all the plans and schemes, but *no.* Look at you: you're fucked, Heath. You need to rest and let your body recover. You're bleeding and broken, so am I.'

'But—'

'*NO.*'

I let the growl be heard in my voice, I let the whole room hear it. My werewolf and I were in agreement on this. He shut his mouth, his lips pressing together as he relinquished to my commands.

'You need a feed too,' I said, carefully slipping my shoulders under his arms so he had support to lean on as I helped him off the table. 'But rest first.'

'*Peak* Auntie move,' Aruhe muttered, tucking herself around Heath's other side so he was wedged between us. It took some manoeuvring, but we were able to get him to the room I had woken up in. The difference was his size: he barely fit on the bed, legs dangling off the end and toes poking out even after I tossed a blanket over him. Yet the second he hit the mattress, his eyelids fluttered as he fought to stay conscious. I went to leave him, but his surprisingly strong grip ensnared my hand.

'Stay with me,' he whispered. I looked back at Aruhe and nodded, my sister returning the gesture as she slipped from the room and closed the door behind her. Pulling up one of the chairs that was left in the room from when I'd held court a few days earlier, I rested my head on the mattress next to his face.

'Get in here with me,' Heath said, the words almost slurred he was tired.

'That would entirely defeat the purpose of "rest" now, wouldn't it?'

There was a pause before he replied with a sigh. 'Aye.'

'But I'm right here,' I reaffirmed, gripping his hand tighter and planting a kiss on the undamaged skin of his shoulder. 'I'm not going anywhere, so let your mind and body rest. For once.'

I was tired too and had to fight the compulsion to fall asleep next to him. Instead I listened to his heartbeat, to his breathing, both slowing down noticeably once he fell into a deep sleep. Carefully, I made for the door and came to a sudden stop when the ghost of Barastin Von Klitzing blocked my path. I mouthed the word 'fuck', resting a hand over my own heart as I recovered from the jump scare. He opened his mouth to say something, but I pointed to the hallway and glared.

'You can't hurt me, wolfie,' he whispered, disappearing through the wall and back to where everyone else remained gathered. They were making plans, Tiaki delegating to specific people in the group as she worked out the best way to get the seven of us to the North Island unnoticed.

'Exactly how safe is this safehouse?' Joss asked.

Tiaki gave him a withering look. 'Safe. No Treize member has ever found this or *any* of our safehouses before, let alone stepped inside. Until now.'

'Hey, I pinky-swore to secrecy,' he said. 'If they find out I've been lying about any of this, I'm dead.'

'You should go first,' Simon mused. 'Go now. It might take them a while to get around to thinking that Tommi was involved in his breakout, but when they do, you want to make sure you're easy to find and doing exactly what you said you've been doing.'

'Hide in plain sight, right,' Joss agreed, before marching off to pack the few things he had with him.

'They'll never believe the Ihi pack helped Heath,' Barastin said. 'They think you're all accounted for on the North Island. It's more likely they'll suspect people from his own team.'

There was a pause as the group digested that thought for a moment.

'You should call his people,' Simon said, handing me a phone.

'Is this—'

'It's a burner. They won't be able to track it. Destroy the phone and the SIM soon as you're done.'

'No,' Wehi spoke up. 'Get him to do it, it's safer.'

He had gestured at Barastin, who shrugged in agreement. 'Who am I ghostin?'

'Find Ginger first,' I said. 'She's the most vulnerable.'

The ghost chuckled. 'Vulnerable? She used to be a Ryanair flight attendant.'

'Ah.' I nodded, understanding.

'What does that mean?' Aruhe questioned, glancing between the two of us.

'It means she can shank a bitch confidently in a small space,' I answered.

'The rockabilly demon,' my sister muttered.

'That's the one. All right, Creeper, if you can get to her quickly I'd start there. Here are the names of the others.'

I listed off everyone I knew Heath had recruited for our personal security on this trip and descriptions of those I didn't. And then Barastin was gone, disappearing instantly as he went wherever it was ghosts went.

'That's how we've been communicating with each other safely,' Wehi said, watching my no-doubt dumbfounded expression as Barastin de-materialised. 'The ghost network.'

'It's one of the ways,' Tiaki corrected, brushing past me. 'If we vary the modes of communication, our messages are safer.'

'And he'll find them?' I asked. 'He'll be able to just . . . *whoosh* and communicate with them?'

'Yes.' Wehi nodded. 'The living leave a trail behind that can be tracked, although it's difficult. That's what makes Barastin so special: he's like his sister. He was one half of the most powerful duo of living mediums. In death, he can be just as powerful, albeit in a very different way.'

'Aruhe,' Tiaki called. 'Come help me get some kai together. Tommi will assist Wehi with putting away the medical supplies.'

'What do I do?' Simon asked, his Auntie clicking her tongue at him with annoyance.

'Clean the table and set it, ay. Honestly.'

'And find some of your clothes for Heath please,' I added, moving towards Wehi.

'That man's a monster,' my cousin huffed.

'He's six foot six, you're what? Six foot two? Six foot one? Wehi's clothes ain't gonna fit him, you're the closest match.'

'Iosefa has clothes here,' Wehi commented.

Simon looked thoughtful. 'That Samoan unit? Might work.'

There was a gentle shake to my hand as I reached out to collect some of the discarded bandages as we cleaned up. Things were in motion and my body – as much as my mind – was still trying to catch up. The wrinkled, dark-brown skin of Wehi's own hand closed around my own and clasped it for what must have been minutes. His skin was warm and comforting, as if silently urging me to take pause and relax amid the chaos. When he released me, I felt better, somehow. Not zen or any shit like that, but warm deep within my blood.

My mind was soon occupied with the myriad of chores at hand, following Wehi to a storage room, packing things away neatly, mopping the floor and throwing out anything that couldn't be saved.

'You'll be seeing more of Barastin and his friends,' Wehi said as we worked.

'Creeper?'

'Yes, not just him but other ghosts. You won't be able to stop seeing them now.'

I paused, gently touching the skin under my eye that was now white as I understood what he meant. 'I saw some already. When we were saving Heath. The others couldn't see them, but I could. And they *knew* I could.'

'Barastin is special. He can choose to be seen or unseen. For most ghosts it's one or the other and if it's the other, unseen, then that's a lonely existence. They're everywhere Tommi, the dead. And it will take some getting used to, but you will need to grow accustomed to seeing them.'

'Will . . . will they hurt me?'

'They can't. They can annoy you.'

I laughed. 'So can people.'

'They can be very useful though and they're always looking for purpose. In the coming months, your brush with death may prove more valuable than we realise.'

That was a lot to sit with, but thankfully I didn't have to let my mind dwell on it for very long as Tiaki and Aruhe emerged from the kitchen with an enormous mound of sandwiches and a huge, tossed salad. It was actually kind of genius, I thought. Everyone was anxious about what was coming, so Tiaki had found a way to focus on a small thing rather than the looming large one. Joss emerged from the hallway, strap of his bag around his shoulder, before Tiaki called him to the table. Simon muttered something under his breath in te reo, causing her to give him a stare that was equal parts deadly and quizzical.

'I'm just saying, trust you to stop the boy as he's running for his life and make sure he has a meal.'

'We all need to eat, Simon,' she replied in a tone that couldn't be mistaken for anything but that of an alpha.

So we dug in. The events of the past twenty-four hours caught up with me as I shovelled corned beef sandwiches into my mouth and tried to fight off fatigue. Barastin returned, leaning coolly against the wall as he watched us eat. I wondered if it was rude to consume food in front of a being who couldn't, but I didn't slow down. Wehi asked him for a headcount and Barastin recited the status of each member of Heath's crew as I tried to remember everything he said so I could tell the giant Scot later.

'They split after what went down at the coming of age,'

he said. 'They're all laying low and staying safe, waiting for the next move.'

'Which is flying Heath out of the country in the next hour,' Simon said.

I choked on the sip of water I had in my mouth. 'I'm sorry, fucking what?'

'Not Heath *Heath*.' Simon smiled. 'Someone who looks like him. I know a chick whose mother was a transfiguration demon, which gives her the ability to change shapes. She can't do faces, but she can transform her body enough to make it look like Heath and then just hide the facial features as if he was trying to stay under the radar.'

'His physicality is unique enough they'd buy that,' I said, thinking it through.

'Clever as.' He nodded, picking the crust off his sandwich. 'She has two associates who can help blow out the number to three people so it matches what the guard saw in the prison.'

'Where are they going?' Aruhe asked.

'Beats me.' He shrugged. 'Point is, they won't be here. While the Treize is chasing them, I thought that would give everyone enough time to get back to Rotorua.'

'I'd avoid Australia,' the ghost mused.

'Why?' I asked, suddenly curious.

'Let's just say there's a whole other issue that will be drawing their eye over there to one of their "labs".'

Simon straightened up, interested in that information. 'The wombats? The Kapoors? *Dreckly*?'

'Leave it,' Tiaki snapped, tapping her hand on the table. 'You need to focus on what's here and happening now. Trust they can handle it, and once we've helped ourselves, we can help them later. If they need us.'

The slow, steady sound of people eating was eventually

the only accompaniment. It was an easy silence, but it wasn't a comfortable one. There was too much weighing on us, both as individuals and as a group. We were at a crossroads and it felt as if everybody was conscious that the decisions we made in the coming days were going to have long-reaching effects.

'What next?' Joss asked, becoming the first person to break the silent covenant.

'For now,' Tiaki said, scraping up the last few crumbs on her plate, 'we take comfort in the fact that we're all here, we're all together, and that everyone we love is safe.'

'And after that?' I questioned, noticing as Aruhe reached out to grip her mother's hand.

Tiaki let out a sigh, but she looked determined. 'We get ready.'

ONCE JOSS LEFT with Barastin in tow to watch his back, the smart thing was to stagger our own exits. Simon and Aruhe vacated first, followed by Tiaki and Wehi, and then eventually Heath and I. None of us were to know when the others would arrive at the Ihi property or what mode of transport they'd be taking, just in case we were intercepted en route. But we all had to get back to where they thought we'd been for weeks. Heath and I were supposed to spend nearly a fortnight slowly trekking our way back to Rotorua and the safety of Ihi land, giving us as much time as possible to heal.

The house had been eerily quiet once we were eventually left alone in it. Wehi had taken me through everything I would need to do to change Heath's bandages and how to keep an eye out for infection, but I was still nervous. I could only afford a few hours' sleep at a time myself, despite being exhausted, because I didn't like the idea of both of us being unconscious for prolonged periods while we waited for our scheduled window to move.

So I explored the safehouse instead and did something I never thought I'd do: I dyed my hair a regular colour. My natural shade was dark brown, just a few tones lighter than Aruhe's, but I used a box dye of dark black found in a cupboard of disguises to cover the remaining whitish blue that clung to the bottom half of my hair now. It had been slowly fading away over time and, as I donned plastic gloves and lined my hairline with Vaseline, I realised with a start it had been twelve months since I'd last put dye in my hair. Usually I'd do it quite religiously, but bigger fish, bigger things to fry.

Blue-haired Tommi was someone everyone knew. Now I had to become someone who could disappear if she had to, covering her scars and her tattoos, covering her most recognisable features. This would make it just that little bit easier to run.

I didn't enjoy waiting and I didn't enjoy this state of flux I felt we were in. Everyone knew what was coming and what we were prepared to do. It was just a matter of when we would all start doing it. I think Tiaki must have sensed my nerves, as, when she left, the last thing she said to me was 'call one wolf and you bring the pack'.

That night, when I was treading the halls and lost in my own thoughts, I heard Heath ask for me. It was little more than a whisper, but my werewolf ears didn't miss it and I dashed through the house until I was hovering in the doorway to his room. It was just after two in the morning and even though it was dark, I knew he could see me as I stood there, watching him watching me.

'What are you doing over there?' he said, his hair fanned out on the pillow beneath him like a golden blanket.

'Just . . . lurking,' I replied.

'Get in,' he whispered, gingerly manoeuvring his body so there was enough space beside him. Carefully, I tip-toed over to the bed and wiggled my way under the doona he was holding up. He extended his good arm above me and I rested my head in the groove between his pectoral muscle and his armpit. We lay like that for some time and I thought he had fallen back asleep until he spoke up.

'You're scared of me,' he said.

'What?'

'You've never seen me vulnerable. I understand.'

'I'm not . . . I'm not used to seeing you this hurt. I don't want to break anything.'

He chuckled, the rumble bubbling up from his chest and surprising me. 'I'm not glass, Tommi. I won't shatter.'

'No.' I frowned. 'But you're not untouchable, either.'

'None of us are.'

'Aye, but you're surrounded by werewolves who can heal and endure more than a normal man can. Your *ex* is an earth demon going on centuries now, and fuck knows the extent of what Casper can do. And you're just a man, Heath. Sure, you're immortal, but you can still be killed. What they did to you—'

He silenced me with a kiss, the kind that prevented any further words forming in my brain or coming out of my mouth. When he finished, I was breathless. My heart was racing and my skin urged for more contact, even though I knew neither of our bodies could handle it in our current states. Heath let out a soft laugh as he examined the effect he'd had on me, his face inches from my own as he continued to stare.

'I've been hurt much worse than this over the years,' he said.

'I didn't know you then. I didn't see it.'

'And now you have. They tortured me for information they knew I wouldn't give them, Tommi. I'm trained to withstand that kind of thing. Plus, I knew you'd find me eventually.'

I snorted. 'How could you possibly know that, huh? I was unconscious for most of the time you were in there.'

Heath's brow furrowed at my words, his thumb running under my right eye, which no longer looked like the one he would have remembered.

'Don't,' I said, turning away so I could hide it under his arm.

'My lass,' he purred, kissing my eyelid. 'It's beautiful. Don't hide it. It's a gift.'

'At most it's a badge of honour, but a gift? Call me old-fashioned, but I'd prefer a diamond necklace or a puppy.'

'Noted.' He grinned. 'I knew someone once, a long time ago, who came back different. They could see what you can. It was a useful tool.'

'Great, now my high school bullies were right: I'm a tool.'

'I want you to tell me everything you saw when you were gone again. Every detail.'

'We have to move in two hours,' I said, checking the wall clock. 'Everyone else is gone, you should go back to sleep for a bit longer.'

'I've slept enough. Indulge me.'

It felt cathartic as I talked Heath through everything I could recall. He listened, not asking a single question as I spoke, just letting me work through the recollections. When I was done, any notion of going back to sleep was well and truly gone as Heath looked more alert than ever. If we were going to unpack this, I would need a cup of tea. Retreating momentarily to the kitchen, I returned with two steaming mugs as Heath was propping himself up in bed and switching on a lamp.

'Do you still have the USB I gave you?'

'Of course,' I said, snatching it from underneath my bra strap where I had been storing it – transferring it from top to top. I didn't know when Heath would want it, but I had sensed it was important enough for him to risk freedom so had kept it close ever since. He took it from me and plugged it into the side of one of two laptops the Ihi pack kept at the property. There was also a PC in the lounge, but this allowed us to stay warm in bed.

'What is all this?' I asked.

'It's a mirror of their local files. Or at least everything I could access in a hurry. Ah, there it is.'

Leaning in, I looked at the face of a middle-aged were-wolf man with a mop of white hair so bright it practically leaped off the screen. 'Who's he?'

'I thought I'd imagined him at first. By day five, they injected me with a hallucinogenic to see if I'd spill any secrets that way.'

'And?'

'Fucking amateurs. At one point, they brought a were-wolf in. He was drugged too, but they didn't touch him, didn't torture him, nothing. Then within twenty-four hours, he was gone.'

'It says there that he was transferred,' I said, tapping the note on his file that was displayed on screen. 'What does that mean?'

'The prison you found me in isn't a permanent facility, it's supposed to be holding cells for prisoners that are in-transit or being interrogated.'

'Okay, if—'

'You know that what you saw wasn't a dream, right?'

'With Mari? With the Three?'

'It was real, and where Mari took you to meet them is a real place too. It exists in Romania, at Treize headquarters. It's where the Three are kept.'

'If that was real, you think what they showed me is real too? The vision in goo?'

'I know the Ihi pack have been looking into missing werewolves.'

'I – hang on, how could you possibly know that?'

'I'm nosy.' Heath shrugged. 'It's my job to know other people's business. Plus, I broke into Tiaki's office on the night of the welcoming rituals.'

'Heath! I didn't even see you disappear for a second!'

'What can I say? I'm good at what I do.'

'Why didn't you tell me?'

'Firstly, it wasn't the information I had come there for – I just stumbled across it. I was trying to make sure everything was on the level with ahi hikoi and that no one from the Ihi pack was going to take you out. Secondly, at that point you weren't affiliated with the Ihi pack any more than a packet of peanuts. If their associates were dropping off the face of the earth, it wasn't my immediate concern.'

'But it's not unrelated,' I said, 'Is it?'

'Other supernaturals are disappearing too, there have been rumours about it for a while and – '

'In Australia,' I interjected. 'Barastin made an offhand comment about something big happening.'

'The rumours and random things here or there are starting to add up. The timing too. I think . . . they might be trying to find a way to save the Three.'

'By what? Stealing everyone's mojo?'

'It can't be done, but yes. They might just be desperate enough to try.'

I snorted. 'I'm sorry, it's not funny, but also it is. They've sealed their own fate, haven't they? Or at least a part of it. The Outskirt Wars might have been specific to werewolves in this part of the world and the things they wanted, but the Treize just gave all species a unifying cause.'

He made a noncommittal noise, as if he was still thinking it through. 'This USB has the location of every holding facility in the Asia-Pacific. More importantly, I need you to describe what you saw to me again: the place the Three showed you. I need every detail.'

'I've got a better idea,' I said, reaching over to grab the notepad I'd left next to the bed. 'How about I show you?'

Over the blue lines of the ruled pages, I had attempted to draw exactly what I had seen: every detail, from those being held to the guards and the shapes of the hallway.

'You drew these sequentially?' he asked, frowning as he flipped through the pages.

'Uh-huh, like a storyboard. Anything familiar?'

'Oh yeah, this looks like one specific cell in Argentina that I visited in the forties. You can tell because the cages are made out of a unique metal you can only get in *one* place.'

'Okay, Mr Sarcastic Fuck,' I laughed.

'But seriously.' He smiled, a glint in his eye returning. 'I've only been there a few times hundreds of years ago, but I know this place. And I think I know why it was shown to you.'

'You ... you do?'

'It's Vankila, Tommi. The top levels of the supernatural prison in Scotland, at least. They're holding more than just paranormal outlaws there, it seems.'

'Where Quaid is being held,' I said.

He tilted his head, looking thoughtful. 'This could be good for us.'

'Us?'

'Aye, *us.* Whatever and whoever is in there, we're going to need to break it out. And up to date information on Vankila is near impossible to find, that place is supposed to be impenetrable, so this is something.'

I expected there to be a crazed, almost maniacal look in Heath's eyes. But the way he stared at me as he spoke those words was that of a deeply sane person. Well, as sane as you could be, given the life we were leading.

'You know what this means?' I said.

'What?'

'We're going back to Scotland.'

24

I groaned, rolling over to find myself in an enormous and empty bed with a mountain of crisp, white sheets and a doona thicker than my thighs. I had woken with a headache and that – frankly – was never a good sign. Closing my eyes for a moment and willing the pounding in my head to stop, I waited patiently for my memories to come back to me. Ah, whiskey. Rum and coke. Possibly gin at some point as well, and . . . karaoke? In our hotel room?

'Oh God,' I murmured, hoping the last bit was a nightmare and not reality.

Propping myself up on my elbows, I winced at the collection of empty glasses across the room and the rest of the past evening came rushing in like water. There was a packet of aspirin, two huge water bottles, and a note that said 'eat me' resting on the bedside table. I greedily grabbed for the water, downing the first bottle at a rapid pace and then popping two aspirin before downing the second. With a heave, I got to my feet and wandered absentmindedly around the five-star accommodation Heath had splashed out on. The hotel had been his idea, naturally.

'It's the last place they'd look,' he had said, smiling mischievously.

We had left the safehouse nearly two weeks ago, locking up and leaving in the wee hours of the morning. We had a deadline to make: get to the Ihi property before the next full moon, which left us a few days up our sleeves. We could do the trip in a day if we weren't being careful, but we had to be so, *so* careful. A quick visit to Gaea – as promised – confirmed what Heath had suspected: the airports were still being watched, even if most of the hunt had moved offshore. We pinched a car off a suburban Christchurch street, swapping the plates over with another vehicle once we neared Hammer Springs and daylight was about to break.

We slept for a few hours in Abel Tasman National Park, before heading up to the coastline to meet a contact of Heath's who had a boat. He was an old guy with ashy black hair and teeth in the single digits: I couldn't sense anything supernatural about him as we climbed aboard. It was a bumpy ride as we crossed the waters between the two islands, docking just outside of Patea before we pressed on with another long drive north. Both of us had been on high alert the entire time, choosing routes that we could defend easily – if we had to – despite our recovering bodies.

We had reached our last stop late in the afternoon yesterday, with the source of Heath's increasing smugness the flash joint he had checked us into. I'd protested at first, thinking it was gaudy and too much of a risk, but the suite he had arranged for us came with a few perks including a private elevator up from the car park and our own concierge. From the moment we checked in, neither of us had set foot out of our room and I couldn't have been happier about it.

I could hear the tinkle of water coming from the enormous shower in the en suite and that – combined with some throaty singing – told me that Heath was slowly waking himself up. There was a gentle knock at the door and I threaded my way through the scattered clothes laying on the floor, tripping on a pair of Heath's Timberland boots. I quickly grabbed the short, blonde wig I'd been wearing when we checked in, pulled it into place, and wrapped a towel around my naked body. Checking the eyehole, I smiled, then I opened the door to let room service wheel in a trolley.

'Good morning, Mrs Brody,' the gent said, the same man we'd been dealing with since we arrived. 'Will that be all?'

'Yes, thank you, Ryan.' I smiled and signed the bill with a fake signature.

'Have a wonderful meal.'

It was going to be hard not to. I was almost over-whelmed by the scents and flavours that emanated from the feast Heath had ordered, which included – but was not limited to – pancakes, eggs benedict, French toast, maple bacon, scrambled eggs, blueberry bagels and orange juice. I dived in, piling the food high on my plate as I stuffed my face. Heath had said that after everything we'd been through, we deserved this and I couldn't disagree as the sweet yet salty bacon hit my lips. There was a wet kiss planted on my bare shoulder followed by several droplets that fell from Heath's hair and onto my skin.

'I see you found everything okay.' He grinned, watching me happily as I ate.

'More than okay,' I replied, swallowing both the egg in my mouth and Heath standing there shirtless with only a towel draped around his torso. My mind was flicking back to the night before, when we'd finally felt safe enough in our bodies to have sex again. In all fairness though, I don't think either of us could have endured much more of a wait.

I'd removed some of his stitches and he had done the same for me, but there were still a few wounds on Heath that remained red and angry as they healed. His finger was gone for good, but I had already watched him practicing with a sword in his left hand as he tried to get used to what wasn't there. My fingertips ran down the broad expanse of his back, inspecting the damage, until his body seemed to arch under my touch. With a quick flick of the wrist, I removed the towel and exposed him in all his naked glory. I loved all of Heath, I realised, every morsel of him. Yet as my eyes came to rest on his pert, round ass, I thought that maybe I loved this part of him the most.

'They really did break the mould when they made you, didn't they?' I asked, slapping his butt.

His eyes were smoky as he turned to face me, yanking me upwards and gently pulling away my own towel until we were both fully exposed and standing inches apart. That space was practically closed, I noted, by Heath's own readiness. He nibbled at my neck, knowing enough about my body by now to go to directly to the sensitive areas and I let out a groan of pleasure. The bandaging on his wrist brushed against my flesh as his arms wrapped around the curvature of my waist, pulling me close enough that my nipples brushed the smooth skin of his chest and his own breathing got ragged.

'Don't you wanna . . . uh, eat some breakfast first?' I asked, barely able to get the words out as his lips worked their way to my mouth.

He leaned back, giving me a dangerous look. 'Oh, I intend to.'

The looming full moon felt quite far away as he picked

me up, my legs straddled around his torso, and carried us both back to the bed. We collapsed in a tangle of limbs and grabbing hands, and his kiss was searing as his tongue met mine and I pulled his face closer to me. His own blond hair snarled up in my own as he ripped the wig from my head and pulled me higher up on the bed. My whole body was aching, but in a good way, as I used my thighs to roll him over on to his back. Straddling him, I relished the tension that was pulsing through his core as I looked down. I ripped open the condom wrapper I'd grabbed, slowly rolling it down his wide penis as he let out a tense breath. His chest was rising and falling with shallow gulps, his mouth slightly open, and his eyes wide as they waited and watched to see what I would do next. Raising my hips, I gave us both what we wanted and took him inside me. Heath wasn't the only one who cried out, our bodies now perfectly connected as I sank lower towards him.

There was the slightest tinge of pain from my body, I couldn't discern where, but I rocked it away and replaced it with a different kind of sensation. It was one that started down in the core of my being and spread outwards with warm tendrils that seemed to infect everything. I wondered if Heath could feel it too, and just as I thought it, he called my name. With one hand on my hip and another threaded in my hair, he pulled me towards him, our lips brushing as he cried my name again, and again, and again.

WATCHING trees zoom past the window as we drove by, I rested my forehead against the cool glass. The moon was nearly here and I sat comfortably with the sensation of my wolf stirring deep inside me. She wasn't impatient, she wasn't itching to break free: she knew her time to reign was less than an hour away. Heath was driving, happily humming to a Lion Babe song I had put on the radio and knew he didn't know the words to. He had one hand on the wheel, the other was reached out towards me, fingers running through the strands of my long, black hair as it flew around in the wind.

'You are not your hair,' he'd said to me back at the hotel, catching me frowning at my reflection in the mirror.

'I know but—'

'You – are – not – your – hair,' Heath repeated, punctuating each word with a kiss on the top of my scalp.

I felt a smile creeping over my face as I thought about that memory while watching him drive, contentment seemingly radiating from him. We had never been more unsafe, more threatened, since we'd known each other. Yet I'd never seen him happier. There was a buzzing sound from within his pocket and I pulled out the burner phone we used only for contact with Joss. There was an unknown number calling and he nodded at me to answer it.

'Hello?'

'Tommi, it's mint to hear ya voice.'

I let out a sigh of relief. 'You too, bawbag. Heath's driving. Where are you? Is it safe to talk?'

'Best if I don't answer the first and yes to the second. Where are *you*?'

'Rotorua. We're almost at the Ihi property now.'

'Do you find that place always smells like eggs?' he asked. 'Rotten eggs?'

'It's the mud baths.' I smiled.

'Ah, nature's farts,' he replied, his satisfied smirk practically audible. 'And I get it, by the way.'

'Get what?'

'Why you and Lorcan never worked out. And what you see in Heath.'

'Christ on a breadstick. Don't you have better things to think about?'

'Everything else I have to think about is depressing and scary. Your love life is much funner.'

'Joss.'

'Aye, hear me out. Whenever you and Lorcan are together, it always ends in a fight.'

'Cos he's a twat.'

'Whenever you and Heath are together there's, like, genuine joy pulsing from both of you just by being in each other's presence.'

I was silent, not wanting to admit he was right, and fighting to hide my own smile.

'One makes you angry, one makes you laugh. I know which choice I'd be making.'

'Thankfully it was already made a long time ago.'

'Damn it,' Joss cursed. 'I always wanted to witness a love triangle. You can't even muster one up, just a wee bit?'

'Ha,' I giggled. 'Joss, my life is less of a love triangle and more of a love straight line. As in, just two points. From A to B.'

'From H to T.'

'Oh my God.'

'I guess that makes sense,' Joss mumbled. 'The only love triangles that happen in real life involve Rihanna.'

I chuckled, straightening as we pulled up in front of the Ihi pack's main home. The Treize had cleared out of the neighbouring town days ago, due to a combination of there being other things to draw their interest and an increased presence from a few of the other local packs the Aunties had managed to recruit. It had been a force of little more than two dozen as it was. Even the Treize were smart enough to sense when things were getting dangerously out of their control. Various packs had tracked their exit from the island for us, like a supernatural game of tag. As the Ihi pack monitored them to their borders, the Lynskey pack took over, followed by the Greigsons, and the Faiti pack, and so on. Once the local Askari were back in their holes, Aruhe had let us know that the coast was clear: we could safely drive straight in to home turf from wherever we'd been holed up.

'We're here, Joss. I gotta go. Do you need me to put Heath on?'

'No, I wasn't calling for anything important. Just mad bants.'

'Stay safe, will you. We'll be in touch, or rather . . . Creeper will.'

'Stay smart,' he replied, before hanging up the phone.

Simon and James had obviously just finished work, the two of them leaning on a car with their jackets tossed over the bonnet and ties loose around their necks.

'You're cutting it close,' Simon said, by way of greeting.

'And you *both* look like you're about to either represent someone in court or rip off those suits and perform at a hen's night. I'm undecided on which.'

'It was Simon's first proper day back in the office,' James replied. 'We had to look the part.'

'Businessmen by day, raging beasties by night.'

'Besides,' Simon said, 'we were waiting for you.'

With a jerk of his head, I followed the men around the side of the house and soon all *Magic Mike* jokes were expelled from my mind as I processed the full sight at the edge of the forest. Some forty people were gathered there, different ages, heights, weights and skin tones. Tiaki was among them and surrounded by the Aunties, who were crowded around Wehi as he talked about something. He froze the second he saw me, raising a lone hand as a form of hello. Tiaki looked up, giving me the briefest nod. The whole Tianne clan – including Keisha – were there as well and Aruhe, who had a warm smile waiting for me. She looked happy to see Heath too, her eyes running over what visible injuries had and hadn't healed since the last time she saw him.

'You look well,' she said. 'Heaps better.'

'I had a good nurse.' He smirked.

She made a gagging sound and I laughed.

'This is as far as you go,' she said, holding up a hand to stop him coming any closer to the pack. 'If you stay inside the house, you'll be perfectly safe.'

He nodded. 'I've got plenty of work to do.'

When the full moon was over, Heath and I would be off. The coming days between the phases was our time to be briefed on the group of rebels the Ihi pack had us going to meet in Western Australia. There were wombat shifters, witches, werewolves and selkies among the group, but the key individual was a woman called Dreckly Jones who was gifted when it came to forging fake supernatural identities and documents. She had information that was invaluable to us and the next stage of what we were planning, Tiaki said.

Heath and I had talked a lot as we travelled. Among other things, we'd talked about the price the Treize had put on his head. It wasn't a monetary figure per se, just 'reward offered' (which was worse, apparently). Heath said that it implied the hunter could state their fee and the Treize would grant it, monetary or otherwise.

'What about your immortality?' I had gasped at the time. 'Can't they just … strip you of that and you'd be dead?'

'It's an alchemist ritual of consent, both parties have to

be willing when it's first performed and the same applies for when it's stripped away. It would be easier for them to execute me.'

'It will be anything but easy.'

We'd talked about the bounty on his head in the context of whether we were safer together or apart. The consensus had been together, but I had added a footnote to that decision: I didn't want us to be apart. Regardless of feelings, we worked well together. We had complimentary skills and a wealth of contacts that we could rely on for help. Yet I had been clear to communicate my point: I was sticking with him for the foreseeable future. His response had been one of enthusiastic passion. Heath had to go on the run, and I'd be running with him. This wasn't a permanent solution to the problem, it was a temporary one while we waited for the birth of Sadie's daughters, but we may as well be useful while we were doing it and draw their eye away from New Zealand altogether. That meant we'd be running in the direction of home, Scotland, and towards a task that was incredibly dangerous. With the strange encouragement of the Three, the resources of the Ihi pack and each other, Heath and I were going to try and bust open Vankila. We were hoping some rebels might join us.

Standing there on Ihi land, I felt sure in our decision. Not safe: what we were going to attempt to do couldn't have been closer to the definition of horrendously unsafe. But both of us felt like it was the thing we were meant to do. I grabbed Heath's hand, standing up on my tiptoes to kiss him before I left. I wasn't quite sure why I was so nervous about the coming moon, after all, this was what I was born to do. And yet . . . He rested his hand on the curve between my neck and shoulder as a soothing gesture before he whispered something only the two of us could hear.

'Tha gaol agam ort,' he said, repeating a phrase he'd first uttered back when we'd been busting him out of captivity. It was spoken in his native language of Gaelic and I hadn't known what it meant then, but I did now: I love you.

'You have nothing to be afraid of,' Heath added.

I smiled, craning my neck to look up at him in the fading light. It was a lie, sure: there was an endless list of things to be afraid of. I could tell that he knew I was thinking about that list and he rolled his eyes at me. I let go of him, walking to join the rest of the pack. Without a word, everyone headed into the forest. It was quiet as we moved, only light chitchat from the group as people started to feel the pressing power of the moon. It was minutes away.

I felt a different kind of presence by my side, that of Wehi, who had left his usual walking stick behind. He was using Tiaki as a makeshift crutch, the Ihi pack's real alpha moving patiently with the older man.

'How are you, Tommi?' he asked. 'Had any visitors lately?'

I met Wehi's gaze and saw the shrewd intelligence glistening there.

'My, whatever do you mean?' I replied innocently.

Ghosts had been popping up everywhere, all the time now. And these weren't like Seamus or even Barastin where they were powerful enough for everyone to see them. At times, it was only me who could. I was getting better at blocking them out, acting natural and ignoring their gaze. Like right then, walking alongside the Ihi pack through the woods, was not one ghost but dozens. Their bodies illuminated the forest around us, but the only other person who seemed to notice was Wehi.

'You'll get used to it,' he said, watching my reaction.

I opened my mouth to reply but the words evaporated as

I felt the first rumble through my body. It began in the pit of my stomach and shuddered all the way up my spine; I gritted my teeth as I breathed through the pain. I shrugged out of my hoodie as I walked, letting it fall to the ground beside me as I moved. The forest was being sprinkled with items of clothing as, one by one, the Ihi pack began disrobing as they too felt the transformation inching ever closer.

The ghosts seemed excited too, chatting among themselves and watching us with keen interest. I shook my hair free of the beanie I had been wearing, letting the long stands fall around me as I heard a sharp cry come from Aruhe to my left. Animal grunts were now mixing with the sounds of human screams as the people around me transitioned into wolves. My own shift came late, with Simon and I the last two in our human skin when we both dropped to our knees and finally gave in to the pain.

Digging my fingers deep into the dirt of the ground I was resting on, I felt my tendons stretch and snap as my legs went beyond the normal human range. My scream was joined by a chorus of others as we all contorted in agony, shifting at different paces. My teeth elongated as I rolled on to my back, arching and shouting as my vocals became a howl. My body vibrated like I was having a fit, convulsing and thrashing as the final hairs pierced my skin. I lay there for several intense minutes, panting. When I rose, I was on all fours. I was no longer a woman: I was the wolf. And the ghosts were no longer in human form either. Wolves both living and dead moved around us, with one exceedingly large ghost wolf padding its way towards me. There was something in his eyes, something familiar yet foreign. He recognised me, but I was only beginning to recognise him.

Suddenly a wet snout sniffed at me, nuzzling into my

side as I rose up on shaky limbs. It was Aruhe and I nipped at her playfully, enjoying the sight of her tiny and slick wolf form sprinting into the undergrowth ahead of me. I took off in pursuit, her tail flashing in and out of focus as I raced after her. It was only then that I realised I wasn't alone: the forest was alive with sound. Branches snapped, twigs crunched and leaves bristled as wolves tore through it at lightning pace. When the first howl rang out around us, the night was silent for a moment as the haunting echo hung there. The void was filled with an answering cry, then another and another before I too finally added my own to the mix.

A pack ran beside me, it wasn't my own, but it was filled with my kind: my brothers, my sisters, my father, my wolves.

GLOSSARY

Alchemist Those who have the ability to infuse and convert materials with magical properties through a combination of symbols, science and ceremony. Alchemists were instrumental in the founding of the Treize, particularly the Askari themselves. Obsessed with immortality, it's rumoured their formula is responsible for the prolonged lives of Praetorian Guard soldiers and Custodians.

Arachnia Traditionally considered a nightmarish vision from Japanese folklore, arachnia emerged from the shadows relatively late compared to other supernatural species and were discovered to have existed worldwide. Their natural state is comparable to a large, spider-like creature, with traits similar to the arthropod.

Askari Foot soldiers and collectors of ground truth. The first point of call in the supernatural community, they simultaneously liaise and gather information. Mortal, yet members often work their way up into the Custodian ranks. Identified by a wrist tattoo, which is the alchemist symbol for wood to signify a strong foundation.

The Aunties A pack within the Ihi pack, this fearsome

all-women group are responsible for voting on and enforcing pack law.

Banshee Thought to be extinct by the wider supernatural community before remerging in Australia, a banshee is a supernatural being cursed with the ability to sense death or impending doom in its various forms. Exclusively female.

Bierpinsel A large, colourful tower in the centre of Berlin: the Bierpinsel is the base of Treize operations for Germany and much of Europe.

Blood pack The family unit a werewolf is born into by direct descent, usually operating on a specific piece of geographical territory.

Coming of age A ritual all werewolves must complete before they're considered mature members of their blood pack. A wolf can only choose to go 'rogue' once they have survived the coming of age.

Coven A grouping of witches within a particular area, covens can include members of the same biological family as well as women of no biological relation. No two members of a coven have the same magical ability, with similar powers spread out over other covens as an evolutionary defence mechanism. Members of a coven can draw on each other's powers, giving them strength and safety in their sisterhood.

The Covenant The series of rules established for banshees to follow once they were deported en masse from Ireland, Scotland and Wales in the seventeen hundreds. If The Covenant is broken, the penalty can range from imprisonment in Vankila to death.

Custodians The counsellors or emotional guardians of beings without other help, assistance or species grouping. Immortality is a choice made by individual Custodians, with those choosing it identified by a necklace with an Egyptian ankh.

Demon One of the oldest forms of supernatural beings, pure-blood demons are known for being reclusive and rarely interact with those outside of the paranormal world. Certain species of demon have a fondness for the flesh, leading to half- blood demon hybrids usually identifiable via physical traits like horns or tusks (often filed down so it's easier to blend in to society).

Elemental Originally thought to be those who could control the elements – earth, air, fire and water – elementals are paranormal beings descended directly from nature. Able to physically become the elements if they so desire, they share a strong allegiance with shifters, werewolves and selkies.

Ghost Translucent and bluish grey in colour, ghosts are the physical manifestation of one's soul after death. Their presence in the realm of the living can be for several reasons, ranging from an unjust demise to a connection with a person or place. The strength of any particular ghost varies case-to-case.

Ghoul Usually found in underground sewer systems and living in nest formations, ghouls are considered a lower class of paranormal creature due to their lack of intelligence or individual personality traits. With razor sharp claws and serrated teeth, they can be deadly in numbers.

Goblin Highly intelligent and supernaturally agile, goblins are known for their speed and lethal nature if provoked. Although not immortal, they have exceedingly long lives and prefer living in urban environments such as cities or large towns. They are one of several paranormal species impacted by the lunar cycle.

Medium A being that can communicate with and

control the dead, including spirits and ghosts. Extremely rare, the full range of their abilities is unknown and largely undocumented.

Outskirt Packs The collective description for werewolf packs from the Asia-Pacific region who fought against the Treize – unsuccessfully – for the right to self-govern and expose their true nature to the human world. Formed in 1993 and disbanded upon defeat in 1998, key leaders included Jonah Ihi, Sushmita Kapoor and John Tianne. This conflict was known as the Outskirt Wars.

Paranormal Practitioner The healers and medical experts of the unnatural world. Usually gifted individuals themselves, they wield methods outside of conventional medicine.

Praetorian Guard A squadron of elite warriors that quell violence and evil within the supernatural community. They're gifted with immortality for their service. Founded by a member of the original Roman Praetorian Guard.

Rogue A werewolf who chooses to live and operate outside of their blood pack.

The Rogues Comprised of rogue werewolves who have decided to leave their blood packs, this group functions from within the nightclub Phases in Berlin and includes global members who have come of age.

Selkie The source of mermaid and merman folklore, selkies are aquatic humanoids that inhabit any large body of water. Despite some human features, tribes of selkie from certain parts of the world have been known to take the form of marine animals like seals, dolphins and sharks.

Shifter Found globally, shifters have the ability to trans-form into one specific creature depending on their linage. Often confused with werewolves due to their capacity to take animal shape, shifters can transform outside of the full moon both fully and in-part.

Spirit Incorrectly compared to ghosts, spirits are their more powerful counterparts. A term used to describe the dead who can travel between pre-existing plains and occasionally take some physical form, they usually preoccupy themselves with the business of their direct ancestors.

Sprite Said to be the result of a union between selkies and earth elementals, sprites are highly secretive and rarely identify themselves to other supernatural creatures. They struggle being around members of their own kind and prefer to live close to nature.

The Three A trio of semi-psychic women who guide the Treize in regards to past, present and future events. The subject of the phrase 'hear no evil, see no evil, speak no evil'. Origin and age unknown.

Treize The governing body of the supernatural world comprising of thirteen members of different ages, races, nationalities, abilities, species and genders. Given their namesake by four French founders, they oversee the Praetorian Guard, Custodians, Askari and Paranormal Practitioners.

Vampire Rodent-like creature who lives off the blood of animals or people (whatever they can get). Endangered in the supernatural community due to widespread disease.

Vankila The Treize's supernatural prison, located in St Andrews, Scotland, and built hundreds of metres below a Cold War bunker.

Werewolf Considered one of the most volatile and ferocious paranormal species, werewolves are humans that shift into enormous wolf-hybrids during the nights of the full moon. Outside of the lunar cycle they retain heightened abilities, such as strength and healing, with the most powerful of their kind able to transform at will and retain human consciousness. Often found living in blood packs, they are resistant towards most forms of paranormal government.

Witch A woman naturally gifted with paranormal abilities that can be heightened with study and practice. Although the witch gene is passed down through the female line, skills vary from woman to woman regardless of blood. Witches believe their power is loaned to them temporarily by a higher being, who redistributes it to another witch after their death. Highly suspicious and distrustful of the Treize due to centuries of persecution, they are closed off from the rest of the supernatural community.

ACKNOWLEDGMENTS

More than anything, I want to thank all the wolfpackers who waited patiently (lol) for the publication of Who's Still Afraid? Like, I know it's not a George R.R. Martin wait or anything, but y'all messaged me every day, constantly, and came up in person to ask when Tommi Grayson would be coming back for a solo book. Massive shakas for letting me know how much you cared, but also for the patience to allow me to expand the Supernatural Sisters universe with women who are very different to Tommi: women like Casper and Kaia and Sadie and Kala and Dreckly and Shazza and Yu. That was vitally important to me, to the health of the storytelling, but also to the myriad of women out there who got to see themselves represented in those characters.

Huge thanks to Blake and Sam Howard, for being the best friends a girl could have. Whether that's while going through a curveball crisis or getting locked down together during a pandemic, I wouldn't have survived the past 18 months without both of you and your chubby children, Hazel Hermione and Keato Mano.

Keri Arthur, who despite everything she has achieved *still* has the time, energy and enthusiasm to help the next generation of lady authors who are legit only doing this because her work motivated them to. Abigail Nathan, sharpest eyes and pen in the bizz. It felt extremely full circle to work with you editing the third Who's Afraid? book when you were so pivotal to editing the first when I was still back in Scotland circa 2013.

Jake Caleb for THAT MOTHERFUCKING COVER! I described it as "kick you in the cunt" level good and I really fucking meant it. It's hard to step in to a job several books in, but I'm forever grateful with how you were able to interpret my shitty sketches and also truly make it your own all while existing within the Supernatural Sisters universe.

My rellies, Tania, Tom, and grandma Teresa who said Who's Afraid Too? gave her a "sex education, even at this age" so apologies for everything you just read :o/ Chur Te Wānanga o Raukawa for continuing my education. Forever grateful for my collective angry brown aunties Ramona Sen Gupta, Jean-Anne Kidd, Rae Johnston, Anna Gough, Sonja Hammer, L.Mo, Rarriwuy Hick, Gen Fricker and so many others for lighting a fire under me professionally and personally. Tēnā koe to Casey Zilbert and Kath Akuhata-Brown for helping unearth new aspects of Tommi and her world over the past few years. Props to Kate Czerny, one of the very first and most feverish readers of every Who's Afraid? manuscript.

Finally, I know I always do this gushy shit, but it's important to stress how grateful I am for the support of book sellers in Australia and internationally for getting behind me as an author and – more importantly - these characters. All the journos and bloggers and podcasters and bookstagrammers who have kept the characters alive with their enthusiasm, not to mention the best motherfucking readers a gal could ask for. Bless and thank ya x

ABOUT THE AUTHOR

Maria Lewis is a best-selling author, screenwriter, film curator and journalist based in Australia. Getting her start as a police reporter, her writing on pop culture has appeared in publications such as the New York Post, Guardian, Penthouse, Empire Magazine, Huffington Post, The Sunday Telegraph, io9 and many more. As a screenwriter she has worked on nightly news program The Feed for SBS and Cleverfan on ABC, as well as children's animation, documentaries and live-action television.

Her debut novel and first in the Supernatural Sisters series - Who's Afraid? - was published in 2016 and is being developed for television by the Emmy and BAFTA award-winning Hoodlum Entertainment. Winner of Best Fantasy Novel at the Aurealis Awards for The Witch Who Courted Death, she is a three-time nominee for titles Who's Still Afraid? and The Wailing Woman. She is the host, writer and producer of the limited podcast series Josie & The Podcats about the 2001 cult film and It Came From The Deep, a narrative podcast series based on her third novel of the same name.

PRAISE FOR MARIA LEWIS

Who's Afraid?

"Gripping, fast-paced, and completely unexpected, Who's Afraid? has more twists than a tornado. I loved this story!" – *NY Times best-selling author Darynda Jones*

"The next True Blood." – *NW Magazine*

"Maria Lewis is a must-read." - *BuzzFeed*

"It's about time we had another kick-arse werewolf heroine." – *NY Times best-selling author Keri Arthur*

"Journalist Maria Lewis grabs the paranormal fiction genre by the scruff of its neck to give it a shake with her debut novel Who's Afraid?" – *The West Australian*

"It's Underworld meets Animal Kingdom." – *ALPHA Reader*

"Truly one of the best in the genre I have ever read." – *Oscar-nominated filmmaker Lexi Alexander (Green Street Hooligans, Punisher: War Zone)*

"Lewis creates an intriguing world that's just begging to be fleshed out in further books." –*APN*

"If you haven't heard about Maria Lewis, you must have been living under a rock." - *Good Reading Magazine*

"Lovers of werewolves and paranormal fiction take note: Who's Afraid? isn't your typical urban fantasy." – *Geek Bomb*

"Really, really refreshing." – *ABC Radio*

"The Sydney-based author takes the reader somewhere they've never been before." - *Daily Record*

Who's Afraid Too?

"Part 2 of Maria Lewis' feminist werewolf antics is even better than Part 1. And she threw in some good old fashioned sex. More books please!" - *Natalia Tena (Harry Potter, Game Of Thrones)*

"We can't wait to see where she goes next as this series continues to go from strength-to-strength." – *SciFi Now Magazine*

"How long until we see Tommi Grayson on the big screen?" - *AusRom Today*

"Thanks Maria for continuing this saga! There are definitely days when being curled up in a werewolf fantasy is a respite and a haven!" - *Teri Hatcher (Lois & Clark, Desperate Housewives)*

"This is an excellent sequel in a series written by a supernatural genre lover for genre fans." – *APN*

"Maria Lewis is definitely one to watch." – *NY Times bestselling author Darynda Jones*

"If you want a fresh, funny, sexy & downright sassy take on the werewolf genre then this series is for you." – *Geek Bomb*

It Came From The Deep

"Lewis's YA debut It Came From The Deep is an unexpected surprise that fills a niche in the Australian market." - *Thoughts By Tash*

"Presenter, producer and writer extraordinaire Maria Lewis, has penned an intriguing and original coming of age tale set against the glittering backdrop of Australia's Gold Coast." - *Lyn Haines*

"She writes kick-ass monsters and things that go bump in the night with a flair for the awesome." - *Reviewers Of Oz*

"This book is Maria's first foray into the YA genre, but she did not abandon her penchant for feminism in her characters and story line." - *GirlTalkHQ*

"It Came from the Deep is one of those stories that sticks with you days after you've read it ... once I started reading, I couldn't put it down." - *Novel Tea Corner*

"The concept is so original." - *Handbag Mafia*

"It's about mermaids and mermen, with a murder mystery, and the procedural elements are her experience as a journalist coming out." - *2SER 107.3FM*

The Witch Who Courted Death

"Easily weaves the magic into each page of this spin-off." - The Nerd Daily

"Author Maria Lewis has created her own pop culture universe." - The Daily Telegraph

"A feminist take on two well-known classics - ghosts and witches - giving them the Lewis makeover and throwing them into her renowned supernatural world." - Aurealis

"The former journalist has staked (pun intended) out a career as one of Australia's best horror writers." - The West Australian

"The Witch Who Courted Death is an unashamedly feminist story about a woman out for revenge." - Readings

"An original and enjoyable read with diverse and relatable characters." - One Bookish Girl

The Wailing Woman

"It's world-building at its finest." - *The Nerd Daily*

"Maria Lewis has created an excellent urban fantasy novel that utilises magic, intrigue and romance." - *Canberra Weekly*

"Lewis continues to smash the patriarchy in both the human and supernatural realms in her latest novel." - *Her HQ*

"Maria Lewis might be an absolute master of the genre." -
Bookish Bron